D0954506

CHRISTIE RIDGWAY

take my breath away

HARLEQUIN® HQN™

Recycling programs
for this product may
not exist in your area.

ISBN-13: 978-0-373-77832-4

TAKE MY BREATH AWAY

Copyright © 2014 by Christie Ridgway

Printed in U.S.A.

Dear Reader,

Take a trip with me to the region known as the Alps of Southern California. Here, an hour from the glamour and glittering lights of Los Angeles, the wealthy retreat to "Hollywood on High," where rocky peaks, tall pines and clean air surround their mansions flanking the shores of Blue Arrow Lake. At this more than mile-high elevation, California has four full seasons and two kinds of people: the moneyed who come for their alpine visits, and the more modest mountain locals, who are rooted to their rugged surroundings.

In *Take My Breath Away,* Los Angeleno Ryan Hamilton seeks solitude by retreating to the rustic cabins managed by lovely single mother Poppy Walker. But her beauty and her can-do attitude draw him out, and soon he finds himself leaning in for a kiss…and then another. Poppy's been burned by love before and has no intention of falling for a guy who seems so out of her league, yet Ryan has a way of getting under her skin and reminding her that being a mom doesn't mean she can't have a man.

I love bringing together two people who think they are absolutely wrong for each other and then letting them wrestle with fate and with their growing feelings. Ready to enjoy it with me? Then come aboard. Destination… romance!

Christie

In grateful memory of Harlow
(aka Best-Dog-in-the-World) for his eleven-plus years
of loyal companionship that included escorting small boys
into dreamland every night. And with thanks to Hank
(aka Sweetest-Dog-in-the-World), who makes us glad
we risked our hearts to love again.

If Winter comes, can Spring be far behind?
—Percy Bysshe Shelley

CHAPTER ONE

Poppy Walker just wanted something good to come from the next ten days. The next ten days, the first ten in March, when she had to do without the company of the only man she'd ever love. Earlier that morning, she'd worn her game face as she'd waved goodbye to her five-year-old son.

The tears she'd saved for the ride back from her cousin's house to the family land, four miles off the mountain highway that served a popular Southern California resort area. One hundred and fifty years before, her ancestors had secured their place seven thousand feet above sea level, and what remained were steep slopes, several acres of pines, cedars and dogwoods, as well as a dozen dilapidated cabins, all currently covered in snow.

Over the Christmas holidays, when she'd learned that her current place of employment, Inn Klein, was about to invest in a big remodel, it had sparked Poppy's own bright idea. Then and there, she'd decided to refurbish the family cabins as vacation rentals to generate a supplemental income to share between herself, her two sisters and her brother.

Unfortunately, her siblings weren't of the same mind. Instead, they believed in the outlandish and archaic family curse: that nothing good could ever come of this piece of Walker property.

Ridiculous.

"C'mon, Grimm," she called to her Lab-German shepherd mix. Dressed in a cotton turtleneck, thick sweatshirt, old jeans and scruffy work boots, she led him out of the cabin where she and her son, Mason, had moved just a couple of weeks before. It was the best of the dwellings and one of five that ringed a small clearing carpeted with snow. The remaining seven were nestled among the trees in the surrounding forest.

Her dog pranced beside her, unsure of the game but a willing participant all the same.

"First order of business is cabin four," she told him. "We're going to clean up the inside." He responded with his doggy grin.

The initial step in the process was to get the water turned on so she could scrub. That involved opening the small door cut into the siding, pretending she didn't see the creepy, ropy spiderwebs then twisting the handle that would let the liquid rush into the pipes.

That went off without a hitch. Inside the kitchen, she pushed a bucket under the spout and turned the faucet handle, expecting a gratifying gush. It didn't come. "Uh-oh," she said, feeling a twinge of dismay.

Grimm seemed much more cavalier than she, wagging his tail as he followed her back to the little door. When they got there, she knew instantly what had gone wrong, as water was spreading from beneath the raised foundation. "Broken pipe," she informed Grimm, dismay turning to real alarm. Surely that would be a costly repair. Braving the cobwebs a second time, she twisted the handle in the opposite direction and started a mental review of her bank balances.

On the heels of that depressing thought process, she allowed herself a fifteen-second wallow in self-pity. Then she straightened her shoulders and once again addressed her dog. "Cabin three, it is, Grimm," she said, reaching for the ring of keys in her pocket.

The one that fit the only entry to cabin three broke off in the knob.

That would probably be a much cheaper fix, but it was yet another to add to an already large pile, so this time she went with a thirty-second wallow during which she saw her brother and sisters in her mind's eye, each of them saying, "I told you so, knucklehead," in their own inimitable style.

Once that was over, she marched off to retrieve the wooden ladder leaning behind her own cottage. "Time to check out the roof of cabin two," she told Grimm as she hefted the old contraption to the dwelling next door to her own. "I'm a little worried about its condition." Not that she knew what to look for actually, but surely something obvious would stand out.

She didn't get a chance to perform her inspection, however. Because even though she chose level ground on which to place the ladder, and even though she took great care to lock the metal spreader in place, when her boot met the third step, its wood tread cracked in two, and she tumbled down, her butt landing in cold, wet snow.

Poppy lay staring up at the peak of their mountain silhouetted against the deep blue sky, thinking dark thoughts about her siblings and their maybe not-so-ridiculous superstitions.

But Poppy Walker, cock-eyed optimist, refused to concede defeat.

"That's it," she said to Grimm, who stood looking down at her in some concern. "The real first order of business is lifting the stupid family curse."

POPPY PUSHED OPEN the door of Johnson's Grocery, her mind on the list of ingredients she needed per her brief stop at the Blue Arrow Lake branch library. Johnson's Grocery was located on the same street, so she thought she'd start there.

Someone hailed her from the back of the store, where a butcher's case held fancy cuts of grass-fed beef, stuffed breasts of duck and free-range chicken, as well as fillets of salmon prepared for grilling. The store was small—real estate in the mountain resort area went at princely rates—but the narrow aisles were packed with gourmet foods, expensive liquor and fancy wines. Everything and anything a filthy rich Los Angeleno couldn't do without during a getaway to what was known as "Hollywood on High."

Cheaper merchandise could be had if she'd driven to a larger community, but that would have cost her in time and gas money, so Johnson's was her go-to market.

The endcap nearest the entrance displayed a selection of expensive children's toys, everything from miniature fishing rods to expansive LEGO sets for snowbound weekends. Gazing on them, Poppy's heart squeezed, sending a rush of tender longing through her veins. *Mason,* she thought, picturing her towheaded boy, who right now was on his way to a vacation filled with such delights as whirling in teacups and flying with Dumbo. *Mason, I miss you so much.*

"Poppy."

At the sound of her name, she glanced over, smiled. "Hey, Bill." Bill Anders was a scarecrow of a man, and wore a bibbed, crisp cotton apron with the store's name stitched on the front, most likely by his wife. She had an embroidery business in addition to the daycare she ran. Like many people who lived in the mountains year-round, the Anderses cobbled together a living out of more than one line of work.

"Heard Mason went to Walt Disney World with your cousin James."

"That's right. James and Deanne wanted company for their own little guy on a visit to Deanne's parents. When Mason heard the magic words *Mickey Mouse,* I could hardly say no."

"Heard, too, that you got laid off from Inn Klein until the remodel's complete. Sorry for it."

"Thanks," she said, hiding her grimace by stepping past the shopkeeper on her way to the fresh fruits and vegetables. Of course, news traveled fast when you lived in a tight community like this one. She knew how this worked, didn't she? People had been in the Walkers' business—and they in everyone else's, she supposed— since the logging family's arrival in the mountains.

But Poppy had felt her friends' and neighbors' interest in a more up-close and personal fashion. Collective eyebrows had lifted and noses had twitched when she'd found herself pregnant by a summer visitor who'd skedaddled back to his moneyed family in Beverly Hills the minute she'd informed him of the test results. Though the truth was, Poppy minded less people gossiping about her sex life than them knowing she'd been dumb enough to fall for a rich and careless man.

Her mother had made a similar mistake before Poppy. Though she couldn't wish her half-sister, Shay, had never been born.

Nor did Poppy regret one moment with Mason.

Mason... She mouthed his name, her heart starting to hurt all over again.

Then she shook off the melancholy. *Think of something else,* she commanded herself, as she stepped up to the tiered rows of produce, glistening from a recent misting. Think of making something of the cabins. *Think of getting rid of that stupid curse.*

"Sage," she murmured to herself, inspecting the selection of fresh herbs. Pulling a bunch of the gray-green leaves from the stack, she frowned at the price. There wouldn't be a paycheck from the inn until it reopened July 4th, and the aromatic was expensive. As a rational woman, Poppy didn't, of course, completely buy in to the idea she could eradicate any negative energy at the cabins. But...

She was determined. And desperate.

Wincing at the mental admission, she dumped the herb into her basket and started her hunt for rock salt. Despite the dire predictions of her older brother, Brett, her older sister, Mackenzie, and her younger sister, Shay, Poppy hoped that by summer the dwellings would be available as weekly vacation rentals. Cabin two—if you didn't count the dubious state of the roof—was already in decent shape and with a fingers-crossed kind of optimism, she'd placed notices on the community bulletin boards around town, including the one here at Johnson's.

Despite the point-of-view of her pessimistic sibs, Poppy would prove to them that the Walker albatross could be turned into an eagle, after all.

The cowbell tied to the store's front door clattered, interrupting Poppy's train of thought. She glanced toward the door.

Her guard instantly jerked up. From twenty paces she recognized the man standing on the mat. She didn't know his identity—that was well-hidden by a watch cap pulled low on his forehead, the fancy Wayfarers that covered his eyes and the dark scarf wrapped around his neck that almost completely obscured his mouth—but she knew his type.

Rich guy.

She'd bet the scarf was cashmere and that those sun specs retailed for five hundred bucks or more. The waterproof jacket and boots came from a high-end store that catered to "outdoorsmen" who spent their summer days sipping martinis on the terraces of their lakeside mansions while watching their fancy boats bob up and down at private docks. They whiled away winter nights beside fires built by other hands, eating meals prepared by personal chefs brought up from L.A. The wine in their glasses would cost more than Poppy's monthly paycheck from running the front desk at Inn Klein.

"Can I help you sir?" A round-faced teen, all perky ponytail and freckled nose, appeared at his elbow.

"Just stopping in for a few things," the man said. His voice was low, but carried easily.

Maybe one of the new moguls that had taken up residence at what was now known as "Silicon Beach," L.A.'s own hotbed of tech industry that was rivaling the famed valley in northern California. While she stared, his head turned her way. His hand lifted, tipping up his sunglasses.

Their gazes met. Poppy's heart jolted. His eyes were a scorching shade of blue, the color that edged the blades of magical swords in fantasy novels or that you could find at the innermost core of fire. Her temperature climbed, heat radiating from the center of her chest and reaching upward to warm her face. It was embarrassing, she thought, still unable to look away. Because it probably appeared to him she was ogling instead of…instead of passing judgment.

Sue her, she didn't trust men like this. Didn't want to be around them more than she could help in a region that catered to the over-the-top affluent.

That thought got her feet moving again. She gave her back to the stranger, only half listening as the teenage clerk chattered to him about the store specials—veal cutlets and cheesecake baked by the kid's own talented mother—and the big March storm the weather service was predicting.

Poppy smirked at that as she added the rock salt and a small bunch of daisies to her basket. The only thing predictable about spring weather in the mountains was its changeability. Her brother said it was like a cranky woman deprived of chocolate, but since he'd been short-tempered himself since returning from his service with the 10th Mountain Infantry Division, she and her sisters just rolled their eyes at him.

Behind his back.

Looking for candles, she turned a corner, almost plowing into the stranger. She drew back to avoid contact, swaying on her feet. He reached to steady her, but she took a staggering step to the rear, instantly sure to her bones she shouldn't be touched by him.

His hand dropped and he muttered something under his breath. Ducking her head, Poppy scooted past him, then glanced over her shoulder. She couldn't help it.

He was a big man, six-two, maybe, to her five foot four inches. When she'd whipped by, she'd caught his scent. That was expensive, too, but not cologne, no. This was a clean, not cloying smell. Handmade soap, she guessed, triple-milled, and with a mild but lingering note of sandalwood. As she continued to watch him peruse the contents of the shelves, a knot gathered in her belly. Her nerve endings seemed to lift to the surface of her skin, tickling the nape of her neck and sending prickling goose bumps cascading down her spine and racing across her ribs.

Startled by her visceral response, she stood another moment, rooted to the floor. Then she saw him stiffen and knew, just knew, he could feel her regard and was an eyelash away from catching her staring again.

Don't let him catch you at anything! her instincts warned.

And Poppy, suddenly a tiny bit spooked, broke free of her paralysis. She hurried away from the stranger, finished her shopping and rushed to the checkout stand.

With her selections paid for and bagged, she paused outside the store, breathing in the cold, piney air. She lifted her gaze to the snow-covered peaks and felt her pulse settle. Inhaling more calming breaths, she picked her way toward her beat-up four-wheel drive, avoiding potholes and patches of icy-looking pavement.

As she neared her car, something made her glance around.

And there he was, the stranger, emerging from the grocery. Now, even from behind those dark glasses, she knew *he* was staring at *her*.

That primal alarm inside of her went off again. Her nerves leaped, her feet tangled on themselves, her arms windmilled and her goods scattered as she fell on her butt—for the second time that day—into a deep, cold puddle.

Damn! Mortified, and aware that color was rising from her neck to her face, she scrambled for her fallen purchases and crammed them into their plastic bag. Then she gathered her feet underneath her, preparing to rise with as much grace as possible.

"Here," that deep voice said.

She allowed her gaze to lift. It snagged on his hand, its wide palm and long fingers outstretched to help her up.

Eyeing it like a dangerous viper, Poppy shook her head and placed a palm on the cold, gritty pavement, pushing off to a stand in one quick move. She relied on herself.

And the only hand she intended to ever reach for, to ever hold, belonged to the little man who also had sole claim to her heart. Mason, who was at this moment probably daydreaming about riding the carousel or chasing down Goofy.

Without a word to the stranger she jumped into her

car and drove off, sighing with relief when the grocery store was no longer in her rearview mirror.

Thank God, Poppy thought on another sigh. Though she might still feel the smothering weight of that family curse, right now she had the distinct sense she'd just dodged a bullet.

NINETY MINUTES LATER, Poppy was in an even better mood as she stood in the clearing outside her home. With Grimm once again at her side, she'd accomplished nearly every step of the energy-cleansing exercise. Rock salt had been scattered near each cabin entrance—these five as well as the seven located deeper in the trees. At each door, she'd clapped loudly, startling Grimm and hopefully any negative energy that resided there.

Now she bent over the makeshift altar she'd established. Earlier, she'd carried a flat-topped rock to the center of the open area. Upon it she'd strewn petals from the daisies she'd bought. A white pillar candle was already flickering and beside it lay the bunch of sage she'd selected at Johnson's. She'd turned it into a smudge stick by wrapping the leaves around a brittle handful of slender pine twigs and tying them in place with twine. The whole thing was supposed to be dried for a week, but she figured if she waited that long she'd feel too silly to go through with the ritual. Though she was considered the whimsical Walker by her siblings, as a single mother she had developed a decidedly sensible side.

She picked up the aromatic bundle. Her final cleansing act was to light the stick and wave the smoke around while thinking positive thoughts. The dry pieces of pine caught easily on the candle's flame and she held it away from her body as the fire licked toward the first of the sage leaves. Smoke curled into the cool air and she moved her arm slowly. "I now release old stuck energy," she said out loud. "I now attract new beginnings and new opportunity to this place."

Grimm stayed close to her side as she turned, leaving her back to the steep drive that led up to the cabins from the road below. "I now release old stuck energy," she said again. "I now attract new beginnings and new opportunity to my life."

The scent of pine and sage rose and a sense of peace settled over her. Poppy closed her eyes, inhaling deeply. Wow, she thought. It works. For good measure, she repeated her last words, even louder this time. "I now attract new beginnings and new opportunity to my life."

Grimm's sudden bark scared the smudge stick out of her hand and shot her heart to her throat. It was his "stranger's coming" bark, and Poppy whirled to see a monster SUV with tinted windows climbing the drive, crunching over the slushy snow.

Her dog barked again, the hair on his neck bristling. He was a very effective, although faux, bodyguard. The fact was, Grimm wouldn't hurt a fly, but he had a deep voice and a brawny chest that gave him a belligerent demeanor. So, curious rather than alarmed, Poppy curled her fingers around his collar and watched the vehicle come to a stop.

Her jaw dropped when the door opened and a long leg in a familiar expensive boot emerged, followed by the rest of the rich stranger from Johnson's Grocery.

Once again, her skin rippled in apprehension and her

stomach knotted. Grimm let out another bark, the harsh sound more welcoming than Poppy felt. To disguise her trepidation, she shoved her hands in the pockets of the jacket she was wearing—her brother's castoff—and leaned back on her heels. "What do you want?"

She couldn't see his expression, as he was swathed in that scarf, sunglasses and brow-skimming cap. Shutting the driver's door, he waved a flyer in his other hand. "A cabin to rent."

Her mouth fell open again. Narrowing her eyes, she recognized one of the half sheets of paper she'd pinned around town in hopes of enticing summer visitors. *Summer* being the operative word, she realized now…and the exact one she'd neglected to include on the advertising. Knucklehead!

"Sorry," Poppy said, commanding herself to stand her ground as the stranger moved from his vehicle and across the snow-covered clearing. "We're not accepting guests right now."

"Is that right?" He glanced around. "The coven using all the cabins?"

"The cov—" She broke off as he nodded toward the small altar and the smudge stick at her feet. Though it had extinguished upon landing in the snow, the pungent scent still lingered in the air. She inhaled a deep breath of it, trying to regain her earlier peaceful feeling.

For whatever reason, this man rattled her.

Deciding to ignore the coven remark, she took her hands from her pockets and crossed her arms over her chest as she tried pasting on a pleasant expression. "As I said, I'm sorry. We're simply not ready."

He glanced around again. Smoke rose from her cabin's chimney, but three of the others ringing the clearing were obviously vacant, not to mention inhospitable-looking with their peeling doors and dirty windows. The one nearest hers she'd decided to work on first, and it looked much better with its new paint and sparkling glass. From here, the iffy state of the roof was not readily apparent, though she'd have to come up with the money to replace it sooner than later.

"I'll pay you twice the going rate," the man said, as if he'd read her mind. His gaze shifted to the flyer grasped in his left hand. "I'll take the two-bedroom 'nestled in the woods.'"

"Sorry again, not available." Squirrels had made a home in the chimney and it smelled like something had died in the second bedroom. It was the farthest from the clearing and the last on her list to refurbish, though she'd foolishly—she realized now—advertised it, anyway. As her father's daughter, she should have realized that unchecked optimism could come back to bite her on the butt.

Speaking of bites, she glanced down at Grimm, who stood relaxed at her side. Usually he took cues about strangers from her reaction and body language. Odd that he wasn't picking up on that now…in which case he would be showing a lot of teeth and emitting one of his best back-off growls.

The long-legged man followed her gaze. "Nice dog."

"If you like death-by-canine," she said. "We call him Grimm, as in the Grim Reaper." A little white lie. Her brother had chosen the name after some famous NFL player he admired.

The stranger patted his thigh. "Hey, Grimm."

Her dog raced forward, his jaw stretched in a toothy smile.

The man ran his hand over her pet's head. "Like I said, nice dog. And I'll pay you triple for whatever place you have available."

Triple? Triple? Poppy thought of her recent layoff, the cost of Mason's plane tickets to Florida and back, the extra dollars she'd given James to dole out on her son's behalf.

"Quadruple, then."

A fool and his money…Poppy mused, tempted despite her jittery nerves and knotted stomach. Mountain people were wary of everything about the rich flatlanders who came up the hill for alpine delights—everything except the money they flung about so freely. It was hard for average Joes and Joannas to make do in a place where real estate and gasoline and foodstuffs were sold at luxury resort prices. But people like the Walkers and the other descendants of early settlers were stubborn about staying among their beloved peaks and pines. Maybe Poppy had once dreamed of oceans and palms and big city streets, but then Mason had come along and sticking to what was familiar had made more sense.

The stranger crossed his arms over the chest of his posh squall jacket, mimicking Poppy's own pose. She couldn't see his eyes behind the dark lenses of his glasses, but she felt them narrow. "Quintuple," he said. "Final offer."

And greed overrode caution. "Done," she answered.

Second thoughts popped up the instant the word left her mouth. "Wait—you realize we're pretty far from civilization. The entrance to the highway is four miles from here."

"I realize. I got lost looking for the turnoff."

Poppy had the sense he was pleased by the fact.

Taking a step back, he tilted his head toward the steep slopes to the north of the cabins and woods. Snow covered the surface that was dotted with few of the pines that grew densely on the other surrounding hillsides. "What is this place? Can you ski up there?"

"If you want to hike up carrying your equipment. The elevation of the nearest town—Blue Arrow Lake—is a little over five thousand feet but here we're at seventy-two hundred, which means plenty of snow in a good winter. My family had a nice ski business on the mountain, but a wildfire took down the lodge, the rope tow and the chair lifts thirteen years ago."

"You didn't rebuild?"

Poppy shrugged. "Not enough insurance money. And a bad financial deal with a certain arch-villain."

He looked back at her then. "Arch-villain? Like Lex Luthor or Two-Face?"

"Like Victor Fremont." Without thinking, she spat in the snow, ground the spot with the toe of her boot then crossed her heart with the tip of her forefinger.

Only when she felt his stare did she realize what she'd done. "Uh, sorry. Walker family habit." The physical manifestation of their vow to never forget or forgive how the old man had ruined their father's livelihood and health was something Brett had come up with long ago. "But, uh, let me show you the cabin."

Maybe he wouldn't like it, she thought, almost hoping that would be true, despite quintuple the going rate. Something was off about him. Or her. Or her around him.

As she dug the keys from her coat pocket, she walked toward the one-bedroom. There were three wooden steps leading to the narrow porch. Inside, it was cold, but warmer than the outside temperature. He walked past her through the small living area to peer into the room that held a queen-size bed and a Shaker-style dresser.

"The bathroom only has a shower," she warned, "and the kitchen…"

With his back to her, he scraped off his hat. His hair was glossy, nearly black, and when he rubbed his palm over it, the strands settled into lines that screamed "This cut cost a mint!" She saw him finger off the sunglasses. As he stuck them into his coat pocket, she wondered if she'd imagined the surreal shade of his irises back at the grocery store. Perhaps they'd be ordinary on second take. Duller, like the color of a faded cotton patio umbrella. Or with gray overtones, like shadows cast on snow.

He turned.

Poppy nearly staggered back. Her mind hadn't oversold them. His eyes were a hot, electric-blue that seemed lit from within. They were compelling. Mesmerizing. The eyes of a magician or a mystic or some supernatural being. Again, an acute wariness shot through her.

Grimm whined and she quickly shifted her attention to the dog, needing to look away before she confessed her sins or offered up her life savings. God. Her pulse was racing and there was a queasy feeling in her stomach.

"And the kitchen...?" he prompted, in that deep voice that carried to the corners of the cabin and maybe to the corners of her heart.

God.

"The kitchen." She focused on the velvety golden hair between Grimm's floppy ears and made a vague gesture. "It's over there."

His footsteps sounded against the hardwood floor before finding the living room's braided area rug. From the corner of her eye, she saw his big hand and those lean fingers curled around the scarf he'd had at his neck. *If you look now, you'll see his whole face,* Poppy thought. Then she heard a rustle of sound that indicated he was removing his coat. *If you look now, you'll see his whole body, too.*

It shocked her how much she wanted to check out both, despite how anxious the man made her.

She was a mother, for God's sake! A Walker, focused on creating something of the family legacy.

A woman who had proven herself an idiot when it came to romance, so had sworn off it altogether.

None of which meant it would hurt to take a peek.

That was the inner optimist in her, always trying to find sunshine on a cloudy day.

It might even be good for you!

Ignoring her little voice, she worked the cabin's key off the ring. "If you're still interested—"

"I want the cabin. Until the end of the month."

Quintuple the rate until the end of the month! Poppy focused on that, and only that, as she slid the key onto the small table next to the sofa. "You'll need to plug in the fridge. The heater should keep you warm enough, but there's wood for the fireplace. I'll make sure to keep some piled on the porch. Oh—and I should warn you. There's no internet and there's no TV."

"No TV?" he asked.

"Don't plan to put 'em in the cabins. We Walkers grew up without television—our mom's idea—and I've never picked up the habit."

"So what do you do for entertainment?"

"I read, and I—" She almost said she played with her little boy, but for some reason she didn't want Mason's name in this room, where she was responding so strongly and strangely to this man's masculine charisma. Those blue eyes had done something to her internal wiring, heating her blood and making it buzz as it raced through her system. "I have a good imagination."

Oh, jeez. Why had she said that? Yet another time, embarrassed heat crawled up her neck.

"We have something in common, then. I have an active fantasy life, too." The sudden note of humor in his voice made her chin jerk up.

Their gazes met.

But there wasn't a sign of laughter on his face. There were just planes and angles—strong cheekbones, a clean jawline—that made her instantly think of elegant European men stepping into lowslung sports coupes and spectacular parties where people in evening clothes ended up jumping into swimming pools while a band dressed in white dinner jackets plays Cole Porter tunes. He was classically, memorably handsome and his features, coupled with those spectacular eyes, put him at the absolute top of her list of the most beautiful—yet still so male—men she'd ever seen.

Her skin was tingling, her stomach was pitching and her palms were probably sweating, but she couldn't tell because her fingers were curled into tight fists. Everything inside her was reacting to him, but in confusing ways. While some of her was going soft and languid, a sense of melting low in her belly, at the same time her defenses were rushing into place and she felt hyperalert and poised to fight her way out of…out of…

Danger.

Silly, she told herself. Stop being so silly.

Still, she backed up, keeping her gaze on him as she retreated toward the door. He remained where he was, though she thought she detected tension in the lean muscles revealed by the thermal Henley clinging to his powerful torso.

Those magnetic eyes swept over her. "I don't know your name," he said, his voice soft now, the near-whisper of that seductive snake in the Garden of Eden.

She shook her head to dispel the image. "Poppy," she replied, trying to sound businesslike and brisk. "Poppy Walker."

He was strolling toward her now and she retreated farther, until her shoulder blades met the wood of the door. Before she could find her way through it, the man had her hand in his. Heat ran like fire ants up her arm. "Ryan Harris," he said, his gaze fixed on her face.

The words barely registered as the burning touch overwhelmed all her other senses. His palm was warm and strong, its size enveloping hers—making her feel small and feminine. That's when she understood. That's when she could finally put a name to what he'd been able to do to her from that first glimpse.

After more than five years, Ryan Harris reminded her of what it was to be a woman.

"I have to go," she said, ordering herself to step away.

"You do," he agreed, nodding. Then he replaced the warmth of his skin with a bundle of bills. "Rent."

Squeezing her fingers around it, she hustled out the door and into the cold sunlight.

The scent of sage lingered in the air. She thought perhaps her ritual had worked. Maybe the negative energy was gone. That would be good.

And bad. Because it had apparently left a vacuum in its place, allowing in an entirely different sort of energy—one that Poppy was much too uneasy to name.

CHAPTER TWO

RYAN HAMILTON WONDERED if he'd make it to the end of March, as surviving the month had been iffy the past three years. Each turn of those particular thirty-one days had exacted a price: he'd wrapped his Maserati around an elm tree the first year; blown up a meat smoker and almost himself while passed out on a lounge chair ten feet from it two years ago; and last year he'd lost most of his good reputation. Now, if it hadn't been for the stunt-driving course he'd taken before shooting his final movie a decade ago, he might not have managed the escape from his own lakefront villa.

But he'd successfully evaded the celebrity photographer who'd been camped outside the gated drive. Had he even known it was Ryan he followed in that roller skate of a car? Ryan had been forced to take a few hairpin turns at speeds that had set his heart slamming in his chest.

He wasn't sure how he felt about the reminder that blood still pumped through his veins and that he retained enough emotional IQ to experience even a small drop of fear. Most of the time he didn't feel much of anything—except, of course, this was March. Fucking March.

He found his way back to the road that led him

through Blue Arrow Lake. While the body of water it was named after was private, and the boat docks only available to those with a deed to one of the pricey surrounding estates, the village itself welcomed tourists as well as the owners of the lakefront properties. Both were out in force, Ryan noted, as the traffic slowed passing the vaguely Swiss-styled buildings that held small specialty stores offering items like fancy cheeses, fancier chocolates and beers from around the world. Despite the snow left in piles here and there by the plows, warmly dressed people were seated under the clear blue skies amid patio heaters at small bistro tables, enjoying their designer coffees and flaky pastries.

The cars in front of him continued at a crawl, but Ryan didn't worry he might be spied by the photographer again. The road was a sea of SUVs in both directions, so his didn't stand out.

A ring sounded through the car speakers, and the touch screen in the dash signaled a familiar number. Ryan considered rejecting the call, but the person on the other end didn't take hints well.

He gave the voice command to answer and at the click of connection said, "What do you want, Linus?"

His younger brother got right to the point. "I want to know where you are."

"How much is *People* willing to pay for that tidbit?"

"Ha ha. Spill."

"It's none—"

"I worry, damn it." Though Ryan couldn't see the other man, he could imagine him forking a hand through his mop of dirty blond hair in a familiar gesture of frustration. Linus was a lankier version of himself, but with their mother's light hair and their father's brown eyes. "Ry, just tell me where you've gone to ground. Your assistant says you're not planning on being back in the Studio City offices until April."

"I decided, spur-of-the-moment, to take a break." Might as well try a new coping mechanism since he'd failed so miserably the past few years.

"Okay. That's good," Linus said. "But where?"

"I don't want company." A car pulled in front of Ryan's, causing him to brake sharply. The vehicle at his rear honked in bad-tempered complaint. "Not my fault," he muttered.

"You're in So-Cal," Linus said, relief in his voice. "I would recognize the sounds of our happy traffic anywhere."

Ryan debated a moment, then decided giving Linus a little more info would do no harm. "I was actually at the lake house."

"Yeah? You think you can stay out of trouble there?"

No, he thought, thinking of that photographer. "I handed over the keys to Anabelle and Grant for the weekend." He didn't need to add last names. They were one of Hollywood royalty's brightest and most watched romances—"Granabelle." Grant had been Ryan's stalwart friend for the past four years, sticking by him when his mood was low, being the designated driver when he was looking for refuge in an alcoholic high. "Can you keep a secret?"

"I've never told anyone you grew up afraid of the purple-haired troll under the bed that only you could see, have I?"

"Its hair was green and you were too much of a pussy to lift the bedspread and take a look."

Linus snorted. "I can keep a secret."

"They're getting married at the house over the weekend. Spur-of-the-moment and strictly family. To keep things as quiet as possible, I'm not even attending."

"Good for them," Linus said, then paused a moment. "How long do you suppose before one of their publicists spills the beans? Doesn't Anabelle have a new movie coming out soon?"

Having reached the end of town, Ryan took the turn that would bring him to the highway and ultimately his rental. "There was already a paparazzo hanging out at the gates."

"Shit," Linus said. "Not that I'm surprised. But you're going to stay clear of it now, right?"

"Right. But once I offered the house to Grant, I found the idea of the mountains appealed. So I've found another place to stay."

"Yeah? Where—"

"I'm using the name Ryan Harris." It was his go-to alias when he was attempting to stay under the radar.

"That's all fine and good, but your face is as recognizable as your name."

"She never watched TV growing up. Her favorite form of entertainment is reading."

The silence on the other end went heavy, then ominous. "She?"

Ryan gave a little shrug. "I'm telling you, the woman doesn't recognize me—has no idea I'm somebody anyone would recognize. She's got a handful of cabins for rent and I'm the first and only guest."

"She?"

"In her sixties, with a little pot belly and her hair in some sort of turban thing," Ryan said smoothly. "She's a chain-smoker."

"For a famous actor, you lie for shit."

"I haven't been a famous actor for a decade."

"You're right. Now you're just the famous part."

Or, after what went down last year, infamous, Ryan thought, which was degrees more uncomfortable. "Anyway, I should probably go—"

"Like I'd let you get away with that. What's she really like?"

Her face is as fresh as the mountain air. At the grocer's he'd thought her no older than the teen clerk, and when he'd caught her staring thought he'd been made. But at the cabins he'd immediately deduced she was well past jailbait. Yet still so…natural. Her cheeks and the tip of her cute nose had been pink with cold, and hanging over the shoulder of her oversize and clearly secondhand army jacket had been a messy braid of hair the mixed colors of honey, sunlight and brandy. Wide gray eyes and a soft pink mouth made him think young again. Her wary expression suggested life had disappointed her once or twice.

"She's not interested in me, if that's your concern," Ryan said to Linus. "I've barely glimpsed the woman in the three days since I had to bribe her with five times the going rental rate to take me in. Oh, and she has a dog she hints might kill me on demand. I'm pretty sure if the dog balks, she'll be willing to do the job herself."

"I think I'm in love."

"Why am I not surprised." At twenty-nine, Linus

was always ready to play with the opposite sex…though when Ryan thought of it, he'd been remarkably woman-free for months.

"Maybe I should come see her—develop my own impression."

"No." His brother was fishing for a reason to check on Ryan. "I told you, I don't want visitors."

"What are you going to do, then?"

"Read books, hike around." And if the past couple of days were anything to go by, stare out the window in case the wood nymph that lived next door made a rare appearance. "Nothing crazy this year."

Linus sighed. "That's great, Ry. Really great."

But his brother didn't sound convinced as he signed off, and Ryan had to admit he, too, had doubts about keeping the crazy at bay. Fucking March.

Back at the cabins there was something to distract him from his morose thoughts, he discovered. His land-lady was outside, dressed in a pair of skintight jeans, sheepskin boots and a nubby sweater that rode up and down her hips as she gathered lengths of wood from a pile then tossed them into a wheelbarrow. As distractions went, it was pretty effective.

Nothing wrong with admiring a pretty sight, he told himself. Shutting off the SUV's engine, he relaxed against the leather seat, taking in the whole scene: the backdrop of mountain, woods, snow. The foreground of the lovely lady. When her dog raced up to drop a clearly well-drooled-upon tennis ball at her feet, her obvious response—yuck—made him nearly smile. He couldn't help but like that she scooped up the slimy ball and threw it, anyway.

When she began trundling the wheelbarrow toward his cabin, Ryan jumped from the SUV and hurried toward her. "Let me do that."

She ignored him, continuing to push the contraption until it was right beside his porch. Then she set to stacking the wood against the cabin's siding. As he bent to assist her, she slanted him a look. "I've got this."

"I can help—"

"Part of the service." The smallest of smiles poked a dimple in her left cheek. "You're paying enough for it."

Though he supposed he should go into the house and leave her to it, he stood another moment, watching her efficient movements. When Grimm came bounding up—no ball this time, but a stick—he rubbed the dog's sides then threw the piece of wood into the trees. "Go get it, boy. Go get it."

Still transferring logs, Poppy spared him another glance. "So…what is it you do?"

Oh, hell. He should have concocted a cover story. Writer of the Great American Novel? No way could he pull that off. A trial period as a Trappist monk? Not that, either, because he thought that would mean a vow of silence, which he'd obviously already broken. "Uh…"

"Forget I asked," she said, her focus returned to the wheelbarrow. "None of my business, anyway."

See, it was that indifference that made her the perfect landlady. As he'd told Linus, she wasn't the least bit interested in him.

And it was stupid, how that rankled.

Just another reason he should go inside to his books and his resolution not to let his emotions rule him this month. Still, he hesitated. Inside, alone, the tearing pain might find him as it had last night, when it dug its talons in him during a dark and flame-filled dream, leaving him to wake in a cold sweat and overcome by grinding grief.

Poppy tossed another piece of wood on the stack. "Are you settling in okay? Our amenities are pretty stripped-down, I admit. Is there something else you need?"

He didn't know what made him say it, and say it in such a low, seductive voice. "Are you offering turn-down service?"

A clear pink color rushed over her face and Ryan realized that was the response he'd wanted. Bastard that he was, this studied indifference of hers was annoying. When he'd arrived at the cabins, and especially when she'd shown him into his rental, he'd felt the thrum of awareness that had pulsed like electrified wire between them. She'd practically run from the place, run from him, and…

And he didn't know why that continued to bother him so and what he thought he was doing, teasing her like this.

Remember? No crazy this year.

It's why he'd decided to go hermit.

Ryan shoved his hands in his pockets. "Sorry. It was a stupid thing to say."

"I won't sic Grimm on you this time." Clearly avoiding his gaze, she grabbed the last of the logs and placed them at the top of the stack. Then she seized the wheelbarrow handles and walked away without a backward glance, her color still high.

Leaving his interest in her still as keen as the moment he'd taken her hand in his and felt a strong, sizzling, decidedly sexual jolt.

POPPY SHOVED HER cell phone in her jeans pocket, her son's excited voice still echoing in her head. *And then we saw Mickey at breakfast and Donald, too, and it was the best pancakes in my whole life.*

How could hearing such happiness make her heart ache so much? Trying to shake off the melancholy, she bent to yank the squeegee from the bucket of water at her feet and returned to the task of cleaning the outside windows of cabin three. She'd managed to extract the broken key from the knob with needle-nose pliers and was intent on getting it clean inside and out.

Thanks to good weather, much of the snow in the clearing had melted, leaving slushy, continent-shaped patches. It was still dazzling white on the ski slopes' mountaintop, but from her vantage point the sun was warm enough that she'd discarded her jacket and was working in a thermal T-shirt covered by a plaid flannel shirt. It was another hand-me-down of Brett's, oversize and with a bleach stain on the front. She'd done nothing more with her hair than a loose side braid.

The mascara and the pink lip gloss were her only concessions to vanity…and to the renter she hoped to engage in conversation if he emerged from his cabin sometime soon.

It had been five days since he moved in, two since they'd had their last verbal exchange over the woodpile. She thought it was time she put on her friendly face and made nice. There was good reason for it. As the manager of the cabins, it was part of her job description to provide a pleasant environment. She knew this from her years running Inn Klein's front desk. Every guest was a possible return guest, not to mention a point of referral. If Ryan Harris enjoyed his stay, he might spread the word about the cabins to family and friends. And if she was going to convince her siblings that she was right to do something more than ignore the abandoned ski resort property, she needed to show them it could be a moneymaker.

At the moment she was a little concerned that Ryan Harris wasn't enjoying his stay. Not that she'd been spying—she'd just been casually glancing out her windows—but she'd noticed the man had her same nocturnal habit. As in, not sleeping. She'd get up and go to the kitchen for water only to see that his interior lights were on, as well. Most relaxed and stress-free people weren't up and about at 2:00 a.m. and 3:00 a.m. and 4:30 a.m.

He'd looked tired when she'd seen him heading to his car the day before. Maybe he needed an extra blanket at night. Or perhaps the house's furnace was working improperly. Wasn't it up to her to address those needs?

Are you offering turn-down service?

Her belly flipped at the memory of those words and for the millionth time she wondered why that harmless sexual innuendo had flustered her so. Her flushed reaction was mortifying to recall, and recall it she did, about once an hour. Each time she wished she could erase it from her memory, but since that wasn't possible, she'd decided another interaction, one normal and congenial, would be the way to stop the other from establishing an endless replay loop in her head.

It was damn silly to get so unnerved around him, she knew that. Sure, he was incredibly good-looking, but at twenty-seven, Poppy had encountered plenty of handsome men, including the one who had fathered Mason. But even Denny Howell hadn't made the hair on her head tingle at the roots.

Are you offering turn-down service?

Her imagination ignited and her mind started off in a dangerous direction as her arm moved the squeegee down the dirty glass. But before any clothes were shed, she heard the click of her guest's cabin door being opened. Showtime, she told herself, pushing other thoughts away. Pasting a smile on her face, she turned.

"Mr. Harris!" she called, waggling her tool to get his attention. "Ryan!"

Even from across the clearing his blue gaze knocked her back a little. Hot prickles rose on her skin and she considered scrubbing her face with a handful of snow.

It would only make her mascara run.

So she kept the smile pinned in place as he made his way to her side. Today, his jeans were as battered as hers, but he wore them with a navy wool sweater that had carved bone buttons riding along one shoulder. His jacket was thrown over his arm. He'd nicked his chin shaving, and a dab of toilet paper was stuck on the cut, drawing her attention to his perfectly formed lips.

She swallowed her sigh and pointed with her forefinger to her own chin. "Um…"

He cocked an eyebrow, clearly puzzled.

She tapped her face. "Looks like your razor's new."

With a stifled curse, he felt for the bit of tissue. For some reason that small sign of imperfection relaxed her.

She could do this. They could have a simple conversation. Maybe she'd even invite him over for dinner...?

No. That was taking hospitality much too far. But friendly she could manage. "How's your morning going?" she asked in a bright voice.

His eyebrow winged up for a second time. "Uh, good?"

Apparently her new game face was something of a surprise. "Terrific!" she enthused. "I'm glad to know my first guest is comfortable. You are comfortable, right?"

"March is not a comfortable month."

As responses went, it was a wet blanket. "Oh. Well." *Be affable,* she told herself, wondering how to follow up. When nothing came to mind, she turned back and started on the windows again. To get the high corners she rose on tiptoes, then jumped a little to reach the final inches.

She jumped a lot when he came up close behind her and grabbed the squeegee. "Here, let me get that."

His smell enveloped her, that clean, woody scent that she found delicious. When temptation compelled her to turn her face into his throat and breathe him in, she forced herself to duck from under his arm. Without comment, he finished the corners of that window and then moved to the final one.

"I can handle it from there," she said, when he'd cleared the highest reaches.

He glanced over at her. "I don't mind finishing. A little exercise will do me good. The push-ups I'm making myself do at night aren't exactly wearing me out."

Poppy's imagination wandered off again, conjuring up his powerful body. Naked. By a bed. Swallowing, she forced herself to think of something else. "My mom always said clean windows make the world look brighter."

"Your mom around?" he asked, dropping the washing tool into the bucket, and idly swishing it in the now-cloudy water.

"No. My dad died twelve years ago. Mom six. But I'm still washing windows and hearing her voice when I do so. I'll clean yours today if it won't bother you."

"You bothering me?" Facing her now, he let his gaze settle on her face. "Well…"

He was doing it again, Poppy thought, going breathless. His piercing blue eyes were stealing her will. Her intent was to be friendly but businesslike, all that a good cabins-keeper should be when they wanted to cement the possibility of return attendance and/or good word-of-mouth. Yet with those beautiful eyes focused on her she could only think of his overwhelming, masculine allure.

His magnetism was undeniable.

"I want to tell you…" That when he looked at her she wanted to confess to him all her secrets. Like that he made her liquid inside. Hot. And the outside of her was hot now, too, so sensitive that her shirt's waffle-weave against her skin felt like a man's finger pads dragging over her flesh. The small hairs on her body rose as if trying to get his attention.

She tried reining in her wayward hormones. What had she wanted to talk to him about again? Oh, she remembered! "I saw you were up in the middle of the night."

She'd watched his lights through her window, wondering what kept him awake, feeling foolishly like a teenager mooning after the boy across the street. But it was a man's kisses and a man's hands on her body she'd thought of until she became so twitchy that she'd retreated to a cool shower. Afterward, she'd visited Mason's room, touching his crayon drawings and his dinosaur collection as a way to remember who she was. A mother. A woman who stood strong, and on her own two feet. One who didn't need a man, not for anything.

He was still staring at her with those mesmerizing eyes. "It appears you're having trouble sleeping," she said, remembering, at last, why she'd called him over. "Is there anything I can do?"

His gaze didn't waver. "You, too, then."

"What?"

"If you know I'm not sleeping, it must be because you aren't, either."

"Well, that's because I—" But he didn't want to hear her single-mother money woes or her yearning for her son or her longing for other things she hadn't realized she'd even been missing until he'd taken her hand in his the day they'd met. "Yes."

"While I'm out, I'll see if I can pick us up some extra z's," he said lightly. "See you later, Poppy."

"See you later," she echoed, shoving her hands in her pockets as she watched him step toward his car. Her fingers found her phone, and an idea she'd formed in the night bubbled to the surface. "Oh," she said, pulling it out. "Hey."

He turned, an inquiring expression on his face.

"Before you go...can I take your picture?"

In one lightning move he was back, his body crowding hers, their noses inches apart. "What for?"

he demanded. "What are you going to do with a photo of me?"

Startled, she blinked up at him, aware of his bigness, the odd light in his eyes, the broad wall of his chest almost pressed to the tips of her breasts. *Grimm,* she thought, flicking her glance toward her cabin where her dog was surely snoring on the couch, *Grimm, I need you.*

What a lie. She didn't want rescue. And she wasn't exactly afraid—or not just afraid, anyway. Even with the man's mood so suddenly dark, his very proximity sent a thrill of adrenaline shooting through her veins. As his breath brushed her cheek, her nipples bunched and she felt a sweet spasm between her thighs.

Ryan's head drew even closer. "Why do you want my picture?"

With his blue eyes filling her vision, her body clenched again. Oh, boy. She definitely was something more than scared. She was acutely aroused, which should be shameful, considering his face didn't express a jot of reciprocal sexual interest.

"Poppy?"

She licked her dry lips. "For a website my sister doesn't yet know she'll be building for the cabins. Because you're the first guest."

He moved back so abruptly she went dizzy, swaying like a drunk on her feet. "No photos, Poppy. I want my privacy."

She put her hand to her head. It felt as if she'd chugged something too intoxicating, too fast. "Okay."

"You—" He broke off, combed his fingers through

his hair, then scrubbed his palm down his face. "You just keep your distance, all right?"

She nodded, though he was already stalking toward his SUV. Without another word, he climbed in, started the engine, drove off.

As he took the turn toward the highway, Poppy kept her gaze on the SUV and fanned her hot cheeks. She should have known they could never be friends. Not when her body had picked up this inconvenient and oh-so-uncomfortable interest in having a lover.

CHAPTER THREE

Six days after taking up residence at the cabins, Ryan tramped through the surrounding woods, taking deliberate breaths of the crisp air. On each exhale, he tried pushing the thoughts from his churning mind. He wanted to clear every corner and rid its rafters of all the sticky webs and their clinging hairy spiders. Eleven months out of the year he somehow managed to blank out the memories and the pain. Sure, he walked around like an automaton, but that was better than the man he became in March, the one who staggered about, falling into sharp-toothed emotional depths, crawling free only to stumble and plunge once again.

His footsteps were quiet on the patches of melting snow and wet leaves. The sound of soft crying didn't register at first—it seemed a natural accompaniment to his March mood—but then he heard a dog whine. Grimm.

Without thinking, Ryan moved toward the noise, and from behind a tree he observed his landlady, seated on a fallen log, her dog at her knee, her face in her hands. Concern propelled him forward. "Poppy?"

Her body jerked. As her hands fell, her gaze caught on him. "Oh," she said, and made hasty swipes at her wet cheeks. "You startled me."

"Sorry." Grimm bounded over and Ryan palmed the soft fur on the dog's head. "What's going on? Are you all right?"

"I'm fine. Fine." She made a little sweeping gesture with one hand. "Just out for a walk. You?"

"Same." He narrowed his eyes, noting one of her boots was off. Her heel, covered in a rainbow-striped sock, rested on the banged-up leather. "What's wrong with your foot?"

"Nothing, really. I twisted my ankle on a stupid pine-cone."

He drew closer. "Hurts pretty bad?"

She shook her head.

"You were crying."

"No—"

"I saw the tears on your face, Poppy." Even the dumb bastard that March made of him couldn't miss that. The lashes circling her big gray eyes were still spiky from the dampness. He hunkered down beside her log. "Let me see," he said, reaching toward her foot.

"No." She drew back sharply, as if his touch might be toxic. "Just go on. I don't need any help."

Ryan sat back on his heels, frustrated by her stubbornness. But what did he expect, he thought, pissed at himself. He'd been a capital-*A* asshole to her the day before, when presuming her request for his photo was something less than innocent. He'd been stewing about that, too, wondering if he should apologize for his harsh tone.

Her eyes had been wide and fixed on his face, the sweet scent of her hair invading him with every breath. Despite his agitation, he'd still cataloged both those details. And more: the heat of her slender body, the nearness of her breasts to his chest wall, the sweet curves of her lips that he'd followed with his gaze as her tongue came out to moisten them.

As angry as he'd been, he'd still gone hard.

Jesus.

Shaking his head, he tried to dispel the memory. But in March, the damn things had sharp claws that dug in, held on. Ryan blew out a stream of air then softened his voice. "Poppy, you need to let me do something for you. I'm not the nicest guy in the world, but I can't leave you here, obviously in pain." Doing her a good deed would make up for his rudeness and settle the score between them, he thought, cheering a little.

Then he could put at least one of the things plaguing him—her—out of his mind for the rest of his stay.

"There's really no pain—" she began.

"Tears. I saw them, remember?"

Her gaze shifted away, shifted back. "Look. What do you know about women?"

The question almost made him laugh. If she followed entertainment gossip, she'd know he'd been linked with the most beautiful women in the world since he was thirteen years old. Suppressing a smile, he said, "They come with parts that are different than mine."

She rolled her pretty eyes. "Let me try a different question. Have you ever allowed yourself a good cry?"

"No." His belly cramped, hard, at the thought.

"I didn't think so. Men can be so repressed."

Ryan snorted. "I assure you I'm not repressed."

Shaking her head, Poppy bent to slip her foot back into her shoe. "I walked into that one, I suppose. What

I'm trying to say is that I twisted my ankle, which brought a couple of tears to my eyes. Then I let the floodgates open for a minute to release some tension."

What was she tense about? He considered asking the follow-up, then shut his mouth and stood when she did. *Just do the good deed, Hamilton. Make sure she gets safely back to her place and then you can forget all about her.*

"I was a Boy Scout once." At least he'd played one on TV. "So indulge me and let me see you home," he said, crooking his elbow in her direction.

Her glance flicked from his arm to his face. "Only if you understand I'll snatch you bald if you ever tell you caught me in a moment of weakness."

He blinked. "Harsh."

"Believe it," she said, then placed her fingertips on his forearm and started limping in the direction of the cabins.

Ryan paced slowly beside her as the clearing came into view. "You know, you can lean on me a little."

She shook her head. "Never." Then her body stiffened. "Oh, hell. Oh, no."

"What?" He glanced around, looking for trouble.

"Pick me up, Ryan," she ordered in urgent tones. "Pick me up and then make a run for your cabin."

His pulse's speed shot from normal to NASCAR. Without taking time to identify the threat, he scooped her into his arms and sprinted forward. Grimm scampered beside them, as if happy to be part of a new game, oblivious to the danger.

It had to be a bear, Ryan thought, adrenaline giving him an extra burst of velocity. Though he didn't dare look for it, he could imagine the hulking, stinking presence with the slavering jaws, mouth open wide in order to take a bite of them.

At his back door he set Poppy down to fumble for his keys. "Shit," he said, then finally yanked them out. She grabbed the ring from his hand and did the unlocking herself. With the door open, he hustled the three of them inside, daring a look over his shoulder as he slammed it shut.

There was nothing there.

His heartbeat evening out, he stared at Poppy as she twisted the dead bolt, her focus still telegraphing emergency. Then she hurry-hobbled to the window, where she drew the curtains. The cabin's rear door led directly into the bedroom and now she slid to the floor so her back was against the mattress. "Get down over here," she directed. "You, too, Grimm."

The dog complied and Ryan did, too, though he couldn't figure out what the hell was going on. Maybe the landlady had been hiding her tinfoil hat. "Uh, Poppy?"

"Shh." She glanced around.

Ryan did, too. There wasn't much to see, the bed he'd made that morning, the stack of books on the dresser, through the open door a slice of the short hall that led to the living area. "Who are we hiding from?" he whispered, since that point was now obvious. "The U.S. marshal? Escaped convicts?"

"A combination of the two," she murmured. "My sisters."

Now Ryan could hear a car pulling up—a sound she must have detected as they neared the clearing.

Doors opened, shut. In the distance, knuckles rapped on Poppy's cabin door. Then silence. When the car didn't start up again, he assumed the visitors were awaiting her return. "Will they go away soon?"

She shrugged. "Hard to say."

Bemused, Ryan settled himself more comfortably on the braided rug, his legs crossed at the ankle. A dozen questions presented themselves, but he reminded himself he was intent on booting her out of his head. No point in learning any more about her.

Time ticked by. Grimm flopped onto his side with a groan and promptly fell asleep. Ryan considered doing the same, but he found himself too attuned to Poppy to find such relaxation. From a foot away, he could feel her nerves humming like plucked guitar strings.

He saw his hand reach out to apply a soothing stroke to her shoulder, then he commanded it to drop. When it landed on the floor with a muffled thunk, she looked over at him.

God. There was just something so damn...sweet about her looks. The wide forehead, the big fringed eyes, that valentine of a mouth. It was a rosy pink that matched the sweater that clung to her small, high breasts. His gaze ran down her slender, jean-encased legs, then back to her lips. She'd taste like cotton candy, he decided, and...

And he shouldn't be contemplating her taste.

"You must think I'm crazy," Poppy said.

"No." That would be him, getting hung up on his landlady when he was here to be a hermit.

"Go ahead, admit it." Her little smile revealed the fascinating dimple in her left cheek.

Looking away from her, he shrugged. "I've got a brother who is often annoying. I've been known to duck him when I can."

"Yes, well…" She sighed. "Here's the deal. They're not entirely on board with renting out the cabins. I don't want to get into yet another discussion with them about it."

"They're against making money?"

She laughed a little. "Walkers are never against making money. We're just not too good at keeping hold of it. This land… The family legend is it's cursed. Can you believe such a thing?"

March was cursed. In his darker moments Ryan thought he might be, as well. He shrugged again. "Is there a good reason?"

"Any number. Because it was Native-American land stolen for the timber it provided. Because in the early years one Walker logger killed another logger over a woman—who then promised retribution through the ages. Simpler version—my father was a piss-poor financial manager."

She said it with a wry affection.

"Was he?" Ryan asked.

"My siblings, everybody around consider him a foolish ne'er-do-well who should have sold out long ago… but then he made a deal with the devil that essentially means we can't." A little sigh caused a strand of golden-brown hair curved against her cheek to tremble. "I'd like to prove that there's still something good here at our mountain." She paused, her gaze dropping to her lap. "Not to mention that I could really use the cash."

"Well—"

Her fingers gripped his forearm as her head shot up. "Shh! I think they're coming over here."

Ryan's eyebrows rose. Was her sibling radar that fine-tuned? But sure enough, now he could detect footsteps on the wooden porch and the *bam-bam-bam* of a fist knocking.

"Insistent, aren't they?" he asked, his voice hushed.

Her mouth moved, the words soundless, and he had to focus carefully to read her lips. "You've got that right." When the rap on the door sounded again, her fingers curled tighter around his arm.

His gaze stayed glued to her face, taking in her glowing skin, small scoop of a nose, the slightly square chin. She didn't have a loud kind of beauty, but the loveliness of her was arresting, anyway. He wanted to rub his thumb along her bottom lip; he could imagine her tongue darting out to taste his skin.

He could see himself bending his head and kissing the thin, tender flesh of her throat.

As if she could hear his thoughts, Poppy's eyes flared wide and there was a new kind of alarm to her expression. But she still gripped his arm and now he shifted toward her, running his free hand from her wrist to her shoulder to calm her uneasiness.

But she quivered under his touch, and her big eyes went even more round. Her pupils dilated and he heard her breath catch as her cheeks turned pink.

To hell with hermit, Ryan thought. He was going to kiss her. And she had to know it was coming, because she had gone as still as a winter bunny with a hawk on the hunt. Yet she didn't attempt escape.

As he bent closer, another annoying *rat-a-tat-tat*

sounded. He flicked a glance toward the front door. "Maybe you should talk to them," he whispered. "Make them go away."

And leave the two of us alone.

A deeper flush broke across her creamy skin. Still reading his mind, Ryan decided.

Her tongue peeked out to moisten that adorable, kissable bottom lip. "They'll insist on meeting you first," she whispered.

"Sure," he murmured, cupping her hot cheek in his palm. "Whatever—"

They'll insist on meeting you.

The words sank in. *Shit,* he thought, dropping his hand and scooting out of Poppy's range. *Shit!* He couldn't meet them. What were the odds that all three Walker sisters would never have glanced at a gossip rag or never watched an entertainment show?

He'd have to make some sort of excuse. "Poppy…"

She was already rising to her feet, the flush now only two flags of bright red high on her cheekbones. "I'll get out of your way."

"What?" He read the embarrassment on her face. "No, wait, it isn't like that—"

"It's exactly how I want it," Poppy replied, her stubborn chin leading toward the front entry as he jumped to his feet and trailed after her.

"Poppy…"

Standing beside one of the narrow front windows, she dared a peek. "Anyway, they're making tracks, so I can, too."

He realized she was right. That humming he heard wasn't a leftover sexual buzz but a vehicle as it drove away from the cabins. "Come on, Grimm," Poppy called, and the dog knocked into Ryan, making him stumble, and letting the woman and her pet get away before he could…

Do what? he demanded of himself.

It was fucking March and everything he touched during that month turned to disaster. So he had to keep his hands off the landlady. Stay hermit.

Even if that meant he now had even more on his mind—like a kiss that hadn't happened.

MISERABLE AND MISERABLY wet, Poppy climbed the steps to Ryan's cabin, a suitcase in each hand and a drenched Grimm pressed close to her knees. The short walk through the icy hail of the predicted March storm—which had arrived, predictably, days later than the meteorologists originally indicated—had frozen her blood in her veins. The low temperature had also petrified her fingers around the bag handles, so she merely lifted her foot to bang on his door with the toe of her boot.

There was no immediate response.

Shivering, she glanced at the adjacent driveway, ensuring that his SUV was, indeed, parked there. Though the weather had rendered the late afternoon twilight-dark, she could still see the vehicle's hulking shape. She didn't bother looking back at her own vehicle, because the memory of it was depressing enough. The heavy oak limb that had crushed a portion of her mudroom roof had also crumpled its front end.

Using her toe, Poppy knocked again with insistent thumps.

Ryan was her only hope for transportation back to town.

Grimm whined, looked up at her, then at her renter's front door. "I know, boy," she said, "I'm going to get us out of this abysmal weather."

Maybe. It wasn't out of the realm of possibility that the man was ignoring her summons. Two days ago, they'd almost kissed. She'd tried convincing herself otherwise, but there was no getting around it. The intent had been on his face and the expectation had been running riot through her body.

Then he'd backed away, which was terribly embarrassing…since she should have been the one to retreat first. Hadn't she learned anything? Didn't she know better than to get mixed up with a wealthy flatlander?

He probably thought it prudent to avoid the sex-starved single woman next door. Not that she was sex-starved in the least, she reassured herself, with another kick at the wooden surface. She was a mother, with other priorities besides—

The door swung open, revealing Ryan, backlit by the cheerful light coming from the living room lamps and the crackling fire. Poppy squeezed the suitcase handles and sucked in her bottom lip to keep her jaw from dropping to her knees.

He was naked except for a skimpy towel wrapped around his hips.

Number one note to self: purchase better quality linens for the cabins.

Number two note to self: maybe she was a little hungry, after all.

The heat from inside his place reached outward to

the porch and Grimm, apparently taking it as an invitation, rushed inside. Poppy hesitated, trying to keep her gaze on anything but Ryan's damp hair, his newly shaven handsome features, the oh-God-how-amazing chiseled pecs, rippling abs and that pair of etched lines that angled from the man's lean waistline toward the bulge that was barely hidden by thin terry cloth.

The wall clock over his left shoulder—which was heavy with muscle and still dotted with water—was fascinating.

"Poppy?" He reached for her and she couldn't help but step back. "Jesus, what are you doing out there? You're all wet."

"Uh-huh," she said faintly.

"Come in."

Because she was warmer now, just from looking at him, she still hesitated. "Could I beg a ride to town?"

"Get inside." Taking hold of the sleeve of her soaked jacket, he pulled her over the threshold then shut the door. "Before we do anything, we need to get you dried off." He glanced down at the towel wrapped around him.

"For goodness sake, don't take that off!" she ordered, the shrill note to her voice not disguised by the raucous drumming of the continuing hail on the roof.

Ryan smiled.

It was the first of his she'd ever seen. Poppy almost gaped again, but she sucked in her bottom lip once more as her blood jacked up another ten degrees. He should smile all the time, she thought, dazzled by its whiteness and the way it drew up the outer corners of his piercing eyes. He had a face made for happy.

His smile could almost make her happy, even under these gloomy circumstances.

"Just a second," he said, then hustled toward the bedroom, only to return a few moments later wearing a pair of jeans and an unbuttoned flannel shirt, and carrying a couple of dry towels in his hand. He draped one on Grimm, who then trotted, wearing it like a horse blanket, toward the fire. Ryan started rubbing the other towel over Poppy's saturated hair.

Still gripping the suitcases, she stood dumbly under the brisk attention. Not only did it feel dangerously good to have someone tend to her, but there was also his naked, great-smelling chest a mere few inches from her nose. It had been a long time since she'd been around a man's unclothed muscles and she found the experience…bemusing.

Yeah, that was it.

And, oh, she really, really needed to get out of here.

Dropping the bags to the floor, she sidestepped from Ryan and snatched the towel away to blot her hair herself. "I have this," she said.

He stepped up to her again, his fingers going to the zipper of her coat. At the fumbling near her breasts, her voice went shrill again. "What are you doing?" She batted at his hands.

"Poppy, you're dripping all over the floor," he said, his tone patient and reasonable. "I'm only trying to help."

"Try to help by collecting your car keys, okay?" she grumbled, unfastening the jacket herself, though they should make their move to town right away. "It would be best to get on the road before it's full dark."

Instead of doing her bidding, he stood his ground. "What's the reason behind the great escape?"

She crossed to the kitchen, where she folded the towel and placed it on the counter. Then she drew off her outer garment and looked around for a place to set the sodden fabric. Ryan snatched it from her hand and draped it over the back of a chair he drew near the fire.

"We don't have time for it to dry," Poppy said, a little panic rising again as Ryan turned to face her, crossing his arms over his chest. Really, it was important she get away from the distraction of his male flesh as soon as possible, especially when she was in this vulnerable state.

"Poppy."

Wrenching her gaze away from him, she focused on her pet, who was settled by the hearth, his head now on the towel he was using as a pillow. "Don't get too comfy, Grimm. We've got to go back into the storm." Then she risked a glance at Ryan. "You probably couldn't hear it over the hail, but a branch came down at my place."

Once again, bearing out the Walker curse. Because she doubted her pocketbook could handle another hit, panic rose again. And not due to Ryan this time, but because she might have just witnessed the end of her dream. "It took out part of the roof," she continued, her voice as miserable as she felt, "and the front end of my car."

In a blink he was before her, his hands gripping her shoulders. "Are you all right?" His gaze ran over her body, causing a shiver. Apparently taking that as a sign of chill, he pulled her nearer the fire, then held her there, her back to his front.

"I'm fine," she said, wiggling out of his grip and away from the heat. Her jeans were clammy against her shins, but that only served to remind her she needed to get someplace safe to change. "I can't stay at my cabin, though. Hence the need for the ride to Blue Arrow Lake. Will you take me?"

"All right," he said, his gaze seeming to assess her condition again. "You're sure you're okay?"

"I will be." The optimist inside her declared... With some dry clothes and time to think, perhaps she could find her way through this latest obstacle. "Can we go now?"

It took only a few moments for him to collect his coat and hat while she struggled back into her wet outerwear. Grimm looked reluctant to brave the storm again, and got up from his place by the fire with a great sigh. By the time Ryan was in his protective gear, she had the bags and was standing by the front door.

He grabbed the cases from her, and shoved one under his arm so he had a free hand to grasp the knob. Without turning it, he slanted her a glance. "You have everything you need?"

She needed to get away from his attractive presence, she knew. Even with all that was on her mind, his half-naked image was burned into her brain. What if she'd leaned forward while he was drying her hair and placed a kiss on the center of his chest? If her tongue had slipped out for a small lick, who could blame her?

"Poppy?" Ryan's brows drew together. "Do you have everything?"

"Sure, sure," she said, giving herself a sharp mental pinch. "Everything." One bag held some of her clothes and belongings. The other was filled with her son's things, including his favorite pillow, just in case she still found herself in other quarters by the time Mason was due back in a couple of days.

Ryan's hand lifted, and he touched her chin with the back of two fingers, angling her face toward his. Her breath caught at the touch, then caught again at the intensity of his gaze. "Why the sad face?"

She shrugged a shoulder. "My residence and my mode of transportation are trashed," she said, worry bubbling again. "Not to mention my brother has a brutal 'I told you so.'"

"Is that where I'm taking you?"

On a sigh, Poppy nodded, then she reached for the door herself, and pulled it open. At the blast of hail-laden wind, she staggered back, only to be bolstered by Ryan's bigger body. Whatever he said was inaudible over the sounds of the storm, but she plowed forward, his steadying hand on her shoulder.

Pebbles of frozen rain peppered her head and face as they fought their way toward his SUV. An unholy howl made her start as a new gust of wind wound its way through the trees. Both she and Ryan glanced upward, and then he pulled her into his embrace, her face pressed against his wet coat, protecting her as a flurry of small branches and leaves whipped around them.

"We'd better run!" Ryan said against her ear, then he gripped her hand in his and they raced toward the passenger side of his SUV. He tucked her inside and threw the suitcases on the backseat. As soon as Grimm had jumped aboard, Ryan made his way around the front.

Once behind the wheel, he drew off his stocking cap

and scraped his hand down his wet face. "Are you sure you want to go out in this?"

"The other cabins are uninhabitable as yet and it's not as if I can strike a tent on the ground in this weather," she said, as the wind rocked the vehicle. "What else can I do?"

He opened his mouth, seemed to think better of what he was about to say and pressed a button to start the SUV's engine. The dashboard came to life, with switches and dials and a touch screen the size of a paperback lighting up. She goggled, wondering if the vehicle could fly through the air or move underwater like a submarine. But now it was on wheels like a regular automobile and soon they were traversing the four miles to the highway, going slowly as they both tried peering through the windshield. The wipers worked madly against the onslaught of the hail and the headlights illuminated the blacktop littered with leaves, pinecones and fallen branches.

The heater blasted warmth, but Poppy still shivered, taking in the ominous conditions. "Are you going to be all right in your cabin?" she said to Ryan.

He didn't spare her a glance. "I don't think your brother would welcome me, too, would he?"

Brett didn't have a kind word for anyone, not since he'd returned home, scarred in places you could and couldn't see. Poppy rummaged through her purse, peering into the dark cavern of it for paper and pen so she could give Ryan her cell phone number. "I'll return tomorrow to assess the damage—and I hope with somebody who can fix the worst of it." Yes, she very much hoped her small cushion of cash was going to cover what needed to be covered.

"Uh-oh." Ryan slowed the SUV. "I don't think you'll be returning tomorrow."

"What?" Poppy frowned, still hunched over her purse as she focused on finding something to write on.

"I don't think you'll be returning tomorrow," he repeated, bringing the SUV to a full stop. "Because you're not going anywhere today, except back to my cabin."

At that, Poppy's head shot up, and in the beam of the headlights she saw the tree that had fallen across the private road that led to the resort, a good two miles short of the turnoff onto the highway.

CHAPTER FOUR

FUCKING MARCH, RYAN thought, as they did the reverse dash from his vehicle to the cabin's front door. By the time they were inside, all three of them were dripping, though Poppy had to be worse off than he since fifteen minutes before she'd arrived wet already. The dog returned to the towel he'd taken to the fire on his first visit. Ryan made his way toward the bedroom with the suitcases, Poppy at his heels.

"Time to get into some dry clothes," he said over his shoulder. "You can have the bedroom."

"I certainly will not." She yanked one of the bags from his hand. "I'll change in the bathroom."

"It's too small for you and your suitcase."

She ignored his warning and strode into the shoebox-size tiled room, then slammed the door. A few minutes later, a thump followed by a yelp told him her elbow had connected with the wall.

By the time he heard a couple more less-than-mysterious bumps, he'd changed into sweatpants and a T-shirt. A pair of thick socks were on his feet.

Standing in front of the fire, he saw her exit the bathroom, a scowl on her face. She stowed her suitcase inside the bedroom, then shot him a fulminating look. "But I'm not sleeping in there, you got that?"

He gazed back at her. She was dressed in a similar style to himself: sweats and T-shirt, with a pair of fuzzy slippers on her feet. "You're pretty bad-tempered for a woman at my mercy."

"At your mercy?" she repeated, waving a hand. "Don't forget I have Grimm."

At the sound of his name, the dog lifted his big head, assessed the situation through half-closed eyes then returned his skull to the floor with an audible thunk.

Ryan looked at the pet, looked back at Poppy. "Oh, I'm very afraid."

"Well, I'm not afraid of you, either," Poppy said. She glanced around the room, then her gaze settled on the window, as the storm continued to rage outside. "It's not letting up." She sighed.

"It's not, no."

"Still, I'm going to call a guy from town. He'll get out here with a chain saw and clear the tree…." Her words trailed off.

"Once the storm lets up," he finished for her.

She sighed again, then rummaged in her purse for her cell phone.

The hail continued to rattle the roof as she murmured into her phone and he went into the kitchen to rustle up some dinner. It was early, but what else was there for them to do? He thought it wiser to keep busy. So he heated soup, sliced cheese, threw some crackers onto a plate. Grimm shambled into the room and when Poppy finished her call she arrived as well with a plastic container of dog kibble.

They all began to eat.

Ryan pretended he couldn't smell the sweet fragrance

from her still-damp hair over the aroma of the tomato soup. When they cleaned up at the sink, he acted as if he wasn't aware of her small female body under those layers of thick cotton. He was successful enough to relax his guard when they returned to the living room fire. As he bent to stoke it with a new log, he didn't even think about the basket that he'd discovered in the corner of the room the day he'd moved in.

So he was startled when he turned to find her poking among the pile of DVDs of movies and sitcoms that went back ten years and more. "What are you doing?" he asked, hoping like hell it hadn't come out like a squawk.

She glanced up at him. "I found this bunch at a yard sale and brought them back for potential guests. I saw you have a laptop. We could watch one on your computer. It would give me a chance to bone up on pop culture."

"Outdated pop culture." Hadn't he seen the first season of *Heaven Come Early* there? If they watched, maybe she wouldn't recognize his just-turned-teen self as one of the stars of the popular dramedy, its title based on the George Bernard Shaw quote "A happy family is but an earlier heaven." Still, there was no reason to chance it. If she discovered who he was, word might get out and then his privacy would go poof! He saw her fingers brush over a DVD of *Main Line,* the last movie he'd made before he'd retired from on-camera work. "I thought you said you liked to read."

Her quizzical look signaled he must sound a little desperate. Ryan tempered his voice. "The only good light is in here and I want to get back to my George R.R. Martin."

"So then I'll take the laptop to the bedroom—"

"I thought you had an aversion to the bedroom."

Yes, desperate. But she didn't push any more, instead crossing to her purse to pull out a paperback. Without another word, she settled at one end of the sofa. Realizing he'd boxed himself into a corner, Ryan retrieved his own book and took the opposite place.

Even the dramatic events of the seven kingdoms couldn't keep his eyes off that basket of DVDs. He should have buried them somewhere when he'd first spotted them. Not that he regretted that part of his life. He'd been a child of Hollywood—well, Malibu, really—with his father a well-known and well-respected stunt director, his mother a successful makeup artist. He and Linus and their pals had started making movies at an early age and during a dinner party his folks threw, a casting agent had seen their latest and wondered aloud if Ryan wanted to try for the part in an upcoming show.

It had seemed like a great way to get out of school, which was damn boring in seventh grade.

A teen star had been born.

He'd gotten a kick out of it, to tell the truth. He'd enjoyed pretending he was someone else and it had taken a while for fame to catch up with him…years before it smacked him hard in the face. But by the time he was twenty-one, twenty-two, he didn't like the long hours wearing heavy makeup, the bullshit from the suits, the celebrity press that wrote ridiculous stories probably planted by studio publicists. The women who came for his face and stayed for his fame.

And he'd garnered enough money to stop making films in order to actually *make* films. And cable series and TV movies.

Maybe people would have forgotten him and he could have gone on to live a nonnotorious life. But then came that March. Fucking March.

"You could scare small children with that expression you're wearing," Poppy suddenly said.

He never wanted to be around small children again. So he grunted, and turned a page he hadn't read.

But her comment returned Poppy smack-dab to the center of his consciousness. He cast a sidelong look at her, watching the firelight play over her innocent angel face, noting her curly lashes and the tail of hair she idly played with as she pretended to enjoy her book.

Because she wasn't turning any pages.

Time passed.

More time passed.

The hail changed to a torrential rain that was a dull roar against the roof. The walls seemed to close in, creating an intimacy that was unwelcome. Risky. Still, Ryan adjusted his position on the cushions, pushing his back deeper into the sofa's angle so he could pretend to read and watch her at the same time. She continued to stare straight ahead, thinking…what?

Then she turned her head quickly, too quickly for him to redirect his gaze. She'd caught him. Their eyes caught, too.

The walls drew closer.

He tightened his hold on his book, though he wanted to throw it aside, then grab her to him and escape March and all its terrible cruelties in her fragrant female body.

He knew what lust was, knew its power, and it was gathering in his loins, in his chest, and he wanted to give in to it. The landlady wasn't afraid of him or immune to him, he could see that by the flush on her face, the quick flutter of the pulse in her neck.

Why the hell couldn't they indulge?

Because after the deed was done he would still be himself, he knew. It would still be this particular month, and if he wasn't able to get away from her in the morning—unlikely, as it appeared she'd remain stuck in his cabin—then he chanced dragging her down into hell with him.

Nothing good ever came of March.

Her gaze still not leaving his, she wet her lips with her tongue.

Ryan's body tightened all over. He was more than half-hard, and he forced himself to look away so that he wouldn't go full-ready. But shit, that mouth— *Don't think about her mouth.*

Clearing his throat, Ryan shot up from his seat. "You want a drink? Coffee? Beer? Wine?"

"Caffeine keeps me up," she said.

Since he was already uncomfortably up himself, he took that as a sign to go for beer or wine. God knew he needed something to take off the edge. In the kitchen, he found the opener and a bottle of red. Since she had stocked the cabinets, he didn't suppose she'd object to drinking out of the large glass tumblers.

He placed one in her hand, careful not to touch her, not to look at her. Careful not to think about her mouth. Kissing her mouth.

Knowing he couldn't go back to pretend-reading, and

because thoughts of bed just made him jumpy, he looked about for an activity to occupy them. A box of jigsaw puzzle pieces sat on a nearby shelf. He grabbed it up.

"You like to do this sort of thing?" he asked, dumping the pieces onto the coffee table in front of the sofa.

Poppy set her book aside. "What's it a picture of? It's something else I found at a garage sale, but I didn't look at it too closely."

He sat beside her and sifted through the cardboard snippets, turning some faceup. They all seemed pinkish in color. "This isn't the original box. Maybe it's one of those really difficult ones that are just the puzzle, no helpful photo."

"Those take a lot of time," she said, starting to move pieces around, as she sipped at her wine.

"And concentration," he added. *We won't be able to think of anything perilous.*

"Look for the corners first," Poppy advised, apparently getting into the spirit of the thing. With a triumphant sound, she held one up.

"Good for you." Ryan found a couple of pieces already joined and set them in the center.

They both continued to work, each of them seeming to find a part of the whole that they claimed as their own. The fire crackled. The very generous pour of wine in each glass was consumed. After some minutes went by, Poppy murmured, "Oh, there is a picture. I think it's a woman. I have some of her face."

He glanced over, noting she'd constructed a nose, and part of one eye. "I'm still getting nothing but pink," he said, trying to work a little faster. As diversions went, the activity was a success, and he congratulated himself on his brilliant idea.

Until...

It stopped being brilliant.

He stared down at the section of the puzzle he'd completed. "Uh..."

"Hmm?" His companion-in-puzzles fit one piece to another, tossed back the last swallow in her glass, then set it aside.

"Maybe we should quit," Ryan suggested.

"What? No." With a frown, she turned her head, then jerked it back when she saw what he'd wrought.

Naked tits. Overinflated, pearly pink and topped with tight, upstanding nipples.

A squeak of horror escaped Poppy's lips, followed by a moment of stunned silence. Then she started to laugh. As she laughed harder, she put one palm over her belly, and the other over her mouth.

Need—rash, blazing and no longer deniable— overtook Ryan. That mouth, he thought again. He was going to have that mouth. It was imperative he taste the laughter bubbling from it, inhale the sound into his shrunken soul. He had to kiss her.

POPPY'S GUARD WAS down, thanks to an outrageous pair of puzzle breasts. Maybe because of the wine she'd drunk or maybe because she'd been walking a tightrope of tension all evening, hyperaware of Ryan's very-male presence in a room that had kept getting smaller by the second, but for whatever reason the sight of those naked boobs had tickled her sense of the ridiculous. Aware she might sound the tiniest bit hysterical, she pressed her hand harder to her lips, still giggling like mad when Ryan reached over and drew it away.

The gesture didn't immediately alert her to a threat. She still couldn't believe that she'd been so anxious to smother the sexual vibrations humming in the room that she'd gladly dived into working a puzzle…of an X-rated image. Even with the knowledge that her car and her cabin were half-ruined lurking at the back of her mind—or because that knowledge was lurking at the back of her mind—it struck her as hilariously funny. Even now another laugh rose in her throat.

"Poppy," Ryan said, his voice soft.

Her gaze shifted to his face, and the glow in his blue eyes sent her to serious in a hurry.

But it didn't send her body anywhere safe. Instead, she sat frozen on the couch, her hand cradled in his much larger one. The contrast made her feel feminine and breathless and…oh, boy, curious. Because she knew what that tone in his voice signaled. She knew what was coming.

And she hadn't been kissed in over five years.

So sue her, she had a curiosity about kissing. Strike that. She had a curiosity about how Ryan would kiss.

And then…and then he was showing her. His mouth brushed over hers, the touch as light as a snowflake, though the brief caress sent heat racing like a flash fire over her skin. When his lips came back a second time, she parted her mouth, hoping to entice him to make it firmer. Hoping he'd brush his tongue with hers.

It had been aeons since she'd been French-kissed.

On the third gentle pass, she speared her hand in Ryan's hair to keep their lips locked. He made a sound, low in his throat. Gratified? Smug? She didn't care. Her muscles tensed, her body quivering as she anticipated his next move.

His tongue, all right, but now it brushed like damp butterfly wings against her bottom lip. Her thighs clenched and he rubbed his thumb over the knuckles of the hand he held. Soothing, every stroke of his soothing, as if he knew she was all of a sudden so keyed up that a stronger touch might shatter her. Who would blame her for that?

Five-plus years without a proper kiss.

Ryan's free arm came around her shoulders to draw her closer. She breathed in his scent as tears stung the corners of her eyes, and she squeezed them tight, mortified that she might have to explain—again—a crying jag. It had just been so long since she'd snuggled up to something this big, this warm, this human.

"You smell better than Grimm," she said against Ryan's mouth.

He drew back a little. "What?"

She discovered her tears had dried up and she was on the verge of more giggles. How much wine did she have floating around in her system? "You smell good," she said, nuzzling beneath his chin.

"You're suddenly friendly," he murmured as she pressed tiny kisses along the edge of his elegant jaw.

"I'm curious," she corrected, drawing her lips over his chin.

"Me, too," he whispered, then tilted his head to take another kiss.

Oh. Oh, God.

His tongue plunged into the cavern of her mouth.

It was no longer a subtle exploration, but a sexual onslaught, masculine, deliberate, hot.

Delicious.

Poppy clutched at the hand that held hers and pressed close to his hard chest as her head fell back and he took what he wanted from her. This wasn't a French kiss, this wasn't anything cosmopolitan or civilized in the least. This was a Neanderthal kind of kiss, one that might involve caves and the pulling of hair and the ripping of fur robes—if only she had the guts to beg for such things.

Just as she ran out of air, he lifted his head and they both sucked in ragged breaths, staring at each other. Poppy's head swam a little, from lack of oxygen or perhaps from a surplus of libido. She wondered about trying to work up some regret or concern about the kisses, but her heart was pounding too hard for clear thinking. A little muddy logic was good, she decided. It kept her mind off unpleasant things, such as why she was at Ryan's cabin in the first place.

For that alone, she owed him. "Definitely better than Grimm," she said.

Still holding her close, Ryan's expression turned bemused. Then he glanced toward the snoozing dog. "I'm starting to worry, Poppy. Do you mean to tell me you let your dog kiss you? Am I going to catch something with you being the conduit between me and getting a sloppy from your pooch?"

Such a silly conversation, she thought. She didn't get kisses from Grimm. But the silliness made it perfect for the giddy, dizzy mood Ryan's thorough kisses had left her in. "Absolutely not," she said, stroking the placket of his flannel shirt with her fingers. Poppy Walker, touching beautiful Ryan Harris's flannel!

"You're not going to make me believe a dog's mouth is cleaner than a human's," he said. "That's an urban myth."

"But you're in the mountains now," she pointed out, smiling a little as she teased him.

He shook his head. "God, you're cute," he said, then pressed a kiss to her nose. "But let's be real. Out in the woods I've seen your dog sniffing some extremely suspicious substances."

Thank goodness he appeared to want to avoid serious or second thoughts as much as she. Poppy wiggled on the cushions and found a comfortable place against Ryan's side. His hand stroked idly over her hair, and the atmosphere turned almost companionable, though the smoke from those powerful kisses lingered like a haze in the air. She stretched her legs, displacing some puzzle pieces as she propped her heels on the coffee table. "The bacteria in a dog's mouth is species-specific," she informed him. "Which means you're much less likely to catch something serious from a dog than another human."

He glanced down at her, the amused light in his eyes making her heart jerk, once. "Where did you come across this bit of knowledge?"

It was the kind of thing the mother of a young son knew, especially the mother of a young son who adored his furry pet. But she didn't want to tell Ryan about Mason. Her little boy and her status as a mother were secured in another compartment for the moment. Mason's mommy didn't cozy up to handsome men by crackling fires. Mason's mommy didn't want to share some more of those potent kisses.

But Poppy did.

Because she was tipsy, or tipsy on Ryan's taste or maybe because she needed further diversion from recalling the damage the storm had wrought on her life. Her mind began to flash on the crack of sound as that heavy limb—

No.

She twisted toward Ryan, grabbed the front of his shirt in a fist and yanked his mouth down to hers. He lurched toward her, catching himself with one hand on the back of the couch before they bashed noses. Their lips met instead and she reveled in this next kiss: the sure thrust of his tongue, the heat of his body, the flame that set fire to her blood. Her fingers curled into his shirt just as she thought about taking off hers, because she was hot, so hot, and—

An icy trail of moisture hit the back of her head, ran down her neck.

Startled, Poppy jolted, then jerked her head upward, only to receive an eyeful of freezing water. "Wha—?"

More trickled into her mouth and both she and Ryan came off the couch in a rush. He shoved the furniture away from the narrow stream that now seeped steadily from the seam between an exposed beam and the ceiling plaster. She ran to the kitchen for a pot to catch the leak.

Another sprang before she returned.

Poppy's mood plummeted as she watched Ryan bend to slide one of the glasses they'd been drinking from beneath the new drip. He looked disheveled and aggravated and absolutely gorgeous.

And completely the wrong man with whom to be satisfying her curiosity after five-plus years of celibacy.

"What is wrong with me?" she said aloud. Her dwelling was damaged, her vehicle was damaged and she'd been playing kissy face with some rich, great-looking stranger who from the beginning had put up her back. Yet she'd almost been on her back! "How did this happen?" she demanded.

Ryan spared her a glance and she could see he was as displeased by the situation as she. "It's March," he said with a grimace. "Fucking March."

CHAPTER FIVE

From *You Send Me*, a screenplay by Linus Hamilton:

FADE IN:

EXT. STREET—DAY

A luxury convertible pulls into a parking space in front of the log cabin-style post office in a tiny, isolated Southern California mountain town. Twenty-nine-year-old LINUS HAMILTON's head turns from side to side, taking in the flanking businesses: a minuscule grocery and an even smaller real estate office. A summer breeze plays with LINUS's wealth of dirty-blond hair.

A woman in shorts and hiking boots exits the post office, catching his attention. She shades her eyes with her hand, as LINUS, in slacks and T-shirt, steps from the vehicle.

WOMAN
Are you lost?

LINUS
Nope.

He grins, an easy smile that is boyish and charming.

LINUS
Just exploring the area. Do you happen to know how many post offices there are in these mountains?

Bemused, the woman shakes her head.

LINUS
Only slightly fewer than the number of rodent-size dogs you can spy on a stroll down Rodeo Drive. In other words, a lot. I've made it my goal to mail my brother a postcard from each and every one.

He ambles past the woman, who turns to watch him as he reaches for the door handle.

INT. POST OFFICE—DAY

Inside the narrow space, a short wooden counter is directly ahead. The left and right walls are covered with old-fashioned post office boxes, their glass faces painted with gold numbers edged in black that look Western in design. Behind the counter is twenty-four-year-old CHARLOTTE "CHARLIE" WALKER, her head with its pixie-cut of flaxen hair lowered as she organizes something on the shelf below. When the door opens, she looks up with a smile. It fades as LINUS crosses the threshold.

CHARLIE
Are you lost?

Staring at CHARLIE, LINUS's hand creeps up to his chest. Then he shakes himself a little, pulls in a breath and beams out another trademark grin.

LINUS
I think I just found exactly what this summer's been lacking.

THE COLD BROOK, California, post office provided counter service for its small community from 3:00 p.m. until 5:00 p.m. in the afternoon, Monday through Friday. Charlotte Walker passed a book of stamps over the scarred wooden surface and flashed a farewell smile for her friend Janelle, who clerked in the deli/grocery next door. It was Monday, which meant Charlie hoped to be seeing the other woman again a couple of evenings from now in Blue Arrow Lake. The two of them and some other girlfriends had a standing date in the bigger town twelve winding miles down the highway—weather permitting. A fierce March storm had been raging on and off but if it let up, then Charlie was going to have a relaxing couple of glasses of wine with her friends later this week.

A girl, even a born-and-bred mountain girl, had to get out and see a little more of the world sometimes.

Charlie took a peek at the wall clock. Fifteen more minutes then she'd slide and lock the metal grille that secured the counter area and back room. She expected one or two of Cold Brook's eight hundred residents would rush through at 4:58 p.m. with the urgent need to get a package weighed or a letter sent off, so she occupied herself by tidying the carousel of postcards that sat next to her station. Hardly anyone ever gave them a glance, so it was a bit anal of her to double-check they were properly organized, but she was studying online for a degree in accounting and details mattered to Charlie.

The customary squeak of the front door came at 4:57 p.m. A bit early, she thought, glancing up to see Walt Eustace bustle through, a box of pamphlets in his arms. Brochure-mailing day, she guessed. It was the time of year when he sent out reminders to previous renters of Cold Brook properties in anticipation of the summer season. *We wish you were here!*

Walt's big belly had yet to make it halfway to her when the door swung open again and twelve-year-old Erin Frye walked through, a letter clutched in her hand. She had a pen pal across the country, someone she'd linked up with through Scouting, and Erin enjoyed perusing the binder of stamp choices to pick just the right one to paste in the right-hand corner of the envelope intended for her buddy in Woods Hole, Massachusetts. Charlie stifled a little sigh. Stamp-shopping could take the middle-schooler past closing time.

Oh, well. Given that Erin's pen pal was a Boy Scout, Charlie got a little kick out of imagining an innocent romance was blooming in the mailbags that crossed the country. It spiced up the mundane routine of her days as the winter doldrums had yet to be replaced by spring fancies.

She was reaching for Walt's carton of glossy leaflets

when the door squeaked a third time, bringing with it another cool draft of moist air. The small hairs on Charlie's exposed nape stood up, an instant before her gaze lifted to take in the newcomer.

Her palms went damp.

Charlie's rite of passage had returned.

In haste, she refocused on the pamphlets and pasted on a smile for Walt. "Hey, you just made it in under the wire," she said, raising her voice. "Don't know that I'll be able to take care of all the customers before closing time."

Behind Walt, Erin let out a little bleat of distress. Feeling guilty, Charlie looked around Walt's rotund form to meet the girl's eyes. "Don't worry," she said softly. "Your letter will go out today."

The man still loitering by the entrance didn't get any of her attention. Why, oh, why, was Linus here? She'd never expected to see him again; had made it clear that theirs had been a short-term summer romance. No way was she onboard with a replay.

Walt was his usual jovial self. She would have chatted him up longer, hoping that Linus might get bored and leave, but Erin was shuffling her feet and appearing anxious. So Charlie finished business with her current customer, then dragged out the fat binder of loose stamps as Erin stepped up to the counter. From the periphery of her vision, she saw Linus hold open the door and say "Good day" to Walt.

Why couldn't he follow the other man out?

Her gaze returned to the plastic sleeves that displayed the available offerings. The young girl studied them with deep concentration. "Can I choose more than one—as many as I like as long as it adds up to first class postage?"

"No problem," Charlie assured the girl. "I'll hand-cancel them myself."

Erin turned the page to inspect the next sleeve's contents. Her fingernails were painted a glittery purple and she had a unicorn-embossed elastic bandage wound around one knuckle—both accessories seemed at odds with her almost-grown-up demeanor.

Had she been so serious at twelve? Charlie wondered. Maybe it took a love interest from far away to turn a girl solemn. Though Charlie's out-of-towner hadn't shown up for over a decade, the instant the tall, charming flat-lander had strolled into her post office last August she'd recognized the momentous occasion.

Many young mountain women went through the ritual event of a summer fling with one of the area's wealthy visitors. Opposite attraction was clearly a po-tent force. By the age of nineteen or twenty, females who grew up in the small, insular communities sur-rounded by peaks and pines had usually dated all the local guys they found attractive. Working as waitresses or shop clerks, in the high tourist season they often came in contact with So-Cal men who came from a higher social strata. Dates were made, fun was had.

Sometimes hearts were irrevocably lost.

But she'd been clear with him, with herself, that hers wouldn't be one of them.

"These," Erin said, stabbing at two different stamps. Her coins clacked on the countertop.

Aware of Linus leaning against a row of post of-fice boxes six feet away, Charlie slowly completed the transaction. With Erin just turning from the counter, Charlie reached high and grabbed the grilled security screen. As Linus stepped up, she slammed it into place.

His head jerked back at the loud clang. Through the metal bars he peered at her. "Uh, Charlie?"

Last summer, he'd often called her "Sal," in a tone of casual affection. Sure, the Peanuts characters Linus and Charlie Brown had been buds, he'd told her early on, but it was Charlie's little sister, Sally, who'd carried a torch for her brother's striped-shirted best friend. When she'd inquired where was his blanket and why wasn't he sucking a thumb, Linus had grabbed her hand and—

"Charlie?"

His voice broke through her reverie. Stepping back, she crossed her arms over her crisp blue uniform shirt and tried quelling the sense of panic that was squeezing her lungs. "Sorry, we're closed for the day."

Linus frowned at her. The expression didn't mar the absolute even perfection of his features. So, her imagination hadn't exaggerated how great-looking he was in those dreams she'd had the past six months. They were what she'd had to rely on, because she'd made herself delete from her phone every picture she'd snapped of him during their brief interlude as a couple.

"I'm not here to buy stamps," he said now, moving closer to curl his fingers over the metal rails separating them.

She stared at his hands, remembering them stroking flesh that was heated by mountain sun—and her body's fiery reaction to that touch, this man. Just a fingertip tracing the vein in her throat could make her mad with desire. Her lungs squeezed again and she dropped her gaze to her black Oxfords. They were unsexy but comfortable, all that she'd felt about her life since Linus had gone back to L.A.

Missing him, wanting him once more by her side, hadn't been an option since it was she who had laid out the rules of their short-lived affair. Coming from such different places, she'd known the magic between them couldn't last.

Her head came up and she forced herself to meet his eyes. "Why are you here?" she asked, trying to keep her tone civil. "Why have you come back?"

He shrugged one shoulder in that elegant way of his. "You know my brother has the house at Blue Arrow Lake—"

"Why are you *here,* Linus?" She lifted her arms to indicate the post office.

"Let me tell you about that," he began, leaning against the counter and beaming that sunny, seductive smile of his.

"I don't have time for the tale," Charlie responded, her voice firm. "I have to lock the front door, finish my duties."

"Then dinner—"

"Absolutely not."

He frowned. "Why?"

"I can't do this twice, Linus. Go away." She kept her gaze steady on his face. "Please go away."

"Charlie—"

"I can't do this to…" She couldn't catch her breath.

Linus's expression hardened and his brown eyes turned to polished stone. "To who?" he demanded.

To myself. But instead of revealing any inner turmoil, Charlie forced her chin to lift. "Goodbye, Linus."

It wasn't regret coursing through her, or anything close to it, she promised herself as Linus stomped out. The tears stinging the corners of her eyes were from mere relief.

Right?

TWENTY-FOUR HOURS AFTER the first leak had sprung, the storm had at last subsided to a soft, intermittent drizzle and the pots and bowls set out to catch the dozen unexpected overflows needed emptying much less often. Ryan poured the contents of a coffee mug into a bucket and walked the half-full container into the kitchen.

The contents gurgled down the drain's sink as Poppy entered the room. She held up her cell phone when he glanced over. "Good news," she said.

Any minute I'll go blind? Lose my sense of smell? Develop amnesia? Because twenty-four hours hadn't been long enough for him to forget how she'd felt in his arms, hot and pliant and eager. And in twenty-four hours he hadn't been able to escape her fresh face and her sweet, signature scent…or the way both tugged at his dick. It seemed as if he'd been hard for her since the moment he'd taken her hand and lied about his name.

Her brows came together and she took a step back.

God, he probably looked as if he was about to close in for a bite. Half-turning, he set the bucket on the counter. "Good news?" he prompted.

He heard her swallow. "My buddy Bob says he'll be out here tomorrow to take care of the tree across the road. We should be able to leave for town by late afternoon."

"One last night, then," Ryan said, grateful that the torture had an end point. It had been hell, not knowing how long he was supposed to repress his urges. His fingers itched to sift through her silky hair as he held her still for his kiss. His palm clamored to cup the curve of her naked bottom. He wanted to be inside her, inside her wet, snug space, where he would move over and over and over, while she moaned and pleaded and clutched at him, begging for release.

The image was so real he felt the sting of her fingernails in his bare shoulders.

Jesus. Ryan cleared his throat, tried clearing the fantasy out of his head. "One last night. That's good."

"Yes." Poppy's mouth turned up. "Though the couch in your living room is likely more comfortable than anything my brother has to offer."

He grimaced. She'd refused to take the bed, making do with a couple of blankets on the sofa. They'd both gotten up in the night to check on the leaks, and Poppy Walker in sweats and with a pillow crease on her rosy cheek was more turn-on than any porn star in her birthday suit. "You don't have to stay there again tonight."

"I can't," she answered quickly. "I can't be in your bed." A flush crawled up her cheeks. "I mean, not that you were suggesting we would share…"

They stared at each other and he saw her face take on that dazed look he figured might be on his if he looked in the mirror. It had never happened to him like this, an attraction so powerful that it made him stupid. Lust poured into his bloodstream and he curled his fingers into fists so he couldn't reach for Poppy and bring her close.

She jumped, breaking their shared gaze. "I'm going to make cookies," she said.

Ryan glanced at the plastic-wrapped plates already sitting on the counter. While he'd taken a shower that morning, Poppy had dashed back to her place—he wouldn't have let her go if he'd known—and returned with a box of supplies from her kitchen: flour, sugar, various other baking ingredients.

When she'd said, "Do you like chocolate chip?" his admonitions about going into a compromised dwelling had died on his lips.

But the delectable butter, brown sugar and chocolate confections hadn't eased his true hunger. He'd still been feeling a bit nauseous from overindulging when she'd flopped down on the opposite end of the couch in front of the fire. They'd tried the parallel-reading thing again.

But then he'd caught her staring at his hands and she'd leaped from the cushions like she'd been scalded and headed back to the kitchen. Though he told himself that he didn't need to eat another thing, and then he told himself that at least oatmeal cookies were a healthy option, once again he'd eaten too many with the end result being the same—he'd been left still dissatisfied.

As he watched her set out more ingredients, he sighed. "Poppy," he said, his voice gentle. "Poppy."

When she didn't respond, he came up behind her and cupped her shoulders with his hands. Her body trembled beneath his touch, and she clutched the open bag of flour. "You need to stop," he said.

"You like my cookies," she replied, not looking at him.

He rolled his eyes. "I think we both know I like everything sweet about you."

"Well, then…"

Such an innocent. "Poppy," he bent his head toward hers so his mouth was against her temple. "You do understand, right? Nothing that you bake can assuage this particular appetite." He punctuated the sentence with an almost-chaste kiss to her ear.

Still, she jolted at the touch of his lips. Her fingers must have spasmed, too, because a little cloud of white powder poofed upward from the bag she held. At her choked sound he turned her, taking in the dusted features, the flour barely obscuring the blush that he found so damn appealing. He smiled at the sight—smiled! in March!—as she raised now-white eyebrows in a rueful grimace.

His dark, withered heart shifted in his chest, inching higher. Lifting his hands from her shoulders, he brushed her face with his thumbs, tracing the arch of those brows, the straight line of her nose, the softness of her cheeks. She stood still under his ministrations, once more in her wild-bunny, don't-hurt-me pose.

Quivering, quivering while hoping, hoping, the predator wouldn't dive for the kill.

Taking the bag of flour from her unresisting hold, he placed it on the counter behind her. Then he ducked his head to catch her gaze. "I'm not going to bite."

She was silent a long moment. Then she heaved in a breath. "What if I wished you would?"

ONE LAST NIGHT, Poppy thought.

One last opportunity to surrender to this overwhelming…thing that Ryan brought out in her. He called it an "appetite" and maybe he was right because she'd never felt so greedy, even when she'd been in the thick of whatever she'd had with Mason's father.

Mason.

Her boy would be back with her, back in her arms again the next day. She'd be "Mommy" once more, with all its attendant joys and obligations. She loved her little boy and couldn't wait to see him, but there was still tonight to get through…as Poppy.

Poppy Walker, who hadn't been touched like a woman in five-plus years.

Ryan was staring at her, the light from his blue eyes burning, mesmerizing her, making her not responsible for what she did—but that wasn't true. In this moment in time she didn't want to *be* responsible. Just for a while she wanted to leave behind all that she'd have to tackle tomorrow: where she was going to live, how she was going to fix the damaged cabins, what she was going to do about her car. How any of that might be paid for.

All those mundane, worrisome issues that made her feel seventy-two instead of twenty-seven.

Ryan opened his mouth, closed it. Opened it again. "Tell me you have a boyfriend."

"I don't have a boyfriend," she said, frowning.

He gave her an impatient look. "You're not helping." His hand came toward her face and she felt her nerves rising to the surface of her skin, welcoming his touch. He skimmed her lower lip with his thumb and she caught her breath, her entire body flushing with heat.

Closing his eyes, he released a soft groan. "I'm married."

Stunned, Poppy went cold as she gathered herself to move away. But then his hand clamped around her upper arm and he was gazing at her again with those burning, hypnotic eyes. "I lied," he said. "I'm not. I've never been."

"Why would you say it then?"

He forked his free hand through his glossy hair. "I shouldn't touch you. I want to—devil knows I want to—but I wouldn't be good for you, Poppy."

"What if I don't want what's good for me?" she whispered. "What if I want…" Her face felt as if it were on fire. "Bad. To do something just a little bit bad."

Ryan's eyes rolled heavenward. "Didn't you just eat a boatload of sugar and butter? Isn't that bad enough?"

"You're the one who said cookies aren't what I need." In another life she'd be horrified at the way she was practically begging this man to take her to bed, but that life seemed far away and Ryan was so close…so gorgeous, and sexy, and…inevitable.

Her reward for over five years of celibacy.

Her recompense for the destruction the storm had wrought.

Her one night.

"Don't look at me like that," he said.

"You're looking at me just the same," she pointed out. And wasn't that heady stuff?

He closed his eyes. "Damn it," he muttered. "It's always something. Fucking March."

"Well," Poppy said, "if that's the case, how can it be March without the—"

And before she could get out the final word, he kissed it right off her mouth, his lips locking on hers, his arms banding around her and lifting her onto her toes and into the wide, rangy strength of his body.

There was no resisting. She didn't want to resist. She only wanted him, to feel his heart against hers, to feel his muscles against hers, to feel his skin against hers. A seamless meld of man and woman.

And it was seamless.

From kiss to caress.

From kitchen to bedroom.

From clothed to naked.

They were on the bed together and he was over her, around her, moving her arm, her leg, so he could tickle the palm of her hand with his tongue and trace erotic pictographs on the back of her knee. Aware she was under the touch of a master, she didn't try to keep up, she only tried to keep silent so she wouldn't reveal her utter lack of sophistication with breathless pleas and stuttered gasps.

Ryan murmured against her skin, not words, just sounds of appreciation, and Poppy was steeped in need for him. But she rode the yearning like a bird might surf an air current, floating on top of it, not daring to dip down or dig in. Terrified, really, to find there might be depth beneath this desire for her one-night stand.

When he mounted—condom on, no discussion of that, either, thank God—she lay splayed beneath him, orgasm already coiled and ready to spring. As he pushed inside her, her hips lifted into his. With tightly closed eyes, she rocked into sensation, reaching for release, but not daring to hold the man who gave it.

When she shattered, he was just an instant behind. After, he rolled away and she stared into the dark as she heard him pad to the bathroom. Nothing had changed, she told herself, as her heart continued to drum as hard as the hail had on the roof. In the morning she'd be back to being Mason's mommy and Ryan Harris would be out of her life.

CHAPTER SIX

HE'D BE GLAD to let Poppy go, Ryan thought the next morning, dressing by the foot of the bed that still held her sleeping figure. Sure, he'd lost the battle and crawled under the covers with her, but that didn't make her yet another of his March mistakes. Today, he'd drive her back to town, drop her where she wanted and then…

And then he didn't know what he would do.

There was still plenty of time left in the month for disaster.

But it wouldn't involve Poppy, and for that he was grateful. In the soft morning light she stirred, and he stopped buttoning his shirt just to watch her come awake. Her hair, the honeyed brandy mass of it, was rumpled and the covers came nearly to her small, straight nose. He'd rarely closed his eyes during the night, and several times considered rousing her for a second round. But then in some corner of his world-weary heart he'd found a tenderness he'd thought eradicated long ago. He couldn't bring himself to disturb her sleep.

Her eyes fluttered open. She lay still for a second, orienting herself, Ryan guessed, then her head rolled on the pillow. She frowned at the empty place where he had lain.

He cleared his throat. "Over here."

Her gaze shot his way and their eyes met. Another of her blushes flagged her cheeks. "Good morning," she said, sitting up a little. Her palm kept the sheet anchored above her breasts, damn it all.

"Back at you," he answered, then forced himself to turn to the closet to find his shoes instead of diving onto the mattress and finding her supple, naked body in the tangle of bedclothes. "Sleep okay?"

"Sure."

When he turned back around, shoes now on his feet, she was still looking at him. "That's good," he replied. Her gaze followed his movements as he strapped on the watch that he'd left on the bedside table.

"You're…you're really not married?" she asked, a little hesitant.

"No." He grimaced. "I wouldn't do that."

"I'm still not quite sure why you said so last night."

"Last-minute attempt at being a gentleman, but I failed."

"Oh, I have to disagree." Her dimple peeked out and her gaze dropped. "You were very much the gentleman last night."

That part was going to haunt him. He had been so careful with her. Though he'd wanted to taste, to touch, to do everything and anything to her sweet body, he'd sensed an inexperience in her that had caused him to hold back. Sure, he'd kissed her, caressed her, made certain she'd got off, but he'd kept the moves mellow, the sex almost soothing, any wildness checked.

"How many men have you been with?" he heard himself ask.

Her brows came together over that cute nose. "I'm not telling."

Some imp prodded him to prod her. "Let me guess then. Seventeen."

"No! Just—" Her mouth primmed. "Not that there's anything wrong with seventeen."

"It's a good number," he responded, pulling open a drawer. The stack of socks inside went into his open duffel.

"Is that how many women you've been with?"

He had no idea. "Men don't keep count."

"Well, why would you think I do?" she said, her voice taking on a tinge of outrage.

"You don't?" He glanced over at her.

She'd found a T-shirt of his and had pulled it over her head. Now she climbed out of bed, the hem of the shirt skimming the tops her thighs. He hoped his tongue wasn't hanging out. "Or are there too many to track?"

"I... My... You..." she sputtered, temper coloring her face brighter. Her arms folded crisply over her chest. "There's just been one before, all right? Happy now?"

He nodded, satisfied with the information he'd goaded out of her. It should put his regrets to rest. More she couldn't have handled. Being the likely first to—

Shaking his head, he hastily cut off that runaway train. Imagining new-to-her positions and activities wouldn't make it easier to let her go. And for all he knew, her first lover had been inventive and adventurous, coaxing from Poppy—

Ryan kicked out of his head yet another incendiary thought and rolled the tension from his shoulders. "I'm going to let Grimm outside and then start breakfast," he said, and stalked out of the room.

A half hour later she strolled into the kitchen, smelling of her shampoo and wearing jeans, a white peasant blouse and a pair of clogs that were a crazy-quilt pattern of colors. A piece of pink yarn was tied around the end of her braid.

Ryan froze, fighting the crazy urge to snatch that fuzzy length of thread from her hair and wind it around one of his belt loops, a public proclamation that he'd had his hands in that hair, that he'd kissed the mouth that was the same bright shade as the yarn. That it was he, as a matter or fact, who had kissed the color onto it.

"Ryan? Are you okay?"

Her voice got him moving again, and he handed her a glass of orange juice. He was going to be damn glad to drop her off and with it this unwarranted and unwanted possessiveness.

They both were quiet as they readied to leave the cabin, Grimm at either Ryan's heels or Poppy's. She was in cell contact with her chain-saw-wielding pal, and as she'd predicted, the road was free for travel by late afternoon. They emptied the leak-catching containers a last time, locked the cabin, then loaded their bags, Grimm and themselves into the car.

Though the rain had stopped, the clouds were low. It didn't hamper their progress to the turnoff, but once on the highway they discovered that stretch of winding roadway wasn't as easy to traverse. They must have been traveling through the clouds. The mist would suddenly lower, surrounding the car, cocooning him and Poppy, and forcing him to slow to a crawl. Around a sharp turn the foggy conditions would ease, until they took another and found themselves once again in near-blind conditions.

He kept the steering wheel in a tight grip, peering through the windshield, his eyes narrowed. "Shit," he muttered, as he almost clipped a Falling Rocks sign that sprang up out nowhere. "I don't like this."

"It's not my favorite, either," Poppy admitted. "I always find it unnerving."

Yeah. Unnerving. Unsettling. Understatement.

Ryan shot a glance at his passenger, noting her fingers were clasped together in an anxious knot. "Hey." He reached over and briefly folded his own hand over hers, transferring warmth to her cold skin—once again succumbing to the strange need to keep care of her. "There's nothing to worry about."

But as they continued toward Blue Arrow Lake, he couldn't shake the feeling that there was. The ghostly mist, the way it made the trees appear, then suddenly disappear again, was wigging him out. When he finally let Poppy go, she would be swallowed up by the stuff, gone from him forever.

What was the big deal? he asked himself. *You don't really know her. She doesn't even know your real name.*

He could at least do something about the first. "What will you do?" he said.

"About…?"

"A place to live, your car, the cabins."

"Oh," she said, in an offhand tone. "That."

Trying to put a brave face on things, he guessed, sneaking another look at her. She was playing with the ends of her braid and staring out the window. "You're going to your brother, right?"

"Mmm."

"That's where I'm dropping you." He wanted to make sure she was safely delivered into someone's hands.

"I've had a change of plans. If you'd just let me out at the Chalet—it's the big restaurant in the middle of town—I'll make my way from there."

"Poppy—"

"My cousin's coming through. I'll be fine." She shifted in her seat. "What about you?"

"Me?" He shrugged. "I'm not sure. Probably head back to L.A." Anabelle and Grant had been due to leave the lake house that morning, but in case they'd attracted some press attention that might be sticking around, he'd be better off staying clear of it. Maybe he'd drive south, find a way to bury himself in the Grand Canyon—but this was fucking March, which meant he might literally find himself buried in the Grand Canyon.

A disturbing sense of relief came paired with the idea, followed by an immediate stab of painful guilt. Ryan couldn't do that to his parents. To Linus.

"Oh!" Poppy shot up in her seat, drawing his attention. "That reminds me." She dug into her purse and pulled out a wad of bills. "Here. You paid in advance, remember? For four weeks."

"I'm not taking that," he said, thinking of her damaged cabins, the crushed back end of her car. "Leave me the cookies and we'll call it even."

"Ryan—"

"The cookies."

She gusted a sigh. "How about this? I'll keep the

cash for now and apply it to your account. You'll have a balance when you decide to come back and visit sometime."

He looked over at her.

Her eyebrows slammed together. "I'm going to get those cabins into shape. You'll see."

"I'm not doubting that."

"Oh." She was silent a moment. "You mean you're not coming back to visit."

"Look, Poppy. I—"

Her hand went up. "I get it, I get it. Don't worry that I think…that I thought last night meant anything, Ryan. You're entirely the wrong kind of man for me."

"That's right." She needed someone who had an open heart and normal emotions on a year-round basis, not a guy who was frozen from April to February and dangerously messed up for all of March.

"It was just a casual hookup." One of her hands made a little whooshing gesture that he caught out of the corner of his eye. "In a week I'll have forgotten your name."

She didn't know his name. Funny, how that irritated him now.

Though they appeared to have left the dense cloud bank behind, traffic picked up as they neared the town of Blue Arrow Lake. His SUV's dash display reported the outdoor temperature as 50 degrees and beautiful people were in their places under the heaters at the outdoor cafés. Ryan thought he knew the restaurant she'd indicated, though he usually avoided public places where he might encounter any of the Hollywood crowd. Even they would stare and worse, if paparazzi were on their trail, the photographers wouldn't hesitate to approach, cameras ready to take shots of the now-notorious Ryan Hamilton. He'd been such an idiot last year.

"Another quarter mile on your right," Poppy directed, leaning forward in her seat. "We're a little early for my meetup, but I'll jump out and you can be on your way."

"I'm not going to do any such thing," Ryan said, turning where she indicated. The Chalet must be a popular eatery because the lot was nearly full of vehicles, luxury models arranged side by side like a dealership in Beverly Hills. A Mercedes backed out of a spot at the end of an aisle and he slid in.

He braked, and Poppy's hand went to the door handle.

"Don't go," he said, clamping his hand on her thigh. At her look of surprise, he corrected himself in a hurry. "I mean, don't go until you're sure your ride is here."

"I'll be fine," she assured him, then slid away from his touch to climb down from the passenger seat.

Of course, he climbed out, too, helping her remove her things, including the goofy dog who gave Ryan a disgruntled look when he clicked the leash to his collar. "Grimm," he said solemnly, bending toward the dog, "you're a good man. Take care of Poppy."

"Poppy can take care of herself."

Ryan ignored the crisp comment and ran his hands over the dog's ears. "Watch out for Poppy. Keep the undesirables away from her."

"If he was any good at *that,* you wouldn't have moved into the cabin next door."

She was in a mood. Straightening, he raised his brows at her. "So I'm an undesirable now?"

Shrugging into that scruffy army coat of hers, she wouldn't meet his gaze. "I wasn't ready—"

"Oh, you were more than ready."

Her gray eyes lifted and there…there was that blush he'd been hoping to make bloom. "Stop," she said, though her dimple peeked out before she managed to flatten her smile.

Stop. He wanted to say that, too. *Stop everything. Don't go.*

"I'll wait over there," she said, indicating the sidewalk surrounding the restaurant. A cluster of people were jamming the exit to the place, causing some sort of commotion, but Ryan didn't give it more than a cursory glance.

"Poppy—"

"Thanks for the ride." She'd stacked her two suitcases in preparation for wheeling them off. Now she took Grimm's leash. "I'll…well, 'bye." Her back turned and she headed away.

On its own, his arm lifted, his hand stretching to stop her. But she was already beyond his reach. Only his fingers made contact, leaving him with that scrap of bright yarn that had covered the elastic band binding her hair.

He stared down at it for a long, long moment.

Then he was loping across the lot, nearly getting plowed by a car that was forced to brake with a loud squeal. He thought he heard someone shout, and then someone else say his name, but he ignored everything except Poppy, who'd made it to the sidewalk and now balanced her suitcases against the stucco wall. She turned at the sound of the ruckus and as she noticed his pursuit, her face registered more surprise. Upon reaching her, his hands cupped her pretty face and he looked into her wide eyes—their color that gray mist he'd worried he might lose her in. He swooped in for a long, deep kiss.

UNBALANCED, POPPY CLUTCHED the back of Ryan's sweater with her free hand as he dragged her closer. Of course she should be pushing him away, but his lips were so hot and then he plunged his tongue into her mouth in a wild frenzy of a kiss that evaporated her common sense. Her fingers loosened on the soft wool and her palm pressed against his hard muscles, anchoring her to him.

She was dizzy from lack of breath when he lifted his head, staring at her with that mystic's gaze. If he'd asked her for the last beat of her heart, at that moment she would have given it to him.

"Poppy," he said, his voice hoarse. "Poppy—"

Then someone shouted "Ryan!" from the entrance to the restaurant. His head swiveled, he cursed, then he backed away from her. "I've got to get out of here," he said, moving faster now. "I'll…"

But Poppy didn't catch the last of the sentence because he turned and dashed for his car. Confused, she stared after him, then looked down at Grimm. The dog had nothing to offer. Shaking her head, she felt her phone buzz in her pocket.

The device's screen declared We're here just as a car pulled up beside her and the back passenger door opened. A smile broke over her face when a little boy leaped from it, a plush Mickey in one hand and his backless booster car seat in the other. With a great surge of love, she gathered him into her arms.

A car came up behind her cousin's, tooted its impatience and Poppy waved acknowledgement when her cousin called he would find a parking space. As his vehicle cruised off, she held her son close, breathing him in with her cheek against his hair. *All's right with the world.* The cabins didn't matter, the car didn't matter, that bewildering, blistering farewell kiss didn't matter.

Mason was back, her one, true love.

She took the booster seat from his hand, dropping it with their other belongings, then kissed him noisily on the top of the head. Yes. All was right with the world.

For about five seconds. Then suddenly voices were shouting and there was a trio approaching them, three people carrying contraptions—cameras? With Mason pressed close and Grimm at her side, she retreated, taking giant backward steps to avoid the advancing group, which unleashed a barrage of mystifying questions that became a single stream of words aimed in her direction.

What's your name? Have you known him long? Is the boy his?

Her son was hers and hers alone, she thought, a fierce need to protect welling up. "Go away," she said, her arm keeping Mason pressed to her. "I don't know what you're talking about." From the corner of her eye, she saw her cousin's car two aisles off.

Poppy considered a run for it, but the asylum escapees were between her and safety. Then an SUV pulled alongside her. The escapees became more agitated. The passenger door swung open and Ryan shouted over the crazy people's din. "Get in the car!"

Grimm obeyed, jumping onto the passenger seat and then over it to the next row. Before she could think what to do, Ryan had vaulted out and run to get her belongings. He tossed them in the rear then shouted at her again as he raced back to the driver's side. "Poppy, come on!"

"I—"

"Get in the car."

The escapees were closing in. Bewildered, heart pounding, she swung Mason into her arms. Should she go with Ryan, a virtual stranger who was supposed to be gone from her life, or face down the curious, clamoring, stranger strangers?

What's your name, sweetie? How'd you meet? Are you the pole dancer we've heard about?

Pole dancer? Poppy glanced over her shoulder, ready to shoot down that notion, but the noisy group's ranks had grown. Bystanders held cell phones that were pointed toward her and Mason.

She directed her gaze back at Ryan, still unsure. "Mason can't ride in a car without—"

"—his car seat," he finished for her. "I'm on it."

He knew about child safety seat laws? She'd think about that later. Now, she watched him make another dash to the rear. In seconds it was installed and as she slid Mason into place realized she'd made her decision. Stomach jumping, she took the seat beside him, not managing to avoid Grimm, who was romping with delight on the cushions as if a threatening horde wasn't just tinted windows-away.

The dog nosed the back of Ryan's head as he edged the SUV through the onlookers, who still held cameras and cell phones and continued to shout questions. As he gathered speed and turned out of the lot, Poppy looked behind. There was a car right on their tail—a small vehicle that was sticking close.

"Oh, God," she said, her maternal instincts going on high alert. She put her arm around Mason's shoulders. "Someone's following us."

"Won't only be one," Ryan said, his voice dark. The SUV gained speed.

Poppy glanced at her son, saw his eyes were saucer-round. "It'll be okay, honey," she said, automatically reassuring him though she was completely in the dark.

She looked at Ryan again, watched as he retrieved his stocking cap from somewhere and jammed it on his head, pulling it low on his brow. Another cap flew over the seat and into her lap. "In case you want a disguise, too."

"What? Why—" But she swallowed the rest of her words and nearly her tongue as he made a sudden sharp turn and then another. What had she gotten herself and her son into? "Ryan—"

"Just let me drive," he said. "Explanations later."

For the next few minutes, she kept her lips buttoned and her arm around Mason. Every few seconds she'd glance behind them, seeing a small parade of cars in their wake. Ryan seemed fiercely concentrated and she didn't dare interrupt as he took turn after turn on narrow, hairpin roads. After ten minutes of evasive driving, their tail still remained in place.

"We haven't lost them," she said.

"For the moment," he muttered, as they wound closer to Blue Arrow Lake. Between the grand homes surrounded by trees situated on its shores, she caught brief glimpses of deep blue water. Ryan took yet another turn, passing a No Outlet sign. Glancing back at their unwelcome entourage, she opened her mouth to warn him of the potential trap when a pair of imposing wrought-iron gates appeared in front of them. Ryan pressed a button on the car's sun visor and the metal contraptions started to swing inward. As soon as the front bumper of the SUV could squeeze through the opening he was on the accelerator again.

As the SUV's back bumper cleared, the gates closed, leaving the other vehicles behind. Ryan sped toward a spacious courtyard, a massive fountain marking its center. As they rounded it, water suddenly shot from the mouths of five leaping trout cast in bronze.

Mason made a little sound of wonder. Poppy might have echoed it as they came to a stop in front of the steps leading to an enormous, elegant villa.

Ryan opened his door and stepped out of the car. He had his cell phone in hand and he tapped on its screen. The door to a stand-alone garage to the right of the courtyard rose. With another tap, one of the house's pair of heavily carved front doors unlatched.

Poppy's own phone buzzed in her pocket. She pulled it out, checked the number. A text from her cousin James.

What's going on? Y are u with HIM?

Her gaze went to the ridiculously handsome stranger standing beside the SUV. The breeze disordered his hair but it didn't soften the harsh expression on his face. He looked pissed.

Lethal, even.

She pressed the button to slide down her window. As if feeling her gaze, he glanced over. "What?" he asked warily.

"Who the heck *are* you?"

It was Mason who answered for him, in an awestruck tone. "What a silly question, Mommy. He's a superspy."

CHAPTER SEVEN

FROM *YOU SEND ME*, a screenplay by Linus Hamilton:

EXT. SCENIC MOUNTAIN VIEWPOINT—DAY

LINUS and CHARLIE sit side by side on top of a picnic table, a spectacular view spread out before them. A summer breeze ruffles CHARLIE's hair and catches at the skirt of her sundress, drawing it upward. She yanks it down, but not before LINUS has taken notice of her tanned thigh. A secret smile pulls at the corners of his mouth.

LINUS
Did I mention I'm really, really lucky?

CHARLIE
No, but I suppose you will now.

He grins, and turns his head to admire her profile.

LINUS
See, you could have been an ogre of a postmistress.

CHARLIE
I'm a postal clerk.

LINUS
(obligingly)
You could have been an ogre of a postal clerk.

CHARLIE
Then you wouldn't have begged me to be your
personal guide to the local sights and hidden
places of interest.

LINUS
By the way, yesterday I emailed the photos of
that old sawmill to the office. They liked them
so much I've been awarded Best Film Location
Scout of the Year.

He surveys the view with a little sigh of satisfaction,
then looks back at Charlie, admiring again.

LINUS
What if I said I wanted to kiss you?

Charlie stills.

CHARLIE
I'd...I'd have to say I'm—(beat goes by)—
involved with someone.

Nonplussed, LINUS begins to scoot away.

LINUS
Uh…

CHARLIE doesn't let him get far.

CHARLIE
But we have an understanding. He's…out of the country and while he's gone, I'm at liberty to…

His trademark charming smile breaks over LINUS's face.

LINUS
Kiss?

And then he's doing it, kissing CHARLIE with the ease of experience while his arm draws her to him. His free hand rises as if to spear the hair at the back of her head, but then he flexes his fingers and forces it to drop. He doesn't want to hold too tight.
They break apart and stare at each other, bemused.

LINUS
You'll continue showing me around the mountain for the rest of August?

CHARLIE
Yes.

LINUS
And you'll continue letting me kiss you?

CHARLIE
As long as you don't forget my situation.

LINUS grins.

LINUS
Besides lucky, I'm a free-and-easy kind of guy.
No strings. It will be the thing you like best.

LINUS STROLLED TOWARD the Cold Brook post office near closing time, his body relaxed, his expression easy. Yeah, he had something on his mind, but he wasn't going to let it show on his face. Not to Miss Unfriendly Charlotte Walker. Just remembering her cool attitude of the other day had him yanking up the zipper of his leather jacket that didn't provide quite enough protection against the March temperatures.

Things had been a lot warmer around here in August.

He pushed open the door and stepped over the threshold. There was a short line of people waiting to be helped at the counter. Linus tamped down his impatience and leaned a shoulder against the wall of post office boxes. They had the old-timey look of props from a spaghetti Western, but last summer Charlie had told him they were the real thing, dating back to the late 1800s.

Last summer Charlie had told him a lot of things.

He ran his gaze over her now as she helped an elderly woman place stamps on a handful of letters. Seven months hadn't dulled the gilt-blondness of her hair. He'd once told her he liked bright and shiny things and last summer Charlie had glowed from the top of her head to her toenails painted a molten gold.

I love the way you kiss, she'd said. *I love the way you hold me with such gentleness and kiss me with such strength.*

The fact was, he'd made it a point not to draw her in too tight.

I'm a free-and-easy kind of guy. Damn it, those words had been—*were!*—true.

Just then her soft laugh rang out. His attention transferred back to the present and he frowned, noting her latest customer was a dark-haired man, thirtyish, who had his hips against the counter and his gaze on Charlie as if he'd settled in for a lifetime with her.

A tide of green-tinged emotion rose from Linus's gut. *Was this him?* Setting his teeth, he took a step forward.

Only to fall back as the man swung around and headed for the door. "I'll give Audra your best," he called over his shoulder.

"Tell her I'm crocheting you guys the cutest baby blanket for the new arrival. I only hope it can be done by her due date."

"She's ready to pop," the man warned. He put his hand on the doorknob—a wedding band on his left ring finger—then paused, frowning as he caught sight of Linus. His fingers slid off the metal and he cast a quick glance back at Charlie.

"Are you lost?" he asked Linus, giving him a suspicious once-over with his eyes.

Why did everyone around here ask him that? And he didn't need to explain himself to some dude-friend of Charlie's. "Are you telling me this isn't Oz?"

The man appeared baffled. "What?"

"I'm looking for the Great and Powerful. The Scarecrow will do. Too damp for the Tin Man, though, and the Cowardly Lion always gets on my nerves."

The dark-haired guy sent another protective glance in the direction of the postal worker Linus had come to see. "Uh…"

"He's pulling your leg," Charlie said, ducking under the opening in the counter. "Don't bother phoning the sheriff, Clint. I know this man."

"I was thinking of calling County Mental Health," he grumbled, then held out his hand. "Clint Owen."

"Linus Hamilton."

"Oh. *Oooh.*" An amused smile twitched at the corners of his mouth. "Linus Hamilton? Weren't you the voice of—"

"Squeaky McPhee," Linus finished for him. "Please cut me some slack. I started voicing that cartoon when I was five. I was lured by promises of LEGOs and kiwis."

"Kiwis?" Charlie echoed, round-eyed.

"I had a thing for the fuzzy fruit in my formative years." He shoved his hands in his pockets. "By the time my voice changed I'd gotten a fat bank account and a dirt bike out of the deal as well as a ration of shit from people for the rest of my life."

"They still air the reruns. I can't wait to tell my wife," Clint said. "I met Squeaky McPhee. Hey, maybe I can get your auto—" He broke off when Linus redirected his glare. "Okay. Yeah. Sorry. Good meeting you."

The man chuckled all the way out the post office door.

"Honest to God," Linus said in disgust, "I'm going to go into therapy and send my parents the bills. They let me play a mouse with an incontinence problem."

"Only when scared by the family cat," Charlie pointed out. "Though that did happen with great regularity."

Linus glared at her. "Yeah, which was why my brother called me Squeaky McPee."

The embarrassing admission made Charlie break into laughter. He decided it was worth the humiliation to hear that sound. He could listen to it all day, all month, the rest of the damn year.

"Squeaky McPee," she repeated, her big blues glinting with humor. "How I've missed you, Linus."

At the words, his chest spasmed, his breath painfully caught.

Charlie's hand came up to cover her mouth, her expression revealing obvious dismay. Clearly she hadn't intended for that to slip out.

But he wouldn't pretend he hadn't heard it. Stepping close, he traced her cheek with his forefinger. "I've missed you, too. Now that I'm here, we should—"

"Let's not go there," she said, moving back.

"Why not?"

She shook her head.

Linus lost his cool. He strode close again and grabbed her hand so she couldn't get away. "Is this about Steven Parker?" The man with whom she had an "understanding" that allowed her to date while he was out of the country. "Is he back then?"

"No." Charlie wouldn't meet his eyes.

"So what's the problem?" Bitterness edged Linus's voice. "I thought Saint Steven gave you a pass to date while he's away."

"I don't want to date you again, Linus."

But the fact was, they'd done more than date. They'd laughed and played and made love and…shit. He didn't want to think about it, but it was all he *could* think about. "Did you ever tell him about us?"

Guilty color suffused her face. "That's none of your business."

He made a mental grab for his usual free-and-easy attitude, but everything inside him felt tied up in knots of those "no strings" that he'd claimed as a hallmark of his character. Shit, shit, *shit*. "It is my business. It's my business because—"

"Don't."

The one cool word set Linus back on his heels. Her hand slipped from his. He stared at her, noting the obstinate expression, the steeliness in her blue eyes.

And he felt like a fool.

"So if that's what you came to talk about—"

"I didn't." Linus scrambled to regain some of his pride. "It wasn't about you or us or—" *that fucking* "—Saint Steven that I came at all."

"Oh?" She raised a brow.

"I'm looking for my brother. I'm looking for Ryan. He's in the mountains somewhere, but not picking up his cell. I thought maybe you'd know something—"

"No maybe about it," Charlie said, pulling her phone from her pocket. "I've even got video."

WHO THE HECK are you? Before Ryan would answer Poppy's question, he had one of his own to pose. He gestured toward the towhead who was staring at him with blue eyes round as marbles. "Who the hel—heck is that?"

Poppy opened the back passenger door and climbed out. "My son, Mason. He's been in Florida with family."

"You have a kid?" He supposed he should regret the note of accusation.

Her pursed lips told him she hadn't missed it. "Well, you apparently have a cultlike following."

He grimaced. "It's about now that I wish you'd watched television."

"I wish you'd take me back to the Chalet."

Ryan shook his head. "Not a good idea...at least not at the moment." He glanced up the long drive, to the gates where the chase team was gathering. "We should get inside."

She eyed the house as first the towhead and then the dog slipped out of the car. Her hand reached down to grasp her son's.

Ryan had to look away, and it was then he saw the first of the photographers climb out with their cameras in hand. Cursing beneath his breath, he took her elbow to hustle her through the doors. "Come on."

Her shoulders squared. "We don't go anywhere with strangers."

He stifled another string of swear words. "Poppy, don't make me drag you up the steps." When she opened her mouth again, he pinned her with a stare. "As for me being a stranger...remember where you were when you first opened your eyes this morning."

Though that sleepy, blushing Poppy of the early a.m. had been replaced by a wary woman with a maternal militancy in her gray eyes, Ryan hadn't forgotten her. That was the woman who'd compelled him into a torrid goodbye kiss that had caught the attention of the paparazzi. It was her fault for being so damn appealing, he decided, though guilt rewarded that thought with a vicious pinch. It was his notoriety that had put her in this position. So he softened his voice. "Look, we need to get into the house."

"Why?"

He forked his hand through his hair. "Because they have telephoto lenses. If they can get Kate Middleton's bare—" remembering the kid, he found a substitute word for *tits* "—parts from an estate away, they can focus down 300 feet of flagstone and snap us arguing."

She glanced over her shoulder. "Are you sure…?"

"I'll show you once we're inside."

Their group tromped into the house, Grimm's leash dragging along the marble floors. Ryan immediately directed them right, into the spacious office with its walnut built-ins, leather furniture and plush area rugs. There, he opened a cabinet and keyed up the views from the security cameras onto their respective screens. In the upper left, three photographers stood near their respective cars, peering through the metal gates.

Ryan couldn't help but notice Poppy's kid seemed fascinated by the security setup, his eyes roaming over the equipment. Poppy turned her own gaze from the black-and-white images, fixing it on Ryan's face. "I don't understand what's going on," she said, crossing her arms over her chest.

"It may seem a bit of a tangle at the moment—"

"Unknot it," she ordered.

He stifled a wince at her sharp tone. "Poppy—"

"Mason." She ruffled the boy's straight blond hair. "See that chair?" She pointed to one by a window. "Why don't you take Grimm over there and introduce him to Mickey Mouse."

"Not there," Ryan put in softly. "Not by a window."

She slid him a look, then focused back on her son. "I mean the other, by the fireplace," she said, indicating a love seat situated far from the glass. "Sit over there and tell Grimm all about your adventures."

As the boy moved to obey, she rounded on Ryan, her face set. "Explain. Right. Now."

He owed her at least some of it. So he told her his real name and about the TV show that had turned him into a teen star. The action movies he'd made in his twenties. The production studio he now ran.

"Today we caught the interest of some paparazzi. The unfortunate fact is there are magazines and websites and nightly entertainment TV programming that spew celebrity news and speculation every day. To get what they need, there are agencies that employ teams to trail A-listers twenty-four/seven."

"That's you, an 'A-lister'?"

He shrugged a shoulder. "I think we got caught in the tail wind of Grant and Anabelle Lester, the latest Hollywood 'it' couple. That's who was coming out of the restaurant when we were spotted. They'd been borrowing my house for a few days."

"Still, the photographers must have an interest in you, if they abandoned this Grant and Anabelle to chase us down."

Here was where things might get sticky. He didn't want to tell her all his history. He couldn't bring himself to speak of it, not with that towhead of hers in the room. Not when he now knew she was a mother. "Who knows what goes through their minds?"

Poppy returned her gaze to the security screen. The photographers had set up tripods now, that were aimed in the direction of the house. "Are they...dangerous?"

He shook his head. "Only to your privacy."

"Ryan—"

"Mommy," her kid called from across the room. "I'm thirsty. And Mickey's hungry. Grimm, too."

"Just a minute, honey." She glanced at Ryan. "Do you mind if I get him a glass of water in the kitchen?"

"You're welcome to whatever is there. If you walk out to the hall turn right, then left, you'll run into it. Scrounge for something to eat, too."

He watched them—woman, kid, dog—proceed from the room, and he fully intended to stay in place where he could keep an eye on the paps and also think through the situation with a clear head. When Poppy was front and center, his thoughts kept wandering into dangerous territory, recalling the sleek heat of her rib cage against his palms, the tight, wet clasp of her around him, the shy way she'd buried her face against his neck when she'd come.

That last fevered kiss that he hadn't stopped himself from taking and even now wasn't regretting, though it had been the cause of this current mess.

But then he heard a stifled shriek and he hustled to find her standing at the threshold to the kitchen, her eyes big, her hand over her mouth. "Oh, my God," she breathed, glancing over at him, then back at the big room. "This is your kitchen?"

It was edging on twilight, so he flipped on the lights

to expose the bank of windows overlooking the lake and the gleaming pots and pans hanging from an iron rack suspended on chains. There were two sinks, two dishwashers, an immense granite-topped island, a refrigerator as big as a king-size bed, a separate ice maker, a wine cooling unit the size of a regular fridge and a beverage center complete with gleaming espresso maker.

"I bought the place from a couple of professional chefs," he told her.

Her head swiveled to take in more of the room's features, which included four ovens, two warming drawers and a range from which an army could be fed. "Do you cook?"

"Uh…"

"You have a cook."

"I have a housekeeper at my Laurel Canyon house in L.A. who leaves me things for me to heat up. I haven't come here very often." He'd bought the place the summer after the first horrible March when he'd held some vague hope that a new venue might shake him from his April-through-February stupor. With quick footsteps, he crossed to the pantry and opened the door to peer inside. "It's pretty well-stocked, however. There's enough food for days."

Poppy had opened the fridge. "I should say so." She glanced at him over her shoulder. "No shortage of chilling champagne, either."

Ryan joined her at the open door. "Or milk or juice or fresh fruit and vegetables." Grant and Anabelle's assistants had laid in for a siege.

Poppy set her son on one of the island's bar stools and served him a glass of juice. The kid's eyes were sleepy as he sipped. With a quick apology to Ryan that he waved away, she hurriedly prepared half a peanut-butter-and-jelly sandwich. "He's on East Coast time, it seems," she explained. "It's nearing Mason's bedtime there."

The boy straightened in his seat. "Not tired."

"Of course not," his mother assured him with a little smile, sliding the food in front of him. "Mason Walker is never tired."

Mason *Walker*. Huh. Ryan figured that Poppy must not have married the boy's father or the kid would have a different last name. He didn't know why the factoid interested him, however, because this was the beginning and the end of his acquaintance with the kid.

Thank God.

Ryan cleared his throat. "Here's how we're going to defuse the situation, Poppy. I'm going back to L.A. tonight, and hopefully our nosy friends will follow me down the hill. Then you can—"

"Bro!" Ryan's brother's voice boomed through the halls, coming from the direction of the terrace. "You got meerkats lurking at the gates. They're standing tall and twitching their whiskers, cameras a-ready. I almost clipped one with my car driving in. Does that mean your nasty porn princess has been singing your praises again?"

Linus strolled into the room, then came to an abrupt halt that might have been comical if Ryan could find a laugh after seeing the aghast expression on Poppy's face at the nasty-porn-princess remark. "Uh..." his brother said, looking from mother to son. "Hi?"

Ryan sighed. "Poppy, this is my brother, Linus.

Linus, this is my…Poppy, and her son." When the dog shoved his head under the other man's hand, he added, "That's Grimm."

"I didn't realize you'd brought company here," Linus said, absently patting the dog. Then, aplomb recovered, he strolled over to the kid, whose hand he shook like it was a solemn promise. The boy grinned, apparently charmed.

Next, Linus turned, smiling in that easy way of his. "Hello, there, my Poppy," he said, bending to kiss her lightly on the cheek.

"Hey," Ryan protested, before he could hold back. At his brother's curious look, he crossed his arms over his chest. "Poppy. Her name is Poppy."

"Oops," Linus said, not looking the least concerned. He slapped his hands together. "What are we all doing, kids?"

Ryan sighed again. Linus on scene was a potential complication the already problematic situation could do without. So with greetings and introductions out of the way, it was time to move the other man along. "This really isn't a good time for a visit."

Instead of taking the hint, Linus draped himself over the nearest bar stool, crossing his right leg over his left so that his foot could swing with a lazy rhythm. He sent a smile to Ryan, the one that signaled his sibling was going to be especially uncooperative. "Oh, I don't know. I'll bet you could use my help in hosting this fine company."

CHAPTER EIGHT

IN A SMALL—by this villa's standards—room off the kitchen, Poppy pulled a woolen throw over her son, who lay fast asleep on a sofa. Grimm settled on the floor nearby, and she tucked Mickey under one of Mason's relaxed arms, then pressed a kiss to his warm cheek. Her sweet baby.

He was exhausted, and so was she. But single mothers couldn't afford to give in to the feeling. Nor, she decided, straightening up, could she afford to rely on Ryan to free her from her current quandary—in her experience men were rarely reliable.

But how had this happened? she wondered, rubbing at her throbbing temples. How had everything gone south so fast?

Clearly, going to bed with him had been a huge mistake.

God. *God!*

After years of celibacy she'd had sex...sex with gorgeous, dangerous Ryan Harris—no, make that Ryan *Hamilton.* And wasn't that just perfect? The man had given her a fake name. She shook her head, chagrined. What an idiot she was, getting physically intimate with the kind of man who would have driven off without ever revealing his true identity.

Just like Mason's father.

Well, sure, she'd known *his* name, but his true colors had only bled through once she'd shared the news of her unexpected pregnancy. He'd sped from her life faster than Ryan had taken the mountain roads to his lakeside estate.

But Ryan didn't leave you, a voice in her head whispered. *When those celebrity hunters came in for the kill, he swooped you away.*

To this house, she reminded the voice, where they were confined behind iron gates. Not a house, a…a mansion, that was *Architectural Digest*-fancy with its marble floors, its soaring ceilings and its luxuriously appointed rooms. She couldn't have dreamed up a domicile more opposite to the Walker cabins if she'd tried.

So? You're dry and warm within walls that are stocked with food and drink, and a dazzling man who knows how to touch a woman.

But she wasn't a woman, she was a mother, and she wasn't going to let herself get all cozy—in the manor, or with the man of the manor, either. That had been a one-time affair, and surely the sexual urges precipitating it had been burned away in the process.

Tiptoeing from the room, she stepped into the corridor and pulled her phone from her pocket. Ryan's and his brother's voices were faint murmurs coming from the kitchen as she thumbed on the device.

Several missed calls from her sisters. Good, she thought. She'd get one of them to drive out here and pick up her and Mason. Or maybe her brother would be better. The scars on his face lent him a savage aura.

One look and the photographers would probably run like hell.

The fact was, though, he intimidated her a little, too, so she dialed her older sister, Mackenzie, who picked up on the first ring. "It's about time. People have called, sent texts, emailed me video from their cell phones. What's going on?" she demanded.

Where to begin? Poppy swallowed. "Well, a few days ago, this man showed up, wanting to rent one of the cabins—"

"The cabins." Mackenzie's voice held a note of near-loathing. "Didn't we tell you no good would come from doing something with them?"

"Some good will come," Poppy insisted, bristling.

"Yeah, it's so 'good' that you've been spied canoodling with the infamous Ryan Hamilton. Rah rah."

"You know who he is." She should have figured that. Unlike Poppy, Mackenzie was a consumer of popular culture.

"Of course. Do you?"

She refused to admit hers was a very recent acquaintance with the real Ryan. "Yes. Could—"

"You know *everything* about him?"

Not the porn-princess part. And she didn't want to even ask about that. Poppy and Ryan were parting ways and the less she knew the easier it would be to forget that brief interlude in his bed. "I know everything I need to know."

Mackenzie groaned. "Poppy…"

She bristled again, annoyed with her sister's condescending attitude. "Why do you say my name like that?"

"Because you're naive, gullible and always overly optimistic."

"Hey—"

"And because you have a terrible track record when it comes to men."

Poppy frowned. There had been her two high school short-term boyfriends who'd bored her to tears. Then Mason's father. Followed by Ryan—

Okay, fine. She had a terrible track record when it came to men.

"All right, little sister," Mackenzie said, "tell me what you need." She punctuated the line with a long-suffering sigh.

But now her sibling's tone and Poppy's own fierce pride made it impossible to ask for help. With temper coloring her voice, she said, "Never mind. I'll talk to you later."

Thumbing off the phone, she shoved it back into her pocket. What now? There was still the small matter of getting out of here.

After a little cooling-off period, she'd phone her brother, she decided, walking toward the kitchen. As she approached, Ryan's brother's voice floated through the doorway.

"…it's March," Linus was saying, "and—"

"She doesn't need to know all that." Ryan sounded as if he were speaking through clenched teeth. "There's no reason to get into it."

Poppy didn't hitch her stride. Surely they'd been speaking of her. "Get into what?" she asked, crossing the threshold.

Linus rose from the bar stool where he'd been loung-

ing. "You look as if you have a headache, my Poppy."
Then he glanced at his brother, amusement sparkling
in his brown eyes. "Did you just growl?"

"Her name is *Poppy.* Just plain Poppy."

Linus seemed to contemplate that as he crossed to the
counter, where a bottle of chilled white wine sat sweating beside a lovely crystal glass. He poured the liquid,
then strolled over to hand it to her. "She doesn't look
plain to me," he murmured, then gifted her with such
a charming smile there was nothing she could do but
smile back. "Come sit down, *Poppy,*" he added, with
another mischievous glance at his brother. "You can
supervise the dinner preparations."

Ryan had a beer in hand that he lifted to his mouth,
then tipped back. Poppy stared at the long, strong column of his throat as he swallowed, just a little bit fascinated. Last night, she thought, her mind drifting as she
sipped her wine, she'd rubbed her cheek there. The skin
had been warm, smooth, until she'd encountered the
dark, raspy stubble of his beard. She'd run her tongue
against it, tasting salt and heat.

Her own body felt a little heated now, as a matter of
fact—no! She'd already been through this. The deed
had been done, the urges satisfied, the want assuaged.

"Whoops, don't drop it." Her glass was removed
from her inattentive hold, refilled and returned to the
granite surface before her. Linus topped off his own,
set aside the bottle then held up his wine. "Hey, gang,
we forgot to make a toast."

"Because I so want to commemorate the day," Ryan
muttered under his breath.

Yet still she heard it, and Poppy found herself instantly annoyed. Under-breath muttering was *her* due, wasn't it? She'd been minding her own business, returning quite happily to her role as Mason's mommy, when she was drawn into some kind of weird fame-warp. "It's not like this was *my* plan," she said hotly.

He narrowed his eyes at her. "You didn't tell me you have a kid."

"I didn't think the fact I'm a single mom was any of your business." Considering she hadn't been acting very momlike…especially in his bed. "*You* didn't tell *me* you're a famous person."

"I didn't want that to be *your* business," he said, muttering again.

"Still you have no right to be angry—"

"People, people," Linus injected in a cheerful tone. "Recriminations get us nowhere, so let's go back to thinking of dinner instead. I'm willing to cook, which is a very good thing since Ryan has no meal-making talent beyond dropping olives into martinis."

"Hey!" Ryan said. "I just spent several days on my own and I managed perfectly fine."

"By heating canned soup and nuking frozen burritos, most likely."

Poppy took a hefty swallow of her wine. "I only got the canned soup," she said. "He must have been hoarding the burritos."

Linus's brows lifted as he glanced between Poppy and Ryan. "You were making dinner for the lady?"

"It's a long story," they answered together.

"I'm perfectly willing to be entertained by learning how you two went from tomato soup to sharing spit for the curious public. Yes," he said, in answer to Poppy's inquiring gaze, "I've seen the video."

"The explanation's not that interesting," Ryan said, his tone dismissive.

Poppy told herself it was ridiculous to feel crushed by the remark. They'd had the one go in his bed. She might have found it…interesting, but for a man like Ryan Hamilton, who apparently had some porn-star princess in his past, as well as who knew how many other women, it likely had been nothing beyond banal.

But did he have to say so out loud?

Maybe she should call Brett right now. Steel herself for his "I told you so," along with a few of his usual "knuckleheads" and "featherbrains" thrown in, then get him out here to take her and Mason to his place. There, she could crash on her brother's couch—well, after he spent the next several hours airing his autocratic viewpoint on the cabins and how she shouldn't have taken up any ridiculous idea to offer them as vacation rentals in the first place.

An opinion she'd heard several times before.

Poppy downed the rest of her wine and decided to postpone that call. The less time she had with her brother before lights-out, the shorter the lecture. Linus topped off her glass again, and she smiled at him. Ignoring Ryan and his dark lurking presence in the kitchen would go easier with a second—or was it third?—glass of wine. "Linus, what can I do to help with dinner?"

He didn't let her do much of anything. So she sipped at her wine, gave Ryan the cold shoulder and finally feasted on a glorious penne, chicken and mushroom dish. Though she checked on Mason before the meal was served, he was deeply asleep and she didn't try to wake him.

She did help with the dishes, and then continued chatting with Linus, who was everything his brother wasn't—charming, talkative and very easy to be around. They talked about Blue Arrow Lake and his summer scouting film locations in the area. They traded their favorite scenic vistas and the best place on the mountain to get breakfast. She shared tales of what it was like growing up in a place where everyone knew everyone else.

All this, while Ryan sat in brooding silence.

For the dozenth time, Poppy snuck a peek at him, then her glance caught on the hands of the watch wrapped around his wrist. She jerked in her seat. "It's midnight. I've got to call my brother to come get Mason and me." Her brother, one of those early-to-bed, early-to-rise types, would not thrilled to hear from her this late, she thought with a grimace.

"Wait until tomorrow, kiddo," Linus advised. He ducked into the next room and came out with a drowsy Mason in his arms. "We've got plenty of rooms here."

Her gaze transferred to Ryan, and she guessed he might resent her continued presence.

As if reading her mind, he pulled her chair from the table. "It's okay. We'll figure things out in the morning."

After a brief inner struggle, she gave in to the idea and clambered to her feet, wobbling a little. Ryan grabbed her elbow and she shot him a look. "I'm fine."

"I know," he said. "Let me just show you to a be— room. You'll be right next door to your son."

She insisted on taking Mason from Linus, then

climbed the stairs to a second-floor bedroom, Grimm right behind her. There, after Linus showed up with their luggage, she got the little boy through bathroom chores before putting him between flannel sheets. By the time the dog jumped up to curl on his half of the mattress, Mason was already back asleep. When she half closed his door, she discovered Ryan waiting for her in the hall. "You'll be in here," he said, gesturing to the next room.

Peeking inside, weariness swamped her as a low light on the bedside table illuminated a wide bed and a bank of fluffy pillows. Okay. Brett's couch wouldn't be nearly this comfortable.

She swung around to face Ryan, his features austere, his expression unreadable in the shadowy hall. "Good night."

With a nod, he turned and headed down the corridor.

Alone, she donned her pajamas, did her duties in the adjoining bathroom and wiggled into another set of soft flannel linens. Then a tiny electronic chirp sounded.

A device built into the wall by the bedside table had lit up, a small panel with buttons and dials. Ryan's voice came through it, low but clear. "Poppy?"

She leaned up on an elbow. "Yes? Where are you?"

"My own suite. The chefs loved their gadgets. The whole house is wired with an intercom system."

"Oh." She relaxed back on the pillows and wondered if he was lying in bed, too—naked, like last night. Not that she'd actually seen his nakedness. It had been very dark and she'd been very grateful for that. After one lover and five years of celibacy it would have been too great a shock to her system to look at Ryan without clothes.

It could have caused blindness. Hives were another possibility. As it was, Poppy thought she might have developed a mild case of contact dermatitis, because her skin was prickling just talking to Ryan while she was thinking about his big body in bed.

After sex, she'd been tempted to snuggle up to that wide chest, imagining his strong arms keeping her close. So instead, she'd forced herself to turn away. Even in sleep she'd maintained a safe stretch of sheet between them. "Did you need something?"

"Just..." He hesitated. "Look, Poppy..."

The sound of him breathing made her think of him breathing on her, and she started tingling all over. "'Look, Poppy'...what?"

"I don't want you to worry. I'm going to take care of everything."

Since they were in separate rooms, he couldn't see her grimace. Her voice was pleasant when she wished him good-night. But she didn't say any more, including that, however well-meaning, she would never rely on such promises from a man like him.

IN THE MORNING, Ryan was the first in the kitchen. He arrived after a short detour to the office, where he checked in on the gang at the gate. Smoke curled up from the tips of cigarettes. Steam rose from paper cups of coffee.

The paparazzi hadn't lost interest yet.

Nor had the rest of the world, he discovered. Once he'd programmed the coffeemaker, he fired up his laptop and clicked on the top five entertainment sites.

Grant and Anabelle—or, more accurately, Granabelle—were front and center. Under headlines like Wowza! Wedding! and Newbie Nuptials were photos of them enjoying a late lunch at the Chalet, their new rings shining as bright as their smiles. Reports were that they'd left the Blue Arrow Lake airstrip for a weeks-long honeymoon in an undisclosed location—which Ryan knew to be San Francisco—and he wondered if he could lure them back sooner. More glamour shots of the couple might eclipse those of him and Poppy that were heavily featured on the sites' front pages, as well. There they were kissing. There was Poppy and her son looking wide-eyed and confused. Several photos of their rushed escape from the parking lot were visible at the click of a mouse, all accompanied by slug lines along the same theme that Ryan found uncomfortably apt: March Madness.

Pinching the bridge of his nose, he looked away from the screen and out the windows. It was a spectacular vista, he supposed, the lake a steely blue, the opposite shore rising to steep terrain covered with dark green conifers and leafless oaks, their silver-gray branches spread like arms waiting for spring to dress them in their new season's clothes. Snow glinted in the sun at the highest reaches. But the beauty felt dormant, Ryan thought, without breath and without energy, just as he did so much of the time.

At the sound of footsteps, he tensed, hurrying to shut down the computer. He relaxed a little when it was Linus, not Poppy, who strolled into the room. "Yo. Bro," the younger man said as he crossed to the espresso machine. "How'd you sleep?"

"Same as always." Like shit. "Surprised to see you up. Thought I'd have the morning to myself a while longer."

Linus grunted. "I've been awake for some time. Saw Poppy and her boy out the window—"

"Crap! The paparazzi—"

"They were exploring the lakeshore with the dog. Paps couldn't see 'em from the front gates."

"Thank God the lake is private or else they'd be out in boats trying for another angle." He once again pinched the bridge of his nose. "Do you know where she and her son are now?"

"Upstairs. She's reading to Mason in his room. He has coloring books and crayons and that Grimm's in there, too. Nice pooch."

"She tried telling me he's an attack dog." Ryan looked back out the window. "And, damn it, she never told me about the kid." The night before, after showing Mason and Poppy into their rooms, he'd explained to his brother why they'd been forced to leave the cabins.

"So? You didn't tell her all your secrets."

"As they say, what she doesn't know…" He redirected his gaze to Linus. "Anyhow, this ends today. She's leaving. I'm leaving. You're leaving."

His brother studied his face as he sipped at his coffee. "Yeah? Because I was thinking, we all could stay here, weather out March together."

Ryan stared. "The *three* of us?"

Glancing down at his hand, Linus appeared to count on his fingers. "Plus the boy and the dog. That's five."

The boy. At the thought, Ryan nearly jumped out of his skin. "Not going to happen."

"I got the impression you kind of like this my Poppy."

The sound of Ryan's back teeth grinding was loud in his head. "Stop that."

"Well, don't you?"

"This is March. We both know I do stupid things in March." Though it hadn't felt the least bit stupid to have her small, firm breasts in his hands. He'd thumbed the tender nipples, enjoying the hell out of the sound of her sweet, baffled moan as she arched into his touch. In that dark room it could have been any month, or no month at all. It was Poppy Time, an interlude that was punctuated by her sighs and her fresh-shampoo scent and the satiny feel of her skin against his hands. With her at his mercy, with her under him, he'd thought of nothing but pleasing her. There'd been no pain, no dark shadows, only the unsullied gladness he'd felt at bringing her to release.

The past four years he'd been so damn self-involved, and nothing he'd tried managed to halt the deep, dreary spiral. Until Poppy. Being with her seemed to suspend the inexorable spin.

Linus crossed to the refrigerator and yanked open the door. "Maybe we can put stupid March behind you for once and for all if we stick together."

Was he fucking kidding? "*Behind* me?"

"There will always be March, of course—I get that." Linus drew out a carton of juice. "For me, too. The whole family. But maybe we can open the drapes and let some optimism in again."

Optimism about what? Ryan thought wearily. "Look, I just want to get out of here." Though he'd discovered during the past four years that there was no place to hide from himself.

The air stirred, signaling a new arrival. Poppy's scent tickled his nose, that shampoo-freshness of her infusing the room a moment before her slender figure entered. Today she wore a fisherman's knit sweater over jeans tucked into laced-up, distressed leather boots. Her hair hung down around her shoulders, though it still retained the wave of her usual braid.

He'd never seen her hair freed like that, except for that night in his bed. At the memory, his blood pulsed heavily toward his groin, and he moved, distancing himself from her and distracting his body from an imminent and embarrassing hard-on. "Linus, get Poppy some coffee or juice."

"Sure, boss. Yes, boss."

Ryan didn't bother to acknowledge the sarcasm. He pulled a chair out at the table and dropped into it as Poppy perched her hip on a bar stool eight feet away. When Linus passed her a mug of coffee, she took a tentative sip, then slid him a glance.

He pretended not to see it, even though he was aware of every move she made. Every damn breath. "So," he began. "The plan is—"

"I can plan for myself," Poppy interrupted. "You don't need to be concerned about me."

"This is what's going to happen," he said, acting as if she hadn't spoken. "I'll go out the gates, making sure the group there sees it's me. I'll drive fast, that always piques their interest, and once I hit the highway—"

"You'll drive safely, right?" Poppy said, a note of

alarm in her voice. "I don't like the idea of you speed-ing down the hill."

"Yeah," Linus added. "Weren't you trying to out-run some paps when you crashed your Maserati three years ago?"

Ryan sent his brother a quelling look. "I'll be fine."

"Broken collarbone, broken leg and a busted spleen weren't so fine."

Poppy jumped from her stool and strode toward Ryan. Coming to a halt before him, she brushed her hair behind her ears, the honey strands framing her delicate features and creamy skin. "That's *not* the way this will go." She put her hands on her hips.

Bemused by the warrior light in her eyes, he stared into her pretty face, feeling his blood heating again. Shifting southward. "Look—"

"No, you look. You wanted some place to stay until the end of the month. You'll have your peace and quiet now that your friends are gone. I'm going to call my sister so Mason, Grimm and I will be out of your hair. You can have your March just the way you wanted it."

He never wanted another March, not ever. He scraped his hand through his hair. "The thing is…" The thing was…what? Inertia stole over him again. What did it matter where he parked his bones and skin? The lake house would be as good as anywhere else. His gaze slid over to Linus. It would probably mean he'd have to put up with his brother.

"I'm staying," Linus confirmed, an obstinate expres-sion overtaking his usually good-natured face. "You should, too."

Ryan gave another half-hearted try. "The paps…"

"The outdoor temp is low enough to cool their interest pretty quick," Linus said. "They'll get bored sooner rather than later."

"What about Poppy?" Ryan asked. "Won't she be hassled if she goes back to her life and I'm still here?"

"Nah," Linus said. "They'll leave her alone. What—" He broke off as Poppy's phone trilled.

She dug it out of her pocket and moved away, though she remained within earshot. "Shay! I've been trying to reach you since early this morning."

Ryan mouthed to Linus *her sister*.

"I— *What?*"

The odd note in Poppy's voice had Ryan rising to his feet.

"They did *what?*" She glanced over at him, a flush of color staining her cheeks. "I'm sorry they blocked your driveway. Just ignore them as much as you can. I don't know where they got the idea I'm a pole dancer, but don't even bother responding."

Ryan slid a look at Linus and spoke to him sotto voce. "They'll leave her alone?"

His brother shrugged. "Hey, I didn't know about the pole-dancing rumor."

"What a load of bullshit." Ryan shook his head. "Does she look like a pole dancer to you?" To him, she was woodland sprite, sexy, sure, but wholesome and appealing and…and fucking adorable in a please-let-me-do-her-again-immediately sort of way. Fine, he'd admit it.

She turned him on like nothing had in years.

And he must be attuned to her mentally, as well, because a chill washed over his skin the instant she stilled.

Then the color left her face. "Denny? Denny called?" Her hand crept up to her throat.

Ryan was by her side in an instant. "Who's Denny?" She swung away from him, he swung her back, holding firmly to her upper arm. "Who's Denny?"

Her hand covered the mouthpiece. "Mason's father," she said, then listened to her sister again. "He saw me on TV. And on the internet? Oh, God. Shay, don't give him my number—okay, good, good. I know. I know you wouldn't."

She closed her eyes in clear distress. Ryan fought the urge to gather her close as the conversation wound down. He didn't have all the details, but could fill in a lot from just one side of the conversation. The celebrity gossip had caught her ex's eye. After years without any contact, he was suddenly trying to get in touch.

When she thumbed off the phone, Poppy stared into space, her teeth worrying her bottom lip.

Ryan allowed her three seconds of silence before he couldn't take it anymore. "Are you all right?"

She glanced at him, glanced away. "He never wanted anything to do with Mason…or me, once I told him about the pregnancy." The fingers wrapped around her phone squeezed so tight her knuckles went white. "I don't know what he's after now, but I don't imagine it can be anything good."

Shit. This was his fault. His notoriety brushing up against her again. Tarnishing her sweet shine.

"He's not going to get to you." Ryan drew her to the table, sat her down. "Nobody's going to bother you."

She appeared to be in deep thought, her gaze fixed ahead, but unseeing. "Shay said Denny left voice mails for Mackenzie and Brett. The paparazzi have also been by their businesses asking questions."

"Shit," Ryan said. "That's not good."

"So I'll keep clear of them and my Walker cousins, too," she mused, "in case the last name triggers unwanted interest."

"That's probably a smart idea," Linus said, placing her coffee in front of her.

She gave him a distracted half smile in thanks. "Maybe Mason, Grimm and I can stay with my friend Lynnette—no, she's allergic to dogs." Her hands circled the mug. "Audra and Clint would take us in, but I hate to ask when her baby is due any day."

Ryan didn't like the way this was going. "I'm worried about word of where you're staying getting out even if you steer clear of the Walkers," he said. "Weren't you describing just last night the active mountain grapevine?"

Poppy shrugged, then her eyes went suddenly wide. "You don't think Denny will come up here, to the mountain, do you?"

Christ, how would Ryan know? But the idea of her ex getting in her face didn't sit well with him at all. He shifted in his chair. "I can't—"

"Naomi," Poppy said, snapping her fingers. "She shares a house with her brother, Tim, who is almost as big as you and would intimidate just about anybody. Plus, he loves my baking."

"That's not going to work," Ryan heard himself say, suddenly certain about this one thing. He couldn't let her go to some "Tim" who loved her baking when it was Ryan who owed her his protection. When it was Ryan, after all, who had gotten her into this mess in the first place. And with that, the separate-ways plan dissolved as a new one took shape.

"You'll stay—we'll all stay—right where we are until this commotion dies down," he told Poppy. "Here at the lake house you're out of reach of any further publicity *and* your ex."

"But Ryan—"

"It's best and safest," he said firmly, disallowing any further objections.

Her gaze roamed his face, her gray eyes once again those huge pools of ghostly mist. "There's Mason…"

"He'll be safe here, too," Ryan said, though the promise felt like a knife to his belly. "We're all going to be okay." It was the first time in four years that he'd managed to say such a thing…and also wish he could believe it.

CHAPTER NINE

POPPY COULDN'T IGNORE the fact that her true love had a crush on someone else. It only made more awkward a situation already uncomfortable. She'd agreed to stay—until she came up with a better solution—under the roof of the man who was supposed to have been her one-and-done. And though Ryan didn't make a big deal about it, she could tell he wasn't at ease around her son.

Which didn't stop Mason's growing case of hero-worship.

Her little boy had stared at the man over breakfast, forking up eggs when he did, biting into toast in tandem. Ryan was halfway through his meal before noticing and then he'd abruptly left the table. Mason had made to follow, but Poppy put her foot down, and then was forced to again, when she caught him loitering outside Ryan's office while the man worked at his desk. His back had been turned and he'd not acknowledged her or her son, but as she led off the little boy, she'd heard the door snick shut, an unspoken *stay away*.

Unfortunately, she realized at noon as she set out sandwich makings on the counter, Mason hadn't received the same message. He'd disappeared on her again, and she was pretty certain where she'd find him.

She retraced her steps to the office. Sure enough,

there was Mason. On this occasion, he was sitting on the floor outside the half-open door, bent over a pad of paper she recognized as coming from the kitchen. He was drawing, she saw, with a marker he must have discovered in a drawer.

With a little sigh, she watched another couple of seconds. At least he was quiet, but she was going to have to talk to him about using things without asking first. Walkers might not be wealthy, but they didn't take what didn't belong to them. She rubbed at the small headache fluttering at her temple. Worry about her boy's moral center was going to have to find a place on a plate already filled with concerns like where she was going to find the cash to fix the cabins, which of her family members she might possibly squeeze in with while doing so and what the heck Denny Howell could possibly want.

As she took another step forward, a marker came rolling through the gap between the door and jamb. Mason slapped his palm down, stopping its course, and with a little smile curving his mouth, uncapped the new acquisition. Then he continued work on his paper.

Bemused, Poppy watched another few minutes. In that time, two more pens made their way through the doorway. Without a word, Mason grabbed them up.

Huh.

"Mace?" she called softly as she approached.

"What?" He didn't look up.

She was close enough to see what he'd been doing with the markers. In his five-year-old style, there was the lake, the trees, the house. "Have you forgotten to say thank you?"

"Superspies must know how to keep silent," he said in a whisper. "And they need an escape route. Hiding places, too. That's why I'm making this map."

"Ah." His espionage interest was fairly new, sparked by a playdate with a friend whose older brother had engaged the younger boys in an afternoon-long game of make-believe. She crouched to inspect his piece of paper. "It's a very good map."

He shifted one bony shoulder, a son's careless acknowledgement of his mother's predictable praise. "I'm making it for Duke."

"Who?"

Mason's hand lifted, and he pointed to the office with a purple marker. "Duke," he said, still in a whisper. "I asked if he could use one, and he said yes."

Poppy thought back. Given all that had happened yesterday and then Mason's jet lag, maybe she hadn't communicated the name of their host. "He's Mr. Hamilton to you. Ryan Hamilton."

"Nuh-uh." Her son's silky lashes lifted and he looked at her with his big blue eyes. "He's Duke."

"No—"

The office door swung all the way open. Poppy glanced up, taking in Ryan's long, denim-covered legs. He wore a white dress shirt, tails out, sleeves rolled to the elbow. He was shoeless, his feet covered in heavy wool socks the color of oatmeal. Even dressed casually, charisma exuded from him. Star power. And sexual power, because her contact dermatitis seemed to be flaring up again.

She swallowed, then busied herself gathering up the pens scattered on the floor to avoid all that allure permeating the air. "I'm sorry. I hope he didn't disturb you—"

"He said he could use a good map," Mason said, clearly offended by the apology. His straight blond bangs fell back as he peered upward. "Didn't you, Duke?"

Poppy sighed. "It's Mr.—"

"The name's from a movie I made," Ryan said, interrupting her. "It's called *Gang of Spies*. My character was Duke."

"We watched it at Curt's grandma's house," Mason volunteered. "Last week. We saw it three times."

Poppy blinked. Curt was her cousin James's son. "Um...did the grown-ups know you were watching?" Visions of guns, explosions and naked women flashed in her mind.

"It's rated PG," Ryan said. "No blood and gore. Low body count. Lots of cool gadgets and flashy escapes, though."

"And maps," Mason said.

"Yeah. Maps." Ryan's gaze flicked to her son, quickly flicked away.

Time to get Mason out of their host's hair. "Let's go, fella. It's lunch," she said to her boy, gathering up the rest of the drawing materials. With the pad against her chest she turned to Ryan. "Would you like me to make you a plate?"

"No, thanks. I'm fine."

Mason began tugging at the pens in her hand. "I'm not hungry, either."

"Superspies will grow up superstunted if they don't eat," she told him.

Mutiny played across his small features. Poppy braced for his temper. He wasn't really a handful, not usually, but the end of a fun-filled vacation plus a new environment plus a continued case of jet lag would make anyone irritable. "Mom…" he began, a whine in his voice.

"I think I'll get something to eat, after all," Ryan announced, strolling past the pair of them toward the kitchen. "Strong men need three square."

He didn't look back.

As a diversion, it worked. "Three square," Mason echoed, looking up at her.

"Three square meals," she explained. "Breakfast, lunch and dinner."

Mason set off down the hall, a bit of a swagger in his step. "Strong men need three square," he murmured, as if trying out the line.

Hiding her grin, she headed after him. If either of them were disappointed to find Ryan had grabbed up a sandwich and was already gone, they didn't share it with each other.

Not that Poppy was let down, she reminded herself. Not at all.

He was the one-and-done who didn't warm up to children.

Her son's crush or no, both she and Mason needed to stay clear of the man.

But her son foiled her plan again.

She groaned aloud when she looked in on her boy's bedroom three hours later. They'd played a card game, she'd read him books and he'd busied himself with a package of pick-up sticks that she'd tucked away in

the bag she'd packed for him before leaving the cabin.
When he'd stretched out with Grimm on his bed, she'd
felt comfortable heading to her own room for a little
downtime.

But now only Grimm occupied the mattress, his quiet
snores ruffling the hem of the pillow cushioning his
large head.

Find Ryan, she figured, and she'd find her enam-
ored small son.

Poppy felt a little like a superspy herself as she sur-
veyed the mansion. When the second floor yielded neither of the males she expected to find, she explored the
first floor next. No one there, either. She smothered the
tiny flare of panic in her belly. Mason knew better than
to leave the house on his own.

And he hadn't. When she discovered a set of steps
leading down to a basement area, she hurried along
them, a maternal radar homing in on her chick. Up
ahead, she heard unfamiliar noises, and she paused at
the threshold of a pair of doors that led into an expansive space.

So this is what they mean by the phrase man cave,
she thought.

The vast space had a little of everything. Pool table,
Ping-Pong table, wet bar. A stand of free weights, a
treadmill, elliptical and some kind of weight machine
with cables. Two rows of theater seats were positioned
in front of a screen currently showing an animated film
starring penguins. One of the *Happy Feet* movies, she
recalled, having caught pieces of it at Mason's day care.

She didn't know if it was playing for Mason's ben-
efit or not, and she couldn't ask her boy, because he

was curled up, fast asleep, in a corner of the room. In another, gym mats were spread on the floor to create a space currently occupied by two bare-footed, bare-chested Hamilton brothers. Once her gaze landed on them, she couldn't look away.

Okay, landed on *him*. Ryan.

His workout pants were strung low on his hips. She had a clear view of his heavy shoulders, the wide plane of his chest, the rippling abs that she'd been up against naked. Wow.

He was damp with sweat, and he used one of his boxing-gloved hands to push back the hair that was falling over his forehead. He was breathing hard as he faced off with Linus, who was similarly dressed, but who had his bare hands slipped through cushioned, padlike mitts.

Their deep discussion hitched for a moment when Ryan suddenly looked around. Poppy drew back, loathe to be spotted playing secret agent. After a moment, their conversation continued, and she had to grin.

They were arguing about krill. And emperor penguins. And whether the small sea creature could actually survive a fall from the mouth of the bird to the snow below its feet.

"It depends on the quality of the snow," Linus was saying. "Is it slushy? Icy? Hard-packed or soft serve?"

"A krill weighs what—two grams at most? It cannot survive a four-foot fall."

"You know the weight of krill?" Linus scoffed. "The height of an emperor penguin?"

"Yes."

"I hate that you think you do."

"Look it up," Ryan suggested.

Linus mumbled something she didn't hear, then he clapped his mitts together. "Ready?"

"Yeah."

She peeked around the corner to see Linus lift the pads. "Left jab, left jab, left jab," he said.

Then Ryan did it, cocking back his arm and punching one of the pads.

"Left jab, right cross, back roundhouse," Linus directed.

Ryan followed the instructions again, each arm movement crisp and deliberate, followed by a kick to the pad extended by Linus's thigh.

It went on like that, Linus verbally directing Ryan's choreography with different kinds of punches and kicks. Then the younger Hamilton said "Faster," and they repeated the chained sequence, this time speeded up. When he said "Faster," again, Poppy didn't blink as Ryan accelerated the pace, executing the moves with a precision and athletic prowess that were...

That made her...

Stirred up.

Oh, God. She was so stirred up by that chiseled body, those shifting muscles, the gorgeous face set with concentration. When he danced back, the series completed, she realized that she was nearly as breathless as Ryan.

Poppy pressed her thighs together and held her elbows close to her body, trying to keep all the heated wildness churning inside her contained. But it wanted free and the heat bloomed on her skin, bursting out in hot patches on her belly, at the sleek flesh at the side of her breasts, on the thin skin of her throat. The hair at her temples went damp and so did the place between her legs.

Oh, God. Her sexual urges were clamoring again, completely ignoring that they were supposed to be one-and-done. She stood there, afraid to move, afraid if she twitched a finger that next she'd run across the man cave and leap into the man's arms. Swamped by desire, she forced her feet to root to the floor as she watched him strip off the gloves, then turn and walk toward a stack of large fluffy towels. He grabbed one, threw it over his shoulder. Then he hesitated, grabbed another and jogged toward Mason. There, he stood over the boy, the muscled expanse of his wide shoulders and bare chest even more rawly beautiful in comparison to the small sleeping child in his Tigger T-shirt and jeans.

Before she could figure out what Ryan meant to do, he'd carefully draped her napping son with the terry cloth.

Poppy's heart moved in her chest, and it completely flipped, revealing a soft underside she thought had toughened up long ago. *Oh, no.* She closed her eyes, trying to block out the truth. *It's only his body that's doing this to you,* she tried telling herself. *You're only thinking about sex.*

But her mind replayed the image of his large hand as it drew up the corner of the towel so that Mason wouldn't catch a chill. Just that simple action, and she was forced to admit that she, like her son, had developed a full-blown crush on the rich guy across the room.

Awkward.

FROM *YOU SEND ME,* a screenplay by Linus Hamilton:

EXT. STREET—DAY

In summer, a shop-lined street in an upscale mountain resort town. On a bench outside an ice-cream parlor, LINUS and CHARLIE work on cones. LINUS keeps stealing glances at CHARLIE, taking in her mouth, then her tanned shoulder. His gaze lands on her free hand, resting on the bench between them. LINUS's own twitches, as if it wants to grab hers up. Shifting on the bench, LINUS transfers his cone so that the yearning hand is now occupied.

A tanned young man, maybe twenty-two, dressed in ragged cargo shorts, a T-shirt that reads Arrow Marine Supply and dilapidated boat shoes is walking nearby when a lemon-colored Volkswagen Beetle pulls to the curb alongside him. Bubblegum-pink suitcases are strapped to the roof. The young man's stride halts as a college-age beauty bursts from the driver's side. In short shorts with a sorority name across the butt and a tank top, she launches herself toward the guy.

COLLEGE GIRL
Tom!

He catches her by the shoulders, holds her off, though she's still on tiptoe, straining toward him.

TOM
What are you doing here?

COLLEGE GIRL
I had to say goodbye.

TOM
(not unkindly)
We said our goodbyes last night, Jules.

The girl drops to her heels, heartbreak all over her face.

COLLEGE GIRL
But Tom...

LINUS glances over at CHARLIE, who seems unaffected by the scene playing out in front of them.

LINUS
(murmuring)
Do you know these two?

CHARLIE, still working on her cone, glances at the pair, focuses back on her ice cream.

CHARLIE
They both work for the university's alumni conference center. Well, worked. She's returning to college after a summer as camp counselor for the alumni's kids. Tom maintains the center's boats. He's a local, and a year-round employee.

LINUS studies the young pair, now engrossed in quiet, almost desperate conversation.

LINUS
They're breaking my heart.

LINUS looks at CHARLIE, who appears unmoved.

LINUS
Doesn't it get to you?

CHARLIE
No.

LINUS
Maybe she'll be back.

CHARLIE takes a lick of her ice cream.

CHARLIE
No.

LINUS
(unwilling to let this go)
Next vacation, or next summer—

CHARLIE
No.

LINUS'S SECOND STOP of the night was the bar attached to the steak-and-seafood dinner house known as Mr. Frank's. Ryan and company were still locked behind the gates at the lake house and he felt a little guilty about that. But the celebrity hounds had no interest in him— his days in the limelight were long over—and he had things of his own to do. Without looking left or right, he approached one of the leather-cushioned stools, took a seat, then smoothed his palms over his hair.

A white square of napkin landed in front of him. "What can I get you?" The man on the other side of the bar wore a crisp red shirt.

Linus ordered a beer, then took a long swallow of the brew once it arrived. It went down cool and easy and he idly watched the game on the television overhead. Though over in one corner a DJ was setting up equipment near a small dance floor, Linus didn't give that man or any of the other guests his attention. There was only one person he'd come here to see, and he figured she'd show up in three...two...one...

"What are you doing here?" Charlie demanded.

She'd always been a timely sort.

He glanced over his shoulder, noting she was in full girls'-night-out gear: tight jeans, high-heeled boots, some sort of tunic top. Makeup was smokey eyes and crimson lips. An arresting look, especially when combined with her gilt-blond hair in its sweet pixie cut.

Charlie had always been a surprise. Last summer, with her golden tan setting off her bright blue eyes and brilliant smile, he'd at first considered her the epitome of hope and cheer. But inside, he'd discovered, she had a skeptical nature, a wry sense of humor and a well-guarded heart.

Or maybe that was because she'd already given it to Saint Steven Parker, Linus thought, scowling.

Charlie scowled back, and tapped the toe of her boot on the floor. "Well?" she asked again.

He glanced from her annoyed face to the posse gathered close behind her. As he'd suspected, her standing midweek date with her BFFs continued. They alternated between Blossom and Mr. Frank's. With a nod to her ladies, he lifted his beer. "I came in for a drink, maybe some company. You?"

Her lips pursed. "Are you following me?"

"I was already here," he pointed out. "How could I be following you?"

"I don't know. I..." She slid a look to her girlfriends, as if hoping they had an answer. When the other women remained silent, she gave a little toss of her head and strode off to a table at the other side of the room, her posse trailing.

Linus followed their progress in the mirror behind the bar. They all settled into chairs near the dance floor and ordered up girly drinks from the cocktail waitress that stopped by. As what looked like an appletini was slid in front of Charlie, she caught him watching her reflection.

He hastily redirected his gaze. No doubt she'd consider him creepy for staring like that, and probably worse, if she ever found out he'd stopped by Blossom first, to see if she and her buddies had been there the week before. They had, which had sent him, tout de suite, to Mr. Frank's.

He'd been that determined to find her.

Good God, he thought, his beer stalled halfway to his mouth. It *was* creepy! Stalkerish, almost. Definitely weird.

His hand tightened around the sweating bottle. Damn it.

Damn Charlie! Wasn't this all her fault?

How had this happened? Everybody knew Linus as a charming, never-serious rogue, who skated through life with a wink and a smile. No backwoods blondie was going to change that about him, he decided, scowling again.

More irritated than he could ever remember, Linus slid to his feet then slammed some cash onto the bar. He'd head back to the lake house and maybe take out a few of the paps gathered at the gates as a way to improve his mood. By tomorrow he'd have forgotten all about the woman and the weirdness she brought out in him.

As he turned toward the exit, he found himself toe-to-toe with a petite brunette in a tight, low-cut sweater. "Uh, hello," he said.

Her lips glistened with gloss and she smelled like spiced sin. "Would you care to dance?"

The DJ was at work, Linus realized. Some hair-band ballad moved through the room's speakers, an odd choice to warm up the room, he thought, until the little lady in front of him began swinging her hips to the sinuous beat. There was warm-up, and then there was *heating up*. From the corner of his eye, he noted Charlie was looking at him and it suddenly seemed imperative that Linus reclaim—with her as witness—his free-and-easy status.

So he grinned down at the brunette and allowed her to draw him to the center of the dance area. It was her girls' night, too, apparently, because she had a gang of females with her. Fun group. He joined them at their table after the first dance finished, buying a round of drinks and later taking each of the ladies for a spin as the music switched from hair bands to Katy Perry to country rock and back again. Poison's "Every Rose Has Its Thorn" segued into "Poison & Wine" by The Civil Wars.

During that slow tune, his current partner left for a bathroom break and as he turned to find another, he came face-to-face with Charlie. They stared at each other as those around them swayed to the slow, drugging beat. Linus drew in a long breath, and even within the mingled notes of perfume, cologne and alcohol, he was able to isolate her unique fragrance. It brought him back to summer and the nights he'd sought the scent with his mouth, dragging it along the column of her throat, licking the insides of her elbows, sucking at the nape of her neck that he'd had a primitive need to cover or at least mark so that no other man could see its bare sweetness and not know she belonged to Linus.

Without thinking, he reached for her hands. Both alarm and desire crossed her face as he tugged her a step closer, their entwined fingers against his chest. They danced like that, barely shuffling to the music, their arms a barrier between their hearts. She had to feel his beating, though, and he couldn't ignore its pounding against his chest wall, the hard tattoo a clear message.

This thing with Charlie wasn't finished.

The problem wasn't that he'd lost his free-and-easy, he thought. The problem was that free-and-easy hadn't had its chance to play out. Last summer, he'd had to get back to L.A. at the end of August. The deadline had ended their relationship instead of the usual, natural, waning of interest that he'd always experienced before. The externally induced conclusion had left their association without the proper ending punctuation.

Something must be done about that. Not a do-over, but a finish-up. They'd pick up where they'd left off and then it could, finally, peter out.

"Charlie." He thought of dropping her hands, of drawing her close. But that would restart their relationship on the wrong foot. This was, after all, about letting go. After six long months, really letting go. "You'll be with me again, won't you? For a little while."

The answer was on her face. In the softening of her mouth, in the darkening of her dazzling eyes. "Yes," she whispered.

Linus nodded, satisfied to know he was not done with her…yet.

CHAPTER TEN

ON HIS SECOND full day back at the lake house, Ryan stripped off his sweat-dampened shirt as he made his way down the hall to his suite of rooms. Just like the afternoon before, he'd had his brother direct a killer kickboxing workout for him. His arms were screaming, his abs were burning from the hundred sit-ups he'd tacked on at the end of the hour and all he wanted was a hot shower and some downtime stretched out on his bed.

The new routine was his way of trying to forget about his impromptu house guests.

As he approached his half-open bedroom door, a soft noise from inside put him on alert. He halted. Three times in his life he'd come back to his hotel room to find a woman lounging against his pillows. On another occasion he'd discovered a pair of nubile young ladies, positioned like naked bookends, on the California King mattress in his first house on Mulholland Drive. They were nineteen and twenty, respectively, and he'd been ridiculously flattered, though also kind of freaked out. Would someone report the incidents to his mother?

But he suspected he wouldn't find female fans lurking within today.

It was more likely the kid.

At the thought, Ryan's sore shoulder muscles

bunched. He'd done his best to ignore the boy, but wherever he was, wherever he went, the towhead hovered at the edges of his field of vision. Like a ghost, Ryan thought, his belly roiling.

Like a ghost he should exorcise for once and for all.

Setting his face into a stony mask, Ryan shoved open the door with the flat of his hand. "What are you doing in here?" he demanded.

A feminine yelp and an empty room put him off his game.

"Poppy?" He glanced about the sitting room, puzzled.

She emerged from the attached bathroom, a plastic basket in hand. "Sorry. I did some laundry earlier and wanted to put the towels away."

Today's pants were of faded olive denim that she wore with her sheepskin boots and a thin white blouse embroidered with tiny pink flowers. She looked young and fresh and so debauchable that he had to clench his fingers into fists or else grab her up and carry her into the next room where he'd throw her down onto the bed in order to...

Debauch her.

Fucking March, he thought, aggravated all over again.

Poppy paused in front of him. "Are you all right?"

"No," he snapped, his gaze snagging on the empty plastic container. "You're not here to wait on me."

One of those delicate flushes of hers colored her cheeks. "I apologize," she said, her voice stiff, "for invading your privacy."

He ground his back teeth. It wasn't her fault he

found her so delectable, but her wood-nymph appeal only served to make him feel like the mean and ugly ogre of the forest. He'd walked in here intending to scare the kid—and wasn't that heroic?—and now he'd insulted Poppy.

As she made to brush past him, he realized he couldn't let her go. "Wait," he said, putting his hand on her arm.

Big mistake. Because her wide gray eyes lifted to his and there was that dangerous mountain mist again, but this time it was he who might be lost. *Let her go,* he ordered himself. *Walk away.* But his fingers merely tightened.

"Uh…is there anything you need?" he asked, attempting to gentle his voice. "I haven't seen you much."

Because he'd been avoiding her as best he could. Not to mention the kid.

"Linus assures me the photographers won't be at the gates forever." She was now staring at his hand on her arm, her feathery lashes half-lowered. "My son and I won't be in the way much longer."

Her son. Ryan looked over Poppy's head and out the bank of French doors that opened onto another of the terraces overlooking the lake. Today, the sun was shining, its light the thin yellow of coming spring. It reminded him of the kid's hair, its silky length fair and pure.

"They're not the only problem, though, right?" Ryan found himself brushing his thumb along the soft cotton of Poppy's shirt. "There's your ex, too."

She slid her arm away from his touch. "From what my sister said, he's been calling around trying to get my number," she admitted. "My siblings have businesses so theirs are available and though my cabin has a landline, I'm not there to answer it. My cell isn't listed anywhere."

"What could he want?"

Her gaze shifted toward the windows. "When he talked to Shay a second time, he expressed to her he didn't…approve of the company I appear to be keeping."

Shutting his eyes, Ryan pinched the bridge of his nose. "Shit. This is all—"

"Look, Denny has no right to pass judgment on anyone," Poppy said in a low voice. "He's never set eyes on his own son."

Ryan dropped his hand to stare at her. "Not even once?"

"No." Poppy walked to the sofa across from the entertainment center and dropped to a cushion, as if suddenly weary. The basket went to the floor. "We… I was a stupid twenty-one."

"Show me a wise person of that age and I'll buy you a pony."

A faint smile curved her mouth. "I have this cousin. At twenty-one, she developed a foolproof plan to keep her from making romantic mistakes."

"Then she hasn't had any fun, either," Ryan said, seating himself beside Poppy.

"It was fun, at first," Poppy said, her expression pensive. "Denny and I."

"How'd you meet?"

"At a party. The mountain kids and the flatlanders don't interact in that way very often…in large social situations. The lake is private, so it's not like we're mingling regularly enough with the wealthy set to get an invitation to the fancy homes."

Ryan supposed there was a natural divide. Those that came up from L.A. for a few days at a time would bring their guests with them or connect with other short-timers like themselves on the decks of boats or behind the walls of gated estates. But natural didn't necessarily mean right. He caught the whiff of undeserved privilege. "I already don't like this Denny," he murmured.

Her hand waved the thought away. "What wasn't to like? He drenched me in compliments and attention. My mother had passed shortly before and he was there to fill some of the gap and take the edge off my sadness. I rushed headlong into every moment."

"Twenty-one," Ryan said.

Her smile was sad. "I thought I was in love with him."

"Twenty-one," he repeated.

She was quiet a moment, then slanted him a glance. "Thanks for that. It shaves a little off my idiot quotient." Her hand found his forearm, gave it a squeeze.

At the simple touch, lust surged up his arm. The idiot was him, Ryan thought. He should have done what he'd first intended, and kicked the intruder—whoever that might be—from his room. Instead, he was inches from debauchable Poppy Walker, and her bare palm was like a brand against his skin. He despised tattoos but he thought he just might have one now, a palm-size Poppy marking on him that would never go away.

When she removed her hand, his skin still pulsed with heat.

"How'd it end?" he heard himself ask. He continued to stare at the invisible throbbing spot just north of his wrist.

"Oh, the usual way. I had missed my period and realized it might mean I was pregnant. I told him about the possibility."

Ryan recalled a similar conversation from ten years before. He'd been scared spitless.

"I took the stick test, still considering it an outside chance. We'd been using protection." She traced a pattern on her denim-covered knee. Daisies, Ryan realized. Her forefinger was drawing chains of daisies, petal by petal.

She glanced up. "When it showed positive, he was much less surprised than me."

Ryan's gaze narrowed at the wry note in her voice. "Because…"

Her shoulders moved up and down on a sigh. "Because he'd known the condom had broken once, but he'd never shared that piece of info with me. 'Oops,' he said. 'I guess some swimmers found that tear in the rubber.'"

"Classy," Ryan ground out.

"And that's the last I ever saw of him," Poppy said. "I called him when Mason was born. Let his parents know, as well, but they never responded. I've continued to send letters and photos annually, but none of the Howells seem any more interested now than they were on the day my son came into the world."

"You could have gone to the authorities—"

"No." She was shaking her head. "You can't make someone care for another person."

And sometimes you didn't *want* to care for any other persons.

"I felt pretty foolish, though," Poppy continued. "It's an old story around here. Mountain rube falling for the slick, sweet-talking visitor. Happened to my own mother—my sister Shay's a half sibling."

Poppy glanced over at Ryan. "I have Mason, though. So I don't feel sorry for myself."

Feel sorry for me, Ryan wanted to say. *Feel sorry for me, who is so damn drawn to you and your don't-cry-for-me attitude, despite the fact it's March and you have that kid and everything feels so fucked up.*

But he couldn't utter a word of that. He couldn't utter anything. The silence turned awkward and he knew she thought so, too, because a pink flush colored her face again and she got to her feet. "Well," she said. "That's much more than you ever wanted to know about Poppy."

"No." His hand caught her wrist before she could get away. He drew her down to the cushions again. "I need to know something more about you right now."

Today's taste of Poppy. The feel of her against him at this moment. What it was like to have her in this room, in the almost-spring sunshine that glazed the green velvet upholstery with a honey light the color of the palest strands in Poppy's multihued hair.

He turned into her then took her down on the sofa, her back against the seat cushions. Instead of protesting, she made a sweet, low sound in her throat as he claimed her mouth. *Aah,* he thought, her taste familiar, addictive, something that he'd been missing. *Aah.*

Her mouth opened under his and he thrust inside her wet heat as she squirmed and he shifted and then they were stretched out and she was making a cradle for him between her thighs. He ground against her there, feeling her moan rise from her belly. He pushed against her again, and the heat between her thighs penetrated his thin workout pants.

She tilted her hips, rubbing against him, too, and he lifted his head to look into her face. The expression was that baffled one that just flat-out got to him, because it clearly communicated that he got to *her,* that the sexual exchange that pulsed between them was both new to her and thrilling.

So fucking thrilling.

Still watching her, he drew one hand up her ribs in a slow path toward her breast. He saw her suck in a breath, hold it, her entire body thrumming in anticipation of his touch.

Through blouse and bra, he tweaked her nipple, saw her twitch in reaction, then flush with arousal. One of her legs came around his hip and he pinched her again. Her body jerked against his cock.

He could make them come like this, he thought. Like two kids—

"Mommy?" A real kid's voice reverberated down the hallways. "Mommy, where are you?"

One instant Poppy was pliant and his, the next she was on her feet, already her son's mother again.

Even though his cock ached like the devil, Ryan had to admire the immediate metamorphosis.

"We should forget that happened," she said, snaring the laundry basket. Without another word, she ran from the room.

Ryan sat up, then tipped his head against the cushions to stare at the coffered ceiling. *Shit.* Yeah, they should forget that happened. Great idea, except the whole "forget" thing hadn't worked for squat for him. Though maybe this time they'd have better luck.

He sent a sour glance toward the door, because a perverse part of him hoped it wouldn't be so.

THAT NIGHT, AS Poppy climbed onto the mattress and slipped between the covers, the intercom built into the wall peeped, goosing her pulse beat. She knew who was only a button away.

Hesitating, she glanced down at her at her sleep-tank, hyperaware that beneath the blankets she only wore a pair of panties. Would he know?

Of course he wouldn't know, she admonished herself. Silly woman. Ryan Hamilton, in rooms on the ground level, couldn't tell anything about her state of undress.

From that distance, he wasn't the least bit dangerous.

Arm extended, she pressed the blinking button. "Hello? Is everything okay?"

"That's my line." His voice, low and rich, tickled her ear. This must be a high-end intercom system—he'd said those chefs liked their gadgets—because it didn't sound mechanical or the least bit loud. His soft tone had no chance of permeating the thick walls and waking Mason. "You didn't have dinner with us tonight."

Poppy switched off the lamp and slid down, onto the pillows. "No. I…" She hesitated, not sure how to explain her absence. The truth was that she hadn't been sure she could face him again so soon after her embarrassing confession. Now he knew the situation with her son's father—that she'd been stupid enough to fall for a man who in the end cared for her so very little.

And of course, there'd been that ill-timed kiss. Thank

God Ryan wasn't close by now, because she had to kick away the covers just recalling it. He'd been so darn hot, in those low-slung pants and nothing else. She blamed all that bare skin for her babble. Distracted by his muscles, she'd been barely aware of the discussion. Instead, she'd been recalling what he did when he was dressed—or hardly dressed—like that. Working out, making all those powerful muscles stretch and flex. Then that body had pressed against hers, long and hard and so delicious against her softer parts. They tingled even now, arousal beginning a low hum.

"Poppy? Did you fall asleep on me?"

"No." Not even close. When she was around him, she felt energized, her purely female side stirred up and at full consciousness. After such a long hibernation she found it confusing. Confounding.

Exciting.

She cleared her throat. "I didn't join you and Linus for dinner because I made an early one for Mason—his favorite, beans and weenies. He was going to crash ahead of schedule, I could tell—your brother wore him out in an afternoon session of a game he made up. Hall hockey."

"Hall hockey?"

Talking of dinner and games had allowed her to cool a little, so she pulled up the blankets again. "Mmm. Some sort of game on stocking feet, with brooms and a crumpled—"

"—brown bag as a ball. Damn that credit-stealing Linus. *I* made that up, though I called it 'wall hockey' due to the number of times our heads or knees or other body part collided with plaster."

"Well, anyway, it was nice of your brother to spend time with Mason. He really enjoyed himself."

Ryan was quiet a moment. "Linus likes little kids."

Poppy wondered what set Ryan apart from his brother in that way. Yes, she'd seen him be kind to her son, but in a distant manner. It was clear he didn't want to actively engage with Mason. A lot of men couldn't relate to children, she supposed, but there was something...off about Ryan's reserve.

She slid one arm behind her head. "Oh, and by the way, over dinner we watched Mason's favorite movie together."

Another quiet pause. "Tell me it wasn't *Gang of Spies.*"

"Well, Duke, I don't believe I can tell a superspy a lie."

Ryan groaned. "I'm not going to ask you what you thought of it."

"That earring sure was something.... And were you wearing eyeliner?"

"I was twenty-one. Remember how we agreed it isn't a clever age?"

Poppy laughed. "I actually thought it was a clever movie," she said. "Fun, as you said. Lots of action. And you got the girl."

"Duke got the girl. In reality, she was doing the married director. Quite the scandal a decade ago."

"You must have lived a very interesting life."

"Not always the word I'd use. For example—those beans and weenies? I wish I'd eaten them with you. Linus, in all his cruelty, thought tonight called for Sloppy Joes."

"So much for the sophisticated palate I imagined you both shared."

"You've had my soup. 'Nuff said."

"But also Linus's penne. I don't see him as the Sloppy Joes type."

"It's a poke at me. While he was busy being the voice of a mouse on an animated series, I got into a few commercials. I was as green as they come when I was cast as a boy-caveman enjoying my Sloppy Joe—the commercial was for a mix—with my cave family around the fire."

Poppy set the scene in her mind. Ryan would have been pretty then, she guessed, the masculine cast to his beauty not yet set. "In furs I suppose."

"Mmm. The costume itched like hell. But I had a line and everything. 'Me eat meat.'"

It made her giggle, the way he said it, with a guttural inflection. "Do you have a copy of it somewhere? I'd love to see it."

"Absolutely not. Just thinking of it makes my stomach pitch. Because here's the thing, it took hours to get those forty-five seconds right. For each take, I had to yell 'Me eat meat' and then sink my chops in the Joe to get a big bite, only to do it all over again if the director decided the lighting was wrong or if somebody wasn't positioned right, or when the buns started to look soggy."

"That sounds like a lot of Joe."

"No kidding. The other members of my 'family' were old hands and knew enough to spit out their bites between takes. Not me. I was a hungry kid and thought I was in hog heaven…until I felt like I had a whole hog in my belly. That was the first and last time I stuck my finger down my throat for a job."

"Poor Ryan."

"I didn't tell that story for the sympathy. Only so you'd understand that the business is not all designer tuxes, beautiful women and overstuffed bags of swag."

Ryan Hamilton in a tuxedo. Poppy nearly swooned at the idea, her imagination conjuring up his lean-hipped body in a well-fitted dark suit. She thought of undoing the tie at his throat and unfastening the bright white shirt. It would have those little stud-type fastenings, and they'd *plink-plink-plink* as she dropped them one by one to the marble floor.

"Uh, Poppy?"

His voice burst the wonderful fantasy and she frowned at the intercom. "What?"

"Should I apologize for this afternoon…in my suite?"

Did he mean the kiss? She didn't want to talk about the kiss. "You didn't twist my arm." Oh, God, that sounded like it was about the kiss. "I mean, I volunteered all that about Denny."

"He's a loser."

She sighed. "Yet I still fell for him."

"You don't get what I mean. He's a loser because he gave up you. And because he gave up his son."

She sighed again. "He was twenty-five when I got pregnant. I suppose he was too young for the responsibility."

Ryan snorted. "Please."

"You don't think most men his age would run from that situation?"

"Real men of any age would not run from that situation."

Poppy made a face. "Only proving, once again, that I'm a terrible judge of them."

"Don't think you're alone. Everybody has regrets of one kind or another."

"Truly? What are you sorry about?"

A long moment passed. "Well, I…"

There was a serious note in his voice that made her suck in a breath. Tucking the covers beneath her arms, she stayed quiet, instinct telling her he was on the verge of some confidence, some admission that might bring her closer to knowing him. She wanted that, she thought. She wanted to understand what lay behind his need for privacy and what was the source of that darkness she sensed deep inside of him. What made a man hold himself so apart one moment, then tenderly cover a sleeping child the next?

"I don't regret that night we spent together," Ryan said.

Poppy released the breath she'd been holding, aware the moment of truth was getting away. Could she get him back on track? "That's nice to know, but—"

"And I don't regret our kiss this afternoon."

"Um…" Poppy squirmed against the sheets. She'd been so easy for him, so quickly melting into his embrace. His hold over her was mystifying. She seemed to get lost in lust for him, out of her element and out of control. But this conversation might make things different if she could steer it back to him. "That's nice to hear, but I think you had something else you wanted to say to me…."

"Yeah."

Poppy held her breath.

"I regret I've never had intercom sex."

The words startled a laugh out of her. *Intercom sex?* "What?"

"I know we thought we'd never see each other again—after that night in the cabin."

"It was supposed to be a one-and-done," Poppy agreed.

"But circumstances changed…." he said in a silky voice. "Though not the way you look at me."

She glared in the direction of the intercom. "You look at me in exactly the same way." Her words had a defensive edge.

"Not denying it, Poppy." His voice lowered, the tone raspy and seductive. "So I'm thinking maybe we could do something about that…from the safety of our separate bedrooms. You know…work through it, but in a different way."

She tried laughing again. "Ryan, really—"

"Intercom sex."

Oh, wicked man. Wicked, tempting man.

"I'm a single mother!"

"Even single mothers are sexual beings," the snake whispered into her ear. *Take a bite…take a bite…take a bite.*

Her pulse was pounding hard, making a whooshing sound in her ears. During the hailstorm, she'd given herself permission to be a little bad…and now she had the distinct urge to be a little bad again. Those patches of fire were blooming on her skin. "But I…I wouldn't know how to begin."

"I'll bet you do, but I don't mind helping out," he said, his soft tone obliging. "Take off whatever's on top first."

"Maybe I'm sleeping in the nude."

"No, that's what I'm doing."

She had an insane urge to giggle again, a hysterical bubble of laughter was crawling up her throat. But then she thought of Ryan—Ryan *naked*—and her mouth went dry. The unclothed curves and angles of him were something she'd felt against her body that night in the cabin. The room had been dark, mountain-dark, as darkness can only be when streetlights are far, far away. But she'd mapped him in her mind, the thick wedge of his shoulder, the pad of his pectoral muscle, the bulge of his biceps as he rested on elbows above her.

He'd touched her breast, the light brush of his thumb, and she traced her nipple with her own now, over the soft cotton of her tank.

"Take off your top," Ryan whispered again.

Poppy did. She felt feverish, her breasts achy and like they'd swelled large enough to miraculously fill a C-cup as she settled back against the sheets. The smooth cotton scratched at the supersensitized skin covering her back and hips.

"What color are your panties?"

Swallowing hard, she glanced down. "Pink."

"Like your mouth," he murmured, "and the color, I'm imagining, of that pretty, pretty place between your legs. Pink and luscious."

Poppy burned.

"It was so dark that night that I couldn't see everything I wanted to. But I felt you, Poppy. You were so damn hot and yielding there. When I slipped my finger inside you, your body tightened on me, and you poured liquid into my palm."

Oh. My. God.

"I went so damn hard I didn't think I could last." His voice became just a rasp of sound. "Are you wet now, Poppy?"

Her breath was caught in her chest. But she didn't need air, she just needed touch and she slid her hand under the elastic band of her hipster panties and stroked her own flesh. Closing her eyes tight, she pretended it was Ryan's hand exploring her. She heard herself moan.

"Caress your nipples, too," he said now, whispering. "It will feel so good."

Like a marionette, her hand lifted and she rubbed her palm against the pearled center of one breast. Her body was humming now, taut with a sweet tension that promised an even sweeter release.

"Say my name when you come," he ordered. "I want to hear you say my name."

She stroked faster, two fingers circling the apex of her sex, even as the edge of her thumb strummed at her nipple. Her breath was loud in her own ears, her heart racing

Then the pleasure peaked and she was fracturing, fracturing, a thousand pieces of Poppy flying about the room, all because of… "Ryan," she moaned. "Oh, God. Ryan."

Through the intercom she heard a quick, indrawn breath and then he groaned, the sound sexy…and satisfying to her ears.

She wanted to see him. She wanted to see him with

a desperate urgency. That night in his cabin it had been so gloomy the sex had been nearly anonymous. But Ryan was no stranger now. He was that strong body that turned her on and the chivalrous man who rescued her from the photographers. He was the one who had said, "He's a loser because he gave up you" and also the one who insisted that even single mothers were sexual beings.

She wanted to see his face, now replete. She wanted to watch his body relax and then drift into sleep.

She wanted to touch him at will and know every one of his secrets.

And that's when Poppy realized how very dangerous he actually was. Because even when he was a floor away, she could still feel him beside her—and she could still want a window into his heart.

CHAPTER ELEVEN

LINUS HAD COOKED dinner, so Poppy performed the cleanup and congratulated herself on dodging Ryan for something like the past twenty hours. Or maybe he'd been dodging her—Linus said he was holed up in his office reading scripts and handling other business matters. The outcome was the same, however: she hadn't been forced to meet his gaze while remembering that searing interlude over the intercom…which had rocked her world in the moment, but in retrospect was entirely embarrassing.

But her exultation over her Ryan-avoidance made clear it was time to craft other plans. Tomorrow, she decided, would be the day she'd leave him, despite the still-lurking paparazzi and the puzzling situation with Denny. With luck, she could make her escape without having to see Ryan again.

A thank-you note could do, right?

Moving to hang the damp towel she'd been using, she heard distant sounds of scuffling and laughter. Linus and Mason had left the kitchen with brooms in hand, intent on another round of hall hockey. When she was finished here, she'd watch them for a few minutes, then convince Mason it was time for a bath, two books then bed. Still holding the length of toweling, her maternal radar pinged just an instant before she heard a loud thud and crash followed by an ominous beat of silence.

Then a small boy's scream.

Heart shooting to her throat, Poppy sprinted from the room. Maybe she flew, because it only seemed a second passed before she found Linus and her son. The brooms were discarded, and her little guy was sitting on the floor in his stocking feet, crying hard as Linus held his hand to Mason's forehead.

Blood seeped beneath his fingers.

Be calm, she told herself, though she felt as if she were choking on her swelling heart. *Don't let Mason see your fear.*

"Sweetheart." She hurried to kneel beside her boy. "Shh. You're all right."

He launched himself toward her, and she caught him in her arms, twisting so she could sit on the floor and cradle him in her lap. The movement dislodged Linus's hand and she took a hard gulp as a new gush of blood poured from a cut on Mason's forehead. Realizing she still held the kitchen towel, she placed it gently against the wound, then applied pressure. *Head wounds bleed a lot*, she reminded herself.

"God, I'm sorry," Linus said, his face pale. "We were playing and he slid too far and hit his head on the edge of that table." His bloodstained hand shook as he pointed toward a narrow table set against the wall. The lamp on it was toppled, and the glass shade that surrounded the bulb was shattered.

Mason was still sobbing. "You're going to be okay, honey," Poppy said, pushing down her initial panic.

She lifted the edge of the towel to get another look at the injury.

Linus pulled out his phone. "I'll dial 9-1-1."

"Wait." Poppy scrutinized the cut, her breath coming easier. "It's not that bad. It's really not that bad at all." The wound wasn't life-threatening and looked to be well within her mom-set of medical skills, thanks to a course she'd taken a few years ago for new mothers. Pressing the towel back to the wound, she glanced up at Linus. "Do you have butterfly bandages?"

"I'll check." In moments, Linus was back, with a large first-aid kit in hand. "I'm sure we've got everything you could need," he said, rummaging through its contents.

Poppy drew Mason closer, rocking him a little. His sobs were quieter, and she pressed a kiss to his hair, still with the towel against his wound. "Okay, honey. You're doing great. So brave."

"The bathroom across the hall has good light," Linus said.

"That's where we'll go then, okay, sweetie?" She pressed another kiss to the top of her son's head. "We'll go into the bathroom and Mommy will fix you right up. Linus will help."

"Noooo," Mason began crying in earnest again, thrashing a little so that she had to tighten her hold on him. "Noooo."

Poppy's chest squeezed and she felt the sting of tears at the corners of her own eyes. No matter what, it was so hard to see her child in pain. "It's okay, baby. Mommy and Linus will be right there with you and it won't take long at all."

"Noooo," Mason wailed, his sobs tearing at Poppy's insides. "I-I n-need the su-superspy. I n-need D-Duke."

Poppy rocked her little boy. "Mommy and Linus—"

"I n-need Duke!"

"I'll get him," Linus said quickly.

She lifted her gaze to meet Linus's. "I don't know. I don't think he'd appreciate—"

"He'll come," Linus said, already backing away. "I'm guessing he's in the basement since he seems to have missed all the commotion up here."

Poppy bit her lip. "Linus—"

"He'll come."

She managed to get Mason into the bathroom and seated on the counter beside the sink. The sound of two sets of quick footsteps coming toward them made uneasiness join the roil of anxiety and worry in her belly. How would Ryan take being forced into service like this?

"Hey, kid," he said, standing at her shoulder. "You took a header?"

Poppy sent him a sidelong glance. His face devoid of expression, he brushed her hand away to take a look at the damage beneath the stained towel. His face registered no reaction to the seeping wound.

Mason whimpered, "Am I gonna die?"

From his place by the door, Linus made an odd, strangled sound.

"Of course you're not," Poppy hurriedly said.

Her boy didn't even seem to have heard her. His drenched eyes stayed glued on Ryan. "D-Duke, am I g-gonna die?"

"No."

At the one syllable, Mason's small frame seemed to relax a little. His gaze shifted to Poppy. "Okay, Mommy. Let Duke fix me up."

She slid another look at Ryan. It was impossible to ignore the tension coming off him in waves. Maybe he was squeamish, she thought. Maybe he was afraid he would go green and pass out. "Duke will be standing right outside," she said, "while you be a brave boy and let Mommy put the little butterflies on your poor face."

"Duke will do it," Mason said, his voice laced with stubbornness.

"Mason—"

"Duke will do it," Ryan confirmed.

"Are you sure?"

He dropped his big hand to her shoulder. "Poppy." Just her name. But that and his reassuring touch were enough to weaken her knees. The stress of the past few minutes made her light-headed, too, now that she had the luxury of someone to take on the bandaging task.

"Linus, come in here and hold the boy," Ryan said.

"No." Poppy stiffened her legs, knowing she couldn't afford to be weak or lean on anyone. "I've got it." Positioning herself behind Mason, she drew him into her arms. "I'll hold you tight, sweetie. Just close your eyes and don't be afraid."

Mason leaned his head against her shoulder. "Not afraid. Duke's on the job."

She could almost smile at that. "Duke's on the job" was a quote from the superspy movie. And Ryan was as efficient as his character. It seemed as if it took no time at all for the wound to be cleaned, then bandaged with the strips that pinched the edges of the cut together.

Linus found another bandage, a large square, to place over them. And when her son wondered if there were any dinosaur ones in the first-aid box, Linus managed to gently draw a passable triceratops on the flesh-colored plastic with a marker.

Ryan had exchanged places with his brother for this part of the process. In silence, he stood in the doorway. There was something almost feverish in his eyes, and though not a muscle moved, Poppy sensed a dangerous edginess about him.

It didn't seem to bother Mason, however, because when she suggested it was time for him to get on his pajamas and go to bed, he held out his arms toward the dark-haired man.

At that, Linus inhaled a sharp, audible breath. Alarmed, Poppy glanced at him, but he was staring at his brother. She had the weird sense that he was prepared to jump between her son and the man who'd bandaged him.

She moved to take up her child, but Ryan got there first. Without a word, he plucked Mason from the counter and strode with him toward the stairs. Following behind, she glanced back to see Linus was trailing the pair, as well, his expression anguished.

But there was no time to grill him about it. Already they were in the room assigned to Mason and she went about helping him with all the before-bed duties, which this time included a dose of children's pain reliever. When they emerged from the bathroom, Mason in pj's and already yawning, Linus was lounging at the foot of the bed. Ryan again hovered in the doorway, as if eager to escape.

"I'm sorry about your fall, Mace," Linus said as Poppy situated the boy under the covers then sat beside him on the mattress. "I think your mom's going to put me in the penalty box over it."

Mason eyes rounded and he glanced at Poppy. "Don't put Linus in a box!"

"It's an expression, baby." With gentle fingers she brushed his hair away from the bandage. Now that the crisis had passed, she still felt jittery, her nerves that had been pulled taut now cut loose and jangling. "It's time to say thank you and good-night to Linus and, uh, Duke."

He repeated the words obediently, but she could tell he was fading. No books tonight, she realized, and turned off the bedside lamp. Now the only illumination came from the night-light in the bathroom. Linus moved to join Ryan at the doorway and Poppy continued to play with Mason's hair as he drifted into sleep.

Crises like the one just weathered could make a single mother feel very alone, she mused. There wasn't a dad with whom to make emergency decisions. No one was usually at her side when she had to cope with anything parental, whether an injury or a discipline issue.

There wasn't someone to steady her when she was bowled over by her deep, deep devotion for the little person she'd brought into the world.

The feeling welled inside her now, and it put her heart, it seemed, on a torture rack, pulling it, stretching it, causing an ache that brought more tears to her eyes. Love. It made your heart bigger and yet so much more vulnerable.

Mason was the only one in the world she was willing to risk all that for.

There was the sense of something shifting in the room, and she looked over to see Linus alone in the entry. Ryan had gone, but his brother remained in place, and even in the meager light she could see the worry settled over his features.

"What is it, Linus?" she asked, now more concerned. "Is there something wrong?"

"I…" His deep sigh sounded loud in the room. "I think… Look, would you go to Ryan?"

"Oh, if there's something bothering him, it's not my place," she protested. She might have wanted to know his secrets before, but now she was scared off by the deep concern on his brother's face.

Linus didn't ease up. "Would you to go to him, anyway? I think he could use you right now."

Poppy opened her mouth to protest again, then heard Linus's voice from earlier in the night echoing in her head. *He'll come.*

And Ryan had. Didn't she owe him for that?

With slow movements, she rose to her feet and headed for the doorway. Linus sidestepped to let her pass and her intuition screamed at her to think twice, to go back, to get far, far away. But she pushed on despite it, down the stairs and then toward Ryan's suite, supremely aware there was something awful up ahead.

Aware that, while she'd intended to avoid him altogether before making her final escape, now she was approaching him instead. As she drew closer to his room, she sensed the trouble in the air—it made the small hairs on the nape of her neck rise. She could see it in the long shadows in the hall, feel it in the weighty, ominous silence captured between the thick walls. It was the acrid taste of brimstone on her tongue.

Her heart wobbled in her chest as she drew near to the man who just wouldn't stay a stranger.

FROM *YOU SEND ME,* a screenplay by Linus Hamilton:

INT. CHARLIE'S BEDROOM—NIGHT

Though the room is dark, we can see that it is very small and dominated by a brass bed. Beaming through the window, the summer moonlight illuminates LINUS and CHARLIE entwined on the mattress. He hovers over her, the bedclothes are bunched at his waist, exposing his naked back.

He's breathing hard and his hair is damp around the edges. He kisses her nose, then on a soft groan keels over, landing supine beside her. His forearm covers his eyes. CHARLIE pulls up the sheet to conceal her nakedness and sends the blind LINUS a secret look of adoration.

LINUS
How was that for you?

CHARLIE
Are you asking for a simple thumbs-up or thumbs-down?

LINUS
(smiling)

A more verbose review would be much appreciated.

CHARLIE appears to think for a moment.

CHARLIE
Bolstered by a strong performance from the male lead, this unpretentious coming-of-age story is creatively rich, even though the audience can anticipate the happy ending from the very first line of dialogue.

LINUS lifts his arm and rolls his head to look at CHARLIE.

LINUS
Pretty clever, *coming*-of-age. But about the first line of dialogue. Was that when I said, "Wanna screw?"

CHARLIE
I believe you were a tad more polite. I think it was "Wanna screw, please?"

LINUS laughs, then closes his eyes again as he stretches.

LINUS
(sleepily)
Have I mentioned how much I love this little room?

CHARLIE
You don't even know what it looks like.

LINUS
Not true.

CHARLIE turns over, goes up on one elbow and
covers LINUS's eyes with her hand.

CHARLIE
What color are the walls?

LINUS
Uh...

CHARLIE
The curtains?

LINUS
Um...

CHARLIE
(with a bit of impatience)
Can you describe any one thing in this room?

A grin overtakes LINUS's face.

LINUS
Oh, yeah. She has hair the color of morning sunlight. Plump little breasts that nestle in my hands
like tame doves. And then there's the sweetest-
tasting p—

CHARLIE's cry of faux rage drowns out the last
word. She launches herself at LINUS and, laughing,

he takes her into his arms, twisting so she's under him again. He kisses her, and she beats lightly at his back with her fists. As the kiss gains in intensity, her fingers unfurl and she clutches at his back.

LINUS RAPPED HIS knuckles against the door of Charlie's tiny house. He hadn't been there since summer, but the one-bedroom cottage looked much the same, including the red-painted Dutch door, the panes of the window on the upper half covered by white lace. Footsteps sounded from inside, and the outside light flipped on. He saw her peek around the curtain edge, then the lock snicked and he was looking at his Charlie, dressed in sweatpants and sweatshirt, with a pair of strawberry-shaped slippers on her feet.

Just the sight of her soothed him a little. There was a pencil behind her ear and she had her bangs pulled off her face with a stretchy headband covered in question marks. He remembered that she'd told him she'd be busy all night with homework for one of her online classes.

"Linus? What is it?"

"Can I come in?"

She hesitated. "I told you I have a paper to write."

"I won't interrupt. I...I had to get out." He couldn't have remained another minute at the lake house. Not only was he upset by Mason's injury, but Linus could also tell his brother's mood was on the fast train heading from bleak to black. He thought Poppy might be able to derail him before the big crash, but if not, Linus needed a bit of space before going back to gather up the pieces.

Charlie glanced around, as if needing to check in with her homework. Over her shoulder he caught a glimpse of her bed, the site of many summer joys. Was that what worried his Sal?

"I'm not here to pressure you about sex, Charlie. You made clear you didn't want to rush into that. I respect your choice."

Of course, he didn't *like* her choice, but at least she'd agreed to see him again. One step at a time.

She took another quick look back, to where her laptop sat open on the mattress. "It's just that there's only the one room and the one place to sit."

"I'll find something to occupy myself and then keep to my side of the bed. You won't even know I'm here."

Her brows rose, as if doubting that very much, but she allowed the door to swing open. Linus stepped inside, reacquainting himself with the cozy room. There was an adjacent tiny bathroom and an alcove opposite it that acted as a rudimentary kitchen with sink, hot plate and microwave.

He waved her toward the bed. "Get back to work, Sal."

Wearing a little frown, she obeyed and he tried to ignore the familiar squeak of the bedsprings as she climbed into place. From the corner of his eye, he saw her position herself against the pillows and pull her computer onto her lap. The staccato clack of keys told him she was determined to ignore his intrusion.

Good. That would give him time to look around. Now that he was here, it occurred to him he could find out about Saint Steven. Not that he should care about the idiot who gave someone as beautiful as Charlie Walker a free pass while he was away, but Linus was a curious sort.

There was a bulletin board hanging on the wall near the kitchen area. He crossed to it and with his hands shoved in his pockets, ran his gaze over what she'd pinned to the surface. A calendar from the real estate office in Cold Brook. The dried remains of a wrist corsage.

Then three pictures. One of Charlie at twelve or so, hugging another girl. They were dressed as matching scarecrows. Maybe Halloween? A second photo showed them older, arm-in-arm, and seated on the hood of a beat-up sedan with a big bow on the roof. Sixteenth birthday, he'd bet. Yet another showed the two wearing matching glitter-and-marabou birthday crowns that were topped with 21 in silver numbers. They had cocktails in hand and wore the glassy grins of girls on their first legal binge.

Linus studied the face of Charlie's friend. Last summer he'd met several of her buddies—and seen her besties again at Mr. Frank's the other night. This person was a complete stranger to him. Hmm. Linus also noted that nowhere on the board was there any sign of her sainted, absent boyfriend.

With a mental shrug, he wandered toward her overstuffed bookshelf. He perused the contents, noting an old Nancy Drew, *Life of Pi* and a chunky *Norton's Anthology of English Literature*. On a lower shelf, a thick scrapbook drew his eye. It had a woven reed cover and *Summer* was written on the spine. Feeling a tickle on the back of his neck, he glanced over to see Charlie watching him. But she didn't say anything as he drew out the thick volume.

He settled with it on the bed beside her. She'd returned to key-clacking as he slowly turned the pages. It appeared to be a chronicle of several summers, beginning with her teen years. There were playlists and photos, ticket stubs and sappy song lyrics.

He felt Charlie's gaze on him again. Without looking away from the book, he said, "Is this your work?"

"No. My friend Rachel makes several new pages every year. She's the queen of die cutters."

Whatever those were.

He still had not seen any record of Charlie's guy. It was on the tip of his tongue to ask her about that when he turned the page to see a double layout titled with sparkly letters that read Summer Beaus. Beneath that were photographs of several young women, some that he recognized as members of Charlie's posse, sporting big smiles and posing with equally happy-appearing tanned young men wearing expensive sunglasses or high-priced watches, or both.

"Summer Beaus," he murmured, glancing at her.

She made a face. "Old-fashioned, isn't it? A friend's grandmother coined the phrase and it kind of stuck."

Linus studied the facing pages again. Little 3-D graphics were arranged around the photos, suns, hearts, a string of *XOXO*s, and in stylized letters the words *Easy Come, Easy Go.*

Easy come. Easy go. Linus stared at those words a long moment.

Charlie cleared her throat. "Those are pictures of the summer guys…you know, the ones who take a vacation at the lake and end up taking out a mountain girl for a week or two or four."

Easy come. Easy go.

He stared at the pretty girls and the handsome guys, wondering why it bothered him so. What was the big whoop? Healthy young people enjoying the summer sun together. Nothing to be concerned about. Still he was glad to turn the next sheet.

Only to see that the Summer Beaus section continued.

His belly clutched, a sensation he tried to ignore as he finished paging through the summer scrapbook. When he closed the cover, he decided he should have remained at the lake house, after all.

This visit to Charlie's had netted him nothing, and as a matter of fact, he felt a little sick. He'd not detected a hint of Saint Steven.

Instead, he'd discovered evidence of himself. Because there'd been a photo of Charlie and him. Requisite tans, check. Requisite wide smiles, check. He'd been wearing his Breitling stainless-steel watch and his favorite Matsuda sunglasses, all that made him only another of the interchangeable, last-for-less-than-a-summer sunglass guys. Just another Summer Beau.

Easy come. Easy go.

CHAPTER TWELVE

RYAN HALF EXPECTED his brother to follow him back to his suite, so when the knock came at his door he remained where he was—sitting on a chair, his head in his hands—and told the younger man to go away in a tone that matched his mood. "Fuck off, Linus," he yelled.

Instead of footsteps receding in the distance, he heard the doorknob turn. *Shit.*

Squeezing shut his eyes, he tried ignoring the raging tension headache operating as a vise around the top of his head. "Linus—"

"I think he's left the house," Poppy said.

Ryan looked up. He'd left off the lights and he could barely make out her figure in the gloom. But her fragrance reached him as the air was stirred by her advance. He breathed in the subtle flower scent and wished like hell she'd go away.

Last night's bright idea of wireless sex hadn't lessened her sexual appeal one jot, and he was dangerous to everyone right now, but maybe most especially to delicate, naive little Poppy. In the mood he was in he'd push for more than intercom orgasms if she didn't get lost quick.

Instead of stopping before him, she walked directly into the bathroom. Moments later she was back, a pair of capsules in one palm, the other wrapped around a glass of water. "Pain reliever," she said.

"I'm not your kid," he growled, his voice mean. "I don't want any pills. I don't want any water."

She set the items on the small table by his elbow. "Is there something else I can do?"

"No."

"Is there something that I've done, that Mason—"

"No." The kid, the blood, his big blue eyes. *Duke, am I gonna die?* The vise around Ryan's skull cinched tighter. "Go away, Poppy."

She kneeled at his feet. "Surely there's something I can do—"

"Yes. It's called leaving me alone." He shut his eyes and started counting off the seconds until she was gone.

At twenty-two, she'd yet to budge a muscle. "Damn it, Poppy," he said, wincing as his loud voice reverberated in his aching skull. "Aren't you listening?"

"You're not talking," she pointed out. "Clearly you have something on your mind. Why don't you open up about it?"

"Look. It's fucking March."

"All right. What specifically about March?"

He wasn't going to tell her. Though it struck him, suddenly, that he'd never had to recount the facts to anyone. Everybody he'd ever met besides Poppy already knew the particulars thanks to media outlets such as *Celeb!* magazine and cable's *Tinsel Town TV.* During the past several months—due to last year's fucking March mistake—the details and all his failings that followed had been hashed and rehashed and rehashed again in a book, on talk shows and at that goddamn, weirdly popular website, PornStarsTellAll.com.

"What specifically about March?" Poppy repeated.

He stared at her, seething in anger and exasperation. Why the hell was she insisting? He was playing the hero, wasn't he, trying his best to hang onto the role he lived in for eleven months of the year—the archetypal strong-and-silent type. Being Duke, on the job, saving the day, keeping the world safe for women and chil—

Not for children.

Not for all the children.

The headache squeezed, the pain stabbing again and again until misery spilled over and slid down his body like a wash of copper-scented blood. Reaching for the glass of water, his hand trembled like a dead leaf in wind.

He already felt a thousand agonies old and they were nowhere near the end of the month.

"Ryan." She whispered his name but he heard it all the same. "Tell me."

Tell me. *Tell me. Tell me!*

Shooting to his feet, he turned his back on her, fighting for control. But it was fucking March, when he too easily lost command of himself. His whole body was shuddering now, from scalp to heels, and when Poppy stood, too, putting her small hand on his back, he lost it.

He wrenched around. "Tell you? You don't know what the hell you're asking for."

"Explain it, then."

He shook his head, but her implacable expression told him she wasn't going to back off. His mood cranked up to another level of viciousness. Pressing his fists to the side of his head he tried once more for calm, but it was swept off in a vortex of pain. So fine, he would give it to her, explain himself, just blast away, be real. The real Ryan Hamilton, who was no good guy. The real Ryan Hamilton, who walked through life a casualty of its cruelties.

"Four years ago this month I lost my son." His mouth tasted bitter. His belly roiled. "He died."

She stepped back, but Ryan didn't let her retreat stem the flow of his words. "On March 1st an electrical fire started at his mother's house. She succumbed to smoke inhalation. My son was rescued, but his injuries were so severe they put him in a medically induced coma."

Poppy put her hand to her mouth, unsuccessfully stifling a small sound of distress.

And still Ryan didn't stop. "Tate died without ever waking up on March 31st…which also happened to be the day after his sixth birthday."

Poppy's face was set, her eyes as wide as he'd ever seen them. Her obvious shock didn't trigger a single regret, though. She'd harassed him into it, hadn't she? That she'd come in here, with her fresh face, sweet scent and stubborn attitude—*tell me!*—was not his fault.

As a matter of fact, her stunned expression only served to piss him off even more. "Now get the hell out," he said, and it sounded like a snarl.

Once again she refused to obey. She stepped right up and put her soft hand on him. It wrapped his forearm, and the very gentleness of the touch detonated the full force of his temper.

He shifted, breaking her contact, only to grip her wrists and then force them behind her back. Yanking her close, he brought her breasts to his chest. As he stared down at her, her breathing turned ragged, and in the dim light he saw there was alarm in her eyes. It excited him.

That was the real Ryan Hamilton, the man he was in March, fucking aroused by the girl in his arms who had finally caught a clue and understood the trouble she was in. He recalled the husky sweetness of her voice saying his name over the intercom the night before, and he wanted that again—but without the sweetness. He wanted to make Poppy Walker hoarse from calling out his name as he took her in rough and dirty ways.

"I'm going to count to ten. You leave before I get to the last number or then you'll find out exactly what else is weighing heavy on my mind, sweetheart." There was nothing endearing about the last word.

"Ryan…"

He ignored her. "One."

Her small body was quivering against his and her gaze was trained on his face as if she were trying to comprehend the fullness of the threat. His fingers circled her loosely—she could break his hold without effort, yet she didn't move.

"Two," he said, from between clenched teeth.

He saw her swallow. Then her face went pink.

Holy hell. It was her flush of arousal. Her I-want-Ryan flush. His erect cock jerked, his body tensed. And then he smiled, all teeth, like a shark. "Ten."

Her eyes widened.

And so did his smile. "Yeah. Too late."

His head bent and he felt her quick exhalation against his cheek before he slammed his mouth to hers. Her lips went soft and he drove his tongue between them, tasting her as his fingers tightened on her wrists, pushing them against the small of her back so her hips tilted.

He ground his hard cock against the softness of her, more lust pouring like gasoline onto the fiery cocktail of dangerous emotions coursing through him. The sound she made in her throat was low and helpless and goddamn, but he loved having her at his mercy.

Holding both her wrists in one hand now, he slid the other under the gauzy blouse she wore with jeans. The skin of her belly twitched as he slid past it on his way to her bra. It had a front clasp that succumbed to his cruel twist, and then he had her heated breast in his palm. He squeezed and stroked, not the least bit worried about gentle because she was moaning against his mouth and pressing herself into his hand.

He drew in his fingers, gave her nipple a firm pinch and felt her knees buckle. Dropping her wrists, he slid his forearm around her hips to hold her steady as he played with her other breast. His mouth moved off hers on his way to her ear.

He bit the lobe.

Crying out, she grasped his shoulders, her fingers digging into his skin. The little pain made his stiff cock jump, then ache with pleasure. He swept her into his arms, leaving the sitting area and striding for the bed.

"Oh, God," she whispered. "I... Mason's alone...."

The boy's name didn't hitch his stride. "We can monitor his room," Ryan said, and flipped a switch on the built-in intercom panel.

Then his mouth was on Poppy's again as he laid her on the mattress and followed her down, covering her body, giving her all his weight. She squirmed beneath him, the friction so good that he groaned, and when she did it once more he slid his mouth to her throat and sucked on the thin, fragile skin.

Her hips jerked high and her fingers twisted in his hair. But he broke free of her hold to sit up, still straddling her. Grasping the hem of her blouse, he yanked it over her head, revealing her naked breasts in the dim light. The loosened bra was dispensed with next, then his shirt was flung over the side of the mattress.

Lowering his head, he tongued one of her stiff nipples and she moaned again, the sound filled with vibrant need. He switched to the other side and sucked in the second crest, pressing it against the roof of his mouth with his tongue.

"Oh, God," she whispered again as his fingers went to the snap of her jeans. "Ryan…Ryan, I…I should…"

He sat up again, working at her zipper while his gaze ran over her half-mast eyes, her flushed face, her reddened and wet nipples. If her brain had objections, his will and her body thought otherwise. "You're staying right where I put you."

He stripped off her pants, then trailed one fingertip up the inside of her thigh from her knee toward her panties. Her leg fell open and he stroked over the damp fabric, pressing into the heated cleft. His forefinger found the jut of her clitoris and he stroked that, too, using the friction of the fabric covering it to arouse her further.

She was panting, her hands clutching and releasing the bedspread. He bent to rim her belly button with his

found her hard, swollen clitoris. She jolted at this new touch, but he didn't let up on this, either, instead continuing to stroke, rub, drive, doing it all in order to draw from her what he wanted for himself.

Pleasure.

Satisfaction.

Forgetfulness, however transient.

And when he felt her go over again, his balls drew up and his cock forged ahead one last time. Connecting one last time with her as he came.

When it was over they lay side by side on the mattress. With a sidelong glance, he cataloged her fuzzy hair and swollen mouth. She would have a bite mark on her inner thigh and memories of that and everything else would likely make innocent Poppy Walker blush for a decade.

She looked good debauched, he decided, not regretting an instant of it. Now she knew nearly all the truth about him—enough, anyway, to keep her away and keep her safe from getting any wrong ideas about who and what was the real Ryan Hamilton.

INHALING A DEEP breath of clean morning air, Poppy thumbed off her cell and hoped she'd just heard the last piece of bad news a man would have to share with her for a long, long while. A school pal who now had his own construction/renovation company had phoned to report on his inspection of the cabins. Though he promised he'd give her a "bro" deal and had time to begin the work soon, there was a lot to be done. As she'd suspected, the place that had been Ryan's required a new roof.

As for her own, her friend said the damage to the mudroom—just a primitively enclosed porch—didn't put her belongings and furniture at risk, but made the cabin an unsafe place to live until repaired. Oh, and while he was there, a tow truck had carted off her busted-up vehicle. In his opinion, total loss.

Following Grimm and Mason, Poppy descended the steps leading from the house's back terrace to the expanse of forest and grass that sloped toward the lake. She had no idea of the acreage of Ryan's property, but stands of pines, cedars and oaks screened the area from any neighboring homes on the right and left. There were other mansions in sight, but they were across the lake and looked dollhouse-size in the distance. From where she stood, it appeared Ryan had the deep bend of this bay all to himself.

The beauty of the view didn't smooth away her stress, unfortunately. Broken roofs and broken cars meant big bills that would require some uncomfortable financial juggling in the short term. Long term, it put into jeopardy her dream of getting the resort into shape. She wasn't afraid of hard work, but she was afraid of what her siblings would say if the cabins turned into a deeper, darker money pit.

The one good news bulletin of the morning was that Mason claimed his head didn't hurt at all and he must be telling the truth given the energetic way he skipped in and out of the trees bordering the great span of grass. He'd unzipped his red sweatshirt and she didn't blame him. Though it might be winter in the deep shade of the conifers, in the sunlight she guessed the temperature would near seventy today.

She strolled closer to the lake, running her gaze over the sickle-shaped area of sandy beach. Beside it, a walkway led over the lake to a spacious canopy-covered platform with a ramp connecting it to a double dock—not surprisingly empty at this time of year. If Ryan owned any boats, they would be stored at the marina, she supposed, or in the estate's stand-alone garages.

Beyond the dock, the lake sparkled in the morning light. It was nearing spring and today the water was a bright, nautical blue, already losing the silvery, cold-season cast that always reminded Poppy of the scales on the freshwater bass fishermen pulled from the local waters. The ragged peaks ringing the lake still had snow on their highest summits, however, and the beauty of the contrast struck her hard. It was said her ancestors first made their way here in March, driving oxen harnessed to carts up steep inclines as soon as the snow began to melt. They would have seen their new world like this—a paradise of natural resources caught between winter and warmth.

"Mom!" Mason called to her. "I just stepped in Grimm's poop!"

Yeah, Poppy thought, with a little laugh. *Paradise.* "Wipe the bottom of your feet on the pine needles, honey. We'll check your shoes before we go back inside the house."

"Thanks for that."

The male voice had her whirling around, her pulse leaping. It subsided when she saw it was Linus, his sandy hair rumpled. He shoved his hands in his pockets, his wary gaze trained on her face. "Hi," he said.

"Good morning," she replied. Mason and Grimm had

found a narrow trail that took them deeper into the trees and Poppy followed, Linus keeping pace.

"Are you all right?" he asked.

"Of course." Through the feathery branches of rough-barked cedars, she spied a rock-sided building. Older than the house, she decided. The rectangular structure was lit from within and its long, narrow windows were partially fogged. Curious, she lengthened her stride.

"Last night…it went okay?"

Last night. Images and memories she'd been trying to block since awakening flooded through her. Should she be appalled? Was so much dark pleasure—at times impersonal, at others so intimate she might not be able to meet her own eyes in a mirror—regrettable or…a revelation? Her naïveté made her feel stupid. Did normal couples share their flesh in such rough and wondrous ways and then get up the next morning and exchange sections of newspaper and their plans for the day?

It sure made marriage sound a lot more interesting.

Not that she was thinking of marriage with Ryan, she told herself. Not that! Still, just saying his name in her head made the mark she'd found on the inside of her thigh that morning tingle. Had he actually *bitten* her there? And had she actually liked it, because she remembered moaning in response to the small sting.

Her face flushed and she rushed up to the building to avoid Linus making note of her discomfiture. Placing her hands on the cool glass, she peered inside. A swimming pool. Tendrils of steam rose from its aquamarine surface. It was oversize, with an adjacent hot tub. A man was spearing through the water, his arm movements aggressive, his feet propelling him though the water with efficient speed.

Ryan touched the tiled wall, rolled into a turn and then kept swimming. There was something almost frantic about his movements and she had the odd sense that he was using the exercise as a means of escape...an impossible escape at that, as he was enclosed by sleek walls of tile and then solid stone.

She glanced at Linus. Again, lines of worry were carved into his forehead as he watched his brother's ruthless pace. "You should have warned me," she told him. "You sent me to him last night knowing nothing."

Without taking his gaze off the pool, Linus grimaced. "It was his story to tell."

She ached as she remembered Ryan's hoarse voice, the brutal words. *Four years ago this month I lost my son. He died.* Her gaze instinctively sought Mason, who was digging in the dirt with a stick a few feet away.

What if she lost him?

Her heart twisted, as if wrung by a brutal fist. Even the idea robbed her of breath. Mason was the love of her life. "How does Ryan stand it?" she murmured.

"As you see," Linus said simply, nodding toward the pool where his brother continued swimming, arm over arm, arm over arm, the punishing speed never diminishing.

Ryan had maintained that same focus the night before in bed. She supposed she should have been afraid—well, it was true that a small thread of alarm had wiggled around in her belly. But that touch of apprehension had, she was almost ashamed to admit, added a layer of spice to the undeniable desire that rushed through her veins whenever she was around him. He was a thousand times more experienced than her, she knew that, but she could tell he'd been overcome by need, too, desperate for her, even if it was only for the relief she could provide. That knowledge had seemed to balance the scales a little.

Ryan Hamilton had needed her, and God help her, she'd wanted to give him everything after what he'd shared. Though Poppy's fascination with the man had been there from the very first, of course. Now that she knew about the pain and heartbreak that lay beneath his beautiful exterior, she was only more conflicted about…everything.

Licking her lips, she glanced again at Linus. "Last night…he didn't tell me much beyond the very basics."

"What else are you itching to know?"

She frowned. "That obvious?"

His mouth quirking in a small smile, he shrugged. "I'm an attentive observer."

Feeling her face heat, Poppy sucked in a breath, then let it out slowly. She hesitated a moment more, then her need to know overcame her embarrassment. "He told me about his son. And I know Tate's mother died, too. But…" Oh, what the heck. "Was Ryan in love with her?"

"No," Linus said, shaking his head. "They met on a set—she was a number of years older, part of the production staff. She pursued him pretty hard. He was twenty-one."

Show me a completely wise person of that age and I'll buy you a pony. So he'd known firsthand about youthful decision-making.

"When she told him she was pregnant, she'd already

moved on to someone higher up in the movie studio. But Miranda did the math and came to Ryan. Between you and me? I think she was hoping to snag a man with a pregnancy, but I can't prove it and my brother would never utter a word against her. The DNA test established Tate was his, and they amicably shared custody. Ryan doted on his son and Miranda seemed to, as well." Linus scrubbed his hand over his face and his voice went scratchy. "When I think about what happened...words fail."

Poppy's heart twisted all over again. Mason came running past and she snagged his arm, then pulled him close for a fierce hug. She ignored his routine protest, closing her eyes to hold back stinging tears. "I love you, baby," she murmured, curling herself over him so she could place a soft kiss beside the bandage on his forehead. "I love you so much."

"Promise you'll stay," Linus said suddenly.

Mason slipped out of her arms to run after Grimm and Poppy drew her sweatshirt sleeve across her eyes. "Oh, but—"

"Just until the 31st. If you're here, he'll remain at the house, as well. That way I can keep an eye on him."

But...but...last night! She wasn't certain she could look Ryan in the eye after that, after her moans, her whispering pleas, her complete surrender to him and all the things he'd done with her. How could she contemplate continuing in his company? She'd stolen out of his bed while he was sleeping, that's how cowardly she was.

"On April 1st, I guarantee he'll go back to L.A. After March, he becomes a different person. No longer volatile, his leash tight again."

"You make him sound like a wild animal."

Linus lifted a shoulder. "There have been accidents in March. Self-destructive decisions—"

"Don't tell me." She wiped her sleeve across her eyes again, remembering Linus mentioning a broken collarbone and leg, a damaged spleen. "That isn't fair."

"I won't apologize for it. I care a lot about my brother, Poppy. I swear having you at the house helps."

"I'm not sure—"

"You're a distraction."

She laughed, the sound a trifle hysterical. What scared her most about Ryan—that he was suffering so deeply—was being used against her now. Though... what if Linus was right and she did help his brother in some way? "Still not playing fair."

He gave her a faint grin. "The provenance of younger siblings. Do you have any?"

"I'm number three of four."

"Then you know. The older ones boss us around but we always find a way to get what we want."

She thought of her brother and sisters. All of them were against the idea of making a go of the cabins, but Poppy had yet to back down. Despite the storm damage and the expense of the repairs, she remained determined.

Glancing over her shoulder, she saw that Ryan was still slicing through the water. His body was big, muscled—she had an intimate acquaintance with it, she thought with a shiver—and he'd yet to slow. Still attempting that futile escape.

Linus stood beside her for a long, silent moment, then he turned back toward the house. "Think about it, Poppy. Not only are you a distraction, but I'm convinced you do him good. You and Mason."

Which was more bad news, Poppy decided, as she watched him stride away. It obligated her in a way she worried she might not survive.

Her phone buzzed in her pocket, and still absorbed in her thoughts, she answered it without checking the display. A familiar voice had her stiffening.

Another male with unpleasant tidings, she concluded instantly. Then he confirmed her fear.

"We need to meet," Denny Howell said.

CHAPTER THIRTEEN

RYAN LEFT THE pool house wearing a sweatshirt and jeans, his swim trunks rolled in a towel as he padded along the path through the trees. An hour of swimming hadn't brought clarity. Lap after lap only served to let his mind wander through images of the night before. Poppy's lovely breasts. The scorching softness between her legs. Poppy on her knees, her back arched as he drove inside her, as he touched her with such blistering intimacy.

He'd done her rough and dirty just like he'd wanted, then woken wanting her all over again. To find her gone from his room had almost made him angry. Then cool relief had coursed through him.

Because what was he supposed to do with her now? An apology was probably in order, but he wasn't sure he could get through it without dragging her back to his bed, where he could ravish her all over again.

She'd probably crept off to nurse her wounds.

God, had he hurt her?

But no, he remembered her moans and cries and knew she'd found pleasure. Though not in the same gentle manner that he'd coaxed her to climax back in the cabin.

Her innocence, however, probably needed a reboot.

He paused at the place where the path ended in the expanse of grass that rose to meet the back of the house. Even in the mere few days they'd been here, the lawn appeared to be rejuvenating, the blades more green and firm-looking. On either side of the terrace steps were raised planting beds, and he could see long green shoots poking through the soil.

As he'd never been here in March, and couldn't distinguish between a weed and a petunia in any case, he had no idea what was sprouting. The natural landscape was coming out of hibernation, though, that was sure, and served as a direct contrast to how dead he continued to feel inside. Only his raw emotions were alive, moving like a raging winter river splashing over and around the impregnable rocks that were his heart and soul.

The jingle of a dog collar snatched him out of his reverie. He jolted, then jolted again when Poppy's towhead caught his sleeve. Ryan stared at the kid's bandaged brow. *Am I gonna die, Duke? Am I gonna die?*

He wanted to turn away from the boy, take off in the opposite direction, but even he couldn't be so callous. "How's the noggin?" he asked, touching his own.

"Good" was the reply, accompanied by a show of white baby teeth.

Ryan had forgotten how small they were. Tate had lost two during one of his custody weeks. With great ritual, they'd wrapped each in a scrap of tissue and placed them under his pillow. Sneaking into the bedroom in the middle of the night, he'd had a hell of a time finding the tiny things without waking his son.

Who would never wake again.

Anguish clawed at Ryan, and he closed his eyes at

the tearing pain. Though no nightmares had plagued his sleep last night, it seemed they could come with daylight, too. Grimm whined and pushed his head against his hand.

Ryan moved away. "I gotta go, kid." Avoidance was the answer. The house had twelve bedrooms, sixteen bathrooms, a gym, a media room, an office, a den, a living room, a dining room and a bunch of other places where he could get lost. Where he could hole up, keeping himself and his foul moods away from everyone. Where he wouldn't have to face whatever was going on in Poppy's head, as well. "I gotta go back to the house. Do some work."

"Me, too," the boy said, skipping to keep up with Ryan's longer strides. "I'm making a new map. I'll give it to you when it's done. Me and Grimm are finding some good escape routes around here. Hiding places, too. I put a red X on 'em, okay?"

"Sure." Ryan rubbed at his temple with the heel of his hand. The sunshine glinted off the kid's blond hair and the brightness was stabbing at his always-incipient headache.

"Do you have a girlfriend?" the boy asked.

The question startled him into halting. "What would you know about girlfriends?"

"From Stu. He's eight and comes to my day care after school. He told me everything about girlfriends."

"Uh..." Ryan glanced around, seeking assistance. Where the hell was Poppy? Had her son sensed something between Ryan and her? And what "everything" could somebody eight know about girlfriends, anyway?

"Stu says his dad, Ivan, wants to be my mom's boy-friend."

"Um." Ivan? He sounded terrible, Ryan thought, re-sisting a juvenile smirk.

"Miss Robin—she's in charge at day care—told one of the other moms that Ivan's a good man."

"Hmm."

"One of the moms told another mom that Ivan looks like he could keep a woman happy. Then the other mom said that if he could keep a job, that was good enough. What do you think?"

"I think you listen an awful lot to what adults say to each other."

"They forget kids have ears."

"You're probably right," Ryan murmured, as his gaze finally landed on Poppy. She stood against the terrace's stone railing, her cell phone pressed to the side of her head. From this distance he couldn't make out her ex-pression, but her slender figure seemed…stiff to him somehow. Was she sore from the night before? God.

"Duke?"

He glanced at the kid's upturned, expectant face, taking in the corn-silk hair and big blue eyes. "Uh…"

"You could superspy, maybe. Find out about Ivan."

Ryan didn't want to know any more about Ivan. "Look, you get I was just pretending for that movie, right? I'm not really a superspy."

The kid's expression didn't change. "You're on the job. I've seen you." He moved, making a decent fac-simile of a left jab followed by a roundhouse kick, just a couple of the moves that Ryan and Linus practiced in the gym. They'd been aware of the boy observing them a couple of times, but had pretended not to notice.

"Yes, but—"

"I don't think I like Ivan," the boy said. "Plus, Stu steals Cheerios from the babies."

"That is low," Ryan conceded, restarting his return to the house. He hesitated a moment, then let curiosity get the better of him. "What don't you like about this Ivan?"

The kid shrugged. "The way he looks at my mom. Sorta how Grimm watches me eat a burger."

"Like...slobbery?"

"Yeah. Icky."

Ryan's belly tightened, though he tried reminding himself that the way he looked at Poppy probably wasn't much better. But he was going to warn her about icky Ivan, he decided as he mounted the steps, Mason and Grimm on his heels. She should at least know the man was raising a cereal-stealer.

Once on the terrace, the sound of their approach caused Poppy to spin their way, cell still at her ear. She looked like spring, Ryan thought, in her tight jeans and a pale yellow hippie-styled shirt embroidered with thread the same color. A blue ribbon was tied around the end of her braid. Then he took in her anxious expression. It hurried him forward, and as he watched she ended her call and slid her phone in her pocket.

"What's wrong?" he said, toe-to-toe with her. His gaze scanned her face, and he thought he saw that she had her own ghosts in her pretty gray eyes. "Who was that on the phone?"

She gave a slight shake of her head. "I haven't a care in the world." The non sequitur was topped with a smile for her son. It was bright as a toothpaste ad but couldn't fool Ryan. "Hey, buddy. How about we make some cookies in that big, fancy kitchen?"

The kid cheered, but Ryan went on further alert. Oh, yeah. Something had pushed Poppy into baker mode... and he had the strong sense that it wasn't what had happened between them the night before. Looking at him, she hadn't colored, she hadn't looked away, she hadn't seemed much aware of him at all. Clearly there was another source of her disquiet.

As she hustled off her son and dog, Ryan called after her. "We'll be having a long talk later." When she threw him a confused glance over her shoulder, he didn't regret the promise.

Though not for a moment did he forget that delving into Poppy's psyche had been a thing he'd been desperate to evade.

POPPY STOOD IN the hall, just outside the archway leading to the lake house's family room. Clamping down on her fear, she tried to keep the shrillness from her voice. "Mason, you just use that one sheet of paper to gently nudge the spider onto the other piece on the floor. Then you can walk it to the back terrace and let it go free outside."

Her son was crouched low, elbows on his knees, as he studied the biggest, ugliest spider that Poppy had ever seen. It wasn't a poisonous type, like a black widow or a brown recluse—she could identify those. This was your average, everyday house spider.

And just looking at it made her sweat.

She gave her son an encouraging smile. "You can do it, Mace."

"What's going on here?"

At the sound of Ryan's voice, Poppy started, and her already jittery nerves did another little dance. She glanced over her shoulder at him then quickly looked away. Now that the distraction of Denny was no longer in her ear, the merest glimpse of Ryan set the memories of last night in his bed shuffling through her head. His mouth scalding her throat, his teeth on her skin, his hands holding her hips steady... A hot rush of goose bumps ran over her flesh and she was afraid if he came a single inch closer she might melt into a puddle at his feet.

Which would bring her much too close to that arachnid.

"Poppy?"

She cleared her throat. "I'm showing Mason how we take care of spiders. He's going to relocate our eight-legged friend outside."

Ryan moved nearer her son and bent to inspect the horrid thing, letting out a low whistle. "That's a big one."

She fisted her hands to fight off a shudder. "Mmm."

"Do you want me to show you how a guy handles a spider like this, kid?"

Her little boy was already shuffling back, his gaze trained on Ryan. She wondered if the man had any idea how Mason looked up to him. "Go ahead, Duke," Mason said.

Ryan stepped up to the spider—and then stepped on it.

Poppy gasped, staring as he used one of the papers to scoop up the flattened carcass. Ryan balled both sheets then strode into the family room, she and Mason trailing behind.

Without giving them a glance, he crossed to the fireplace and tossed the crumpled mass into the crackling, leaping flames.

"I—I—" Poppy wet her lips. "I was intending a more humane method of disposal."

He sent her a look. "Sorry. No hero here." Then he passed by her on the way to the wet bar. "Shame on you," he murmured for her ears only, "getting your kid to do the dirty work."

Her face burned. "It's a phobia," she muttered to his back.

He returned to her holding two stemless wineglasses half-filled with a garnet-colored wine. "Now that dinner's over and Linus has repaired to who knows where, I thought we could have that chat I mentioned before."

Poppy's fingers automatically closed around the glass before the intent of his words sank in. A *chat*? She glanced around the room to find Mason paging through a picture book they'd left there earlier. A chat about what? Ryan had mentioned one before, just after she'd wrapped up her phone call with Denny. She certainly didn't want to tell him about that conversation.

And surely Ryan wouldn't want to talk about...

Last night. In his dimly lit suite. Her mind wandered there once more and images flashed through it, again slide-show-style. His hand binding her wrists. Her fingers twined in his hair. Ryan, still half-dressed, between her legs, his wide shoulders keeping her naked thighs spread for the exploration of his mouth.

Her body went hot all over at the memory. Yes, they didn't need to have any kind of chat about anything.

Ryan already knew enough about her.

She took a bracing sip of her wine. "I'm sorry—no time to talk. Mason and I have before-bedtime plans." And knowing Ryan—and knowing why—he'd find an excuse to avoid being with her son. Another swallow of the liquid in her glass went down her throat, the taste like raspberry and smoke against her tongue. "I found some board games in a closet today."

"What games?" Mason asked, looking up from the book.

"There's Candy Land."

Both males in the room made the same disgusted face. Okay, it wasn't her favorite, either, but surely it would send Ryan running.

"Candy Land is for babies," her son said. "I'd rather draw."

A gleam of satisfaction came into Ryan's eyes. "Then—"

"We'll play Go Fish. I found that, as well."

Mason considered, nodded then shot a look at the spider-slayer. It occurred to Poppy that Ryan's decisive action had only given her son another reason to admire him. Sigh.

"You'll play, too, won't you, Duke?"

Knowing the forthcoming answer, Poppy took another swallow of wine. Then choked on it when the man agreed. She goggled at him, but his expression was unreadable as the three of them found places on the expansive, soft-cushioned couch placed before the fire, with Mason in the middle.

The males played the game with much seriousness. Ryan accused her of cheating to help her son win—and since he was right she had to deny it with a vigor that made amusement spark in his eyes. Their gazes met over Mason's head and a horrible, dangerous longing bloomed in her chest, making it hard to breathe. What if she could have him like this every day, every night?

But since she knew that was impossible, she tore her attention away, looking everywhere but at him. The family room was as elegant and well-appointed as anything in a glossy magazine, with its gleaming floors and enormous marble-fronted fireplace. A baby grand piano sat in one corner of the room and there was an entire wall of mullioned windows that in the daytime presented yet another breathtaking lake view. Now the fire was reflected in the glass, the gold and red as rich as everything else about the estate.

Poppy supposed a woman like herself, raised in a home much more humble, might feel intimidated. But the fact was, the Walkers were an arrogant lot, unimpressed by baubles and stacks of cash. They'd come to the untamed peaks with their oxen and their iron will, facing down any and all who got in the way of their holding a piece of the California mountains. Once they had it, they'd considered themselves wealthier than the whole world.

"What have you heard from your family?" Ryan asked, as if he'd read her mind—or was trying to initiate that chat he'd claimed to want.

But this was a safe topic. She glanced at Mason, who

had gathered the cards and was separating them into piles with little-boy busyness. "My brother, Brett, has been out of town, it turns out. I've been ignoring my sisters' calls and instead have been taking their scoldings via text message."

"Tell me about them."

"Why?"

Ryan shrugged. "You know Linus."

"Not that much." Other than he was charming, boyishly elegant and deeply concerned about his brother. Oh, and that he thought she should stay with Ryan for the rest of March.

"You know Linus cooks. He can also do a decent soft shoe."

Poppy blinked, fascinated. Her own brother refused to sway on the dance floor even at weddings. "Can you?"

"When you get me drunk enough."

She directed her glance to his wineglass sitting on the end table by his elbow. He'd refilled both of theirs not long before.

"It would take a lot more than a couple of glasses of grape juice," he said, and a smile played at the corners of his mouth.

The sight of it made her belly tense and the bite mark on her thigh suddenly throbbed. Oxygen seemed bottled up in her chest as that dangerous longing surged through her again. Afraid he might see it on her face, she looked away. Mason had abandoned the Go Fish cards to curl up on his cushion and was quickly heading toward sleep. It was a good excuse to get up and carry him to bed. After that, she could hide out in her room.

But the fire was beautiful and the wine had mellowed her and…and she didn't want to leave Ryan's company quite yet. Running her finger around the rim of her wineglass, she stared into the liquid. "My brother has a landscaping company. He used to be in the army—10th Mountain Division. He's back now, at turns quiet and cranky."

"And your sisters?"

"Mackenzie, she's older than me, runs a housekeeping business. I saw one of her cards in your kitchen."

"I'm not sure who we usually use. I have an assistant who makes a call to a service when I plan to be up here."

Poppy grinned. "If you get the chance to meet my sister, she'll likely talk you into using hers."

"And the other…Shay?"

"Tutors when needed, does nanny work. She just got a new job as a…well, it sounds sort of like a governess, actually. One of your neighbors at the lake has a teenager. Shay is living at the estate and homeschooling the girl."

"I still don't understand why they're so against developing the cabins."

She shrugged, thinking of how to explain family history and family dynamics. "Our dad was a dreamer. An impractical one, and it caused a lot of contention between him and our mom, on and off throughout their marriage. He was so focused on keeping that last tract of land that he made bad financial decisions. When everything fell apart, he took a mining job in South America."

"Tough," Ryan said.

"And it got tougher." She sipped at her wine. "My mom—and to be fair, she couldn't be certain Dad would come back—had an affair that resulted in Shay. That relationship went poof and then our father returned… and he and Mom patched things up. He accepted my sister as his own and never treated her differently than the other three of us."

"Then he was a good man."

"Yes." There was a sting of tears in Poppy's eyes. "It's one of the reasons I don't want us Walkers to abandon the property that meant so much to him."

"But your siblings are adamant about not cooperating with you?"

"They think I'm a dreamer, same as my dad. But all his ideas weren't failures—and I want to prove to them this one isn't."

"Do they really believe the land's cursed?"

She shrugged. "With bad memories for sure. After the fire there, dad's stress over the situation caused the heart attack that killed him. But I think if we can make something of the cabins, then we can make some good memories, too. It would be dad's true legacy. And my mother's, too, when it comes to that. I'm so glad Mom gave him a second chance."

Which was why when Denny phoned today, she'd not instantly hung up. At some level, ever since she'd heard he'd been asking about her, she'd expected the call. In a small community like theirs, her number was easy to uncover. Her surprise had been from what he claimed to want—a chance to get to know his son.

While part of her recoiled at the idea, given that he'd never expressed any interest before, her conscience couldn't immediately put the kibosh on it. What if he'd changed? She would never take up with him again, that was over, but could she deny him a chance to be a father to Mason?

Ryan had influenced her there. His love for his boy and his grief that Tate was gone made her not immediately refuse her ex. But she was being careful, and had told Denny she needed time to fully consider the situation.

"I hope that's what you'll find, Poppy," Ryan said in a quiet voice. "A man who'll love you and have an open heart for your son."

Glancing over at him, her own heart stopped, then did another of those pancake flips in her chest, exposing once again its soft, vulnerable underbelly. Because, though Ryan was staring into the fire, his fingers were lightly sifting through her son's hair. The gesture was tender and sweet and she knew he had no awareness of it whatsoever.

A man who'll love you and have an open heart for your son, Ryan had said. The words raked at her. Poppy knew for certain Ryan's statement wouldn't ever, couldn't ever, refer to himself.

Because when it came right down to it, she now knew him quite well, too.

CHAPTER FOURTEEN

FROM *YOU SEND ME*, a screenplay by Linus Hamilton:

EXT. BLUE ARROW LAKE—NIGHT

LINUS and CHARLIE are snuggled side by side at the rear of a small powerboat. The lake gently rocks them as they gaze upward, enjoying the weekly fireworks display while surrounded by other boaters, some in kayaks, some on large, flat-bottomed party boats. The rockets are launched from a platform in the middle of the lake and the various hues of the subsequent explosions wash over the faces of CHARLIE and LINUS. Once the incendiaries flame out, ash and some still-glowing tiny embers rain into the water, landing with little hisses.

LINUS
That was a good one.

CHARLIE squeaks in mild alarm as ash falls around them again and LINUS tucks her closer, kisses her temple. Another boom sounds, and colors flower in the sky above.

CHARLIE
I've never been this close. Are you sure it's safe?

LINUS
Anything spectacular requires a bit of risk.

LINUS looks over at CHARLIE, whose face is
turned up to the sky. His fascinated gaze doesn't leave
her as the red and blue and yellow light up her face.

LINUS
(casually)
I've been meaning to tell you...

CHARLIE
What's that?

LINUS
I have a couple of invitations to an upcoming red
carpet movie premiere. Big after-party following
it, too. We can dress snazzy, drink too much, then
fall asleep in a limo on the way home at dawn.
How does that sound?

CHARLIE stills.

CHARLIE
Where and when?

LINUS
(even more casually than before)
L.A., natch. Labor Day weekend.

CHARLIE
September?

LINUS
(tightly, he suspects this won't go his way)
That's when Labor Day normally occurs, right?

Ash falls down around them, but this time CHAR-
LIE doesn't seem aware.

CHARLIE
(quietly, almost to herself)
September.

Then CHARLIE looks at LINUS and shakes her
head.

CHARLIE
I couldn't, Linus. There are…boundaries.

LINUS
What kind of boundaries? Geographical? Chron-
ological?

CHARLIE
Come September, yes.

CHARLIE SCOOPED UP another spoonful of crème brûlée
and caught Linus staring as she brought it to her mouth.
Making a face, she halted without taking the bite. "It's
weird to eat when you're not."

"I told you," he said, leaning back in their horseshoe-shaped booth at Mr. Frank's. "I already had dinner."

"With my cousin and her son and your brother. How's them staying with you guys working out?"

He gave a light shrug, but she could tell it didn't dislodge the heavy weight he carried on his shoulders. In summer, they'd hardly spoken of family and friends. It had been an interlude belonging only to them—a time for sunshine, sweet talk and sizzling kisses.

An August affair. Then it had been over, at her insistence. He'd returned to L.A. just a few days after she refused to attend that movie premiere.

It should have stayed over. But he'd returned to her world and she'd been powerless to resist his appeal. Linus, brimming with all that casual, unfussy charm, had sneaky ways of getting past her guard.

But not into her heart. She had strict lines drawn around it. Boundaries he'd never pass.

Then he rubbed a hand over his eyes, in a gesture so weary that the heavily protected organ in her chest squeezed a little. Linus had never shown a hint of fatigue, not even when they'd burned the candle at both ends last summer.

"What is it?" she asked, dropping her spoon and reaching for his free hand. "What's the matter?"

"Things on my mind, Sal. Sorry. I'm probably lousy company tonight."

Another first. Linus had always been the best kind of company, ready to share witty observations, yet equally content to enjoy a comfortable silence. She squeezed his fingers. "Is it about Ryan? And…and his son?"

At his nod, Charlie's heart constricted again. Like

just about everyone else in the world, she knew about the tragedy and then the trouble his brother seemed to encounter every March. But Linus had lost a loved one, too, hadn't he?

"Would you…would like to tell me about your nephew?" she asked.

Linus's fingers twitched in her hold and his gaze, trained on the tablecloth, lifted to hers. "Tate."

"Tate," she repeated. "Tell me about Tate."

He was silent another moment, then began to talk. "We were all crazy about him." A half smile curved Linus's mouth. "Well, at first I considered him just a blob, you know? I watched Ryan cart him around and thought bo-ring."

Charlie squeezed his hand. "I've yet to meet a man who instantly went ga-ga over newborns."

"Then one day Tate was in this carrier on the kitchen table at my mom and dad's. I was sitting there with a bowl of cereal when a sneeze crept up on me—one of those kind you can't swallow down."

"Ah-choo."

"Yeah. I ah-chooed, all right. So loud the pots and pans rang. And Tate…"

"Screamed? Cried?"

"He laughed." The corners of Linus's mouth lifted in a real grin. "It was the first time he ever laughed. Mom, Dad, Ryan, everybody just gathered around him then, and we took turns fake-sneezing to hear that laughter over and over and over again."

Charlie ran her thumb across his knuckles. "Sounds like he enjoyed an audience. A true Hamilton, huh? Another performer."

"Yeah. Maybe. I guess we'll never know." At that, he sat up and slid his fingers from hers. "But downer of a conversation, huh? Got any good stories about the best little post office in Cali?"

Instead of letting him deflect the direction of their discussion, Charlie slid along the booth's seat until her hip brushed his. "You can talk to me, Linus."

He glanced over, as if judging her truthfulness. "Yeah?"

"We're friends, aren't we?"

His second assessing glance made her bristle. "Well, I consider myself your friend," Charlie said. "And if something is bothering you, I'd like to hear about it."

Linus hesitated a long minute. "Okay." He blew out a breath. "It's just this time of year is hard, you know? My folks fret about Ryan, and I fret about Ryan, and..."

"And then there's your own grief."

He was still again. After a moment he slid an arm around her shoulders, drawing her into him to press a kiss to her hair. "And then there's my own grief. Thanks for realizing that. He was a good little kid. I miss the hell out of him."

Charlie leaned against Linus, hoping he drew some comfort from her warmth. "I know what that's like, you know. Losing a loved one. Having to accept you'll never see them again."

With gentle hands, Linus pushed her away, putting a small distance between them. A frown drew his eyebrows together. "I'm so sorry. Who...?"

"My best friend, Laurie. We were inseparable from middle school until...until she died."

"That must have been so hard," Linus murmured.

"Yes. We did just about everything together." Except Charlie had made sure she never fell in love with one of the Summer Beaus. "She was like a sister to me."

Linus's thumbs caressed circles on her shoulders. "What happened?"

"Car crash. She was heading downhill off the mountain one night and went through the guardrail." Over the cliff, Laurie's body breaking, just as her heart had already been shattered.

"God." Linus pulled her to him again, hugging her close. "I'm so sorry, Sal."

She allowed herself to lean there, absorbing consolation, returning it, feeling closer to him than ever. His heartbeat was steady in her ear, his breath warm on her temple. *This closeness is dangerous*, a little voice whispered to her. *Remember, it's what your rules and boundaries have been all about preventing.*

"Was she the girl in the photos on your bulletin board?" Linus asked.

"Hmm?"

He drew back to meet her gaze. "I saw some pictures on the bulletin board in your room. You and another girl. Laurie?"

"Yes. Laurie." Even after three years Charlie missed her like a phantom limb. She'd think, *gotta call L, gotta tell L the latest*…and then belatedly remember that L wouldn't pick up ever again.

As if he sensed her distress, Linus kissed her forehead, her cheeks, her mouth. "It can be just so damn hard."

She nodded, and they gazed into each other's eyes, his brown ones looking so warm and tender that she felt tears gathering inside her like a storm. But they weren't threatening to spill over and roll down her cheeks. Instead, she felt them as a force against her heavily defended heart, a flooding pressure great enough to fracture what was within. *Hold strong*, she cautioned herself. *Keep steady.*

"Sal," Linus said, his voice soft. "You said you were willing to hear what was bothering me."

Sal. That nickname was killing her. But what could she do but nod? "Is there something else?"

"It's just… I'm just…" Linus looked away, then looked back at her, and there was a flush of— embarrassment?—riding his cheekbones. "I need to see Steven. There wasn't a photo of him in your room, not that I saw, anyway, and I don't know…for some reason I've got to put a face to the name…."

His voice trailed away as she reached for her purse. Her movements felt sluggish, like she was surrounded by mud instead of air. But her fingers managed to close around the leather and then they found her wallet and then she flipped through the plastic sleeves. A guy in uniform smiled for the camera.

She tilted the photo to give Linus a better view. "Steven Parker."

FROM *YOU SEND ME,* a screenplay by Linus Hamilton:

INT. CHARLIE'S BEDROOM—NIGHT

At the foot of CHARLIE's brass bed are two piles of clothes, his and hers, the same wardrobe the couple had been wearing on the boat. As before, the summer

moonlight streams through the window, illuminating
LINUS and CHARLIE. This time, they lie side by side,
not touching, though the disarray of the sheets indicate
they'd been very close a few moments before. Silent,
they both stare at the ceiling and soon CHARLIE's eyes
drift closed. LINUS has been waiting for this moment.
With slow, deliberate movements, he picks up her hand
and places it on his chest, directly over his heart. His
fingers cover hers. He releases a sigh, indicating some
of his tension has eased, but his eyes stay open. He's
not planning to sleep and waste a second of one of the
last times they'll be together.

LINUS HAD NEVER felt less free-and-easy than when looking into the face of Charlie's man. The request had just
tripped from his mouth and so he had no one to blame
but himself for the way the sight of the soldier dragged
him to a new, crappy March low. "Yeah. Okay. Thanks,"
he said, pushing Charlie's wallet toward her.

Put it away, he urged in silence.

Just like he would put away whatever dumb ideas
he was starting to think about him and the blue-eyed
blonde. Again.

"I'm just here until the end of March," he told Charlie. "Did I make that clear? April 1st it will be safe to
drag Ryan back to L.A. and get on with our lives."

She nodded, occupying herself with her purse. To-
tally cool with him imposing another deadline to their
affair. But she was accustomed to that, and had intro-
duced the notion herself, as a matter of fact. *Come September, there are boundaries.*

Linus wanted to hit something. His ugly mood, this

depressing month and the picture of fucking Saint Steven suddenly coalesced into a ball of fiery energy in his belly. His blood started zipping through his veins, charging him up, filling him with restless energy that needed an outlet.

Sex, he thought. He needed sex to put everything back in order in his head. To give this thing he had with Charlie true perspective.

When she turned back to him he was ready. Taking her shoulders in his hands, he yanked her close to lay his lips on hers, claiming her mouth in a greedy, scorching kiss. When air became necessary, he jerked her away and stared into her eyes with unmistakable intent.

"I've got something I want to do to you," he growled.

She blinked.

"Any objections?"

Her mouth opened.

He dove in for another ruthless lip-lock. Her face was flushed when he once again lifted his head. "Any objections?" he repeated.

Slowly, she shook her head from side to side.

"Let's go," he said, using his body to herd her out of the booth. As he stood, he realized he'd yet to take care of the bill. Glancing around for their waitress, he pulled a money clip from his pocket. "This will only take a second."

"I'll use it to go the ladies' room," Charlie said, then hurried away.

Linus watched her leave, the sway of her hips doing nothing to temper his lust. When his server said she'd be a moment with his bill, he headed toward the bar, figuring he'd order a shot of something while he waited.

A foursome huddled together at a nearby table, two young women accompanied by two men in their mid-twenties. The guys were snowboarders, Linus decided, their goggle sunburns giving them away.

The girls excused themselves, strolling slowly past Linus as they headed in the same direction Charlie had taken. He couldn't help but overhear them.

"Are you going to be okay?" the brunette said to her redheaded companion. "They're only here for five more days, and Craig said he wants to put you at the top of his list."

"You caught that Craigslist reference?" The other girl smothered a giggle. "Okay, it's a pretty lame line, but he's seriously cute."

"Which is why I ask again, are you going to be okay?"

They both paused to glance over their shoulders at their escorts, who were still shooting the breeze at their table. "Sure," the redhead said. "I've got Steven now."

The brunette's eyebrows arched. "Wait. I thought Charlie Walker—"

"Nope. She's all done with him."

They continued on as Linus absorbed the implication of the conversation. Charlie was "done with him"? Had Charlie and Saint Steven broken up? But...

She hadn't shared that with Linus.

He hadn't asked that exact question, though, had he? Recalling his second March visit to her post office, the essence of their exchange had been this: Was Steven back in town? No.

Linus had never asked if they were still together.

Why had she kept it from him? Why was that phot

her butt and Linus realized she'd accomplished more than he'd deduced. Charlie was completely undressed.

After six months, he had her naked again.

Impulse overtook caution. He drew her against him and found her mouth, kissing her with heat and tongue while his palms ran over every inch of her flesh, exploring soft curves and taut muscle. In the past, he'd gone to great effort not to hold her too close, but as his fingers took hold of one glorious ass-cheek, he reminded himself that Sexy Girl #1 was no danger to him.

Sexy Girl #1 was a faceless, strings-free entity.

Who had some moves of her own. Even as he continued to kiss her, his tongue thrusting deep between her lips, she was busy with her hands, unfastening the front of his button-down, working at the snap and zipper of his jeans.

Then she had him in her palm, and his dick surged in welcome, offering its own wet kiss to her stroking flesh. His head fell back and he groaned, enjoying the hell out of the pleasure of Charlie's touch.

Sexy Girl #1's touch.

Her mouth found his nipple, her little tongue darting out to tickle him there and his skin rippled in response, a hot shiver of desire sending goose bumps across his body. She chased them with her lips and then she was kneeling on the floor and now Sexy Girl #1 was starring in *that* kind of movie, performing with perfect mud-flap abandon, and Linus groaned again.

He had to see this, he thought, desperate for the visual. He was a man, wasn't he? He had to see this.

His hand stretched out, fumbled then found the

switch of the bedside lamp. Yellow light spilled into the room, brightening his companion's hair like a halo.

An angel on her knees.

Linus's heart slammed against his chest wall, nearly buckling him. He reached back, hand grasping the bedclothes to steady himself. It was too much, he thought, gaze glued to the sight of Sexy Girl #1, her mouth around him, her eyes closed.

Charlie not looking at him.

It wasn't right.

Leaning down, he grasped her by the elbows and drew her to her feet. She made a low sound of disappointment—*God, what a turn-on!*—and he hushed her with his own murmur and rolled them both onto the bed. The squeak of the old springs made him smile as he tossed off his clothes. Then he pulled Charlie against him once more and she burrowed close, her mouth at his throat, her short, silky hair catching in the rough whiskers on his chin.

"Sal," he whispered. "Oh, Sal."

Then he slid his hands to her breasts, feeling them swell into his palms and her nipples stiffen to gain the attention of his thumbs. He inched down on the mattress to tease that sweet flesh, her low moans the soundtrack to this new movie.

Linus and Charlie's movie.

"The color of the walls are pistachio," he murmured against the cleft between her breasts. "The ceiling is eggshell."

Her fingers sifted through his hair as her back arched. He sucked a nipple and worried it with his tongue. When she gasped, he lifted his head. "The curtains at the windows are pinstriped. Green again, and chocolate-brown."

A line was dug between her brows and he crawled up her body to kiss it away. "What's the matter?"

"That's not my room."

"No," he admitted, then found a condom in her bed-side drawer—his brand, that he'd left behind when he'd thought he could leave her behind, too. "It's mine, at my house in L.A."

He wanted her there.

Before she could formulate a response, he was be-tween her thighs. His fingers found her ready, so ready and soft, and his cock slid inside. She lifted into the thrust, her body offering no obstruction to his.

A dozen Charlies raced across the screen of his mind: in her pressed postal clerk uniform, in a sundress and hiking boots, eating ice cream, admiring fireworks, frowning over her homework, smiling at him when he called her Sal.

He looked down at this version of Charlie in his arms, the halo of hair, the mouth swollen from his kisses, those blue eyes that had remained dry-eyed the day he left her.

And Linus knew he couldn't do it again. He couldn't let her get away.

I'm in love with her, he thought. Full stop. *Without any kind of limits or boundaries whatsoever.*

CHAPTER FIFTEEN

RYAN WALKED THE path from the pool to the house, aware his morning swim hadn't put Poppy from his mind... again. For the second day in a row he was stewing over her, this time because he'd failed the night before in finding out what was bothering her.

She'd spilled nothing about the mysterious phone call that he felt certain had put her off her game and into her baker's apron. Though he'd cornered her after dinner, she'd used the kid as a shield and ultimately as an excuse to escape upstairs.

Sure, Ryan could have tried once more after she'd tucked in the boy. He might have cajoled her downstairs via intercom or dragged her out of her room by the ankles, but he'd been aware she was on guard. He was going to have to catch her unawares to wring the truth out of her, but he'd find a way to do it. For whatever reason, he was determined to learn what was going on inside her head.

As he approached the terrace doors, a sound from the front of the house made him cock his head. A vehicle—big, by the sound of it—was trundling along the drive. He let himself inside and made tracks for the front of the house. If the paps had dared to trespass, he was going to contact the police and press charges.

At the front door, he met Poppy. "Um," she said. "There are visitors."

"I'll take care of them." He pulled his phone from the front pocket of his jeans. "They'll be under arrest in minutes."

"I wish you wouldn't do that," she said. "I don't have the money to post bail."

He stared at her. "Who—?"

"My brother and sisters." She gestured toward the entrance.

He opened one of the double doors a few inches to see a heavy-duty work truck with an extended cab and a bed bristling with landscaping tools slow to a halt in the courtyard. A small sedan, with Maids by Mac written on its side, braked nearby.

Then Ryan's foyer was full of Walkers.

He stood back as Mason and Grimm rushed down the stairs to join them. The boy was given attention first, his uncle and aunts asking questions about his Disney trip. When he scurried off to retrieve Mickey for show-and-tell, the Walkers took stock of their cloistered sibling.

And Ryan took stock of them. Mackenzie, the oldest sister, was taller than Poppy, her face shaped the same but with coffee-dark hair and irises a pale blue. She gave her sister a hug even as her gaze slid to Ryan. Her suspicious expression reminded him of early Poppy, when she'd been as cool to him as the winter air.

Shay stepped up next. She was slender like her sisters, but with chin-length auburn hair and Mackenzie's eyes in a model-elegant face. Her hug for Poppy was warm and she took another moment to study her older sister as she stepped back. "Okay?" she asked, a line digging between her brows.

So Ryan wasn't the only one thinking there was something to be concerned about.

Poppy waved away the question. "I'm fine."

Then her brother moved in. A short scrub of light brown hair topped his tanned and weathered face. He had gray eyes like his sister's, narrowed now. A wicked scar cut from his brow in a dramatic diagonal over his forehead to disappear into his hairline. Another slashed across the bridge of his nose. On a sigh, Brett pulled Poppy in, then pretended to pound the top of her head with his fist as she slapped at him. "Screwup. Why are you always causing trouble?"

Ryan's hackles rose in her defense. "Hey," he began.

As one, the Walker tribe turned on him.

Shit. Still, he stepped forward, looking each of Poppy's siblings square in the eye. "None of this is her fault."

"Oh, right," Brett said. "For a moment I forgot that sloppy kiss you landed on her for the cameras."

"It wasn't intentionally for the cameras," Poppy protested, as one of her blushes crawled over her face. "And it was just a thank-you," she mumbled, inspecting something on the floor at her feet. "For my cookies."

"For your cookies." Brett Walker looked from his red-cheeked sister to Ryan. "Really. For her cookies?"

Ignoring the sarcasm, Ryan strolled to Mackenzie and held out his hand. "Mac, right? I'm Ryan Hamilton."

She traded a brisk shake then made a face at Shay as he reached toward her with an outstretched palm. "It's not right. A guy who looks that good on screen should be butt-ugly in person."

Ignoring Mac, the auburn-haired sister shook his hand. "I'm Shay."

That left Ryan facing the big brother. "Look," he said. "I'm sorry about the trouble we found ourselves in, but—"

"Yeah," Brett said, gripping Ryan's hand. The squeeze wasn't a strangle, but close. "It's probably not all on you. First there's the knucklehead over there. And we're aware that those cabins and the land they're on bring nothing but trouble."

Poppy released a small sound of distress. "Brett—"

"Admit it. That place has always been a problem. You should just leave it be. Let those cabins go to rot."

"Not going to do that," she said, her squared shoulders in opposition with the clear dismay on her face.

For the second time, a protective urge rose inside Ryan. Was her worry over the cabins' future the cause of her disquiet? Maybe he could do something about that, he thought, and shifted his attention to her poker-faced big brother. "When was the last time you were out there?"

He shrugged. "Who cares?"

"You should go see the land. Check out the cabins," Ryan said, moving his gaze to include Mackenzie and Shay.

"Shay and I have seen them," Mackenzie replied, dismissing the topic with a wave of her hand. "We're not here about the resort. With Brett back in town, we decided to stop by and make sure Poppy and Mason are all right. They've been here, what? About a week?"

Poppy frowned, and ignored the question directed at Ryan to ask one of her own. "You thought he might have boiled us for supper? Look, I can take care of myself."

Ryan crossed his arms over his chest, determined not to let the subject go. Pinning his gaze on the other man, he sent out a challenge. "I'm serious," he said to Brett, "you should give the place a look."

Brett's brows rose. A tense moment passed, then he seemed to make a decision. "Fine, then," he said with a nod. "We'll go right now."

"Now?" Poppy worried the hem of her sweater. "*Now* now? You know the storm did some damage—"

"Only more reason to look things over." He turned toward the door, then glanced back at Poppy and Ryan. "You coming?"

Poppy's eyes rounded. "Leave the house?"

"We pass through that press gauntlet by the gates," Ryan warned, "we'll only feed their prurience."

Brett shrugged. "You're right. They're crawling all over town, asking nosy questions and staking out popular corners in hopes you drive by."

In hopes they'd catch him flaming out again, Ryan thought. "So—"

"So, don't you know how to duck?"

That's what they ended up doing. After deciding to leave Mason at home with Linus—Poppy didn't want her son to worry over the post-storm condition of their cabin—Brett swung his truck around so they could make the dash from the front door without being spied by the paps. In the backseat, they slumped against the cushions. When they neared the gates, Brett cautioned

"Lower," and Ryan pulled Poppy over his lap and bent over her.

Her hair tickled his nose and he breathed in its delicious scent, its sweetness now familiar. She took her own breath, her fragile shoulder blades lifting into the cage of his body. *So damn delicate*, he thought, and was compelled to curl tighter around her, giving in to a tender urge that he thought had died with Tate. Not good, he decided instantly, and tried sweeping it away by recalling his knowledge of other parts of her body: the subtle curve of her breasts, the tight bud of her nipple against his lips, the sleek heat between her thighs. But that only served to start working him up and, Christ, he couldn't afford to get in that kind of condition with her lean and mean big brother only inches away.

"Fuckers," Brett muttered as his speed slowed to a snail's crawl. "Your mug can't possibly be worth this stakeout."

"Photos of A-list weddings and celebrity babies can bring in a million or more," Ryan said, pitching his voice low. "Picture of a famous figure during a time of personal turmoil…high six figures. Add a new romantic interest, add a zero."

The other man cursed under his breath, then it was pedal to the metal as, Ryan presumed, they made it past the gathering at the gates. Glancing up, he saw Brett check his rearview mirror. "Shay and Mac are clear, too."

Poppy's brother turned a sharp corner then blew out an audible breath. "All right, people. The captain has turned off the Fasten Seat Belts sign. You're free to move about the cabin."

Ryan wasn't so certain. Though he unbent from his current position and so did Poppy, he put his hand on her arm to prevent her from sitting straight on the cushions. "Keep your head below the window level."

"Fine," she said, but he could feel the tension in her, her muscles stiff beneath his palm.

"Why are you so keyed up?" he said, beneath the cover of the country music blaring from the radio her brother flipped on.

"I'm mentally refining my sales pitch."

"Give me a chance to help," he offered.

Her head turned toward him, her eyebrows rose. "Why do you care?"

He opened his mouth to answer...and then found he had no answer other than that unwelcome protective sense looming again. Scowling, he brooded over it until they chugged up the hill to the cabins. When Brett braked, he jumped out. Ryan opened his door, intending to follow, then glanced back at Poppy, still glued in place. On a sigh, he turned back to her, unable to resist her and her worried face.

"Come on," he said, releasing her seat belt then pulling her out by the hand. "You'll see, it'll work out."

Though clearly she knew her siblings better than he did. While Brett grudgingly remarked on Poppy's painting efforts of the two refurbished cabins, Mackenzie didn't hesitate to proclaim "What a mess," while surveying the damaged mudroom roof.

The fallen limb was cleared, though; the wood chopped, split and stacked for future fireplace use. Ryan pushed his hands in his pockets and studied the surroundings. "I think you Walkers are seeing the place through the wrong lens. I spent over a week here and couldn't get enough of the view. If there were skiing and snowboarding..." He tilted his head to take in the mountain that loomed over the cabins, the summit still covered with snow. "It could be a great little winter escape."

"We don't have exclusive rights to the mountain," Brett said, and the four siblings looked at each other, then spit in the dirt, used the toes of their shoes to rub it into the ground and crossed their hearts.

Having seen the ritual before, Ryan didn't flinch. "There's no way around it?"

Brett shrugged. "Even if there was, there's also the small question of—what is it again?" He snapped his fingers. "Oh, yeah, money."

"You can find investors. Maybe someone like me—"

"God, no." Though it was Mac who spoke, all four Walkers stared at him with identical horrified expressions.

"Flatlander money would only bring more bad luck to a place already cursed," Brett said.

"That's where our father went wrong," Poppy continued. "Dad had big ideas for this place but no ready money to sink into it. So he sold an interest to Victor Fremont—" here she paused so they could do the whole spit and heart-cross thing again "—and after the fire took everything you-know-who wouldn't invest any more cash."

"And he says he won't give us permission to redevelop the mountain even if we win the lottery and come up with the scratch ourselves," Mac added, her face stony. "Dad gave him that power."

"But we can fix up the cabins on our own," Poppy

said, then looked at her siblings. "I can fix them up. Just don't actively oppose me, okay?"

Her earnestness made Ryan's chest ache. To avoid it, he studied the clearing, the cabins ringing it, and remembered the more remote ones he'd run across on his hikes in the woods. Everything looked different now. The snow-covered landscape had been spectacular, but without the white stuff and without the rain, he could see the potential of other seasons. The sun-heated pine needles would smell pungent and clean. Moonlight would edge the foliage with a silver light.

"You have something special here," he said, hardly aware he was talking aloud. "Think of summertime. Open windows. Quiet voices in the darkness."

Brett groaned. "Not another one. You've been hanging around Poppy too much."

She glared at her brother. "Come on, Brett. Can't you keep an open mind?" Then she turned her gaze on her youngest sister. "What do you say, Shay? Will you give me the go-ahead to finish what I started?"

The woman shrugged. "Since I'm not an actual blood Walker, I go with the majority."

"Shay," the other siblings said together.

But though they were unanimous in their reproach of their sister, the jury stayed out on the resort property. Not one of the three gave Poppy the words she wanted to hear. After a few minutes, they all climbed back in their respective vehicles, with Mac muttering about getting an appraisal on the value of the part of the acreage they were legally able to sell and Brett sharing the observation that Poppy had always been the family's crazy, cock-eyed optimist. Clearly he didn't consider it high praise.

Frustrated, Ryan stared out the window as they returned to Blue Arrow Lake. He glanced over at Poppy, noting her preoccupied expression and the way she was once again worrying her sweater hem. "Maybe your brother and sisters will change their minds. Be more cooperative."

Her big gray eyes turned his way, their expression puzzled. "What? Oh. Don't mind them. I'll figure something out."

It was the offhand way she said it that made him realize the cabins weren't the sole source of her tension. She'd mentally moved on to other trouble and damn, it bothered him that she wouldn't open up about whatever that was.

He went back to staring out the window and began formulating plans to woo the truth from her. Maybe he'd get one of the boats in the water and take her onto the lake. The relaxation might do the trick. Or perhaps he'd build up a big fire and sweat the truth from her. She'd strip out of that sweater and then...

And then his mind went in the entirely wrong direction.

Yanking it back, his gaze finally took in what he'd been staring at for miles of winding highway. "Whoa," he said. Clusters of long-stemmed, vibrant yellow blooms marched along both sides of the road, their brightness a sudden shock to his system. "Daffodils."

Poppy glanced over. "Pretty, right?" And then she smiled.

The power of that startled him, too. Its warmth slayed him. She slayed him. Impulse overcame him once more, and a deep need moved in his chest. He wanted to make things right for her. To make her happy.

In four years he'd never felt the need to do anything in fucking March but escape himself. So he might not know what was going on with Poppy, but what was going on with him was something entirely new.

And it bothered the hell out of him, because the man he'd been since his son's death didn't have the chops to do any good for anyone.

FROM *YOU SEND ME,* a screenplay by Linus Hamilton:

INT. POST OFFICE—DAY

CHARLIE's at the counter, helping a customer. One person awaits service, and now two, as LINUS steps up to the back of the line. The patron in front of him is an old man clutching a handful of letters. He glances at LINUS.

OLD MAN
Are you lost?

On a sigh, LINUS shakes his head.

CHARLIE
Next.

LINUS's attention wanders as he waits his turn.

CHARLIE
Next.

LINUS steps up to the counter.

CHARLIE
I thought you were already on your way back to
L.A.

She's struggling to maintain her stoicism.

LINUS
I need to mail this.

He tosses a picture postcard onto the counter. It's a
glossy photo of a mountain setting. Across the top it
reads Mountain Greetings!

LINUS
A souvenir of my stay.

CHARLIE flips it over. Her gaze lifts to LINUS.

CHARLIE
You're mailing it to yourself?

LINUS
With a message from you…I hope.

He produces a pen, tosses it down, too. A challenge.
CHARLIE retrieves the ballpoint, clasps it a moment,
then bends over the postcard. LINUS holds his breath.
    When she puts down the pen, the camera focuses on
what she's written. "Glad you were here." And then,
"Goodbye."

LINUS FIGURED CHARLIE knew something had changed after the night in her bed. The next morning, when he asked if they could have a quiet dinner alone that evening, he'd read the panic in her eyes a moment before she suggested they go out again instead, this time to another of her favorite hangouts, Blossom.

Laid-back Linus had agreed…though for the first time in his life he was thinking in a careful, not careless way. If at the moment she was more comfortable with him in a public setting, then that's where he'd take her. Making this declaration was the most serious thing he'd ever contemplated, and he wanted to get it right.

But he'd get it done tonight, he assured himself as he held open the restaurant's door for Charlie. Now that Steven Parker was no longer between them, Linus didn't want to waste any more time. He was in love with her and by putting that on the table he'd be one step closer to the future he wanted them to have together.

His fingertips at her back, he followed her inside—and immediately wished for a do-over. *Damn.* The place was packed. With Charlie's friends.

There was not going to be any romantic table for two in a corner, he realized, as she moved toward her pack of young women. Though it wasn't a regular girls' night, for some reason a couple dozen mountain ladies were socializing with either light beer or some kind of sweet-tini in hand. Platters of bar food were being passed around.

They weren't so busy with their buddies that they ignored male company, however. A couple of the girls were already flirting with guys watching the game at the bar. One of Charlie's gal pals that Linus had met the summer before snagged his arm and urged him into a chair at a large round table.

Though his love had been snared by another group, he didn't refuse her friends' invitation. This was one of those kinds of events, he surmised, where people constantly rotated position. He'd start out between Amy and Ann, have a chat with Mindy and Melly, and soon enough he'd be sandwiched by Zoe and Zelda. Charlie would end up beside him eventually.

So he ordered a beer for himself, a glass of wine to be delivered to the gilt-haired girl laughing at the other end of the room, and then prepared to wait for his opportunity.

Charlie's orbit neared him ten minutes later, but she ended up lighting on a chair at the farthest point from him. Even from that distance, though, he enjoyed listening to her. Men made conversation like they were at the bowling alley, sending the heavy ball of their idea onto the polished floor with a spin designed to knock everyone else's down. Charlie floated her thoughts into the discussion like feathers set in motion by her breath. It wasn't that they had no weight…they just landed with delicate grace.

Someone called her name and she rose, then passed his chair to greet the newcomer. Linus caught her hand as she went by. Glancing down, she sent him an apologetic smile. "You're being patient."

"For the moment," he said, then instantly regretted the remark, because it sent her on the run from him.

Sighing, he nursed his beer and tried distracting himself by people-watching. More men had arrived and he identified their kind by their luxury shoe wear and expensive taste in beer. The winter's equivalent of Summer Beaus.

He refused to let the thought leave a bad taste in his mouth. He'd been one of those short-timers and there was nothing wrong with enjoying flirtations and transitory affairs. Still, something about that Summer Beaus scrapbook continued to trouble him. Deciding to soothe himself by seeking out Charlie, he started to rise from his chair when a young woman slipped into the one on his left, virtually pinning him into a corner.

Her drink was pink, her dress was short and she was much too young for him. "Hi," she said, with a nervous wiggle of one forefinger.

Barely twenty-one, he thought, and new to this scene. After a moment's hesitation, he settled back in his chair, and turned on the charm. That he was now a one-woman man didn't mean he was a man who no longer enjoyed the company of women. And this little darling could use a safe guy like himself to see her through what he surmised was a brand-new adult experience.

He held out his hand. "I'm Linus and I'm from L.A."

She was Grace and a receptionist at the local bank.

They talked about interest rates, the weird stuff people kept in their safe-deposit boxes and her current mission in life: to get the security guard at her branch to laugh. "I'm sure he thinks he's part of the Swiss Guard," she confided, leaning close.

Linus thought she was adorable. When another pink drink was slid in front of her, he got a little worried. A guy at the bar had sent it over. Linus gave the other man an assessing glance, taking in his cashmere sweater and deep dimples. Someone as young as Grace could get her heart stomped on by someone so slick.

"Do you have a special guy?" he asked.

She looked flustered, then glanced down at her lap as if she might have stowed a cheat sheet there. "Well…" Bringing her new drink to her mouth, she took in a healthy swallow, then coughed a little. "I…"

"You…?" Linus prompted.

"I kind of have someone, but…" Grace sent him a flirty glance through her lashes.

Damn, Linus thought on a silent groan. *I wasn't fishing for myself.* Before he could make that clear, Grace plowed forward.

"We have this understanding, you see. While he's out of the country."

Linus went still. He stared at the youngster.

"While he's out of the country, Steven and I have an agreement that I can…you know, date other people."

"Steven?" *Steven?*

"Steven Parker."

What the hell? Linus thought. Just last night the brunette, tonight sweet thing Grace. Before that, Charlie. How many women did Steven Parker the Prick string along at a time?

Grace was fumbling with her purse. Then she had her wallet out and was holding up a photo. "Here he is."

It was a man wearing swim trunks and holding a surfboard. He had a wild tangle of sun-bleached blond hair.

"He's in Australia on a surfing trip," Grace added.

And he looked nothing at all like the soldier in Charlie's picture.

Head reeling, Linus mumbled an excuse, rose from his chair and struggled to get past her. He was taller than most in the crowd and his gaze sought out bright blond hair. When he found it, he kept his eye on the target and wove his way to her side. She was smiling at something her companion said and when she glanced up at him, her face went blank, all the humor dying.

He grasped her upper arm. "We need to talk."

"Oh, but—"

"Now," he said, his fingers tightening on her bicep.

Towing her behind him, he found privacy in the short hall leading to a door marked Employees Only. He turned her to face him, and she stepped instantly back, the wall meeting her shoulder blades.

"There's nowhere to run," he said.

She lifted her chin. "I'm not going anyplace."

He barked a short laugh. "That's what Steven was all about, right? Your justification for not getting too close. Your reason for never giving too much of yourself. With him hovering in the background, you never had to risk leaving your comfort zone of short-term romance."

Charlie opened her mouth, but Linus stopped her by putting up a hand. "I only want you to confirm one thing. Steven Parker isn't real, is he? He was never real."

She was silent a long moment, then Charlie directed her gaze to somewhere over Linus's shoulder. "No. No, he was never real."

"Jesus." Linus shook his head.

"You see, Steven Parker was…is…" She smoothed her short hair with her hand. "He's what you might call a prop."

A *prop*. Though he'd guessed it already, hearing her

say it out loud made Linus feel foolish and used. Angry. Foolish and used and...hurt. *You were lying to me while I was falling in love with you!* he wanted to shout, but his pride and his ego made him stifle the words. "God, Charlie," he said, shaking his head. "God. How could you invent—"

"Before you criticize Steven Parker, remember that thanks to him you were comfortable getting to know me." Temper kindled in Charlie's blue gaze. "Steven Parker made me unthreatening to your casual bachelor ways because through him I was as no-strings, as free-and-easy as you. Don't pretend that wasn't what *you* liked best."

Okay, at the beginning that was true. But then what he liked best had become exploring the mountains with Charlie, floating on the lake with Charlie, kissing Charlie. Making love to her. But it had all been pretense on her side. Disgusted with himself and his stupid, stupid heart, he turned from her and walked away.

CHAPTER SIXTEEN

POPPY WAS READING Mason a book when Ryan stuck his head in the kitchen. "You have visitors," he said.

"Me?"

"Unless your sisters are here for Grimm." At this, the dog got to his feet and shook, his collar making merry noise. "I saw them via the security cam at the docks. They came by boat."

Puzzled, Poppy set the book aside and looked at her son. "I suppose we'll have to see what they want."

Mason was already on his way to the door that led to the terrace and from there to the lake. Grimm trotted behind. She hesitated.

"Want backup?" Ryan asked.

"No." It was a kind offer and reminded her that he'd gone along on that trip to the cabins a few days before. But she didn't want him thinking she needed help with anything—including handling her own siblings. If they were here to give her more of their opinions of what should be done about the Walker land, she'd make clear to them she steered her own course.

They met on the lawn halfway between the house and the water. It was another warm day by mountain spring standards and Mason ran circles around his aunts, the dog following behind. A young teen watched the action with dispassionate eyes, slouching in jeans and a black hoodie. This would be Shay's charge, the girl she was living with and homeschooling. After greeting her sisters, Poppy offered a smile to the youngster. "Hi," she said. "I'm Mason's mom, Poppy. And you're...?"

"Tucson," the girl said, and looked away, as if bored by even that brief snippet of conversation.

Shay tucked her hair behind her ears. "Actually, it's London, but she's trying out different city names for... entertainment purposes."

The girl rolled her eyes. "Entertainment," she muttered.

Rebellion, Poppy figured. "Tucson's nice," she offered.

"I like it better than Elko," Shay said. "Clyde didn't do much for me, either."

The teen shrugged. "When are we getting out of here?"

Mackenzie stepped in. "Right now. Let's go, Poppy."

Suspicious, she stepped back. "Where? And what for?"

"We're going to Tucson's house. A neutral location for conversation."

Poppy narrowed her eyes. "Why does that sound like 'intervention'?"

Her older sister flicked a glance toward Ryan's villa. "Are you addicted to something?"

"Certainly not. But I don't want to—"

"Mason," Shay said, catching his attention as he ran past. "You want to go for a ride in a boat?"

"Yes!" he said, and without pausing changed course toward the dock. Poppy was obligated to go after him, aware the rest of the group swarmed behind. She made it to the boat before her son had the chance to jump inside.

Resigned but still annoyed, she glanced at Shay. "You have a life jacket on board that will fit him?"

Tucson turned cooperative on this front. Once inside the gleaming powerboat, she fished out a small life vest and helped Mason into it. Then she lifted him aboard and even managed a smile for Grimm, who took that as his own invitation.

In minutes they were reversing away from Ryan's landing. Poppy saw him standing on the terrace and she lifted her arm in a wave, only to catch Mackenzie staring, a speculative gleam in her eye.

"Well, well, well," she began.

Poppy shot her a look. "Don't even start."

Any response she might have made was whipped away by the wind as Shay accelerated, taking them out of the small bay. The trip was a short one. After rounding a headland, they made their way toward another lakeside estate. Unlike the classic, old-world style of Ryan's home, this was built on contemporary lines. Two walls were entirely windows and a sleek deck wrapped the place.

"Nice digs," she told Shay as her younger sister tied up the boat.

"Tucson's dad's a big-time builder," she said, watching as the girl helped Mason up the ramp leading to the house. "I've not met the man. I send him emails on her progress. To get the job, his assistant interviewed me via Skype."

"Ah," Poppy murmured. "Goes for the personal touch, then."

Shay's tone turned dry. "Exactly."

An absent dad, then, like Denny?

He'd phoned again, and again Poppy had put him off. Her mind was not yet made up on letting him into her son's life.

Contemplating the situation, she followed their crew to the sunshine-filled deck. Shay brought out a tray with glasses and lemonade. Tucson dragged behind her a laundry basket of plastic preschooler toys that she presented to Mason. He dug in with unreserved enjoyment while Grimm looked on.

"Thank you," Poppy said to the girl.

She gave another world-weary shrug. "They were left by the people who lived here before." Then she threw herself onto a chaise lounge and hid behind a pair of black-lensed sunglasses.

Poppy and her sisters settled around a table. When Shay passed her one of the lemonades, she sipped, waiting for her sisters to start. When the silence grew long, she shifted her gaze to them. "Well? Why am I here?"

Shay sent Mac a pointed look, and the eldest Walker sister huffed out a sigh. "We thought we should get you away from that house. From—"

"Discussing him is off-limits."

Mac frowned. "C'mon. We only have your best interests at heart."

"If that were the truth, you wouldn't be fighting me on the cabins."

Shay squirmed on her seat. "Look—"

"You haven't even listened to my plans." Poppy

pinned her younger sister with a stare. "By the way, I want you to build a website."

"That's a lot of work—"

"If she won't do it, I will," Tucson offered, still stretched on the nearby chaise, her expression unreadable behind the glasses. "I've won awards."

"True," Shay admitted. "But is that really necessary?"

"If I'm going to get rich Los Angelenos to the cabins, yes."

Mac made a face. "Not our favorite crowd, Poppy."

"They're the ones with the money," she said. "I'm revising my plans because…because I've identified a new need." She'd been mulling over Ryan's wish for a retreat the past few days. "Rustic chic."

"Rustic what?" Mac's eyebrows drew together. "Chic? Isn't that an oxymoron?"

"This is lovely," Poppy said, waving her arm around to indicate the luxurious house and the lake view, "but not everyone has access to properties such as this and maybe some would appreciate a place more out of the way."

"There are bed-and-breakfasts—"

"Too cutesy. No privacy. Lots of people don't want to chat up the guests from the room next door over breakfast parfaits and egg strata."

"The inns offer more anonymity," Shay said.

"The cabins can offer seclusion. Think about it. If I go a little more luxurious—fancier sheets and towels, that kind of thing—it can be a place away from it all, but with it all, except for the intrusion of internet and television."

She thought of Ryan's cans of soup, and another idea sparked. "And maybe I can offer a meal service of some sort...nutritious gourmet fare as well as top-shelf liquors and fine wines." Excitement fluttered in her belly as she gazed off over the lake. "You know, when I was thinking of just clean and quiet, I was thinking too small."

Mac groaned. "You sound like Dad. And I blame Ryan Hamilton for that. Your brush with celebrity is giving you grandiose ideas."

"Dad loved that land. He did what he could to make something of it, and I'm doing the same," Poppy said. "Don't blame that on Ryan."

"Still, we think you should leave his house," Shay said. "He's bad news."

Such bad news that he'd never doubted her ability to make something of the cabins. Such bad news that he'd even tried to persuade her siblings to see them her way.

"I recognize that stubborn expression of yours, Poppy," Mac said, frowning. "You know he's not like us, right?"

"He eats. He breathes." He grieves.

"He's the kind who'll tromp all over your heart then go on his happy way. Didn't Denny Howell take care of that lesson?"

Denny had never touched her heart. Only her pride. "Ryan is not Denny."

Mac pinched the bridge of her nose. "Tell me you're not in love with him."

"I'm not in love with him." That was an impossibility, because he wouldn't be able to deeply care about Mason, her number one requirement of a man in her life.

Her sisters exchanged glances. "Look," Mac began, "you're…"

"Too naive?" Poppy volunteered, her voice bitter. "Too foolish? Too soft-hearted? Do those really make me the family screwup?"

"You're a die-hard optimist," Shay corrected gently. "We worry about those rose-colored glasses you wear."

"Fine." Poppy mimed lifting a pair from her face and dashing them to the ground. "Happy now?"

"We're worried about you becoming *un*happy," Shay said. "Ryan Hamilton is…"

A wounded man.

And perhaps it was naive and foolish of her, but she thought she just might be good for him, like Linus had said. *I care a lot about my brother, Poppy. I'm convinced you do him good. You and Mason.*

Could she walk away from him, from the possibility of that? He was a father who had lost his son. Couldn't she remain at the lake house a few more days with the prospect of helping him heal?

Mac made a sound of disgust. "Hell. We're wasting our time. You're at least half-gone already."

Poppy felt color rise up her neck. "I'm not." Still, she thought of the desperate grasp of his hands on her body in the dark. And then the gentle play of his fingers through Mason's hair.

Linus's voice again, those words he'd said to her nearly a week ago. *You're good for him. You're a distraction.*

Maybe Ryan was her distraction, as well. Instead

of wallowing in self-pity about what had gone wrong during that hailstorm, she was already coming up with better ideas and new plans. It seemed he was good for her, too.

"You're not in love with him," Mac said, skepticism in her voice, "yet you won't leave that house."

"Not until the end of the month," Poppy replied, making her decision right then and there. And it wasn't Linus's words that persuaded her or even the wish to show her sisters she knew her own mind. She wanted to do this for Ryan.

But what if you end up back in his bed?

Poppy let herself contemplate that and in that moment she went from sunshine-warmed to sexual heat. Without thinking, she lifted the lemonade and pressed the cool glass against the side of her neck. "What if?" was feeling a lot more like "Why not?" to her libido.

For a moment she was back in that shadowed room, her heart beating in her throat, her skin trembling with the fever only intense desire could bring. Ryan between her legs, his mouth insistent and ardent. Ryan over her, his chest's heat burning her spine and his touches blowing her mind. Making her feel womanly and possessed and…wanted. God, being wanted had felt so good.

Even single mothers are sexual beings. Oh, yes, they were.

Mac made another small sound. "I don't want to even know what you're thinking about now."

Poppy could feel the slow smile curving her lips. Perhaps she was a cock-eyed optimist. A knucklehead. But this optimistic knucklehead just might be getting herself a lover until the end of the month, in the form of one gorgeous, experienced and talented hunk of man with the kind of sexual star power that a woman would risk getting singed to experience.

She was going to quit trying to avoid the burn.

"I'm thinking exactly what I want," she told her sisters. "I'm doing exactly what I want."

And it felt good, steering her own course. She wouldn't allow herself to spoil it by worrying she might be aiming straight for disaster.

FROM *YOU SEND ME,* a screenplay by Linus Hamilton:

EXT. LOS ANGELES—DAY

Sad music plays, and LINUS is in his convertible as September heat shimmers from the asphalt. He's traversing L.A.'s famous streets, Mulholland Drive, Hollywood Boulevard, Sunset Boulevard, as if looking for something. His gaze lands on a post office and on impulse he pulls into the parking lot. For a moment he stares ahead, his fingers tightening on the steering wheel. Then he pulls back out.

With the top now up on his convertible, LINUS is driving again, this time in the suburbs. As he passes by a school, there is a line of small children dressed as pilgrims and Indians. The teacher carries a turkey-filled platter. He turns a corner and a U.S. flag catches his eye. Another post office. He pulls in, and again doesn't get out of the car before leaving.

Christmas decorations are everywhere as LINUS is again driving. Carols are playing through his car stereo speakers. He's dressed in a red sweater and there are packages to be mailed on the seat beside him. LINUS pulls into the parking lot of a post office, brakes, then goes inside.

INT. LARGE, BUSY POST OFFICE—DAY

With the packages in his arms, LINUS waits in line. More cheerful Christmas music plays, at contrast with his mournful expression. Appearing lost in thought, LINUS steps up to the counter, where a male postal worker is waiting. On top of the clerk's head is a fuzzy Santa hat.

The clerk smiles.

CLERK
Can I help you, sir?

LINUS looks at him as if he's speaking a strange language.

CLERK
(louder)
Can I help you?

LINUS's head turns and he gazes about him. Clearly he doesn't really know why he's here.

LINUS
I'm lost...I'm lost without her.

He wanders toward the exit, unmailed packages still in his arms.

CHARLIE WAS WELL aware of the disadvantages of life in small mountain resort communities. Beyond the guaranteed transience of tourist romances, there was also the fact that the locals watched over everybody at every moment. Today, though, she embraced that particular drawback. A mere ninety minutes after putting out the word she was on the hunt for someone, a text told her where to find him.

Her stomach as tight as a fist, she walked along the sidewalk in the direction of the coffee bar. Spring had arrived with a vengeance, riding high on a heat wave. The shops were doing a brisk business and people were dressed in shorts and flip-flops, their sweatshirts tied at their waists. Charlie had opted for one of her favorite sundresses, a cherry-red knee-skimmer that wouldn't allow her to fade into the woodwork in case she lost her courage. Instead of sandals, she wore it with a pair of cowboy boots.

Another safeguard from cold feet.

Still, though, they stuttered to a halt when she spied Linus seated on a small bench against the front wall of Oscar's Coffee. His fingers were curled around a cardboard cup and his chin was tipped up, his head leaning against the shop's white-painted siding. Behind his sunglasses, she imagined his eyes were closed.

So she took some moments to simply look at him, in all his male glory. The planes and angles of his handsome features were only topped in appeal by the easygoing charm that he wore as close to the bone as his golden skin. The combination was such a powerful one that when he'd walked into her post office nearly seven months ago she'd waltzed into a romance with barely a qualm. After all, she'd thought, with that photo printed off the internet in her wallet, she had her fortifications in place.

What a fool she'd been, to think a flimsy scrap of paper could keep her safe. Like Laurie, she'd gone straight over the cliff.

A passerby bumped her shoulder, shoving her forward so she was forced to take a step. At his apology, she turned her head to half smile and wave a hand, and when she looked back at Linus's bench, she saw he'd straightened. Even from behind his glasses she was aware he watched her every move.

So there was nothing to do but continue her approach. Charlie tightened her hold on her purse and stepped into the railed area designated for the sidewalk seating. Though the bench was large enough for two, she dragged a free wrought-iron chair closer and then dropped into it.

She squirmed as the sun-heated metal touched the backs of her thighs. A literal hot seat.

Linus looked on with polite inquiry on his face. "Can I get you something? Coffee? Iced tea?"

Oh, so damn considerate, she thought, unsteadied by his insouciance. Maybe he was as disinterested as he sounded. But that wasn't the point, was it? She'd come here to be honest with him. The sight of the hurt on his face during their confrontation at Blossom's had scraped at her every hour of the four days that had passed since that time. Steven Parker had never been about causing Linus pain...only about protecting herself from it. So now it was time to come clean. Explain everything.

Swallowing hard, Charlie brought her purse to her

lap and told herself to be brave. "I have something for you."

"Oh?" One of his eyebrows winged over the frame of his sunglasses and his voice sounded so very, very cool. "Is this where you hand over a cardboard box filled with my books you borrowed, the mix tape I made you and the pair of shoes I forgot at your place?"

When he'd returned to L.A., Linus had left nothing of his behind. Not even an old T-shirt to keep her company or a discarded toothbrush that she could stick in a glass on her counter to pretend he might return. She curled her fingers into fists and when she felt the pressure building behind her eyes, she told herself it was temper, not tears.

Because Linus had gone off for six months and then had the gall, the utter gall, to walk back into her life and criticize her for doing what she could to protect her heart. Annoyance added an edge to her nerves.

"Look," she said, staring him down, "what you don't understand is stories like ours happen all the time around here."

He set his cup on the ground and crossed his arms over his chest. "Our story is not like anyone else's."

"Like hell," Charlie muttered. "You've been in the bars. You've been with me at Blossom and Mr. Frank's. Tell me you haven't noticed the flirting, tell me you haven't witnessed the first stages of numerous hook-ups."

"That happens everywhere, Charlie, not just here in Blue Arrow." He pushed his sunglasses to the top of his head, still such a cool customer. "People meet, explore their chemistry. Sometimes it works, sometimes it doesn't."

She leaned forward. "But here it never works—not long-term, not when it's between a local and a visitor. You see that, right? For men like you, it's always a vacation romance, over when you go home. But for those of us from here, this *is* home. If we're not careful, what you considered a short fling, for us gets…rooted."

"So you dreamed up Steven Parker." Linus said the name like a curse, some of his seeming indifference falling away. "You dreamed up a dishonest ploy to prevent any of these flings from having a chance at turning serious."

"Don't you think that's a good reason? Because hurt happens here all the time. My aunt was shredded by a short-term affair. My cousin Poppy fell for a guy who walked away when he learned she was pregnant." Her eyes were stinging now, but she went on. "And then there was Laurie. My Laurie."

Charlie's chest was so heavy no air could make it to her lungs. Maybe she couldn't do this, after all. She started to rise but Linus's hands were on her shoulders, pushing her back down.

They were knee-to-knee now and he held her in her seat. "What about her?" he asked, his voice as soft as his hands were unyielding. "What about your Laurie?"

Closing her eyes, Charlie saw it in her mind. That little sedan her friend had received for her sweet sixteen. Laurie had loved that car, but not as much as the man who'd come to Blue Arrow Lake five years later. Still, it was what she'd taken with her over that cliff.

"Laurie…Laurie fell for one of the Summer Beaus.

What she didn't know was he'd come for a few weeks of bachelor fun before returning to his fiancée and their autumn wedding. When Laurie realized it was over, and why, she…went for a drive."

And in her mind, Charlie saw it all, her best friend's desperate unhappiness, the likely tears on her face, the broken shards of her heart, the speedometer needle edging higher and higher and then that little car sailing over the rail and flying into space before dropping down… down…down. Burying her face in her hands, Charlie curled into herself.

"Oh, God." Linus stroked her shoulders, her arms. "Are you saying she killed herself?"

"I don't know," Charlie said, her face still covered. "We'll never know."

"Let's get out of here. Let me—"

"No." She lifted her head and rubbed the heels of her hands across her cheeks. "I came to do this. To give you something."

Inhaling a shuddering breath, she dug into her purse and pulled out a sheaf of letters. Staring down at them, she hesitated once again. "A few months after Laurie was…gone, we were at a girls' night and I came up with Steven Parker. I thought he could be the defender of our souls, the strong warrior to guard our hearts."

"That's why he's a soldier in your photo."

She nodded. "Other people imagine him differently."

"Grace has got herself a surfer."

Charlie smiled a little. "To navigate the rough seas of love." She looked up. "That's how you figured it out? I saw you talking to her the other night. She tossed out

Steven Parker? We're only supposed to use him one at a time, but…"

"There's all those rough seas out there."

There was understanding in his eyes, Charlie thought, the tightness in her chest easing a little. Still, what had to happen next wouldn't be easy. So she did it like you ripped off a bandage. On a quick inhale, she shoved the bundle of letters at Linus.

"What's this?"

"I wrote them, addressed them, hand-canceled each and every one. Picked out the pretty stamps, too."

He studied them in his hands. "You wrote me letters."

"After you left. But I never mailed them." Charlie noted Linus's fingers were trembling as he sifted through the envelopes. That very uncool, very undetached sign of emotion made her want to cry all over again…or twirl in circles like a delighted child. *Oh, Linus.*

He looked up. "What do they say, Sal?"

Sal. Oh, *Linus.* "Various things. Accounts of the weather, post office trivia—"

"What do they say, Sal?" he repeated.

It was time to tell the whole truth. "Between the lines…and sometimes right on the lines, they say… they say that last summer I fell in love with you, Linus."

He cocked his head, his gaze trained on her face. "And now?"

Her hand slipped into her purse and pulled out one last missive. "This one I wrote yesterday. It…it says I still love you." After a moment, she blinked. "Wow. I wasn't sure I could do it. But I was honest. I took the risk."

Linus continued to stare at her. "Anything spectacular requires a bit of that."

Blood was rushing through her veins, hot and cold by turn as terror and gladness alternated through her. *"Well?"* she said, the only word she could manage now that her mouth had gone desert-dry.

Now he blinked. "Well…what?"

Okay, it was only icy terror now. "Is there something—"

"I didn't say it? I didn't tell you that I love you back?"

The sun came out from whatever cloud it had been hiding behind. "No," she whispered.

Linus smiled, so handsome, so charming…so sincere. The gladness that was pouring through her was reflected in his eyes. "Because I've thought it, Sal. Almost from the very first instant I saw you."

And now Charlie let the pent-up tears free again as she launched herself to him. He took her into his arms, and kissed her with a passion that made her laugh with joy once he lifted his head.

And laugh again, when the people surrounding them, at the tables and on the sidewalk, started up an appreciative applause. Standing, Linus took an elaborate bow—performer to the bone—then, drawing her up by the hand, indicated she should make her curtsy. Feeling silly and sentimental, goofy and girly, she did just that.

And then everyone else fell away and it was just Charlie and Linus, staring into each other's eyes. "What happens next?" she asked him.

He rested his forehead against hers. "We go behind

some closed doors and let me do that thing you *really* like best about me."

"That sounds—"

"Excuse me," a voice said, causing them to look up and realize they were blocking the entrance to Oscar's. As one, Charlie and Linus stepped aside so another young couple could make their way inside. In a moment of sweet astonishment, she recognized the pair as none other than local boy Tom, arm in arm with his Summer Girl, the college coed who had driven away in tears six-plus months before.

Charlie had been so sure that relationship was over.

Linus leaned close. "Now what do you have to say?" he asked, his voice rich with good humor and smug satisfaction. Then Charlie's rite of passage slid his arms around her and squeezed her very, very tight.

That's when she realized that even though she intended to keep Linus forever, he still represented her transition from one status to another. From risk-averse girl to brave woman. From guarded heart to open soul.

From skeptic of love to daydream believer.

CHAPTER SEVENTEEN

IT WAS EARLY EVENING, and Ryan walked into the kitchen. Poppy, in jeans and stocking feet, stood near the counter pouring coffee into a mug, having returned from settling her son into bed. She glanced over at him, her hair coming a little loose from her usual side braid. Mussed, he decided, because she'd been propped against Mason's pillows while she read him *Where the Wild Things Are* or *Goodnight Moon*.

"Want some?" she asked, holding up the carafe.

He shook his head, the image of maternal Poppy still not enough to slow the pulse of sexual attraction that started beating anytime they were in a room together. It throbbed in his blood and drummed against his breastbone like a deep bass note. It shimmered in the air, moving the atoms like a sound wave.

Poppy's face went pink and that guileless, enchanting bewilderment crossed her face. He wanted to tell her he couldn't understand it, either; that he had no more power over it than she, but how would bringing it out in conversation help matters? He was determined not to take her back to bed, so he stayed silent and watched her struggle against the attraction's influence.

Bastard that he was, he found the effort it cost her gratifying.

She returned the carafe to the burner, then picked it up again. "Maybe Linus and Charlie want some coffee," she said, taking a step toward the family room.

"Don't go in there," Ryan warned, remembering why he'd escaped from them in the first place. His brother had brought Poppy's cousin to the house for dinner and they were clearly more than friends. "One moment Linus and I were talking about the time-waste that is a car's power seats—it takes fifteen seconds to move from the fore position to the aft, you see..."

Poppy was laughing.

"What?"

"You two carry on the most inane conversations. Not long ago I overheard you talking about krill."

He frowned at the comment. "It's how men relate to each other. Through sports, cars and inanities."

Her smile poked that small dimple into her left cheek. "I didn't realize it was so different than how women relate to each other. Or how a man and a woman relate to each other for that matter."

"Yeah?" He found himself strolling toward her, so he shoved his hands in his pockets to keep from touching. "Have you been spending time recalling just exactly how we've related?" That seductive note in his voice was completely beyond his control. Damn.

Her smile died as her long eyelashes dropped. She looked up at him through them and her fingertip brushed his forearm as he came to stand beside her. "Well, it didn't seem absurd in the least to me."

His hands bunched into fists as lust poured another pail of burning heat into his blood. What was he doing?

What was *she* doing with that flirty glance? Her finger stroked him in another secret touch.

Damn, damn, damn. He thought he could hold himself back, but he couldn't be responsible for the both of them. Still, another round in the sack was too risky. If she wasn't so bright and buoyant, if he thought somewhere beneath that fresh face there might be a single cynical bone...then maybe.

But he didn't want to be the one she built pretty dreams around only to have him toss them aside with some fucked-up March bullshit, or when April arrived and he beat feet down the mountain. His grief over Tate had siphoned everything out of him and he only had a shallow pool of caring left for anyone.

Not enough caring for Poppy. She deserved a well of emotion, a man who had a lake's worth of love to lavish on her. His shriveled heart hadn't anything like that inside it.

Her head bent and as her fingertip drew another circle on his flesh he stared at the part in her hair, the exposed, pale line of her scalp just another sign of her vulnerability. His belly tightened.

The least he could do was step back.

So he did.

The corners of her soft mouth turned down, but she didn't comment on the distance he put between them. "So...you were telling me about Linus and Charlie."

Ryan cast his mind back, trying to clear the haze of want from his system.

"Something about cars?" Poppy suggested in a helpful tone. Mischief sparked in her eyes, as if she were perfectly—happily—aware she could discombobulate him, too.

"Right. Power seats." Ryan cleared his throat. "One minute we were conversing like normal men and the next my brother had your cousin on his lap and his tongue down her throat."

Poppy's brows rose. "I see."

"Well, *I* didn't want to see. Clearly Linus is coming off a dry spell."

She leaned against the countertop and picked up her coffee to take a sip. "During dinner, I got the impression there was a bit more to them than a booty call."

He stared at her. Booty call? Did Poppy even know what that phrase meant?

With a little smile, she shook her head at him. "Honestly, Ryan, I haven't been living in a nunnery. I'm up on all the cool-kid lingo."

"Yeah. Fine." She was the ultimate in sophistication. She and her one other lover besides himself.

"Charlie told me privately that Linus wants to bring her back to L.A. They're talking…future."

Whoa. Ryan couldn't wrap his mind around it. "Really?"

Poppy shrugged. "I admit I have my reservations about a mountain girl tying herself to a flatlander, but I don't think Linus will hurt her." She hesitated. "I think he might even marry her, Ryan."

He frowned, trying to see his brother as a husband, realizing it shouldn't seem so strange. The younger man was twenty-nine, after all. Time didn't stand still for everyone. "Our parents would probably like that."

"There might be children."

Ryan forced himself to imagine that, too. He'd never given it a single thought, he'd been so engaged in his own emotional war these past years. But there could be other small Hamiltons. Little girls. Little boys. Would a child of Linus's look like Tate, with his freckled nose and crooked grin?

The question gripped him for a moment and he sucked in a breath, waiting for the inevitable sharp-edged anguish....

That didn't come.

The knowledge of that rocked him. *Tate*, he thought again. *Tate. Tate. Tate.* Instead of torment he heard a child's laughter, saw a trailing pair of shoelaces, smelled bubblegum-scented shampoo and felt...warmth. Tate.

A soft touch returned his attention to the present. Poppy stood at his elbow. "Are you okay?"

He didn't know. After years of existing on the un-steady knife's edge between despair and deep grief, the cessation of it left him in an unsettling limbo. He glanced away from Poppy, saw that sometime since sun-set one of those mountain mists had settled around the house. It pressed against the windows, hovering like a multitude of expelled ghosts.

Should he celebrate their banishment or rush to the doors and let them back in? Because who was he with-out his specters? Without his pain?

"Ryan. *Ryan.*"

His focus took a long time to return, as if he'd been very far away. Poppy had her arms around him and he realized she must have been saying his name for quite some time. He was stiff in her grasp, but as he came back to the present he wanted nothing more than to hold her against him, to absorb her delicate sweetness, to slide into her heat.

When she went on tiptoe, her clothes abraded his. Her arms wound around his neck and the soft notch of her sex nestled against the place where he was growing hard. Throbbing. Alive.

"I'm bad for you," he said, even as his hands moved to cup her ass and press her closer against him. "I'll take you to bed and gobble up all your good cheer and it won't change a thing besides leaving you without it."

"I can make more good cheer." Her fingers pushed into the hair at the back of his head to bring his mouth against hers.

"I don't know why you're doing this," he said against her lips.

"Must have to do with your troll-like looks."

He bit her lower lip in retaliation, and felt that telling melt of her body against his. If only he believed it could be something so surface for her. "Poppy, really, you don't—"

"I'm very annoyed with people thinking I don't know what I want or telling me I shouldn't do what I want." She put a little space between them. "Give me some credit for knowing myself."

It was him she didn't know. If she did, she wouldn't offer to share her wholesome goodness with him. The first time they'd gone to bed together he'd managed to excuse himself because they'd clearly agreed to a single session, stranger-to-stranger. The second time, he'd been in the clutches of his raw emotions, unable to battle back the lust.

But now…now his good sense and his conscience

were fully operational and they were telling him, in no uncertain terms, that he couldn't have her again.

Even if he wanted her so damn much.

He stared down at her, torn. In this room, the sexual attraction was as alive as the two of them and it had no compunction, only need. God, and he had need, too. He wanted another experience in Poppy Time, badly enough his hands were shaking. With a little sound of frustration, she lifted into him again, taking his lips, licking into his mouth with her hot little tongue.

He groaned, clutching at her hips. Then he heard a new sound in the distance. Lifting his head, he groaned again. "Linus and Charlie. They're still here. They have the TV on."

"Linus and Charlie," she repeated, clearly still kiss-dazzled.

"My brother? Your cousin?"

"Oh." Poppy's eyes drifted closed and she rubbed her body against his stiff cock. "We should say good-night or something."

They should get out of this room before he took her on the table. Grasping her wrist firmly in hand, he towed her in the direction of the family room. "Let's go."

"To your bed," she insisted, tugging back.

Whoever said he was a hero? Hadn't all the recent Marches proved exactly the opposite? "To my bed," he confirmed, kicking his conscience to the curb while continuing forward. At the threshold to the family room, he paused, hoping from this distance they wouldn't notice his blatant arousal.

Glancing over, he took in Poppy's thoroughly kissed

state and battled a renewed urge to tear the clothes off her. He wrenched his gaze away and instead focused on Linus and Charlie, who weren't aware they were standing behind them. The other couple's attention was focused forward, on the large TV over the fireplace. He just had to do the host thing, Ryan decided, call out a quick "good night," and get Poppy down to his suite.

A woman was front and center on the flat screen, in one of those arms-baring dresses that female TV reporters wore these days no matter what the season. She asked some question and then the shot switched to another woman, this one with platinum hair and Jessica Rabbit tits. Ryan froze, recognizing the voluptuous female.

She'd been born Suzanne Waddell, had matured into normal proportions, but then thanks to a combination of plastic surgery, ambition and a certain remarkable flexibility, had gone on to make millions in porn as Suzee Wad.

He told himself to move. To yell to Linus to switch off the TV. To run the forty feet across the carpet to do it himself or at least grab Poppy by the hand and race her away from the room.

But his muscles refused to move and his mouth couldn't seem to form words. A high whine began buzzing in his ears, so loud it drowned out what the woman on the screen was saying. It didn't matter, because next they showed a head shot of him, and then some moments of the film Suzee had directed last March in that opulent hotel room in Vegas. Her co-star was a shadowy figure, and the network tastefully blurred out the salient portions of his anatomy for their TV audience.

But you could view the uncensored version on the internet. Suzee had been using it as an advertising tool for her memoir, titled, coyly, *Wad's Up?*

Hot and cold ran over Ryan's skin as horror, embarrassment, shame and anger coursed through him. Finally, it freed his frozen muscles and without even knowing he did it, he dropped Poppy's hand. With the television still recounting the sordid story, he stalked to the wet bar across the room, where he poured himself four fingers of tequila, tossing half back in one go.

"Hell," he heard Linus exclaim, and the TV went dark.

Then his brother was there. "I didn't know you guys were in the room," he said, placing his hand on Ryan's shoulder.

He shrugged it off. "Get Poppy out of here. Make her go upstairs."

"Ry—"

"Just get her away," he said in a low, raspy voice. "Get her away from me."

Linus glanced over his shoulder to where Poppy still lingered by the entry. "Maybe you should explain the situation to her."

"And say what?"

"And say the truth," Linus said. "If there's one thing I've learned from my return to the mountains, it's that being honest is the only path to being happy."

Being honest with Poppy would mean earning her disgust. She was too unsullied, too bright for the decadence he'd lowered himself to last year. He shouldn't ever kiss her again. He wasn't good enough to touch her with his hands.

And she wouldn't want him to, if he was up front about what had happened last March.

Ryan absorbed that thought as he swallowed down the last of his tequila. Then he squared his shoulders. All right. He'd be honest.

Because it was the thing guaranteed to save her from himself.

RYAN HERDED POPPY toward his suite, aware he was about to kill the fascination they had for each other. Well, the fascination she had for him. He'd still think she was the sweetest and sexiest woman he'd ever run across. But once he shared the video with her, she'd pack up her belongings and her son and escape the lake house. Then he'd see out March as he always did…miserable and miserably alone.

Crossing the threshold into the sitting room, as he dialed the overhead light to a low glow, a delicate scent assailed him. It was decidedly floral, but also included notes of black pepper, honey and mint. Looking around, his gaze lit on the probable source, a pottery vase centered on the coffee table by the couch that was filled with trumpet-shaped flowers on slender green stems, the blossoms white, yellow and deep pink. The scent drawing him, he moved forward and traced the edges of one fragile bloom with his finger.

"They're freesias," Poppy said.

He touched another and its clean scent wafted upward. "I'm not familiar with them."

"They grow from bulbs and like the daffodils, make a short appearance in spring. I found a patch against the side of the house and couldn't resist bringing some inside. In flower terms, they symbolize sweetness, friendship and trust."

All of which he'd lose from Poppy once he showed her that salacious video. His fingers curled into fists and he glanced over, catching her wary expression.

He steeled himself against those big gray eyes. "There's something you need to see."

"All right."

He ran his hands through his hair, then forced himself to move to the other side of the room, where he switched on a lamp. The TV in the entertainment center went on next. It was connected to the internet and mere seconds were required for him to locate the link to the video.

Yeah, he could have played it for her on his laptop, hoping the small-screen dimensions would diminish some of the squalidness. But the point was to use the ugly, unvarnished truth to push her away.

"Okay," he said on a deep breath. "You should sit down."

Her stocking feet were silent on the thick carpet. Over his shoulder, he saw her settle on the deep green velvet sofa. She tucked her knees to her side and he thought she looked like a dainty fairy curled up in a garden. As he watched, she shivered a little and he took quick steps to the fireplace, where he flipped on the gas flames.

Then there was nothing left but to allow last year's March mistake to play.

Taking a seat at the opposite corner of the couch, Ryan refused to look away. Months ago, when it had first hit cyberspace, he'd forced himself to watch the whole thing. Seventeen edited minutes of sex in a shadowy room. Tonight it seemed to go on as long as the entire lost weekend he'd spent in that hotel.

Through all of it he was naked.

Through most of it Suzee was wearing a jeweled bra and matching G-string that he'd been told were later auctioned off. Not for a second did he believe the $75,000 they garnered were donated to charity.

She'd also sold a pair of boxer briefs that she'd claimed were his from that same interlude, but since he wouldn't be caught dead in Calvin Klein, he'd known that for the lie it was.

When the video ended—final image the red-and-yellow cover of *Wad's Up?*—Ryan closed his eyes, waiting for Poppy's indictment.

Which didn't come.

As the silence continued, he opened one eye. She hadn't moved.

He couldn't abide the quiet. "Last year's bright idea was to survive March with a month-long bender in Las Vegas."

Poppy's nonexpression didn't change.

"I think I ran into her the last three or four days. It's a bit hazy."

"Not for her," Poppy said. "She's clearly looking at the camera several times."

"It was hers. I wasn't aware she was filming."

"Mmm." Poppy picked a piece of nonexistent lint off her sweater. "I guess that means if I ever see her in person I'll have to smack her silly."

Ryan drew back. "That's all you have to say?"

She seemed to consider. "And that I believe she could mix cement with those hips."

The comment startled a half laugh out of him. "Poppy…"

"You're mostly just lying there, Ryan. Do you expect me to condemn you for a video in which you appear just one click away from comatose?"

"I…I showed a remarkable lack of judgment hooking up with her. Suzee Wad—"

"Shows a remarkable lack of judgment choosing to go by that name."

He shook his head, trying to understand her reaction. "The sex tape is why the paparazzi are so rabid, Poppy. I didn't come clean with you about that."

"Because it makes you feel dirty."

"And stupid." And sad, so sad, that he'd allowed Poppy to brush up against it. To brush up against him. "I'm sorry."

Then, to his astonishment, she turned on the couch and started crawling toward him. "What are you doing?" he asked.

She kept advancing, even when he reared back. "I'm returning to where we were before we were so unpleasantly interrupted." Now Poppy was in his lap, looping her arms around his neck. She pitched her voice toward the closed door. "Good night, Charlie. Good night, Linus."

"What—"

"We missed that part. Now let's get to this part," she said, and kissed him.

His hands closed over her shoulders and he thrust her away. "That's it? That's all you have to say?"

She tilted her head and the ends of her braid tickled the back of his right hand. "About the video?"

Maybe he was baffled because he could never think straight with his arms full of this pretty woman. "Yes."

"Well…only that I've known you to do much better work than what was caught on that tape." She brushed at his hair. "So I'd suggest you start rehabilitating your rep."

He stared at her. Then, laughing, he caught her hands in his. "God, Poppy." With his lips, he touched her forehead, the tip of her nose, the round apple of each cheek. "God, Poppy."

Drawing her close, he buried his head against her neck. "If I wasn't me, I think I could fall in love with you."

If I wasn't me, I think I could fall in love with you.

They were just words, Poppy thought, running a gentle hand over Ryan's hair. A meaningless expression of gratitude. He'd expected recriminations about that ridiculous video because clearly he'd been beating himself up about it all year. But the only anger she felt was for the woman who'd taken such advantage of him.

Ryan's mouth pressed another kiss on her, a gentle buss to the side of her throat. Still, she shivered, the slight abrasion of his evening whiskers teasing her sensitive skin. His tongue chased the chills spreading over it. "I love the way you taste," he said.

Love.

She squeezed shut her eyes, rejecting the word. Then Ryan kissed her again, lips-to-lips, and she opened for him, welcoming the carnality of a hot, deep kiss. She could lose herself in their physical connection. Be carried away from dangerous thoughts by the clamoring want of her body for him. His hands were at the hem of the sweater and she lifted her arms to allow him to draw it off her.

Her bra was tossed away next.

Reflexive modesty had her crossing her arms over her breasts, but Ryan grasped her wrists and held them away, baring her to his gaze. She shivered again.

"Let me warm things up," he said, slipping from beneath her.

She watched him cross to the fireplace. In seconds, the flames were leaping higher. With his gaze on her, Ryan reached behind him with one hand to yank his T-shirt over his head. Her breath caught as she took in the heavy set of his shoulders, the rise of his pectoral muscles, the rippled contours of his belly. His blue eyes were as hot as the center of the fire.

Anticipation made her breathless and she squeezed her thighs together, the juncture of her legs already feeling swollen and soft. Ryan settled in the opposite corner of the couch, then beckoned her to him. "Come here," he whispered, more heat in his smile.

Her nipples furled into hard points and her breasts swelled, too, every inch of her skin preparing for his touch. When she crawled toward him this time, he welcomed her into his arms, bending his head to take a firm tip between his lips. She cried out, cradling his head as he sucked. His mouth was molten, the suction bliss. When he moved to her other breast, his fingers toyed with the flesh he'd dampened.

Poppy wiggled in his hold, unable to keep still, and

his hips lifted, his erection a delicious pressure against her bottom. His fingertips slid under the waistband of her pants and her belly hollowed, allowing his hand deeper access.

They both groaned when one long finger found the first wetness waiting there. He pulled free and before she could whimper he had her pants at her knees. His hand was hot as it brushed her calves to push them away. And maybe she should feel silly in only her scrap of panties and a pair of socks, but the way he looked at her made her feel as desirable as any tackily dressed porn princess.

As if he moved through water, he took his time stripping away her wool socks. Then he hooked his forefinger on one side of her underwear and he drew them down, down, down.

Poppy was naked, the denim of Ryan's jeans just slightly rough against the soft skin of her derriere. He ran his palm over her flesh, cupping the curve of her shoulder, following the slope of her breast, testing the resiliency of her thigh. His fingers tickled the underside of her knee and burning shivers flared from his touch to the soles of her feet and to the top of her head.

She closed her eyes, reveling in the feeling. Then something cool and fragrant passed over her skin. Her lashes lifted and she saw he'd plucked a handful of the freesia blossoms and now was stroking their scent into her skin. The peppery sweetness of it rose around them and she felt bathed in Ryan's touch…and in spring.

He kneeled beside the couch and stretched her out on the cushions. More blossoms caressed her skin: the under-curve of her breasts, the bend of her elbow, the tender inner surfaces of her thighs. He pressed his lips to her belly and breathed her in. "I love this scent."

Love.

To get away from the word, Poppy scrambled up.

"Wha—" Ryan began, but she smothered the word with a kiss of her own. He groaned into it, accepting the stroke of her tongue and clutching at her with hard hands.

Taking them, she drew him to a stand and then her mouth was busy exploring his hard chest. She ran her teeth along the bulge of his biceps, she traced the lines of his ribs with her tongue, she sank to her knees so she could rub her cheek against the hard column of him beneath his jeans. Rather than worrying about her inexperience, she just went with what her body wanted.

A relative novice could do a lot with enthusiasm, she decided.

"Poppy," he said, his fingers tangling in her hair, sifting through it so it was loose around her shoulders.

Looking up, she shook it back as she worked at his snap and zipper. His eyes were wizard-bright again, and a wild shiver ran across her body as she freed him from his clothes. Then she reached for him with her tongue, brushing the soft crest of his erection with the lightest flick. His fingers curled, the tug on her scalp just more pleasure.

There were crushed freesia blossoms scattered about and she scooped some into her palm and then stroked his hard shaft, pressing the bruised petals to his hot, satin skin. He groaned again, and she let the flowers fall once more so she could take him into her mouth.

The taste was both fresh and spicy, both salty and

sweet. Like she was catching water, she cupped him from below, rubbing her thumbs across the twin sacs as she continued to draw him in and then let him slide out, her tongue circling his flesh. She edged forward, her nipples making contact with his muscled thighs. Her heart pounded so hard she was sure the drumbeat was loud enough to drive away the last vestiges of winter, the destructive greedy grief, any words that shouldn't be spoken.

His magnificent eyes continued to watch her, compel her, and she had the desperate satisfaction of knowing that though he'd be gone soon, now, in this moment, she filled his vision. She rolled her tongue over the sensitive head of him, and with an oath, he broke.

Next thing she knew, he was lying on the couch, wearing nothing more than a condom, and he was drawing her over him…the position of him and that nasty piece of woman who'd been on the sex video. But it was nothing like that movie.

His hands were warm on her hips. Not rough, but urgent, and so careful as he drew her down. She sank onto him by degrees, each millimeter ratcheting the desire. Ryan groaned, low and soft.

"I love the way you take me in," he said.

Poppy shuddered as he entered, and then knowledge fell like a soft spring rain, gentle enough not to damage frail blossoms but with enough power to reach her heart. To change it, irrevocably. *And I love you*, she thought, as the climax began to build, making her tremble in his arms.

I'm in love with you.

CHAPTER EIGHTEEN

HEAD MUZZY FROM lack of sleep, Poppy headed straight for the coffeemaker. As she poured, for the first time she noticed Charlie sitting on a stool at the kitchen island, her hands cradling her own mug. With coffee in hand, Poppy gave her cousin the best good-morning smile she had available.

It must have been pretty lousy, because Charlie's eyebrows rose. "You look wiped out. Are you all right?"

Avoiding the question, Poppy sipped at the dark brew. "No need to ask you that." Charlie's glowing face was the only evidence necessary to conclude the younger woman had enjoyed her overnight with Linus.

A grin drew up the corners of her mouth. "I didn't know I could be this happy."

"I'm thrilled for you," Poppy replied, meaning it to the marrow. "Linus is great."

"And what about his brother and you?" Charlie asked.

Mason skipped into the room, paper and pens in hand. Sending her cousin a significant look, she tipped her head toward her son. "Morning, buddy. Cereal okay?"

"I want the kind Duke eats," Mason said, climbing up onto a stool beside Charlie's. "The sugar one."

"The sugar one is bad," Poppy said, crossing to pull a bowl from a cupboard.

Mason's brows pinched together. "Duke wouldn't do anything bad."

Little do you know, darling boy. Duke did a very bad thing to Mommy. He made her fall in love with him. Poppy slid the bowl and a spoon in front of her son. "Oat flakes or rice puffies?"

Her son was focused on another of the many "maps" he'd made of the lake house and surrounding estate. "The kind Duke eats," he repeated, making a careful red X in what looked to be a stand of trees.

"Oat flakes or rice puffies?" she said again, putting a stern note into her voice.

Mason looked up, his lower lips signaling imminent mutiny. "Mom—"

"For goodness sake, let the kid have the cereal he wants," Charlie insisted, sliding from the stool and moving toward the pantry.

"I love Charlie," Mason said, beaming her an angelic grin.

"Love you, too, boyo," her cousin called over her shoulder.

Poppy crossed her arms over her chest. "Easy for you to say. You won't be dealing with the midmorning sugar crash."

The long-legged blonde came back with the cereal box and proceeded to pour the equivalent of nineteen candy bars into Mason's bowl. "I can be. You look as if you could use a breather. Why don't you let Linus and me take him for the day? Would you like that, Mace?

We can find fun things to do. Try out that pool I've heard about. Maybe have ice-cream sundaes for lunch."

"Yay!" Mason raised his arms, clasping his fists overhead like a champion.

"Oh, great," Poppy said. "More sugar."

"You let me worry about that." Charlie lowered her voice. "Call Shay. I hear she has access to a boat. Get her to spring you from the estate."

Poppy hesitated. It was true, leaving via the lake would keep her out of the paparazzi's sight. "But…"

"Do it," Charlie said. "Take a man-break."

The concept was much too tempting to pass up.

Maybe a man-break would give her the time and opportunity necessary for an emotional rewind, Poppy thought an hour later, waiting on the dock for her sister to arrive. Last night, she'd snuck away from Ryan, slipping between the sheets in her bed, where she'd lain awake until morning, lamenting her own knuckleheadedness while examining and reexamining how she'd managed to turn her heart over to him.

That he couldn't reciprocate was supposed to have protected her!

But watching him have sex with another woman had changed all that, which, when she thought of it, was extremely messed up. If Mac knew she'd be shaking her head and once again pointing out Poppy's terrible track record when it came to men…

Though it wasn't that stupid sex tape. It was his hands, she decided. Covering a sleeping Mason with a towel. Bandaging a wounded Mason with such confidence. Cupping Poppy's shoulders while he whispered in her ear, *Nothing that you bake can assuage this par-*

ticular appetite. Then last night, the tight grip of his long fingers as he tried to push her away, yet only managed to hang on tight. Those moments had brought her to the tipping point.

To when she'd surprised a short, startled laugh from him because she hadn't condemned him for last March's futile effort to cope with his son's loss. *If I wasn't me, I think I'd fall in love with you.*

As Shay eased toward the dock in her employer's boat, Poppy rushed to meet her. With luck, a man-break would permanently fracture her fascination with the dark-haired, blue-eyed flatlander who'd come to mean too much.

But trading one lakeside estate for another wasn't a cure-all. While her sister and her charge—for today, she wanted to be known as Winooski—carried on with the youngster's studies, Poppy was left on her own. She read a book, perused a magazine, borrowed Shay's headphones to listen to music. Lunch was a shared affair with the other two, and afterward Poppy dipped into yet another book.

In late afternoon, she let herself out of the house to wander the grounds. She made patterns with pinecones, she tossed rocks into the lake, she admired the flower beds that showcased yellow daffodils, white and pink tulips, purple hyacinths and…freesias.

She had to get away from them.

Pulling her sweatshirt hood over her head, she let herself out a side gate. Winooski's house was located on a narrow, winding lane that was bisected by long driveways leading to other mansions. Flowers brightened the front gardens, but there weren't any other signs of life.

Midweek in the low season likely meant most people were spending time in their primary homes down the hill.

Swinging her arms, Poppy set out on a brisk walk. The air tasted fresh and she breathed in great gulps of it. Dappled sunlight fell over her, filtered by pines and oaks. Squirrels chattered as she strode by, zipping up tree trunks so fast they startled blue jays from the branches. After fifteen minutes, she was too warm for fleece and stripped off her sweatshirt. Dreaming of a cold drink, she turned back, suffering another scolding from the bushy-tailed rodents. With the house just a few yards away, she glanced down to adjust the knotted sleeves at her waist when the sudden skitter of a pinecone across asphalt came out of nowhere.

Her gaze jumped up, landing on a man lurking in the shadow created by the massive cedar located beside the entrance to Winooski's drive. Poppy moved back, instincts on alert. Then the man stepped into fuller light. It took her a moment to recognize him. His hair was darker, his face bonier, his smile just that much falser.

Trying to hide her dismay, she nodded at him. "What are you doing here, Denny?"

"Poppy." He strolled forward. "I had no idea I'd run into you."

"Then why are you here?" His family's place wasn't situated at this end of the lake. As a matter of fact, she had no idea if they still owned it or even if they visited Blue Arrow anymore.

He shrugged. "Heard through the grapevine your sister was working at this address. I thought I could make my case to her. Have her put in a good word for me."

"Don't bother Shay anymore."

"I don't need to," Denny said. "Now that we're face-to-face." He glanced around. "The kid with you?"

"No." The air took on a new chill and she unknotted her sweatshirt and shrugged back into it. She wasn't any warmer. "I haven't come to a decision yet about you spending time with him."

"Well, what's it going to take?" he asked, his voice annoyed. "I'm the kid's father, right?"

"The kid's name is Mason."

Denny waved that away. "Yeah, yeah, yeah. I want to see him."

"Why?"

He hesitated and she knew he was trying to come up with the best way to sway her. Crossing her arms over her chest, she pinned him with her stare. "Don't bullshit me. What's going on?"

"My mother," he finally said. "She'd like to know her grandson."

He said it too fast. "I have a hard time believing that," Poppy replied. "I've sent her photos every year and she's never bothered to contact me."

"My mother should want to see her grandson."

On that they could agree, she thought, but this whole scenario, now that she was looking him in the eye, wasn't ringing true. "Denny—"

"Okay, fine. I need money."

She raised her brows. "Your job at the family firm…"

"I was let go." His gaze shifted away from her. "My parents don't understand."

So he wanted to use Mason to…what? Well, hell, no,

to whatever he was scheming. "I don't see how bringing my son into this situation changes anything for you."

"My mother might fall for the kid. Soften up, you know? Does he look like me?"

"He looks like himself." She didn't bother mentioning that she'd sent Denny photos every year, too. It had seemed the right thing to do, but no longer. Poppy edged toward the path that would bring her to the front door. "I think we should leave things as they are."

"We can't!" He winced, then softened his voice. "Look. I need money. I owe some people. So if my mom likes the boy, then she'll probably loosen up on that checkbook she's clutching so tight."

When Poppy didn't reply, he took a step toward her, that smarmy smile stretching his mouth. "Hey, if she does, I'll share some with you."

"No." She strode for the front door, the hairs on the back of her neck going on end as he began to follow. "I don't want your money."

"Oh, that's right." He paused at the bottom of the stairs. "You've got that rich and famous new boyfriend."

She didn't have any of Ryan. "Leave him out of this, too."

"I don't think I can. I'm a little desperate, see? Do you want me to go away?"

"Fervently."

"Then get me fifty grand."

She laughed. "Denny, you know I don't have that kind of money or any way of getting it, either."

"Of course you do. You've got Ryan Hamilton."

As the implications of what Denny was saying sank in, Poppy started to shake. She shoved her hands in the kangaroo pocket of her sweatshirt to hide their telltale trembling. "Do you actually mean—"

"Get me the money, Poppy, and I'll leave you alone. Otherwise I'm going to have to bring my parents their adorable little grandchild for a visit. My brother and sister don't have any kids, did you know that? Granny and Papa could very well decide they want ours full-time and sue for custody. Maybe *I'll* sue for custody."

A sick feeling swamped her insides and it took all she had to stay upright. Paternal grandparents wouldn't have any legal standing to take a son away from his mother, she tried assuring herself, even if they were very wealthy and very well-connected. As for Denny— he was too self-centered to want to take care of a small child. "No," she said, hoping her voice didn't quaver. "Not a chance."

"Yes," Denny countered. "But you have your way out. Go sweet-talk your lover. Give him a kiss or two and he'll give you whatever you want." He turned to saunter back down the path to the street. "Fifty grand, Poppy," he said over his shoulder. "And real, real soon."

Poppy leaned against the front door, trying to pull herself together before going inside and facing her sister. She had to get back to Mason. Avoid Ryan. And figure out what she was supposed to do next.

Man-break had been a disaster.

AT DUSK, SHAY piloted the boat, skimming over the water on the return trip to Ryan's, as Poppy cautioned herself to keep her composure. She would come up with some way to handle the Denny situation on her own—taking care of herself and her son as she always did. Her pride precluded her from discussing it with her brother and sisters—if they thought she screwed up by falling for deadbeat Denny in the first place, imagine what they'd think if she shared he was a blackmailer! Telling Ryan of the other man's threats wasn't a possibility, either. The idea that he might think she'd ever consider taking advantage of him by asking for money horrified her.

But the encounter had her insides raw and quivering—not a good state to be in when seeking a solution. So she'd calm herself with some cuddle time with Mason and then retreat to her room. There, she'd think things through…and keep her distance from Ryan. Her emotions were too ragged to be around him now.

Though she remained firm about retrieving her heart ASAP. No way could she allow him to have it forever.

Once inside the house, she found Mason in his room, where he put up with her tight hug for approximately three seconds. Then he proceeded to tell her about his action-packed day with Charlie and Linus. He'd spent time with Poppy's cousin before and she knew all the things he liked best. They had indeed swum in the pool. And though ice-cream sundaes hadn't been on the lunch menu, they'd had pizza for dinner followed by a cone of rocky road.

"You've eaten already?" Poppy asked, perching on the end of the bed so she could reach Grimm, sprawled on the mattress. He opened one eye as she fondled his soft ears, then closed it as he resumed his light snoring.

"Yep. Charlie says swimming makes a boy hungry, and she's right." He yawned hugely, then returned to the piece of paper he was coloring at the nearby desk.

"I'm tired, too, but I have to finish this map and give it to Duke before bedtime."

"I can take it to him." She'd leave it in the kitchen, where Ryan was sure to run across it.

"Has to be me. So he knows I'm on the job, too." He lowered his voice, speaking almost absently. "I'm on the job, too."

Poppy bit back a smile. His tendency to repeat little phrases that appealed to him was one of the things that made him such a joy. She couldn't imagine her life without her little guy.

Would Denny's parents really—*no*. It wasn't a legal worry and was just something Denny said to scare her. Shoving the concern away, Poppy watched Mason cap the markers then stand. "I need to find Duke now."

So much for avoiding the man altogether, Poppy thought. She got to her feet, too, and reached for Mason's hand. "Let's go."

Mason's feet dragged as they went down the stairs. He yawned again. "You really are sleepy," Poppy said.

"Will you put me to bed after I see Duke?"

"Yeah, honey." With her free hand, she stroked his straight blond hair. "Mace, you know that we're only here at Ry—Duke's for a couple more days, right? A friend of mine's working to fix our cabin after the big storm. We'll be back there soon."

"I know," Mason said, and yawned again.

He perked up a little when they found Ryan in his office. He was surrounded by what appeared to be reports and other stacks of paper. When she knocked lightly on the doorjamb he glanced over, then his gaze sharpened and he got to his feet.

He wore dark jeans and a dress shirt tucked in, sleeves rolled to reveal his forearms. They were roped with muscle and dusted with dark hair and she stared at them, wondering how that simple length of bone and flesh could represent so much maleness and so much power. She felt her pulse pounding at her wrists and her throat. Looking up, she caught Ryan's hot gaze running over her slowly, taking in every inch. *Oh, boy.*

"Hey," he said, his voice soft, his focus now trained on her face.

"Hey back." She felt another baffling blush heat her face. Embarrassed, she looked down at Mason and squeezed his hand. "Don't you have something to give Duke?"

Mason thrust out the colored sheet. "This one I did today after Linus and me scouted around."

Nodding, Ryan took the paper. "I appreciate your hard work."

Her boy sent Poppy a triumphant look. "Hard work," he repeated, then turned back to his idol. "Don't forget about the *X*'s. The best hiding places are there. Escape routes are yellow."

"Sure, kid." Ryan set the paper on his desk.

"We'll say good-night, then," Poppy said.

Ryan's gaze sought hers. "Come back when he's down for the count, okay?"

"Uh…"

"I have something for you."

Perhaps her heart. Perhaps he'd found it somewhere among the mussed sheets and now he intended to return it. *Oh, Walker,* she thought, *you are really reaching.*

"Poppy?" He stepped close. Touched her face.

Scrambled her thoughts. Made her skin prickle with a rush of almost painful awareness.

"Come back."

And because she was weak when it came to this man, she agreed.

Still, she stalled after getting Mason into his Spider-Man pajamas and under the blankets. Showers were always a good thinking place, so she took a long, hot one, letting the water fall over her as she leaned against the cool tile. But instead of the Denny problem, her mind kept returning to the man downstairs. He was so wrong for her, as she'd known from the very beginning in his dark glasses and expensive clothes. But he'd taken off his disguise around her, hadn't he? She knew him now, his tragedy, his cell-deep pain, the way both tried to destroy him in March.

And that didn't make it easier to keep away.

So she found herself walking toward his office once again, dressed in her most comfortable jeans, a long-sleeved pink T-shirt of the softest brushed cotton and her sheepskin boots. As armor, it probably wasn't particularly effective, but she figured anything short of chain mail wasn't going to protect her from his touch, anyway.

No more skin-to-skin with him, she promised herself, even as she pressed her palm against the place he'd caressed just an hour before. The four points where his fingertips had met her cheek continued to tingle.

Getting her heart back and getting over him prohibited any further physical contact.

This time when she approached the office door, there was no need to knock. He was seated in his chair, staring off into space, but his gaze snapped to hers when she stood framed in the entrance. As he rose, he gave her a smile.

She could count on her hands how many of his she'd seen. A Ryan smile boosted his magnetism by about three thousand degrees and it already started out at a number she couldn't even name. As it widened, her pulse skipped and then settled into a solid thrum. *Watch yourself, Walker*, she thought, and stuffed her hands in her pockets. "I'm here."

"Now." He cocked her head and studied her face. "But you were gone all day. Something about a 'man-break'?"

Charlie. Poppy shrugged.

"Well, as you said, you're here now." He walked toward her. "This way."

She hesitated to follow him as he made a turn in the hall that would take her toward his rooms. "Uh…"

He glanced back. "Please, Poppy."

Though her concerns were not allayed, her feet had their own mind. When they reached the door that led to his sitting room, he pushed it open, then stepped aside.

Her breath caught. The room was lit only by the low flames in the fireplace and the candles in holders on a table for two set up nearby. There was soft music playing and the scent of good food in the air. A bottle of wine cooled in a bucket of ice next to stemware that gleamed like diamonds.

She was drawn toward the pretty sight. "What's all this?" she asked, pulling a hand free of her pocket to touch a linen napkin.

"I thought…I wanted to treat you right tonight. Special."

"It's all very pretty." The plates were covered with silver warmers. She lifted one and the scent of mushroom-and-chicken penne made her mouth water. "Linus cooked?"

"I set the table myself. Picked the wine." He crossed to her and drew out a chair.

"Well, then." It was impossible not to be charmed. She sat. Once he took his place, he poured them both wine. With the delicate stem of the glass in her hand, she looked at the fire through the straw-colored liquid. "This is nice."

The rim of his glass pinged when it met hers. "To us," he said.

She froze. He must have read the dismay on her face because he replayed the moment. "I mean, to…"

"Spring," Poppy offered.

"To spring," he repeated.

And with that awkward moment out of the way, the meal proceeded. They ate slowly, sipped at the wine, let quiet moments of companionable silence stretch the interlude.

It was all too comfortable, Poppy suddenly thought. Too…domestic.

Romantic.

Wrong.

But she didn't protest when he poured her coffee from an insulated carafe and led the way to the couch, where they'd made licentious use of freesias the night before. The remaining flowers were still in their vase and Poppy wouldn't allow herself to look at them as she settled into a spot on the cushions far from Ryan.

Still, it remained too cozy.

"Tell me about your life," she said, to burst the mood. "Tell me about what you do in L.A." Anything to stop herself from picturing him with her.

His eyebrows rose as if he were surprised by the question, but he answered readily. "Pretty much what you've seen me do here. I read a lot of material, examine a lot of reports. We have a production company— a couple of partners and I. For some projects I'm the executive producer...essentially the guy who gets the money. My real interest is on the development side, though. That's when I work at identifying and acquiring good material."

"Ah. No acting anymore?"

He shook his head. "It became something I didn't enjoy any longer. Being in someone else's skin—the skin some writer had dreamed up—didn't feel like living to me. As a profession it was more like wallowing... and the lifestyle attached to it no longer appealed. So there came a time when it was important for me to move forward."

But he was stuck again, Poppy thought. Stalled. Wallowing. Unable to fight free of the dark nightmare he'd entered four years ago. *Oh, Ryan.*

"What's wrong?" he asked.

"Nothing." With a little shrug, she put her coffee aside.

"Your emotions cross your face like clouds cross the sky," he said. "Something's up. I saw the shadows in your eyes when you returned from your man-break."

"I…" And then it all descended in a deluge like that last-of-winter hailstorm: Ryan's bottomless grief and his inability to escape it. Her devotion to Mason and the unexpected reappearance of his father. The love she felt for Ryan and the fact that he was the last man she could have.

"Poppy." He moved swiftly. One moment he was four cushions away, in the next he was close enough to make contact.

To protect herself, Poppy pressed back against the sofa's arm. "Don't."

He cursed under his breath. "Baby. Something's wrong. Can't you tell me, sweetheart?"

At the endearments, tears stung her eyes. She was accustomed to *Mommy* and *knucklehead*, not *baby*. Not *sweetheart*. Nobody called her such tender names. Desperate to hold herself separate from him, she shook her head.

His fingers speared through his hair. "All right. All right. Keep your secrets. Just…let me hold you, Poppy. Please. Let me do that one small thing for you."

That's when she realized he didn't have to be touching her to touch her. That he didn't have to know he held her heart to rend it in two. That she was weak, weak, weak, because she let herself be taken into his arms, scooped against a wide, strong chest.

Her cheek turned into his throat and she pressed a kiss there as he carried her into the bedroom.

CHAPTER NINETEEN

A SOUND YANKED Ryan awake. His eyes snapped open and he stared into the dark, still bleary from sleep.

A child's voice cried out in terror.

Acting on instinct, he rolled from the bed. Another whimper had him shoving his legs into his discarded jeans and running from the room. Fear was fully engaged, not his mind, and it drove him down the hall then up the stairs. Not until he pushed open a bedroom door and saw the small blond figure lying in bed did he come conscious to the present.

Lake house. Night. Earlier, he'd taken Poppy to bed, flipping on the switch to monitor her son's room.

It was his cry he'd heard, not Tate's.

Then Poppy's son moaned again, his legs thrashing beneath the covers. For a moment Ryan hesitated, but a sharper cry had him moving again, crossing to the mattress. He put his hand on a small bony shoulder.

So familiar, he thought, his belly knotting.

Ignoring the sensation, he shook the child. "Kid. Wake up, kid."

Little hands clutched at the sheets. Another sound of distress.

Ryan dropped to the mattress and brushed his hand over the boy's damp face. "It's just a bad dream."

His eyes fluttered open. He blinked. "Duke? Duke!" Then he launched himself into Ryan's arms.

What could he do but fold them around the small figure? Though his belly cramped tighter, he let the boy press against him, little-kid tears falling onto his bare chest.

In a muffled voice Poppy's son told a story about scary monsters and snowmen on wheels and how he couldn't find a good hiding place from them. What would happen if the bad things came back?

"You have your maps," Ryan murmured, "remember?" To get more comfortable, he propped his back against the pillows and stretched out his legs.

"Yeah." The boy accommodated the new position, plastering himself to Ryan's side, a skinny arm stretched across his waist.

"You have your escape routes. You need to hide, you head for those places you marked with an *X*."

"Right, Duke," the kid agreed in a sleepy voice.

Ryan's hand passed over corn-silk hair. "Go back to sleep."

"You'll keep me safe?"

He stiffened, the question stabbing him straight in his clenching gut. Surely Tate had expected the same from his daddy. Ignoring the pain, he cleared his throat. "I'll do my best."

It didn't surprise Ryan that Poppy's son still had his suspicions. "Duke'll stay on the job?"

Hell. "I'll stay on the job."

The boy was back to sleep in five minutes. Ryan remained in place, however, propped against the headboard with the child slumped against him even as the room lightened with dawn's approach. He stayed awake by imagining his eyes propped open with toothpicks, afraid if he fell asleep he might fool himself into thinking that he was beside his own boy.

That his son was still alive.

I failed you, Tate. I'm so sorry. I'm so damn sorry I didn't keep you safe.

Anguish took its dark hold on him, like a skeletal hand reaching from a grave. It would be so easy to fall six feet deep, he thought, and pull the dirt over himself like bedcovers.

His own way of keeping the scary monsters at bay.

The air moved, signaling a presence scented like Poppy. He glanced toward the door as she came to stand in its frame, looking hardly more than a child herself in flannel pajama pants and a tank top.

He shoved away the sense that he was caught doing something he shouldn't. "Don't get the wrong idea," he warned her in a soft voice. Because it was all wrong, how his unconscious had sent him racing to the child, how easily he'd fallen back into the paternal role and how…how much he missed it. But he wasn't able to love again so it was very wrong, very, very wrong to feed anyone's dreams, including his own. With Tate gone, so was hope.

"ALL RIGHT." POPPY's eyebrows rose. "What's the right idea?"

Extricating himself from the boy's hold, he climbed off the mattress and stalked toward Poppy. He towed her into the hall, then shut the bedroom door. "You should have stayed in my bed." It was true, wasn't it?

If she didn't insist on sneaking away from him at night, she would have been the one to go to her son. "He was having a bad dream. I heard it through the intercom."

She grimaced. "I'm sorry. You could have woken me—"

"It's all right," he said, aware he sounded like a graceless ass.

"He's my responsibility," she said stiffly. "So forgive me."

"Christ, Poppy." Though he'd not asked to play the part of nightmare-eradicator, her apologies still pissed him off. "Relax. It's not a crime to let someone else step in once or twice."

Her eyebrows rose. "Someone like you who's going to be out of my life in just a few days?"

Now she was really trying to make him angry. "Forget all about me," he said, stalking away.

"I'm trying to," she called to him even as he redoubled his pace.

Damn woman couldn't stop herself from underscoring how this interlude was nearing its end. How afterward he'd become just some fleeting memory that she'd most likely regret. Damn him for being so irked by the fact. He'd tried addressing his conscience by the candlelit dinner, tried to ensure she knew he didn't consider her just some kind of convenient fuck buddy, when what he really thought about her was…what? That he couldn't put his finger on it only made him more nuts.

So he took himself to the pool, hoping to calm his inexplicable anger. As he stroked, his emotions felt as churned up as the water. Fucking March. Good thing he was supremely aware of how the month was his personal disaster or he might be concerned how one fresh-faced little mama was messing with his mind.

A ninety-minute swim did nothing to improve his mood. He exited the pool house, intending to lock himself in his office for the rest of the day. As he walked across the grass, he felt the sun's warmth on his shoulders. There were boats on the lake, powerboats, party boats and sailboats slicing across the blue. The obnoxious roar of the exhaust pipes of a Hallett boat drew close and he glanced around. There was no reason for someone to enter his bay. Over his shoulder, he saw the pointy nose of the racing-style vessel nearing his dock. He squinted against the sunlight, saw it wasn't Shay or anyone else he recognized.

It was a man. A paparazzo?

Temper shooting high, he ran toward the lake and onto his dock. The boat floated on the water six feet from one of the tie-up cleats. Ryan grabbed the lifeguard's shepherd's crook clipped to a metal lockbox, extending it like a weapon to keep the stranger from getting any closer.

"Who're you?" He ran an assessing gaze over the pilot of the boat. There was no camera in evidence, so it was unlikely he was a celebrity journalist. Photos or video were the stock-in-trade in that business. They never bothered with interviews as the basis for print articles—those they just fabricated from thin air. "What the hell do you want?"

The stranger was lean, with thinning dark blond hair above a handsome, almost pretty, face. He bared perfect teeth but the smile didn't reach his eyes. "I'm Denny Howell."

Denny...Poppy's ex? "I repeat. What do you want?"

The man made a gesture toward the dock. "Can I tie up?"

"No." Ryan didn't relax his guard. "You can tell me why you're here. Uninvited." Unless Poppy...? The thought added more kindling to the fire of his temper.

"I saw photographers at your front gate. Our conversation needs privacy, so I borrowed a boat." He tried another of those fake smiles. "Did Poppy explain the situation?"

That she'd invited this smarmy jerk to Ryan's home? But she wouldn't have done that, he thought, commanding himself to chill. "What situation is that?"

"I knew it." Denny shook his head. "That girl..."

That *woman*. Sexy, strong, delicate, independent, maddening, prickly. So pliant once he had her in his arms. Ryan shoved all that out of his head and narrowed his eyes. "Why don't you tell me what you think I should know."

A breeze put a little chop in the water and Denny had to grab the wheel to maintain his balance. "Well... uh...see, I bet the boy is kind of important to Poppy."

Ryan stared. "You think?"

"And, uh, I have this bit of a problem." Denny hesitated.

"Jesus," Ryan said. "I don't have all day. Spit it out."

"I owe some people. Fifty large."

Fifty *large?* Ryan stifled an impulse to laugh. Did the dude think he was starring in a gangster movie? "How does this involve Poppy?"

"It involves the kid," Denny said. "I gotta get the money from somewhere. I think if I brought him to my parents, showed him around a little, they might give me some cash for his upkeep."

Ryan wished he'd let the guy onto the dock, just so he could knock him off of it now. "Cash that would go to your…creditors, I presume, not to the mother who has cared for him on her own these last five years."

Denny frowned. "Haven't you been listening? I owe fifty large."

"Jesus." Ryan shook his head. "Poppy's not going to let you take her son so you can parade him around like that." He turned to walk away.

"She won't have a choice," Denny called out. "I'm the father. I can get a lawyer. Maybe me or my parents want custody."

Ryan turned, something in the other man's tone sending ice slithering down his spine. "What the fuck are you talking about?"

"You can make all that go away, though," Denny said. "I told Poppy she has a choice."

More cold cascaded down Ryan's back. "You discussed this proposal with her?"

"Yesterday afternoon," Denny said. "I laid it out. I'll leave her and the kid alone. I promise I won't pursue custody or visitation. You just get me the fifty, and I'll go far, far away and stay there."

POPPY WAS RUNNING the vacuum in the family room while Mason played with his Mickey doll, dancing him over Grimm, who lay sleeping in a yellow patch of sunshine streaming through a window. The nightmare seemed to have left no lingering effects…except in her conscience. Not only had she slept through the moment when Mason needed her, but she'd also been unkind to Ryan after he'd been there for her son.

The visual of that moment was permanently branded on her brain, she supposed. She'd come awake and some sixth sense had sent her to the other room. There had been bare-chested Ryan Hamilton in all his former movie-star glory, with her sleeping son glued to his side. Duke on the job.

Doing a job on her. The sight had made the heart she'd given over to him—the heart he'd broken the night before by offering to merely hold her—tear into even more pieces. So she'd struck out at him, upset at having to absorb yet more pain.

With only a few days left in their stay, though, she regretted lashing out. He was going back to his real life then, and wouldn't it be so much better if the remainder of their time together could be spent in harmony? Then he might remember this March differently.

A shadow crossed the glowing jewel tones of the rug, and she looked up. Ryan, in jeans, sweatshirt and running shoes, was pacing toward her, his face an expressionless mask. Still, her nerves jittered. Was something up?

He pointed toward the vacuum, clearly signaling she should turn it off. Swallowing, she held up a finger. Okay, she was stalling.

Instead of waiting her out, Ryan crossed the room and yanked the cord from the wall. The sudden quiet hurt her ears. "Poppy, I told you I don't expect you to work here like this."

"Unless you want to knit a sweater from Grimm's hair, it's got to be sucked up on a regular basis."

At the sound of his name, the dog came out of his morning stupor, jumping to his feet and shaking so that his jingling collar drew Ryan's attention. Looking on the dog and the boy on the floor beside him, Ryan scraped his hand over his bristled jaw. "Kid, I need another one of your maps."

Mickey was paused midcartwheel. "You do?"

"Yeah." Ryan rubbed again at his beard. "Why don't you go into my office. There's plain paper by the copier. Pens in the holder on the desk. Work there."

"Okay." Mason clambered to his feet, his gaze shifting to her. "Mommy?"

"That's fine. Don't touch anything but the blank paper and the pens, okay?"

"I won't."

"And kid," Ryan called after his retreating figure, "make sure you don't leave the house."

Poppy frowned. "He won't. Is there a problem?"

Now Ryan palmed the back of his neck. "Poppy…"

She recalled she wanted to put them back on a friendly footing. "Wait, let me go first. I need to apologize for earlier. My dad was a great monster chaser and I'm sure Mason appreciated your assistance. I was just a little…taken aback."

"That makes two of us," he muttered. Then he blew out a long breath. "Look…is there something you want to tell me?"

"Something like what?"

"Okay. I'm trying to give you a chance here." He inhaled and exhaled again, as if trying to get a hold of himself. "Something about yesterday?"

He couldn't know about yesterday. In case her expression might give something of it away, she grabbed the microfiber rag she had tucked in her back pocket and began dusting the fireplace mantel.

"What the hell are you doing now?" he asked.

"This is dusting. You do it with a rag, or in this case, a special cloth designed to capture the dirt."

"That snotty tone of yours isn't improving my mood."

Her nerves weren't just jittering, they were waving now, operating like semaphore, signaling danger ahead. "If you have something to say, just say it."

"Damn it, Poppy, that should be my line."

Ignoring him, she continued running the cloth along the mantelpiece, then focused her attention on the deeply carved surround. When he snatched the microfiber cloth from her hand she gasped.

He threw the rag into the fireplace. "Denny paid me a visit."

Her head jerked toward Ryan. She took a quick step back. "Wha—?"

"Met him down at the dock."

She felt her palms go damp. "He shouldn't have come here."

Ryan shook his head. "The man doesn't seem to have boundaries."

Shame rolled up from her toes and she stared at them. "Just forget about him."

"Not going to be so easy, given that I'm part of his plan to meet his gambling obligations."

Poppy's gaze lifted.

"Yeah," Ryan confirmed. "He's got terrible luck. First losing you, and now that money."

Unsure how to respond now, she busied herself by

gathering the abandoned electrical cord. Winding it in figure eights around the pegs at the back of the vacuum gave her something to do, even as she felt the intensity of Ryan's gaze on her.

"When were you going to bring up his blackmail?" he finally asked, his voice tight.

"I wasn't planning on discussing it with you at all."

"Poppy—"

"In a few days you'll go back to L.A. and your not-March life and he and everyone else in the world will realize they were mistaken. There's nothing between us. What is it that they say? There's no here, here, so he'll give up on getting something from you."

"And then what? Denny's still going to want money. Were you planning on asking Brett to use his muscle to shut him down?"

"Sure." She realized she'd said it too fast.

"Shit, Poppy."

Guilt burned her face. "There's nothing for you to worry about."

"You know what?" he asked, sounding exasperated. "You *are* a knucklehead."

Instead of listening to this, she decided to move along. But he caught her arm before she'd managed three steps and shook her a little. "Poppy, you're going to need help with this situation. You can't survive on your optimism and your ridiculous independent streak alone."

"You mean my knuckleheadedness," she said bitterly.

"In a word—*yes.*"

She wrenched her arm from his hold. "Well, I don't need you."

"You need someone, Poppy."

Whirling, she pinned him with her stare. "Who do you need? You seem to think you're just fine living with no one besides your ghosts and your grief."

His expression went grim. "We're not talking about me."

"Maybe we should be," she muttered.

He ignored that. "I'm not facing a desperate ex who appears to have some wacky ideas about how he can fill his wallet. You should have talked to someone about this situation yesterday...." His eyes narrowed. "No, before that. He contacted you a while ago, didn't he?"

She shrugged a shoulder. "He expressed an interest in getting to know his child. I was considering it." She'd been taken in, she saw now.

"Without discussing that with anyone? Not Mac or Shay?"

"I don't need other people resolving my problems for me."

"Christ, Poppy!" He ran his hand through his hair. "You make me nuts. How hard is it to be honest? But you don't do that. You don't tell your family about your troubles. You don't tell them what you want for the cabins—"

"They know."

"No, they don't. You keep saying you want them to stay out of your way, let you proceed with your plans for the place, but what you really wish is for it to be a family project. For you to be a family focused on making that legacy something good again. By all of you. For all of you."

She stared at him, disturbed by how clearly he could read her. "It's none of your business."

"You're right, the cabins may not be. But by God, when a man is threatening your child, threatening something that will hurt you, it sure as hell *is* my business."

"What? Why?"

"Because…" He forked his hand through his hair again, making it stand up in a very un-Ryan Hamilton manner. "Because…"

Poppy waved a hand. "Never mind. I got it. It's your hero-complex at work. You've beaten yourself up for four years for not saving your son and his mother from the fire. Even though you had nothing to do with it. Even though you had no way of anticipating it or of preventing it. Even though no one in the world could ever lay the blame for that at your door. It wasn't your fault, Ryan."

"Don't bring Tate into this." He sounded furious.

"Why not? Because I'm right?"

"Poppy—"

"Let go of your guilt," she said. "Let go of your rigid sense of responsibility. For Tate and his mother, and now for Mason and me. The first are gone, may they rest in peace. For me and mine…we'll find our way without you."

He shook his head. "You've taken this to the wrong place. I'm talking about being honest, about asking for help when you need it. About asking for what you want."

Looking at his beautiful face and perplexed expression, all the emotion drained out of her. "Ryan. I'm sorry, but you don't know what the heck you're talking about."

"Meaning?" he said, gazing at her with wary eyes.

"Sometimes people don't want to hear the truth. They really don't want all that up-front honesty you're talking about." Weariness made her reckless, and she tilted her head. "Shall I prove it to you?"

Now it was his turn to step back. "If this is about Tate again…"

"Absolutely about Tate again. But I won't repeat all that. You heard my thoughts on him the first time. This is about me."

At his next step, his heel hit the couch and he dropped onto the cushions, his eyes never leaving her face. "You?"

Everything her family accused her of was true. She was the soft-hearted screwup, the feather-brained knucklehead, a sometimes foolish woman with no sense of self-preservation. Because she was going to tell Ryan Hamilton the truth. And even though she was a cock-eyed optimist, too, she didn't imagine it was going to change the outcome of anything.

But Poppy was Poppy, and accepting that, she looked on him with pity and felt it for herself, as well. "Yeah. Me. I'm pretty certain you don't want me to be honest about my feelings. But I've fallen in love with you, Ryan. And I'm pretty certain you don't want me to ask for what I want from you…. Which would be an April, by the way. And a May. Maybe a whole summer and another season after that. For me, and for you, and for Mason I might even want a forever."

He put a hand over his eyes. "No," he said. "I can't… I won't… There's no more love inside me. I've got nothing to give back."

"Maybe. Maybe not." She thought of him throwing sticks for Grimm, rolling markers to Mason, taking her in his arms. *Let me just hold you, Poppy.* Freesias at play on her skin. A sleeping Mason on his chest. Silly conversations with his brother about krill.

She thought he could love more than he was aware, she thought he might have plenty to give. Neither changed what Ryan thought, though. "But like I learned a long time ago, you can't make someone care for another person."

"Poppy, I—"

And before he could finish the sentence, the front bell rang, the dog barked, Linus yelled something and then a sultry female voice vibrated through the house. "Darlings! The newlyweds have returned!"

CHAPTER TWENTY

To RYAN'S MIND, his friends couldn't have better timed their interruption, though he was surprised by their change of plans. "I thought you were intending a few more days in San Francisco before heading straight back to L.A.," he said to Grant as he helped cart Anabelle's pile of matched luggage into one of the guest rooms. "Christ, what does she have in these suitcases? Bricks?" He grimaced as he swung one bag onto the luggage rack he'd yanked from the closet.

Grant wiggled his brows. "No complaining. There's some very…inspirational lingerie in those bags."

"Since I assume I'm not going to see her in any of it, I get to grumble all I want."

"Isn't the delectable Poppy enough woman for you? If you ask me, she's…" Grant's voice trailed off, but the grin that sold millions of movie tickets every year spoke volumes.

Ryan pointed a finger at him. "No picturing Poppy in little nothings—or nothing at all, for that matter."

"Ho. So that *is* the way the wind blows. Linus hinted—"

"You've been talking to Linus?" Ryan frowned.

"It's March, man. Anabelle and I are your best friends. We can be concerned. When we caught wind of what was happening, we decided to check in."

"Well, as you see, your concerns are baseless."

Grant draped a garment bag over the back of a chair. "Poppy's made a new man out of you?"

"What do you think?"

His best friend eyed him. "Your temperament appears its usual sugar cubes and whipped cream."

"Yeah," Ryan muttered. "That's me, sweetness and light." But who would be happy given Poppy's disturbing revelation?

I've fallen in love with you, Ryan. And I'm pretty certain you don't want me to ask for what I want from you.... Which would be an April, by the way. And a May. Maybe a whole summer and another season after that. For me, and for you, and for Mason, I might even want a forever.

What was *wrong* with the woman? She was nuts if she thought Ryan could handle any of that. It worried him, it really did, that she walked around with all that emotion pinned to her sleeve. She'd get over these misbegotten feelings for him—likely brought on by a hailstorm and single-mother celibacy—but she was bound to get really hurt someday, so he was left to fret about the next man who'd come along, play with her heart a little and then pass out of her life.

Like he was going to do on April 1st.

April Fool's Day, a voice inside his head pointed out.

Of course, he had to admit, it was entirely possible some good man would find her at those cabins where she hid herself, four miles from the fucking highway, but...

But it had better not be Ivan the asshole with his cereal-stealer of a son. Or some other uncouth, bearded, mountain man. Worse yet though, it could be a smooth operator out of L.A., who would take her to bed and…

Leave her like Ryan was going to on April 1st.

April Fool's Day, that voice whispered again.

"What's going on in that thick skull of yours?" Grant demanded.

And because he didn't want to think about Poppy's confession anymore, let alone speak of it, Ryan told his friend about the blackmailing ex. It was testament to the odd turns of a famous life that Grant didn't even blink. "Of course, you refused to hand over a dime."

"Right."

"What *did* you do?"

He slid a look at his buddy. "You're so sure I made some move?"

"It took thirty seconds of me seeing you and Poppy together today—not to mention that wildfire of a kiss caught for posterity that Anabelle and I viewed twenty zillion times in our hotel room overlooking the Golden Gate—"

"Perverts."

"—to know there's something special going on between you two."

He wasn't addressing that remark. "I made a call to my attorney. He's got a private eye on retainer and between them they'll determine what I need to do to shut down Denny-the-Dick Howell."

"Sounds sensible."

"Yeah? I'd rather just beat the shit out of him." He headed for the door. "Don't tell Poppy, all right? She believes she can handle any and every situation by herself."

Grant followed him out of the bedroom. "Why can't these self-reliant, loner types ever see when they're wrong?" he murmured.

Behind his back, Ryan flipped his best friend the bird. "Shut up."

They joined the others in the family room. Anabelle sat beside Poppy, who held Mason on her lap. Linus had Charlie at his side, who seemed starstruck into a sudden shyness. But the actress wielded her usual charm and soon they were swapping funny stories—Anabelle about her San Francisco honeymoon and then the Walker women about small-town life.

Anabelle sighed. "I love it up here. I think we need to find a house in Blue Arrow, Grant."

"Sounds good to me." Seating himself on the arm of her chair he glanced over at Ryan. "Fancy us as neighbors?"

"You like this place? I'll give you a good deal on it."

At his impulsive offer, the room fell quiet.

Then Poppy was on her feet. "Excuse me." Taking Mason by the hand, she hurried away, Grimm following.

Everyone else turned as one toward Ryan, staring at him as if he'd just kicked something small and furry.

"What?"

Anabelle rolled her eyes. "Think. If you're leaping at the chance to get rid of your house…"

You're showing Poppy how quickly you also want to get rid of the memories you have of her in it.

Which was actually the case.

But, while true to his black, withered heart, was less

than she deserved. Ryan pinched the bridge of his nose. "Fucking March."

"Don't blame the month, you jerk," Anabelle said hotly. "Instead, take a look in the mirror."

Grant winced. "Babe—"

"No, she's right," Ryan said, pinching tighter. Hell, he wished he could make things better, smoother, simpler between him and Poppy, but since the beginning, and especially since the moment when he ran after her for that farewell kiss, he'd only created complications that tangled them tighter.

"You know what I think we all need?" Anabelle said after a moment. "Some fresh air. Why don't we head outside and we'll break out the goodies Grant and I bought in San Francisco?"

Her new husband smiled at her. "You're a brilliant woman."

Though Ryan didn't feel much like fresh air or anything else now that he'd insulted Poppy, he felt obligated to follow the group onto the terrace. He threw himself into a chair while Linus, Charlie, Grant and Anabelle descended the steps to the grass with their mysterious packages bound in butcher paper. Brooding, he watched them without seeing, until Poppy, Mason and Grimm suddenly appeared out of the woods.

Poppy looked as fresh as she always did, a small breeze tugging bright tendrils of hair from her usual braid so they danced around her exquisite face. Though she didn't appear any worse for wear, the thought of the blow he'd just delivered made his stomach roil. Tipping back his head, exhaustion rolled over him like a lead blanket. It was as if he hadn't slept in four years.

How the hell could he repair things with her if he didn't have the energy to get out of the chair?

A delighted squeal redirected his attention to the lawn below. Poppy's son was dancing around a trio of kites spread on the ground. One was in the shape of an airplane, another was an octopus, the third a butterfly. Ryan smiled a little at the kid's enthusiasm. Maybe Anabelle's idea *was* brilliant.

Except it turned out the assembled crowd had absolutely no idea how to get anything airborne. Charlie seemed to think she had the rudiments down, but all her short runs across the expanse of grass never got a single kite aloft. Grant proved to be equally inexpert, and Ryan was embarrassed for the Hamilton family name when Linus drove the plane on a straight, low flight into the trunk of a tree.

Good God. Someone had to save the situation.

He jogged down the terrace steps. "Give that to me," he said, snagging the octopus and the spool of kite string from Anabelle's hand.

Then he stilled a moment, determining the direction of the wind. With it at his back, he held up the kite, feeling the breeze's first tug. As the octopus hovered in place, he let the line play out and the creature flew higher, then higher. Glancing down, he saw Poppy's son was at his elbow. "Here, kid," he said, and handed over the spool.

"Me?" the boy said.

"Just hold on to it. You'll be fine." Ryan met Linus's gaze and nodded him over to supervise.

Grant, following Ryan's lead, had managed to get

the plane into the air. He grinned. "I have my man mojo back!"

That left only the butterfly. It had a wingspan of six feet and was a rainbow of colors. Using the same simple technique as before, Ryan launched the kite, watching as it rose, bright against the blue, blue sky. The sight dizzied him for a moment, and he blinked rapidly, trying to orient himself. His gaze dropped, and for the first time he noticed how…green the lawn had become. It was almost emerald now, vivid and healthy-looking. He traced it with his gaze, turning to admire how the thick carpet of it met the planters flanking the back steps. More color abounded there: what he remembered as green shoots were now yellow daffodils and pink tulips and some other spring-hued flowers he couldn't name.

And freesias. They nodded in the breeze as if acknowledging his notice.

They were beautiful.

He spun back, taking in the wide expanse of the lake. It spread before him, dappled with gold discs made by the sun that warmed his face. Taking a fortifying breath, he moved his gaze upward again, to that jewel-hued butterfly hovering above him.

Something stirred in his chest. He might have worried it was a heart attack, but there was no pain, only… awakening. The crushing exhaustion drained away and new vigor rushed through his bloodstream. He smelled growing things and clean water and they brought to life a seed that had been hiding, dormant, deep inside him.

As he breathed, he felt that seed begin to grow. Was it contentment? Satisfaction? Or…happiness.

God. In this moment, it seemed he was happy.

Surrounded by natural beauty, family, friends, he felt gratitude, too. For the first time in four years, he felt an appreciation for his five senses and the carbon shell that housed them.

For the first time in four years, Ryan Hamilton was grateful to be alive.

Afraid the feeling was too fragile to survive, he moved gingerly through the rest of the day. He remained on the periphery of the group, second-by-second assessing if the new energy and new appreciation were dissipating. As the day wore on, however, both stayed steady and strong, rejuvenating him.

A couple of days of this, he thought, and he'd find the right words to say to Poppy. He could communicate how much she'd meant to him and how sorry he was that it could never be anything more. Never anything in April.

Lost in thought, he didn't join in the dinner conversation. He didn't notice anything about it really, until a charged silence settled around the dining room table. He blinked, then ran his gaze around the now-quiet company.

"What?" he asked. "What is it?"

Poppy folded her napkin and placed it beside her plate. "I just told everyone that Mason and I are taking off tomorrow. Mackenzie's coming for us in the afternoon."

He frowned. "But it's not—"

"April. I know. But you've got your friends here and…"

And he'd made her feel unwelcome. But he needed more time to make amends for that. More time to get his head together so he could say the exact right thing. "Poppy—"

"I've made up my mind."

From the look on her face, he wouldn't get his chance. "But Mommy…"

Ryan shifted his attention to the kid. Maybe his protest would change her intentions.

"You said we could have a goodbye party. With cake and everything."

Grant perked up. "I like the way Mason thinks."

Poppy pushed a tendril of hair behind her ear, looking flustered. "It's a little custom we have…inventing reasons to have a party."

"Please, Mommy," her son said.

She hesitated, then gave in with a little sigh. "I suppose."

Grant smiled the smile that launched a thousand tabloid covers. "Cake and everything," he said, his gaze sliding to Ryan. "Like a real celebration."

Woo-hoo, Ryan thought, pressing the heel of his hand to his temple. A party to salute her leaving him before he could find a way to make things right. A celebration to commemorate another March he'd royally fucked up.

LATER THAT NIGHT, a mouthwatering scent drew Ryan from his rooms. He was unsurprised to find Poppy in the big kitchen, looking like something edible herself in pale pink pajama pants and matching tank top. The socks on her feet were printed with fat lambs. He leaned one shoulder against the wall, watching as she moved between refrigerator, pantry and counter. Two layers of a cake sat on separate racks while she used a spatula to move butter from its paper wrapping to a metal bowl. Powdered sugar went on top of that, then she stilled, her body language making clear she sensed someone behind her.

"Ryan."

She knew it was him without looking.

It was like that for him, too, his body aware when she was near. He walked into the room, approaching her from behind as she continued to work with the ingredients on the granite top. A glass measuring cup hit the counter with a sharp crack, and it was the sound of his best intentions fracturing. Sure, he should be keeping his distance because he still didn't have the words to make things right. But in this moment, like always, he couldn't stay away.

"Do you think aliens abducted us from our cabins that first night?" he asked.

"What?"

"It could have happened. I read a script with just such a premise. Hapless male and female leads are asleep in their solitary beds when they're beamed up to the mother ship. The extraterrestrials mess with their chemistry to see if they can stimulate an insatiable attraction."

"How does that work out?"

"Not so good. They unwittingly cause a love triangle when one of the aliens is affected by the mind control they're using on the humans. Think *Men in Black* meets *Twilight*."

She stole a glance at him over her shoulder. "Is there a happy ending?"

"You decide. In an attempt to break up the human

pair, the alien part of the triangle destroys the lab equip-ment that controls the experiment, which in turn causes an explosion that takes out the entire mother ship and all those in it. The next morning, hero and heroine wake up, realize they no longer feel the pull, and return to their pre-abduction, unpaired lives." When she didn't comment, he offered his own analysis. "Lame."

"I don't know." She was stirring the concoction in the bowl. "The alien's pretty cool. It tried to change things."

"You're right. No status quo for ol' Scaley."

"Ew. That was its name?"

"How it looked." He came close enough to peer at what she was blending. "Vanilla frosting?"

"French buttercream." Then she shot him a warning look. "Don't touch."

As if there was any choice now. He swooped in a finger, took it to his mouth. Butter and sugar melted on his tongue. "Good. I want more."

"Control your insatiable appetite, mister," she said, sidestepping to move herself and her bowl farther down the counter. "Don't force me to destroy the mother ship."

Bemused, he watched her whip the frosting a few more times, then pick up a new utensil to efficiently begin icing the cake. Had she recast the tale? Putting herself in the role of the extraterrestrial? Maybe so. He'd always seen her as something otherworldly—a flower fairy or a wood nymph.

That left him as the male human lead...with who as his human counterpart?

Or...what.

You seem to think you're just fine living with no one besides your ghosts and your grief.

"Here," she said, sending the bowl on a slide down the counter.

His hand caught it reflexively.

"You can have the rest." She came close enough to present him a wooden spoon.

She came close enough for him to see how his nearness affected her. As had happened so many times before, a blush infused the fine-pored surface of her face. Her breath quickened and when her gaze lifted to his, her pupils were already dilated.

His own arousal surged in reaction and he went hard, just like that. To keep her near, he caught her upper arm. She trembled in his hold and her visceral responses made him feel strong and weak and everything in between. "Poppy," he said, feeling more desperate for her than ever.

Her gaze shifted from his eyes to his mouth and back again.

Then he spoke the only words that came to mind. "One last night."

In the tense pause that followed, planets collided, worlds went to war, new galaxies formed. His ears were so full of its cacophony, he could only read her lips.

"One last night."

POPPY LEFT THE kitchen with Ryan, intentionally leaving second and third thoughts behind. He hadn't responded to her "I'm in love with you," with anything close to the same—but she hadn't expected that. Later, his remark about selling the lake house had stung—but she'd never expected to see him again after this month ended, anyway.

So this was it. This was the last chance for her to be with the man who'd shown her a single mother was still a woman. And she was going to revel in it.

Ryan directed her to take a turn in the hallway, with one hand at the small of her back. It raced hot chills up her spine and made her wonder again about the bowl of leftover icing he was carrying.

She stole a glance at it. Surely… "Um, what's with the bowl?"

The look he returned was smoldering, the blue of his eyes that inner-flame shade that made her insides turn to jelly.

"Ryan…"

He put the icing on the bedside table, twitched back the covers to reveal the soft sheets, then he turned to her. One hand slid down her back to cup her bottom, the other tilted her face as he bent his head for a searing kiss. His tongue drove into her mouth and she welcomed it with her own, any last thoughts lost in the lavish exchange. He drew back for air. "You were saying?"

"Um…"

Whatever protest she might have made was lost in the cotton of her sleep tank as he pulled it over her head. His fingers found the fastener at the end of her braid and he pulled it free so that he could fluff her hair around her shoulders. "You're so beautiful," he whispered, gazing at her face.

She clutched the sides of his T-shirt and brought herself to tiptoe, pressing her lips to his, taking for herself another kiss. His palms slid beneath the waistband of her pajama bottoms, angling her hips into the aggressive jut of his sex.

Its heat, its hardness, made her shiver. His mouth took over the kiss and she let her head fall back, going dizzy with want of him.

He used her giddiness to get her full naked and then she was on the bed and he was naked, too, except for a wicked glint in his eyes and the bowl of icing in his hand. She scrambled across the cotton, a giggle bubbling in her chest. "Keep that away from me. You'll... you'll get the sheets all sticky."

He shook his head. "Only if you keep moving around. Poppy, stretch out and stay still."

"Oh, Ryan, no—" But the protest stopped on a gasp as he brushed a fingerful of the sugary stuff on the tip of her breast. His mouth followed, and she dropped her head to the pillow as the heated suction produced exquisite pleasure that mimicked the strong pulls of his lips. When he performed the same act on her other nipple, she curled her nails into her palms to keep from begging.

He gave her what she wanted, anyway.

"It's like finger painting." He drew a design on her belly. "Or invisible ink," he said, following the pattern with his tongue to lick it away.

She tried to take her turn at the game, but he refused to allow her access to the icing. "It's all mine," he murmured. "One last night, you're all mine."

Then he took her mouth with another kiss, the sweetness of it almost unbearable. Poppy wrapped her arms around his neck and gave herself over to the sensation, the moment, the man. He pulled away and dipped his finger once more into the bowl.

He drew it over her skin, making lazy shapes, tight

circles, wide parabolas. She wondered if it might be a sorcerer's spell, a magician's runes set on fire by the light in his supernatural eyes. Was it an incantation he was murmuring? But no, they were normal words. *You're so pretty, sexy girl. You feel so good to me. Be still, be still, I have important business to do.*

"What business?" she asked, breathless, as she once again tried to pull him over her, into her.

"I'm drawing you pictures," he said. "I'm telling you stories."

His seductive voice made every cell of her body tingle. She felt open to him everywhere and she watched through half-closed eyes as he marked her with that gentle touch and insistent tongue. With a finger, he scooped inside the bowl one last time and then set it aside.

His gaze on her face, he came between her legs, bending one knee flat to the mattress, opening her to place the final dollop on her private flesh. She flinched, her sex so sensitive that just one stroke brought her to the brink. Then his mouth was there and she was sure she'd go over with the first touch, but he licked at the sugary paste with such delicate strokes that another flush layered over her heated skin and the arousal was pushed higher. And higher.

Poppy was visibly trembling as Ryan continued to pleasure her, his tongue becoming more insistent, his mouth moving over the soft, wet, pleated flesh. Her fingers found purchase on the sheets as she lifted into the goodness of it, and then he speared two fingers into her and she arched, shuddering with spasms of incredible, bewitching bliss.

He stayed with her through every pulse, his mouth

easing her through several more mini-explosions. Then he was over her, a condom on, his expression anything but playful. He looked down at her, his chiseled face so handsome it almost hurt to look at him. Shadows hollowed his cheekbones and the dark grit of beard roughened his chin. This was Ryan of the winter, a man of long, dark nights, of black demons, of barren landscapes. The one she'd first met who had both frightened and attracted her at the same time. But now she took him in her arms and welcomed him into her body, tightening herself around his deep thrust. He grunted, pressing his bristly cheek to hers as he retreated and drove himself in her again.

His body was heavy on her, he was all male, with thick bone and burning skin and she wrapped her legs around his hips to bind her to him. Perhaps he sensed her purpose, because he lifted his head, those hot-blue eyes boring into hers. His body kept pounding into hers and he gasped between words. "Tell me…tell me something back."

One hot tear rolled from her lashes toward her temple as she realized what he was asking for. He wasn't looking for another confession. It was absolution he wanted.

Poppy hesitated, and then…then she realized how much of a giver she could be. Because in this moment she wanted to shower him with all he needed, no matter what the cost to herself. Closing her eyes, she pictured herself tossing handfuls of love at him as if they were bunches of dandelion fluff. She saw little white parachutes drifting down around him.

And then she told him exactly what he wanted to hear.

"Come April, I won't love you anymore."

The gratitude in his gaze made the lie worth it. The man lived with enough pain.

CHAPTER TWENTY-ONE

HANDS IN HIS jean pockets, Ryan gazed out the windows toward the lake. Sun streamed through the panes, brightening the pale yellow of the family room walls. Outside, the sky was a sharp blue and as he watched, he saw Linus cutting through the water in the white-and-red Hurricane inboard-outboard on his approach to the dock. They'd elected to liberate the boat from storage at the marina today, and anticipating himself behind the wheel later, speeding through the light chop, poured a caffeinelike buzz of eagerness through Ryan's veins.

Whoa, he thought, surprised by the thrill of anticipation.

Yesterday, while kite-flying, of all things, he'd experienced a sudden burst of exhilaration and now this. Even aware that Poppy would soon defect wasn't quashing these new feelings. Maybe because after she'd spent the night in his bed, they'd come to a resolution of their relationship.

Come April, she'd said, *I won't love you anymore.*

Because it was for the best, he was choosing to believe her. After all, the end had been foregone from the beginning, so he was going to go with the flow and just enjoy the hell out of these last hours. As Linus walked up from the dock, his arms full of grocery bags, Grimm came loping from the woods to greet him. Besides getting the boat from the marina, his brother had been instructed to make a grocery run, and on the list were hot dogs, hamburgers, buns and chips. Grant considered himself the king of the 'cue—his words—and intended to do the grilling.

At the sound of female laughter floating from the kitchen, Ryan cocked his head. The women were making side dishes.

On his way to check on their progress, he froze at the threshold. Tears were streaming down Poppy's cheeks. Alarm had him leaping forward. "Sweetheart!" What had happened? Who had hurt her? He glared at Charlie, then Anabelle, then grasped the truth of the situation, almost falling on his ass as he halted his headlong run.

"I…uh…" With a sheepish shake of his head, he was forced to address the three women staring at him in concern. Gesturing toward the mountain of onion in front of the prettiest woman in the room, he slipped onto one of the bar stools. "I thought you were upset about something, Poppy."

She blotted her cheeks with a napkin as the actress chopping potatoes beside her slid him a sly smile. "That's so…caring," Anabelle said.

He sent her a quelling look. "Look at you. I've never seen you wield a kitchen knife except in that teen slasher movie that was your debut."

"Take that back," his best friend's wife protested. "I was just telling your mountain girl that we don't live the kind of rarefied existence she might imagine." Anabelle turned to Poppy, who was scooping the diced onion into an immense glass serving bowl. "That whole

Hollywood clubbing lifestyle—not us, at least not any-more. We have a small, close circle of friends, includ-ing that ugly guy over there, and we conduct ourselves like real people."

"Real people who have a thousand pairs of shoes in their closet," Ryan said, "half of which I think I lugged into your bedroom yesterday."

"Not a thousand!"

Charlie dumped a handful of sliced celery into the glass bowl. "I saw it on a celebrity lifestyle show. They were filming in your closet. And counting. At least a thousand."

"Complete fabrication," Anabelle said, waving a hand. "Charlie, we'll have you and Linus over, and you'll see."

The younger woman beamed a shy smile. "Yes? You really think I'll fit in?"

"Of course. We'll make sure of it."

Poppy observed the interaction, clearly pleased her cousin had found a champion. Though Charlie would be fine; his brother was a goner for the woman, so Linus would never make it less than so. Poppy would thrive down the mountain, too, he thought. Why not? He could see her on the deck of his house in Laurel Canyon, sur-rounded by eucalyptus, fan palms, scarlet bougainvil-lea and the white-starred jasmine. He'd build a fire for her in the clay chimenea, and as night fell they'd watch it burn down to glowing embers before heading inside.

"Look out, Duke!"

Her son's voice shook him free of the vision. He lifted his feet so they didn't impede the trajectory of the soccer ball the boy was chasing. Grimm tagged behind, pausing a moment to swipe Ryan's hand with a long pink tongue as he galloped by.

There was room for that pair at the Laurel Canyon house, too. The dog would sprawl on the terra cotta tile floor in the kitchen, always in everyone's way. The blue guest room across from the master could be turned into a boy's hideaway—

God. That was never going to happen. There would be no Poppy. No dog. Absolutely no boy.

Disturbed by the path his mind had been wandering, Ryan exited the kitchen and headed outside. Grant had rolled the grill onto the lawn near the lake, and he now wore a neon bib apron proclaiming I Play With Meat. Linus showed up, and between the three of them they pulled chaise lounges and an umbrella table and chairs from a storage locker and arranged them on the grass. With a broom and a rag, Ryan made sure to eradicate any eight-legged invaders.

Linus suggested they set the kites aloft again, and Ryan took that to be his job. Poppy's son came out onto the grass to watch the launches. Staring upward, the kid shoved his little hands in his little pockets. "It's been good knowing you, Duke," he said, like he was thirty and they'd been on an assignment together that had now reached its conclusion.

The sun glinted off the kid's blond hair, the brightness making Ryan's eyes sting. "Uh, it's been good knowing you, too. You stay on the job for your mom, all right? Look after her. She doesn't think she needs anybody."

The boy nodded. "We're Walkers, we're tough," he said, then wandered away.

Ryan remained where he was, head tilted back to watch the bright shapes flying.

His brother strolled up, nudged him with an elbow. "How you doing?"

Ryan looked over, lifting a brow.

"We're coming down to the wire."

Did he mean to the anniversary of Tate's death or to the moment of Poppy's leave-taking? He didn't want to dwell on either. "Let's not go there." He returned his gaze to the kites, watching the butterfly dip and twirl in the breeze. "I'm not thinking of calendars. Just taking pleasure in this, moment by moment."

He stuck to that as the day wore on. The entire group—except Grimm—donned sunscreen, sweatshirts and hats and took a cruise around the lake. There were plenty of other boaters out enjoying the balmy spring day and after Ryan tired of driving, Linus set Poppy's son on his lap, allowing him to act as captain. Then it was time for lunch, and they clambered back to the grass, where they filled up on picnic fare.

Afterward, Linus and Charlie stretched out on one double-wide chaise, Grant and Anabelle on the other. Earlier, they'd retrieved a bocce ball set from storage, as well, and Poppy and her son played a pre-K version of the game. Ryan lay on the grass, dozing in the sun.

He drifted into a dream where he was once again at the Laurel Canyon house. It was dark, and he was walking around the interior, securing it for the evening. A night-light glowed in the bedroom across from his but he bypassed that door to push open his own. Poppy was propped up in pillows on the bed, reading. As he stood there, dumbly taking her in, she looked up from her book. Smiled.

His breath caught, his heart expanded in his chest, euphoria rushed like a flash flood through his blood.

Then a hand was shaking him awake. "Wha—?" He opened his eyes, the sun nearly blinding him.

"Cake's been served," Linus said.

Sitting up, he pushed away the sense of disappointment. *Relish this moment by moment.* The others were gathered around the table, paper plates in hand. Ryan took up his own, inspecting the baked layers. Their slight pink cast reminded him of Poppy's blush.

He glanced up, saw her looking back, though she quickly redirected her gaze. "It's strawberry cake," she said to everyone. "Mason's favorite."

Her boy was already digging in. The rest of the group followed, accompanied by *mmm*s and groans of appreciation. "Love the frosting," Linus added. "Delicious."

"Agreed," Ryan said, and this time Poppy's eyes didn't shy away from his, though he could see that telltale color on her cheeks. He tried messaging her through their shared connection. *I'm sorry I couldn't be more for you.*

She smiled, gave a little nod, and his flagging mood lifted again. It was a beautiful day. A beautiful moment. Nothing was over yet.

Then he felt a tug on the hem of his T-shirt. The kid stood at his side, his big blues latched onto Ryan's face. "I made you something, Duke."

"Yeah?" He noticed there was a folded sheet of paper in his hand. "Another map?"

"No," the boy said, holding it out.

Setting down his cake plate, he sent Poppy another look. When she shrugged, indicating she was out of the loop, he inspected the front side. It was more marker-work, bright colors and shapes. Kites? Or balloons, maybe. Then he opened the sheet.

Inside were words that were like an elephant kick to the gut.

A solar eclipse occurred as he stared at them. The day turned dark and cold, mirroring what was happening inside him. A shudder wracked his body, his bones rattling beneath his clammy skin.

Linus said, "Ry...?"

The child's voice piped through the high whine in his ears. "I copied the letters from a book we have. I heard Charlie and Linus talking about your boy. It's his day. I know he's not here, but we can make this party be for him, right, Mommy?"

"Oh, Mason." Poppy's voice sounded thick with tears. "What did you do?"

"I made Duke's boy a card."

As Ryan stared down at it, the childish print wavered, distorting the uneven letters spelling out Happy Birthday Tate!

The kid kept talking. "Because everybody should have a celebration on their day."

RYAN RETREATED TO the farthest corner of the basement, his back to the wall, his ass on one of the boxing mats. Grief ravaged his insides like a monster, with snapping teeth and swiping claws. He didn't flinch, he didn't scream, he sat through the savagery dry-eyed. *Tate*.

His mind had skipped over the significance of the

date. For the past four years, the next day's tragic anniversary had overshadowed it. When it came to misery, March 31st became the one day to rule them all.

Something changed in the big room. Ryan's skin prickled in awareness. Poppy. His inner radar recognized her before she came into sight.

Her feet were silent as she crossed the foam, Grimm at her heels. Ryan rested the back of his head against the wall and watched her approach.

She stopped before him, her soft mouth turned down, her big gray eyes moving from the birthday card discarded on the mat beside him to his face. "I'm so sorry," she said. "I had no idea. Linus and Charlie feel terrible. They didn't realize he overheard all of that about Tate. They told him how to spell his name."

"Adults forget kids have ears."

Her tongue ran over her bottom lip. "What can I do?"

"Just go away, Poppy." He didn't say it unkindly.

Instead of obeying, she crouched near his feet. "Please, let's talk. Tell me—"

"I won't put any of what's in my head in yours."

"Ryan." She touched his shin with light fingers, but he could feel their warmth through the denim of his jeans. "Don't play the hero with me."

"No." Pressing the heels of his hands to his eyes, he tried to block her and that word from his mind. "Don't say that." *God.* Hero.

"Ryan—"

"Go, Poppy. Go away." He felt his hold on himself unraveling. "Just get the fuck away from me."

"Bottling it inside isn't working." She moved, settling

on the mat beside him and the dog flopped nearby, too. "Talk, wail, screech, whatever you need. I can take it."

Her shoulder brushed his, and damn him, the scent of her shampoo made him want to bury his face in her hair. But he had nothing to offer in return. He'd siphon away her sweetness and it would get lost forever in the bleak landscape inside of him. Her warm, generous spirit would be swallowed up by his ice and gloom.

"Listen to me," she said. "You're a good man."

Her words tipped him from resignation to near-rage. "There you go again," he said, his voice harsh. "Good man. Hero. Get that out of your brain."

"Ryan…" She laid a soothing hand on his arm.

He brushed it away. "You have no idea what I am, what I became when I had to watch over my child in that hospital bed, see him with a breathing tube, a feeding tube, forty-five percent of his skin burned."

"Oh, Ryan." Her voice was filled with compassion.

It only tore at him more. "I never saw his eyes open again. They kept him in a medically induced coma because that much damage causes so much…so much pain."

She ducked her head.

But he wasn't having that. She'd wanted him to talk this out? Then she'd hear it all. Grasping her chin, he turned her eyes to his. "For thirty days I was terrified he wouldn't wake up. For thirty days I was just as terrified he would. Do you still think I'm some kind of hero?"

"Yes," she whispered.

He made a sound of frustration. "Would a hero feel so damn helpless?"

She stroked the hand still cupped around her face. "Of course."

The monster went to work inside him again, slicing, dicing, wreaking havoc. His fingers tightened on Poppy and he saw her flinch, then hold steady. So fucking brave, willing to be this close to the ogre that was him. So fucking bright and bighearted.

And he was so mean, he suddenly wanted to lay waste to it all. He wanted to turn her into barren, frozen ground like him. Smash her hope. Crush her idealism.

More so, even, when she fixed those big gray eyes to his and said, "I'm a parent. I know you have to be a hero to survive the greatest loss of all."

Destroy every ounce of her optimism.

"Oh, yeah?" He sneered at her. "You think? You think that a man is a hero when one of those doctors approaches, coming down a fucking endless corridor, her white coat whispering, whispering, and when she stands before him and tells him that his precious son's heart no longer beats, do you think that a hero would feel…would feel…" The word got stuck in his throat, choking him.

He hoped to die.

"Relief?" Poppy asked. "Did you feel relief?"

God help him. Somebody help him. "Yes," Ryan confessed, snatching his hand from her face and closing his eyes. "*Yes*. Would a hero feel relief?"

"Oh, Ryan." Her voice was hoarse. "You're also human, you know. It's human to want to spare your child such anguish."

"It emptied me out. There's nothing inside me." But the monster. Even it was receding now, too, though having exacted this year's punishment to great effect. Exhausted, he let his head fall back against the wall.

"Maybe…maybe something, someone, will come along. Fill you up again. Remind you what it is to love."

Really? He rolled his head to look at her, unsure if he should laugh or rap her skull with his knuckles to jostle some sense into her. She still was thinking in rainbows and unicorns? "Love, Poppy? Foolish girl, you've got to know I'll make sure that never, ever happens."

She stared at him for a long moment. Then he saw the truth dawn over her face. *It's good she's wised up,* he told himself. *It's good she understands I'm a hopeless case.*

Her gaze still on his face, she got to her feet and Grimm clambered up, as well. "I guess this is goodbye, then."

"Yeah. I guess this is."

As she turned and headed for the stairs, her dog at her side, Ryan's future descended. One of bleak silences and endless nights. A life empty of Poppy's smiles, her blushes, her spring.

The last he saw of her was a flutter of the sunny yellow ribbon tying off her hair.

A new record, he thought dully. Worst March ever—because this time he'd hurt someone besides himself.

POPPY STOMPED UP the stairs, angry at herself. She ached for Ryan's misplaced guilt and irreparable loss, but she should have played out the scene better. What she'd wanted was to comfort him, to ease him, but instead she'd forced him into a declaration.

Love, Poppy? Foolish girl, you've got to know I'll make sure that never, ever happens.

She understood that he felt empty, but it was a much bigger problem if he welcomed it, even wished it for himself. Yanking at her braid, she stood at the top of the stairs, torn. Think. *Think!*

Would it work if she marched herself back downstairs to confront him once again? And then what? Tell him she'd lied the night before and that she'd love him in April and in summer, in autumn and when winter came again?

He didn't want love.

And he didn't want her.

A sharp pain pierced her breastbone. Pressing her fist there, she breathed through the waves of hurt. No, she thought, refusing to surrender. No. *I'm not giving up just yet.*

She'd been wrong to lie to him the night before. And she'd be wrong if she left now, she decided, heading for the kitchen to find her purse and her phone. After a quick check on Mason, she'd call her sister and postpone the pickup. Then she'd find her way through this.

The French doors to the terrace opened, and Mac, Shay and Brett moved inside. Poppy stared. All of them? And early? *Damn.*

"You're here," she said.

"Barely," Mac said. "The photographers are still at the gates."

"More than before, now that Grant and Anabelle have arrived."

"We just met Granabelle," Mac said, wiggling her brows. "Shay's starry-eyed."

"I am not," their sister retorted, frowning. "I'm not taken in by—"

"So what's with the family reunion?" Poppy asked, interrupting the impending squabble.

"Always the peacemaker," Brett murmured, then shoved his hands in his pockets. "We thought we might need an entire posse to rescue you from the clutches of your desperado."

Poppy narrowed her gaze at her brother. "He's no villain." *Would a hero feel so helpless?* Ryan had asked, his voice rough, his expression desolate. *Would a hero feel relief?* Remembering, hot pressure formed behind her eyes.

Shay stepped up and put her hand on Poppy's shoulder. "What's going on? Are you all right?"

"S-sure." Pushing the back of her hand under her nose, she managed to suppress the tears. "I'm fine."

Brett cursed under his breath. "You knucklehead," he said, exasperation and affection twined in his voice. "What has your soft heart gone and done now?"

Be honest with them. Ryan's voice, again in her ear. *Tell them what you want.*

Mac's brows drew together. "Little sister, what is it you need?"

Tell them what you want. "What I need, what I want, is all of you," Poppy said, her gaze traveling over their faces. "I need you at the resort, with me, behind me, beside me, helping me make it something our family can be proud of."

Brett groaned. "Poppy—"

"I may be a soft-hearted knucklehead," she said, glaring at her brother. "But I'm *your* soft-hearted knucklehead, *your* cock-eyed optimist. I'm the glue who's willing to go all the way to hold this family together."

"We're already a family—"

"That three out of four of us share a cynical streak as treacherous as a black diamond ski run doesn't make us a family."

Her brother frowned. "Hey—"

"That three out of four of us are unreasonable Negative Nellies—"

Mac elbowed Brett. "She called you Nellie, big guy."

"—doesn't make us a family."

He scowled. "Fine. But we don't need that land—"

"We need that land," Poppy insisted. "We need those cabins. We need to work together to be the Walkers. We have a legacy, and I'm holding on to it with every stubborn bone in my body."

Brett shook his head. "It's a shame that the ones who lack common sense are always the most mulish."

Mac shoved his shoulder with the flat of her hand. "Knock it off. Are you serious, Poppy? You've been Miss Prickly about this and everything else. Miss Independent."

"Because...because when Mason arrived I had to prove to everybody, including myself, that I could handle the situation I got myself into. I'm a good mom, I know that now, so I don't have to be afraid anymore to ask for help." She looked at Brett. "Help." And then at Shay. "Help." Finally, she turned to Mac and reached out her hand. "Help me do something about our heritage."

Her older sister stared at Poppy's fingers. Then her own hand rose. "I—"

Charlie burst through the French doors. "Poppy!" A leaf was caught in her short hair and her eyes were saucer-wide. "Poppy, we can't find Mason!"

CHAPTER TWENTY-TWO

AT THE SOUND of slamming doors upstairs, Ryan's head lifted from his knees. Then heavy footsteps pounded down the stairway to the basement and the cloud of gloom hovering over him drew lower. He slowly stood, moving through its inkiness as his brother ran into the room with disheveled hair and distress written all over his face.

Fear clutched at Ryan's belly. "What is it?"

Linus panted. "Mason's lost."

"What?"

"He was out on the lawn with us when you went inside, then Poppy and Grimm. I swear, Ry, he was there one minute and then…he wasn't."

"Shit." His mind leaped to the worst possible scenario. "Did you check the lake—"

"First thing. Grant inspected the water, the dock, the boat. We don't think he's been that way."

"Okay." Ryan told himself to stay calm. Kids had a way of wandering off in the blink of an eye. "C'mon," he said, but when he made for the stairs, he started running.

In the office, he flung open the security cabinet doors and keyed up the images on the monitors. Front gate, paps gathered there. Dock, the boat bobbing up and down. Camera focused on the woods to the south, showed no boy. North woods, the same. "I wish I'd set these up to record," he muttered, then his gaze went to the video feed of the lawn, where Poppy and everyone else was fanning out toward the trees. "Go get Poppy, will you? Make her come inside."

"Me?" Linus said. "At this moment you can't tell that woman anything."

Instead of arguing, Ryan went back to running. He tore along the hall to the terrace and raced down the stone steps. If her son was hurt…or worse, he didn't want her to be the one finding him. Under the soaring kites, he caught up with her. His hand grasped her arm and turned her toward him.

Her pale cheeks and the wild expression in her eyes hit him like a blow. She stared at him. "Ryan, he's missing," she said.

"I know, baby." He cupped her face in his hands. "We'll find him for you. Go inside until we do."

She shook her head, golden tendrils dancing over her wide brow. "I have to look for him."

"No—"

"He's my everything," she said, her voice tight. "He's my only."

Ryan closed his eyes, her desperation squeezing his withered heart. Didn't he know this pain all too well? "All right, sweetheart," he said, taking her cold fingers in a firm grip, lacing them with his. "We'll find him together."

"Ry." Grant stood at his elbow. "Let the paps help."

He glanced over. "What?"

"Unlock the gates. Let 'em in. They can search, too."

Poppy was already tugging on him, straining for the trees. "Okay," he said over his shoulder. "Keep them to the front, though, will you? Take Linus or Brett for backup. Watch them like hawks."

"Come on," Poppy urged. "The women are going to the other side of the woods. This one's ours."

It was cooler in the shade of the conifers. Poppy shivered and he slid an arm around her shoulders. But she shrugged free as they worked their way around tall trunks and looked under deep sweeps of evergreen branches. "Mason!" she called. "Mason, come to Mommy!"

Grimm seemed up to the task, as well. Instead of his usual exuberant gambol, he crisscrossed the area with purpose, sniffing at piles of leaves and around tumbled boulders. Squirrels skittered up trees. Birds flew to higher reaches.

No small boy appeared.

"Mason!" Poppy called, her voice hoarse. "Mason! Mommy's waiting!"

Frustration mounting, Ryan kicked at a mound of dried pine needles, scattering them and a gathering of industrious ants. He cupped his hands around his mouth. "Mason! It's Duke! Yell if you can hear me! *Mason!*"

Poppy halted to stare at him. There was a streak of dirt on her cheek and more of it dusting her hair. Even in her worry, he didn't think he'd ever seen a woman so beautiful. "What?" he asked, when she continued to gape. "Why are you looking at me like that?"

"You've never said his name before," she whispered.

He frowned at her. "Sure I have."

"No." Then she shook herself and started forward again. "Mason!"

Ryan joined his voice to hers. "Mason!"

Three minutes later, his phone buzzed in his pocket. His eye on Poppy, moving ahead of him, he put it to his ear. "Did you find him?"

"No." Linus's voice. "But we found someone else who shouldn't be here."

Emerging from the woods, Poppy and Grimm at his side, Ryan saw Linus, Brett and Grant on the grass, the last two each grasping one of Denny Howell's arms. The blond man's expression was a combination of rebellion and sulkiness. Thirteen didn't look good on a guy heading past thirty. When his gaze lit on Poppy, he struggled against the other men's hold. "You should have done what I said, Poppy," he called out.

Ryan saw red. He strode up to the asshole and fisted his hand in the guy's shirt. "What the hell are you doing here? I made it clear yesterday—"

"He came for Mason," Brett said.

Poppy gasped. "What did you do with him?" She looked about her. "Where is he?"

"I told you I wanted him to visit my mother," Denny said. "Or get your boyfriend to hand over fifty grand. So when he refused—"

"Don't you blame this on Ryan!" Poppy said hotly. She marched up and pushed Ryan aside. Now her small fingers curled in Denny's thermal. *"Where is my son?"* she asked, in lethal tones.

Her ex tried leaning away from her, but she held fast. "I don't know, okay? I was waiting in the woods, you know, looking for my chance to…to talk to him—"

"You mean kidnap," Grant said.

Denny slid a furtive glance toward the guy who'd played a CIA assassin in his last movie. "I was just planning to ask him if he wanted to go for a ride."

Poppy narrowed her eyes until they were slices of smoke. "My son would never go off with a stranger."

"He didn't," Grant said.

A little smile curved Brett's mouth. "Kid's a Walker, through and through. According to Denny, here, when he tried to snatch him, Mace punched him in the stomach, kicked him in the knee and managed to run off."

"Where?" Ryan demanded. "Which way?"

"I didn't notice," Denny said sullenly. "It's like that kid's some sort of kickboxing ninja. Never seen anything like it."

"Good for him," Ryan said, thinking of all the workouts the boy had witnessed in the basement.

Poppy released her ex's shirt. "We've got to get back to searching."

"Just one thing first," Ryan said, and looked at Brett and Grant. "Let him go for a moment, will you?"

They complied.

Denny, his wary gaze on Ryan's face took a step away, in Brett's direction. Poppy's brother responded by shoving the guy toward Ryan. "I don't want any trouble," the ex said, whining as he stumbled.

"Too late," Ryan replied, then punched the jerk in the face.

Denny windmilled back and would have gone down if Brett hadn't caught him under the arms. "I think I should have done that," Poppy's brother complained.

"Or me," Poppy said, and then before any of them could blink, she stepped up and kicked Denny Howell, wanna-be kidnapper and deadbeat dad, straight in the balls.

Those sheepskin boots must pack more of an umph than at first glance, because the man let out a small shriek, then crumpled. Brett let him fall this time, his shocked expression saying it was more by surprise than design. Ryan loomed over the man lying on the ground, his knees drawn up. Blood oozed from a cut on his mouth and he was cupping his groin.

"*That's* the woman you left behind," Ryan told him. "I hope you regret it for the rest of your sorry life."

Then he glanced at Poppy, who was already running back into the woods, Linus at her side. "Mason!" she was yelling again as she gained the trees. "Mason, Mommy needs you." The yellow ribbon at the end of her braid fluttered in the breeze before she was lost in the shadows.

"I think I've underestimated her badly. She can be mean," Brett said, then started after his sister. He threw a look over his shoulder. "You coming?"

Ryan's gaze was focused on the last place he'd seen Poppy before she disappeared. In his mind's eye, he saw that rippling yellow ribbon. Then it morphed into a yellow marker line on a sheet of paper that was covered with green trees, a blue lake, tall mountains.

Yellow escape routes, Ryan thought. Red *X*'s marking the hiding places.

Spinning toward the house, he called back to the other man. "I've got an idea. Keep going, I'll be in touch."

RYAN EMERGED FROM the house in mere minutes, a sheaf of papers in hand. Grant stood on the lawn, his head close to Anabelle's. "Any luck?" he asked his best friend's wife as he approached.

"No." She grimaced. "Not yet."

Ryan glanced around. "Denny take off?"

"If you call limping away with his hands cuddling his dick 'taking off,'" Grant said. "I figured you'd be okay with that."

Ryan nodded. "Lawyer will do the rest, cops if that doesn't work." Then another thought struck. "What about the paps?"

"I'm keeping them happy," Anabelle said, as she struck a pose, then relaxed. "They're still working the front of the estate in exchange for a few shots of my newlywedded self."

"Thanks," Ryan said, and passed some of the sheets he'd carried to his friends. "Can you guys get these to the others?"

Grant turned the ones he held this way and that as if trying to make sense of them.

"Maps," Ryan explained. "Mason makes them for me all the time. Those yellow lines are escape routes. A red X designates a hiding place. Maybe one of them will lead us to him."

Grant glanced up. "You've saved all these?"

"Of course."

Shaking his head, Grant exchanged a look with Anabelle. "Huh. Weird."

"You talk to me when there's some little Granabelles running around. You'll be saving artwork, too."

"Huh," Grant said again, and he shot his wife another look.

"Let's get going," Ryan said, deciding to ignore their unspoken communication. Every second that Mason remained lost was torture for those who loved him. "I'll head out after Poppy and Brett, you find the others."

They split up, moving fast. Ryan gripped a few of the sheets, including the last ones Mason drew. The presence of a big blue blob made it easy enough to get oriented to the mapmaker's perspective. Keeping the lake to his left, Ryan studied one of maps even as he strode through the trees.

The kid drew well for five years old. Excellent motor skills for a child not yet in kindergarten. And he could write his letters, too, even if he'd only copied the happy-birthday message on the card he'd made. Poppy had a precocious little dude on her hands. At nearly six, Tate would rather play catch than sit down and take pen to paper. Ryan's steps slowed as he thought of his son, smiling as he remembered a small baseball mitt, a child-size Dodgers cap, a father-son outing to the ballpark, where Tate had displayed his mischievous side by managing to find an empty cupboard in their luxury box and folding himself inside.

Ryan's smile died. Had Mason done something similar?

The pool house was looming ahead. According to Linus, Brett had checked the door—locked—and peered through the windows. Thank God, no small figure was found at the bottom of the pool. In any case, Ryan tested the door himself now, finding it still secure. His gaze fell to the map again, it showed where he was standing as a brown square covered in black bubbles—representing stones, he supposed. Something in the small dark circles caught his eye. Squinting in the shadows, he thought he saw a red X beneath the black orbs.

His pulse leaped. In a nearby patch of sunshine, he looked again. Yes, definitely an X.

But the door was locked. Of course, the key was secreted behind one of the stones near the door, but Mason wouldn't have a way of knowing that...

Unless he'd watched Linus retrieve it on the day he'd gone swimming with Ryan's brother and Charlie.

Heart pumping hard now, he ran to the door then pried at one of the rocks beside the jamb. It fell to the ground, revealing an empty niche.

He pounded on the door. "Mason!" he shouted. When there was no response, he moved to the nearest window, peered inside. It looked empty. He rapped on the glass. "Mason!"

Back at the entrance, he rattled the locked doorknob. "Mason!" Could his brother have pocketed the key instead of remembering to return it to its rightful place? Was he just wasting his time? But his gut said no, and still shouting Mason's name, he set his shoulder against the door.

The first ram didn't work.

The second time he put a little more desperation into it, by thinking of Poppy's big gray eyes and Mason's silky towhead. Wood splintered and he was inside, sucking hard to bring warm and humid air into his lungs. The first thing he did was inspect the pool once again, his heartbeat calming a little more when he saw it still empty.

"Mason!" he called out, and the syllables echoed back to him.

Hell. The kid must not be here.

Or, Ryan thought, he might be afraid to show himself. The attempted kidnapping would seem like that nightmare he'd had, the one with scary monsters and snowmen on wheels. "Mason," he repeated, trying for loud but not threatening. "It's Duke."

He prowled around the room, looking under chairs and behind the stack of chaises. There was no sign of a small body, but he thought the quality of the silence had changed. "Mason?"

At the back corner of the pool house was a narrow closet. His gaze on it, Ryan approached swiftly, then tried the knob. Locked. "Mason? Are you in there? It's Duke."

He thought he heard a scurrying sound behind the wooden door and hoped like hell it wasn't rats or spiders. "Mace? It's me. It's Duke. I'm on the job now. Here to keep you safe."

Sudden, loud noises erupted from behind the door. The sound of small fists on wood. "Duke! Duke!"

At the boy's voice, Ryan's heart shuddered once, then expanded with relief, painfully filling his chest that had been empty for so long. He swiped at his damp forehead, his pulse skittering. "Are you all right, kid? Tell me you're all right."

"I'm okay," Mason said, then started to cry. "But it's dark in here and I can't get out."

"Try the knob." Did the closet lock from the inside? It didn't seem likely, but Ryan had no idea.

"I d-did. I think it's stuck." The sobs turned heavier.

"Don't worry, don't worry," Ryan said hastily, looking around for a tool. "Remember I'm great with escapes."

"Yeah," the boy said. "I know. G-great with escapes."

Ryan considered using his cell to call for reinforcements and a crowbar, but from the sound of the renewed crying behind the door, the boy had reached the end of his tether. But he couldn't work the same ramming magic as he had on the front door—this one swung out, not in.

"Duke. Please...p-please get me out!"

The little boy's sobs would soften stone. "I'm going to, I promise. And remember, Walkers are tough." He looked around for door-breaking inspiration. "Can you sing something for me, Mace?" he asked, hoping to distract the crying child.

"S-sing?"

"My son, my Tate, he liked to sing when he was scared." At the doctor's office, on the way to preschool the first day, the time he'd broken a window at Grandma's and Ryan made him apologize. It was why Ryan had crooned himself hoarse at his boy's hospital bedside.

"Tate would sing?"

"Yeah. You know a song?"

A silence. Then a hiccup. Then... "Y-yes."

"I could really use a song while I work on this escape."

So as Mason started in singing, Ryan did a frenzied search of the drawers of the wicker bar that was angled in a nearby corner, matching bar stools before it. He found shrink-wrapped packages of paper cocktail napkins. The top half of a bikini. A moment of triumph when he uncovered a wine opener, but the corkscrew was broken and probably wouldn't have been long enough to do any good if intact, anyway.

Then his fingertips landed on a rusty screwdriver. It was old, the handle mangled, but the shaft was thick and long and was going to get Mason free if Ryan had to use his teeth, too. As he ran back to the door, he heard the kid still singing, and the words sank in.

"B-A-N-G-O," Mason sang. "B-A-N-G-O. B-A-N-G-O and Bingo was his name-O."

Okay, Ryan thought with a grin. Maybe not so precocious. But who couldn't love a kid who could sing his heart out like that?

The prying was the work of minutes. Then Mason flew through the damaged door and into Ryan's arms. It was like that night of the boy's bad dream. He sank to the floor, his back to the wall and let the boy hang onto him. The kid's hair was damp, but soft under his palm. Ryan didn't cringe when Mason wiped his wet cheeks and running nose against his shirt.

Such was fatherhood.

Ryan froze.

Who couldn't love a kid—

Shaking himself, Ryan fished for his phone. "We need to call your mom, pal. Tell her you're okay." He pulled up his contacts, got Linus on the line. "Hey, put Poppy on, will you?"

Then he handed his cell to Mason. "Mommy?" The boy's face glowed with the light of angels. "Mommy."

Who couldn't love this kid?

"I'm okay," Mason was saying. "Duke found me in the pool house. I was hiding from the bad guy." He listened for a moment, then glanced up at Ryan. "Yes, we'll wait for you right here."

His big blue eyes stayed trained on Ryan's face while he listened again. "Yes, I'm good, honest. I don't know about Duke, though, Mommy. I think he's crying."

The kid was right, Ryan thought, trying to blink away the tears as the phone was returned to him. He swiped at his face with his hand as more fell. Jesus. He hadn't cried since he was Mason's age.

The kid continued to look at him curiously. "Are those cuz of your little boy that got deaded?"

Adults definitely forget that children have ears.

Ryan looked into the small face. The boy had Poppy's nose and her mouth. Probably her optimistic attitude, too, which wasn't a bad thing at all, when it came down to it. He cleared his throat, again drying his face with his palm. "Some, maybe," Ryan admitted. *Tate, I loved you with all my heart and soul. I will miss you every day for the rest of my life.*

Then he cleared his throat again. "But I think they're about you, too, Mace. I'm pretty darn relieved to find you."

Who couldn't love this kid?

Then Linus, Brett and Poppy came rushing through the door and Mason raced into his mom's arms. She swept him up, squeezing him tight, her eyes closing as if savoring the goodness of having her boy with her.

Ryan slowly rose to his feet, staring at the assembled group that got larger as the rest of the Walkers and Granabelle arrived. The air in the pool house had made his clothes damp and he shivered as a cool spring breeze blew through the broken door. His approach went unnoticed as everyone was exclaiming over Mason, who appeared to be recovering more from his ordeal as each second passed.

Who couldn't love these people?

Then Poppy looked up. For an instant their gazes met, then she leaned down to kiss Mason on the top of his head while at the same time she curled her fingers into the fur of the dog leaning against her legs.

Who couldn't love this woman?

And that's when Ryan knew that he did. The love

inside him hadn't died, after all. It was there, for all of them, his friends, his family.

For Mason and Poppy.

And then he knew something else.

He wouldn't really, truly get to love them if he didn't forgive himself for not being a hero when faced with impossible odds. He wouldn't really, truly get to love them if he didn't let go of all the bad March stuff and replace it with happy March memories so his boy could finally rest in peace.

So while the Walkers et al continued rejoicing in Mason's return, Ryan made himself recall the day of Tate's birth, the miracle of that, the elation he'd felt when his baby had been put in his arms. Next he remembered all the birthdays after, and how much he'd loved his son through each and every one. And every day, every year.

Standing in the humid pool house, with a cool spring breeze ruffling his hair, Ryan rejoiced over his son's life…because everybody should have a celebration on their day.

Then he thought of how that love for Tate had prepared him to be a good dad to another little boy who needed him. How that fathering was going to open his soul and allow him to love that other boy's mom as she was supposed to be loved. With all the depth and breadth she deserved.

And that, he was certain, was going to be the very best part of the rest of his life.

POPPY LEARNED THAT the Hamilton brothers had a secret language. A silent language. One minute she'd been standing in the pool house, surrounded by her siblings, her cousin, Linus and Granabelle, with her hands on

Mason's shoulders. The next she'd glanced up and Ryan and his sorcerer eyes were staring back at her. They'd flicked toward his brother. Instantly Linus began rounding up the troops. "I need another burger. And more cake. Who's with me?" he said.

There was cheering. Anabelle made a reflexive comment about watching her figure. Grant said that was his job now and swatted her bottom. Brett offered to be his backup, Charlie giggled and then Shay and Mackenzie were drawing Mason from Poppy, each of them with one of his hands. "Oh," she said, automatically reaching to take him back.

"We won't let him out of our sight," Shay assured her.

"Let us help, little sister," Mac said.

"I don't need help," Poppy said, in automatic protest.

"This time, accept the offer," Ryan said in her ear. He'd come up behind her and she gave him a quick glance, then looked away. His blue gaze was more intense than usual, and it made her nerves do another of their jittery dances. Had he really been crying?

"Thanks, ladies," he said to her sisters.

Did they share a secret language with Ryan, too?

"Duke..." Mason began, craning his neck to look at his savior as he was being urged out the pool house door.

"Be there soon, Mace. Just need a couple of private moments with your mother."

Then they were all gone and there was no one between her and the man who had found her missing son. So number one, she must properly express her gratitude. She whirled to face him. "Thank you. Thank you so much—" Her lungs lost all air as the events of the afternoon caught up with her. Then her knees lost their starch and she found herself on the damp pool deck, her face in her hands.

"Sweetheart…" Ryan crouched beside her.

"He was only missing for less than an hour," she said, still hiding her eyes, "and it crushed me. You… your loss is forever."

"Poppy—"

"I understand better now." She looked up. "Not completely, of course, but I was mad at you before and now…now I'm not."

He ran a knuckle over her cheek, his expression bemused. "You were mad at me?"

"And me. I thought there was something I could say. I thought there was something you should feel because I…"

"Because you…"

"Feel so much myself." She looked up. "For you. But I get why it's just too hard for you to care for me, for anyone."

"Hmm…" Ryan said, smiling a little. "What if this pretty woman with big gray eyes came into my life and she had this not-scary dog and this cute kid and this can-do attitude that in the end filled me up? That in the end reminded me of what it was—how good it can be—to love?"

Poppy stilled.

Ryan cupped her face with his big hand. "You said about Mason, 'He's my everything. My only.'"

"Yes." Her face heated under his touch, as always.

"Let me be that, as well. Let me be your other everything. Your other only."

She blinked. "I can have two?"

"You can have it all. Just let me love you, Poppy." His

gaze was tender, his thumb soft as it stroked her cheek. "Oh, sweetheart, I'm so in love with you."

Her mouth dropped. She stared at him. Could she believe her ears? Could this be real? And then the cock-eyed optimist in her asserted itself and she flung herself at him. He wrapped his arms around her and murmured words against her temple.

"You saved me, Poppy," he said. "For that you'll always be my hero."

March 31

POPPY WATCHED THE man she loved from the pillow beside his. "It's the 31st...are you okay?"

"Very okay," he said, brushing her hair from her brow. "Having you makes it that way."

"You're not upset the paparazzi got those pictures of us yesterday?"

He shrugged. "They helped search for Mason. I consider it their reward." Cupping her chin, he directed her gaze to his. "What about you? They'll call us RyPop or something ridiculous like that."

"Because you told them I was your fiancée." She was ridiculously happy about it. Ridiculously.

"Much better than being my pole dancer, right?"

She made a face at him, then sobered. "So you think you'll make it through this March without doing anything crazy or wild?"

"No."

She frowned. "No?"

He smiled, then rolled to take her under him. "Because I'm about to get very crazy and wild while I bingo the woman I love." He laughed at her perplexed expression. "I'll explain later," he said, and lowered his mouth to hers.

April 1

RYAN WATCHED THE woman he loved from the pillow beside hers. She was worrying her bottom lip. With his knuckle, he freed it from her front teeth. "What's going on in your busy brain?"

She slid him a look. "Linus says you become someone else in April. Do you feel...different?"

He rolled his eyes heavenward as if he were taking stock. Then he tilted his head to gaze into her beautiful gray ones. "Nope. Still feel like me. A lucky SOB with a beautiful woman who has promised to be his wife. A lucky SOB who hopes to make her smart boy his boy, too."

Poppy found his hand, and brought it to her lips. "That means I've found that man who'll love me and who has an open heart for my son. I'm lucky, too."

He ruffled her hair. "Knucklehead," he said, just to tease her.

But she was worrying her lip again.

"What now, baby?"

"How's this going to work?"

"You and me?" At her nod, he smiled. "The usual way, I guess. We'll love most of the time, fight a few times, occasionally worry over our kids—"

"Kids, plural? We'll have more kids?"

"Don't you want that?" he asked softly.

"Yeah," she whispered. "Oh, yeah."

"Me, too," he said, trailing a finger over her cheek.

"So...where was I? Oh, yeah. We'll love, we'll fight, we'll worry over our kids. And we'll laugh, too. We'll enjoy our families and our friends and always feel a little smug and a little sorry for them because we'll believe they can't possibly be as happy as we are."

"But we're from two different worlds."

"We'll make our own world. It's going to be great."

"How can you be so sure?" she asked, an edge of anxiousness in her voice.

Ryan pulled her close, and breathed in the sweet scent of her hair. Breathed in spring and hope and the incredible idea of a future with his mountain girl. "Because I'm a realist, honey. Since I love you so very, very much, Poppy Walker, there's just no other option."

* * * * *

Look for Shay's story,
MAKE ME LOSE CONTROL,
coming soon from Christie Ridgway
and Harlequin HQN!

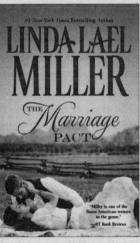

REQUEST YOUR FREE BOOKS!

2 FREE NOVELS
FROM THE ROMANCE COLLECTION
PLUS 2 FREE GIFTS!

YES! Please send me 2 FREE novels from the Romance Collection and my 2 FREE gifts (gifts are worth about $10). After receiving them, if I don't wish to receive any more books, I can return the shipping statement marked "cancel." If I don't cancel, I will receive 4 brand-new novels every month and be billed just $6.24 per book in the U.S. or $6.74 per book in Canada. That's a savings of at least 22% off the cover price. It's quite a bargain! Shipping and handling is just 50¢ per book in the U.S. and 75¢ per book in Canada.* I understand that accepting the 2 free books and gifts places me under no obligation to buy anything. I can always return a shipment and cancel at any time. Even if I never buy another book, the two free books and gifts are mine to keep forever.

194/394 MDN F4XY

Name _____ (PLEASE PRINT) _____

Address _____ Apt. # _____

City _____ State/Prov. _____ Zip/Postal Code _____

Signature (if under 18, a parent or guardian must sign)

Mail to the Harlequin® Reader Service:
IN U.S.A.: P.O. Box 1867, Buffalo, NY 14240-1867
IN CANADA: P.O. Box 609, Fort Erie, Ontario L2A 5X3

Want to try two free books from another line?
Call 1-800-873-8635 or visit www.ReaderService.com.

* Terms and prices subject to change without notice. Prices do not include applicable taxes. Sales tax applicable in N.Y. Canadian residents will be charged applicable taxes. Offer not valid in Quebec. This offer is limited to one order per household. Not valid for current subscribers to the Romance Collection or the Romance/Suspense Collection. All orders subject to credit approval. Credit or debit balances in a customer's account(s) may be offset by any other outstanding balance owed by or to the customer. Please allow 4 to 6 weeks for delivery. Offer available while quantities last.

Your Privacy—The Harlequin® Reader Service is committed to protecting your privacy. Our Privacy Policy is available online at www.ReaderService.com or upon request from the Harlequin Reader Service.

We make a portion of our mailing list available to reputable third parties that offer products we believe may interest you. If you prefer that we not exchange your name with third parties, or if you wish to clarify or modify your communication preferences, please visit us at www.ReaderService.com/consumerchoice or write to us at Harlequin Reader Service Preference Service, P.O. Box 9062, Buffalo, NY 14269. Include your complete name and address.

ROM13R

TERI WILSON

Ever since she was a little girl learning to make decadent truffles in her family's chocolate shop, Juliet Arabella has been aware of the bitter feud between the Arabellas and the Mezzanottes. With their rival chocolate boutiques on the same street in Napa Valley, these families *never* mix. Until one night, when Juliet anonymously attends the annual masquerade ball. In a moonlit vineyard, she finds herself falling for a gorgeous stranger, a man who reminds her what passion is like outside the kitchen. But her bliss is short-lived when she discovers her masked prince is actually Leo Mezzanotte, newly returned from Paris and the heir to her archenemy's confection dynasty.

With her mind in a whirl, Juliet leaves for Italy to represent the Arabellas in a prestigious chocolate competition. The prize money will help her family's struggling business, and Juliet figures it's a perfect opportunity to forget Leo…only to find him already there and gunning for victory. As they compete head-to-head, Leo and Juliet's fervent attraction boils over. But Juliet's not sure whether to trust her adversary, or give up on the sweetest love she's ever tasted….

CHRISTIE RIDGWAY

77745	BUNGALOW NIGHTS	___ $7.99 U.S.	___ $9.99 CAN.
77740	BEACH HOUSE NO. 9	___ $7.99 U.S.	___ $9.99 CAN.
77715	THE LOVE SHACK	___ $7.99 U.S.	___ $9.99 CAN.

(limited quantities available)

TOTAL AMOUNT
POSTAGE & HANDLING
($1.00 FOR 1 BOOK, 50¢ for ea
APPLICABLE TAXES*
TOTAL PAYABLE

(check or money ord

To order, complete this form an
order for the total above, paya
3010 Walden Avenue, P.O.
In Canada: P.O. Box 636, F

Name: _____
Address: _____
State/Prov.: _____
Account Number (if applicable): __

075 CSAS

*New York residents remit applicable sales taxes.
*Canadian residents remit applicable GST and provincial taxes.

H HARLEQUIN® HQN™

™ www.Harlequin.com